ERRORS OF OMISSION

Errors of Omission

A novel
by

MUKUND GNANADESIKAN

Adelaide Books
New York / Lisbon
2020

ERRORS OF OMISSION
A novel
By Mukund Gnanadesikan

Copyright © by Mukund Gnanadesikan
Cover design © 2020 Adelaide Books

Published by Adelaide Books, New York / Lisbon
adelaidebooks.org
Editor-in-Chief
Stevan V. Nikolic

For any information, please address Adelaide Books
at info@adelaidebooks.org
or write to:
Adelaide Books
244 Fifth Ave. Suite D27
New York, NY, 10001

ISBN: 978-1-953510-58-7

Printed in the United States of America

To those who feel invisible: Wherever you are, I see you.

*To those who offer the lifeline of acceptance when
it's least expected.*

*Most of all, to my family, who define for me each day the true
meanings of love and constancy.*

Contents

PART ONE

Chapter One

Irina walked past the bar of the smoky nightclub. Anatoly made eye contact with her and nodded. She knew what this meant, and walked through the beaded curtain to the booth where he sat with his well-connected friends. Clad in a tan suit with slicked-back brown hair and dark eyes, Anatoly preferred for the girls to call him Tolya. He sat in a semi-circular leather booth with several acquaintances, just the sort who brought with them large quantities of money and deviance.

"Irina, be a dear and wait in room number two," said Tolya, smacking her on her bare buttocks with his rough right hand. She tried not to shudder at the touch of his greasy palm.

"You look bewitching tonight," he said, smiling. "Vasiliev will be very pleased. I'll bring him to you."

Wearing nothing but black lace lingerie and white stilettos, she felt the chill of the late autumn winds that leaked through the single-pane windows. It had been this way for more than a year. How much longer could she go on as Tolya's toy, his human sacrifice to friends and cronies? She didn't want to test that limit.

Irina transferred a thin silver dagger from her palm to her garter belt, then walked down the nearly dark hallway and entered the second room. It was painted red and lit with two yellow wall lamps and a faux-antique chandelier. Under different circumstances Irina wouldn't have minded the room. But under Tolya's heavy hand, the space portended a threatening and uncertain future. Some of the men who entered were harmless and pathetic, but others were keenly focused on inflicting injury for pleasure, and they did so with no apparent remorse.

How had things arrived at this point? All she desired was a singing career. The idea of doing what she loved while making people happy seemed simple and pure. And Tolya had the money and connections to make it happen. That's what he told her when he wooed her and her father with promises of future fame. He spoke well, dressed well, and quoted Tolstoy and Gogol. Surely a man like this had to be trustworthy.

Then he got her on stage. It was a big club in downtown Moscow. She wasn't the headliner, but the crowd had to be over 2,000 people. Some may prefer alcohol or heroin, but Irina's drug of choice was attention. Nothing felt better than applause, the roar of a crowd, and an audience begging for more. He had delivered, and she was hooked.

She was unaware at the time that there would be a price, that Tolya only gave in order to take, and that he would take over and over again, as long as it suited him to do so.

Singing on stage was followed by dancing on stage, ever more provocatively with progressively fewer clothes. Not long after that the men were introduced, and by that time Irina felt all of her freedoms had been stripped and tossed away with her dignity. It wasn't comfortable but at first Irina was willing to pay this price in exchange for her lofty end goal. After all, as Tolya said, "You can be bathed in pig's blood with your father, or in a bright future with me." Considered in that light, the cigarette-stained breath of drunken rich men felt necessary.

Left naked and desolate physically and otherwise, the joys of singing for a crowd seemed far away as she massaged lotion on the scars her "special" customers inflicted on her thighs. The memories of the painful episodes made her want to cry and scream, but there wasn't time to do so. Now was time for action, time for an escape.

Tolya knocked on the door. She knew it must be him because he always used the same rhythm: "tap-tata-tap-tap".

She opened the door.

"Are you ready for Vasiliev?" Tolya asked. "He is very eager tonight."

Irina grasped Tolya's hand and led him into the room. She fluttered her eyelashes and caressed Tolya's cheek.

"I think he can wait, don't you?" she suggested. "Come."

She tapped the end of the bed and Tolya obediently sat down.

"Close your eyes," said Irina. "And put this on."

Tolya put the black blindfold on. Irina knew he loved games. She undressed him a button at a time, stopping to assess his anatomy as he sat breathlessly awaiting her.

She brought the dagger out and slid her index finger along its side. She knew she would only have one chance. She had to make it count. Otherwise disloyalty would be repaid with death.

One thing she'd learned from being compelled to sleep with different men each night was that each man has a weak spot. And for all, the inner thigh was vulnerable. She once watched as Tolya stabbed a man in the groin and left him lying by the curb, blood spurting everywhere. If all went according to plan, Tolya was in for an identical fate.

She walked toward him.

"You're going to love this surprise," she cooed.

Swiftly, she drove down the dagger into Tolya's left groin. He screamed in pain, blood streaming from him as he tried to pursue her but instead fell to the ground.

She kicked off her heels and ran to the back door. She slipped out into the night, but she could hear the commotion behind her.

A blue sedan screeched to a halt beside her.

"Get in!" said the driver.

Irina peered inside.

"Father!" Irina leaned over to kiss her father on the cheek.

"There is no time for kisses. This is time for father and daughter to run. Love is for later."

As they drove away, Irina saw two beefy bouncers brandishing weapons in the doorway behind them. But as the car sped away, she saw that nobody was following.

"We did it, Father!" Irina exclaimed. "It's really true. So why is it I feel so awful for what I did?"

"You did what you must," said Alex. "We all must first survive. He gave you no other choice. And now it is finished."

"Truly?" asked Irina, hesitant to believe that she had broken loose from the net that had ensnared her for the past year.

She began to cry tears of relief. Since the death of her mother, the only reliable force in Irina's life had been her father Alex.

"You are done with those people," said Alex. "I swear upon my life, upon your mother's grave."

"Yes," said Alex. "And that also means we are done with other things?"

"Do you mean what I think you mean?" Irina asked. They had spoken of emigrating to New York before, but nothing ever came of it.

"Yes, we must leave," said Alex. "And we must never return."

"I'm sorry father," said Irina. She frowned and placed a hand on her father's shoulder. "You sacrifice so much for me. Now my choices make you turn your back on Russia."

"This is no time for apologies," said Alex. "We must only look forward. Forward to America."

Irina forced her lips to smile. She stared at her hands, still flecked with Tolya's blood.

"To America," she said.

The stuffy New York summer air felt heavier with each successive breath as Irina walked up the stairs to the abandoned second floor apartment in the burnt out building that she and Alex currently called home. It was anybody's guess who might be occupying the dwelling from one day to the next, but today they had the good fortune of being alone.

The security of their former apartment, a cramped and tiny two-bedroom shared with ten others, was long gone. Security had vanished with the demise of the butcher shop where Alex had been employed. The promise of a bright future no longer seemed as possible as it had when they arrived in New York City.

Still, she was fortunate to be here, Irina reminded herself. Looking back at the lashes and beatings, the ominous words spoken in darkness of night, it was true. But today she ached with every breath and good fortune seemed distant. She coughed and wheezed, then doubled over and grabbed her knees.

Alex came up the stairs behind her just in time to catch Irina as she buckled to the floor.

"You are not well," he said. "We must go to hospital."

"We cannot afford hospital," said Irina. "Not until you get another job. I can wait until then."

"Do you hear yourself?" asked Alex. "You can barely speak. We go. No arguing."

Alex started to lift Irina, but she demurred.

"I can walk," she insisted. "I am not dead, yet."

As they waited for the city bus, fits of coughing and wheezing shook Irina's thin body. She could feel her ribs vibrating. The painful inhalations felt like punishment. For what, she wondered? Was it greed, selfishness, or the justified but shameful violence of retribution that she regretted? Whatever it was, it seemed to constrict her like a corset.

She leaned on her father's shoulder as he helped her up the steps of the bus.

The other passengers made way, clearing a seat for her to sit down. She wasn't sure if this was due to sympathy or fear of contagion, but in any event she was grateful to be allowed to rest her body against the firm seats. She had suffered from asthma since childhood, but this, like much else in her life, had gotten worse in the smoke-filled clubs of Moscow. The reminders of the shame and pain seemed to make breathing more onerous.

"We are here," said Alex as they arrived at the hospital. "No protests. We get you seen."

Irina was soon triaged into the emergency room. From the concerned looks he saw on the nurses, it appeared that they easily recognized the severity of her distressed breathing. As much as she had resisted coming, Irina was now relieved to be in a safe, nurturing place. Neither Moscow nor her recent homeless existence could be described in such terms.

The doctor, a handsome dark-skinned man who she guessed to be of about 30 years of age, furrowed his brow. The embroidered inscription on his white coat read "Dr. Rajesh Patel."

"This is bad," he said, looking at a sheet with some numbers on it. "Your pulse ox, which shows how well your lungs are working, says you're at 88% oxygen. A young, healthy person should be at 98 or better. You're at risk of going into what we call respiratory acidosis, which is a fancy way of saying your lungs are on the verge of giving out. We need to get you to ICU, where they can give you the level of monitoring required."

He smiled and squeezed her hand. She recoiled slightly, but was reassured when she saw that his eyes were warm and kind, the eyes of a man who she imagined to have a good soul.

"I am scared," she said. "This place, it is like I can feel the sadness of death here."

"People are often frightened by the hospital," said Dr. Patel. "But they'll take good care of you up there. They're some of the best doctors in the city, so don't be nervous, OK?"

"OK," she said. "I trust you."

"I'll be waiting," said Alex. "If you need anything, I'm here."

"You have a good dad," said the doctor. "Take care. They'll be here to take you up to the third floor shortly."

Chapter Two

"Dr. Patel, Dr Rajesh Patel to ICU. Dr. Rajesh Patel: Please report to surgical ICU immediately."

Raj was accustomed to the blare of the hospital's antiquated overhead paging system. But today it was distorted: in the operator's nasal twang, he imagined a car engine beginning to backfire. The pounding in his head and buzzing in his ears indicated an acute change. The discomfort made him wish he followed his original passion of computer science instead of entering the high-stress world of medicine at his parents' behest. Was the hospital audio deteriorating, or was this the beginning of a bad migraine?

"Raj. Raj."

He was stirred from his internal preoccupations by the gentle voice of a nurse with luminous ebony skin and grey hair gathered into a long ponytail.

"Raj, they want you in ICU. It's important."

"Thanks, Mabel, I'll be right there," he said.

Raj unfurled his body from the coffee-stained, brown armchair and rubbed his clean-shaven scalp as he loped down the corridor. Why was ICU calling? He had graduated from med school little more than a month ago. As an emergency medicine intern he was out of place in intensive care.

Orientation week just started this morning. No, there was no obvious reason for him to be called to the unit.

Clad in his customary white oxford shirt, golden yellow tie and blue pleated trousers, Raj proceeded down the hall through the automated double doors.

When he arrived, a flood of familiar faces stood before him. Foremost among them was Dr. Leonard MacIntosh. "Dr Mac", as he was known, seemed as old as the venerable teaching hospital itself. A pale, stout man with tufts of gray hair emerging from the perimeter of his skull, he bore an uncanny resemblance to a koala bear. Now in his late 60s, MacIntosh was a name loved by patients and feared by medical students. As a student, Raj spent more than a few mornings standing before the anesthesiology team answering questions until he got one wrong. At that point the crusty old doctor would shout, "Patel, I thought you were one of the smart ones! What's wrong with you? You better study up if you ever want to be a doctor, Patel."

Next Raj turned his attention toward the bedside, where the trauma surgery team stood masked with heads bowed. The senior surgeon, Dr. Marcus Thompson, lowered his mask and beckoned.

"Marc," as he introduced himself to patients and colleagues alike, was a burly man in his early fifties. After emigrating from Haiti to New York, he ascended the surgical ranks by virtue of his unparalleled combination of work ethic and bedside manner. Marc was renowned in hospital circles as the doctor appointed to bear bad tidings in sensitive cases. The morbid humorists of the hospital dubbed Marc, "Dr Gooddeath," a term Raj found mortifying.

The ICU is always a serious place, but on this day he noticed the sad faces of the nurses as they watched Marc walk away with him. A wave of fear rose in his chest.

"Have a seat," said Marc, guiding Raj to the one unoccupied region of the large urban intensive care unit.

They both sat down on shabby plastic chairs in the corner. The chairs reminded Raj of the South Bronx elementary schools where he did health screenings in medical school.

"Raj, this is really, really hard for me to say to you, but your parents were in a serious car accident," said Marc. "It looks grim."

"You're sure it's them? Can I see them? Hopefully there's no internal trauma, no end-organ damage, nothing like that?" Raj asked.

Marc shook his head. His face assumed a mournful cast, his eyes darkening as if under a thunderhead. He rubbed his chin and cleared his throat.

"Raj, the accident was really serious. They got T-boned. It took the Jaws of Life to get them out of the car, and they're both in comas. The other driver was dead on impact."

Raj felt his whole body tremble. He grasped at a nearby bedrail to steady himself.

"Good news is that the chopper got them here quick. Bad news is they each sustained a lot of internal trauma," said Marc. Raj observed that Marc's eyes looked away from his own, as if hiding from the truth. "Even if they do wake up, they're not out of the woods. We're going to do everything we can, as long as that's what you want."

The word "comas" slowed the pace of time to a crawl. Raj felt as though he had been thrust head first into a whirlpool. He paced the length of the floor, kneading his temples with his fingertips.

"We need to do something," he insisted. "Has mannitol been started? When are they scheduled for the OR?"

Marc paused and let silence hang in the air for a few seconds before he continued to talk. He washed his hands and dried them on a paper towel. "Raj, I get it. You want to get your hands dirty. But this is what our surgeons are trained for. Best thing you can do is let us work, OK? You're a professional. You know how it is."

"Of course, you're right." Raj sighed and wrung his hands. "I'm sorry. I trust you. Do whatever you can, whatever you have to. You can't let them die. It's not their time yet. They have so much more to do. It can't happen, you hear me?"

Marc's large hands grasped Raj by the shoulders.

"You know me, Raj. Your parents are special people. I'll give it all I have, man. Brain, hands, and soul. We'll keep you updated on everything. In the meantime, if there's anything you need, let us know, OK?"

Raj nodded and wiped away the tears with his forefingers. He felt cold, naked, and sick as he cleared his throat and wobbled to the waiting room, craving some fresh air to clear his head.

He sat down, trembling and disoriented. As he stared at the floor in front of him, Raj recalled how parents insisted on giving the doctors he worked with tokens of their thanks. Sometimes Mother plied his supervisors with tins of rich, buttery barfi, custom-tailored kurtas or gold bangles. He found such mawkish gratitude embarrassing. Now he regretted his irritation. Why find such a petty reason to argue?

He recollected the final conversation with Mother. She was bursting with pride and insisted that he stop by for dinner. Their dream of having a doctor in the family had come true, and she wished to shout it to the world. He loved her cooking and the way her straight teeth shone when she saw the satisfaction guests derived from her curries and sweets. And yet he begged out because of his aversion to the crowd of people he anticipated.

"I can't come," he had insisted. "I don't even know most of those people, or care about them. They're your friends, not mine. And this is my accomplishment, not yours. You can't just parade me in front of your friends for your own pride. I'm a doctor now, not some trophy to be admired and gawked at. If you want to see me, come down and we'll have dinner here, just us."

He slumped forward under the weight of his guilt. For what had he been too busy? Was he too important to show thanks to his parents, who spent all their savings on his medical school tuition? Selfishness created this nightmare. He wasn't driving the other vehicle, but might as well have. After all, they wouldn't have found it necessary to travel to the city if he had swallowed his pride. All he had to do was take a goddamned train to the suburbs, instead of being a prima donna and insisting that they come to him.

He visualized the collision as his imagination dictated. He saw his mother's eyes dilating with fear as the onrushing car approached, then heard the screech of tires. There were bitter plumes of smoke and emergency crews running with stretchers to the accident scene. The emotionless efficiency and heightened attention of paramedics usually drew admiration from Raj, but envisioning them now, he felt only panic and dread.

The scene shifted, and he saw his father's short, plump body being extracted from the car, placed on a stretcher, and loaded into the emergency chopper. Soon his mother followed, her fine long black hair framing her delicate sienna-colored face now smeared with blood.

He closed his eyes and shook his head. This couldn't be happening. They had to make it through this crisis. In all their doting over their only son, his parents had never prepared him for their departure. Throughout life they convinced him that they were all he needed, that they were constant and powerful forces of nature. Friends and social groups were unnecessary. He had always been content to embrace the idea, which made life's path less twisted and easier to comprehend. How could fate rip them away so suddenly?

He buried his head in his hands. A few tears leaked out of the corners of his eyes. Rajesh was not unfamiliar with tear-drops. But frustration was the usual motive for his tears, a product of impatience and high expectations. Today his eyes anticipated ultimate sadness, the loss of the only important people in his life.

After a minute, Raj suppressed his grief. A public emotional display wouldn't do. He had to pull himself together and be present. Raj perched his head on his hand in the manner of Rodin's "Thinker" and looked through the unit's window at the river a few blocks away. A tugboat crossed his line of sight, calling to mind his childhood flights of fancy when he vowed to circumnavigate the globe in a tugboat. He smiled through his sniffles. If only life could be as simple and joyous now as it was in childhood.

A tap on the shoulder interrupted his grief-ridden meditations. By his side stood Doctor MacIntosh.

"I thought I might find you out here," said MacIntosh with uncharacteristic gentleness. "Listen, if you're feeling a little bit better, we're ready for you now in ICU."

Raj nodded and unfolded his body from the chair. The room tilted, and his legs strained under his weight as he moved through the hallway. Anxiety sucked the breath from his lungs, and he was unable to keep pace with Dr. MacIntosh. When they finally arrived, he paused and leaned against a wall.

His eyes scanned the unit from left to right, back to front.

In one bed lay an old withered black man with tubes pro-jecting from every orifice. His thin, frail body drew irregular breaths, shaking from the effort. Probably end-stage CHF, Raj thought. A shudder ran down his spine and he looked away. In medical school Raj harbored an aversion to the ICU, with its insistent alarms and the constant threat of imminent death. Seeing the black man's labored breaths made him nauseous as he envisioned what lay ahead at his parents' bedsides.

Another bed held a lithe young woman with blue-grey eyes who was receiving nebulizer treatments. Even through his desperate anxiety, Raj noticed her smile and her cascading reddish hair. She smiled weakly and her pale hand waved at him. It was the girl he'd admitted three days earlier. What was her name? Irina, that was it.

Raj felt his heart flutter as he took three strides forward toward the bedsides of his parents, who lay next to each other as they always preferred to be. In front of him he beheld sights he had dreaded since his first childhood nightmares: his father and mother unconscious in neighboring beds, swathed in bandages, with various monitors keeping vigil over their flagging vital signs. Their swollen, misshapen faces were bruised to the point that they bore no resemblance to the people who had fed him, embraced him, and provided him with all the emotional connection he'd ever needed.

He approached Dr. McIntosh, who stood by the bedside, glancing at the monitors that tracked patient vital signs.

"What can I do?" Raj asked. "Surely there must be something? I can't just stand here. They're all I have."

He looked at the swollen, bruised faces of his parents. Their cheekbones were displaced vertically and laterally, and the grotesque distortion of their features repulsed him. "Please Dr. Macintosh."

Dr. MacIntosh looked at the floor. The old Scotsman cleared his throat, coughed, and began to speak.

"Things look bleak. Your father had a hemopneumo-thorax and went into cardiac tamponade. You know how serious that is. Your mother may even be worse off. It seems that the head trauma she sustained was pretty severe and she's herniated. We're doing what we can to relieve the pressure, but the chances don't look good. You know me. Marc and I will do whatever's possible; I hate to lose a patient, much less the family of a friend."

Raj turned away. The news felt like a cold, blustery day piercing him through every sensory avenue. He walked past the foot of the bed, over toward the nurse's station.

"I trust you," said Raj. "Do whatever it takes."

As he wandered, stunned and fearful, Raj heard a brusque, gravelly voice calling out to him. He turned and saw a pale man with a fresh scar on his leg.

"Hey you! I need some help, goddamnit!" the pale man railed at anyone (and everyone) who would listen. "Hey you in the nice pants! You work here?"

Given the circumstances, Raj preferred to ignore the man, but his medical training prevented him from doing so.

Raj turned around and stared at the man's face. His frowning, pursed lips and aquiline nose gave the impression that he had eaten something noxious.

"Yeah, I'm a doctor, but I don't work here on the unit," said Raj. "It's not really my area. I'm an emergency room physician. What's the problem?"

The dyspeptic-looking patient scowled.

"Problem is that," he said, pointing to a crooked, zigzagging incision along his left leg. "Why the hell is my scar all crooked?"

Raj answered as well as his foggy mind would permit.

"Well, sir in your case I really don't know, but sometimes they have to cut irregularly to get the saphenous vein out right."

Just in time Gail, a nurse who Raj knew from medical school, rushed to the bedside to intervene. Her smooth, freckled skin and light blue eyes gave her a child-like appearance. She wore jungle-themed scrubs with smiling monkeys hanging from trees, and she spoke with the sort of voice one hears on automated messages.

"Sorry about Mr. Cranston, Doctor. Don't mind him," she said, ambling over to refill the man's water pitcher.

"Shame on you for bothering this poor man," she chided Mr. Cranston, smiling at Raj. He imagined it was the sort of smile one sees at a funeral.

Dr. McIntosh walked over to Raj and placed a hand on his former student's shoulder.

"It's still touch and go," he said. "Cardiac and neurologic functioning isn't improving, and there's no saying when or if it will. I guess what I'm saying is stay close, we may need you soon, since there is no other next of kin."

"Next of kin."

He knew what those words meant. It wasn't fair. They were only in their early fifties. This was not when sons were meant to face this. Just as his life was taking flight, this happened. They couldn't leave now. He had so much to say, so many reparations to make.

Chapter Three

Raj looked around the ward. The room spun around him and he collapsed against a bedrail.

He awoke, stunned but unhurt. As he glanced up, Raj saw the concerned faces of MacIntosh and Gail looming over him.

"I think I'm OK," said Raj, rubbing his sore neck and shoulder.

"Gail," said MacIntosh to Gail, "Make sure Dr. Patel is OK. Give him some water and help him to the waiting room, OK?"

"I don't want to go," Raj protested. "This is where I need to be. They need me. And I need them."

Gail nodded.

"Doctor, don't be stubborn. If you don't want to go to the waiting room, you're going to sit down and stay here till you're better, OK? I know it's hard for you doctors not to be the hero, but it's time to just be family."

Raj nodded at Gail as he digested the nightmarish contents of the day.

He sat down in one of the brown armchairs stationed between his parents' beds. It complained as he collapsed backward onto its worn, stale cushions. Raj was exhausted, but he could not allow sleep to take hold. Not now.

Inside his mind swirled pictures of his parents lying motionless and open-mouthed in their hospital beds, surrounded by a sea of wires. The faces of the doctors and nurses were distorted into knowing, malignant grins, and the continuous, strident blare of an ambulance siren drowned out all other noises in his head.

And so proceeded his internal universe for the better part of 36 hours: his body, exhausted and yearning for a moment's peace, in pitched battle with a psyche that sounded continual alarm bells. At long last, his thoughts were interrupted when a cart carrying IV supplies banged into his leg.

"Oh, I'm so sorry," said Gail. He fancied that he perceived pity in her face. Did she know something she wasn't telling him?

"You have to sleep. Just get a couple hours," said Gail. "Tell you what, go to the waiting room and I'll wake you in a couple."

"I don't need to," Raj protested, but soon his body gave up its resistance and he shuffled to the waiting room and slumped back in a Barcalounger.

"Ah!"

Raj woke with a start to find a portly red-faced man with a ring of matted grayish hair surrounding his sunburned scalp sitting next to him. The man flashed a broad smile, assuaging Raj's apprehension.

"I am sorry. Did not mean to make you jump," said the affable stranger in a heavy, eastern European accent.

Raj groaned and righted himself in his chair.

"It's OK. These chairs aren't really made for sleeping," he said.

"Mind if I sit?" the stranger asked, still smiling.

Raj shrugged and stared straight ahead.

"Go ahead, seat's free. I need to go check on my folks anyway."

The stranger sat down with his hands on his knees and emitted a prolonged sigh.

Raj assessed his new neighbor. The old man's twinkling blue eyes were blemished with streaks of worry. He was clothed in an ill-fitting frayed windbreaker that at one time must have been dark blue in color but had faded to a dusky gray. His ample belly peeked out from beneath a stained white T-shirt. He had chunky legs that strained the seams of his faded army fatigues, the sort one might find in a second-hand store.

"By the way, I'm Alex Petrov. Remember me? My daughter's in here." His eyes began to well up with tears, but with a quick blink and swallow he stopped their descent. "You were the one who helped her, in emergency."

"Oh yes," said Raj. "How is she?"

"She is still sick. But getting better. Thanks to you and other doctors here, she will make it. As a child, she is always sick, but always make it. She is a fighter, my Irina," said Alex, his right fist banging the chair's armrest. "As you say here, 'small but mighty'."

"So, what about you?" Alex shifted in his chair to face the young man head-on.

"My name's Rajesh, Rajesh Patel," he murmured in a disengaged manner.

"Well, Dr. Rajesh, whatever you are going through must be pretty hard. Your eyes tell tales of sadness. But you are a good man, I can tell. A good man in pain," Alex said.

Good was a relative term. As he heard Alex's words, Raj questioned himself. There were reasons for him to doubt the

Russian stranger. Was his image accurate? Good men have friends. Not Raj. He had acquaintances that he used for his own purposes. Was his virtue authentic? It was true that he saw medicine as a noble vocation. But he also craved respect and status. That was a large part of the field's allure, maybe most of it. Was helping people a pretense? If that was so, he might be receiving his punishment for living a lie.

All these years he fixated on his own objectives. Advancement and achievement became necessary to him even as they inconvenienced others. His parents spent their life savings on his medical school tuition. He could have declined and taken out student loans like everyone else. But he took the gift with no questions asked, no pause to question his worthiness for such generosity. What if the image he projected were nothing more than a hologram?

Though Raj doubted Alex's character assessment, the old man was right about pain. This mental anguish and panic consumed him in a way no emotion ever had. For years he maintained a comfortable distance from emotional extremes, but today overwhelmed his normal defenses. He stared off toward a nearby hallway, pensive and dazed.

An old, leather-faced nurse with dark, beady eyes poked her head out the door of the ICU.

"Is there a Mr. Petrov here?" she croaked toward the waiting visitors.

Alex popped out of his seat with the agility of a lynx.

"I am Petrov," he announced, chest protruded.

"Your daughter wants to see you," said the nurse, ducking back into the busy unit.

"Well, friend, good luck to you. I must go now," said Petrov.

Petrov ambled away, leaving Raj alone with his thoughts. Alex must have challenges in life, yet he seemed humble, hopeful, and full of love. Irina was fortunate to have a father like Alex, and Raj reflected that he had been fortunate too, though he rarely bothered to recognize the fact.

Raj recalled the day he received his medical school acceptance letter. He'd arrived home from the basketball court, hands covered with dust and body drenched in sweat. As he entered the house his parents rushed to embrace him. "Read the letter, son, go on!" his mother coaxed, unable to contain her excitement as she shoved the paper into his hand. Her light brown, egg-shaped eyes sparkled. As he read the words, "We are pleased to offer you a spot in our incoming first year class."

He was pleased to have realized his parents' aspirations, dreams that were implicit but obvious. All the hours that his father and mother put into their import/export business were for him, and his parents spoke in worshipful tones about the medical profession. They strived to offer him the educational options they were not afforded and took on the burden of putting their only child through the college of his choice. Each morning they rose at 5 AM, working at least six days a week for him to have whatever he might need or want. All this was done so he could transcend their achievements.

What could be a better return on their investments than becoming a doctor? At last he had validated their sweat and toil by gaining acceptance into the esteemed profession of medicine. It wasn't enough to repay his entire debt, but it was a start.

A scant month ago he strode across the stage, grabbing his medical school diploma and brandishing it high overhead like one of the championship trophies he had won as a high school athlete. His parents stood up and ran over to embrace him simultaneously. They celebrated afterwards with generous portions of laughter and Epicurean delights. It was a day of exuberance, intoxication, and unbridled joy.

Now he fast-forwarded to the present day. He shook his head and wondered if all their sacrifice was worth it. What if they never got to see him practice medicine? He was supposed to take care of them in their waning years. Now that might not happen.

He shook his head to clear the distress. It didn't pay to think of death. It was not an option, and the doctors would fight. Medical science must triumph, and he needed to join the fight. Raj followed a nurse through the doors of the ICU and rushed to the bedside.

As he stared at his parents, he remembered their mantra: "Family is everything. Family is all you need." If that was true, his life might soon be devoid of all meaning.

He recalled the days of childhood, watching television on his mother's lap and reciting silly improvised rhymes with his father. He remembered combing his mother's long, silky hair, a pastime he enjoyed for reasons that were beyond description.

He saw them, in his mind's eye, jumping to their feet when he slammed a winner during his tennis matches. For years, he knew they lived for him, and he wished to return the favor.

As he slumped forward in his chair, staring at the distended bodies of the people who formed his anchor in the world, past glory days seemed foreign, distant, and hollow. The only time he had ever entertained the idea of personal loss was during the late nights of his early childhood years. But those childhood nightmares about losing his parents paled in comparison to the real world fear. As a toddler he ran to their bedroom and they made everything better. If only things were that easy tonight, he thought. But this was no dream.

Several hours passed as he sat by the bedside absorbed in a contemplative trance. Though he did not rest, time assumed a dream-like quality, punctuated by the rhythmic drone of alarms sounding and the hum of IV drips turning on and off. All the events of the day were replayed in a fragmented manner, broadcast against a hazy white background.

"Mother, father," he addressed his parents. "If you can hear me, hang on. I know I haven't been the best son. I took you for granted. It won't happen again. Just survive. You've got to."

Physical exhaustion sapped the storm of thoughts and fears that raged in Raj's mind. He walked down a sterile white hallway that was deserted at this late hour. He stopped at a large window that afforded a panoramic view of the city. The skyline was dotted with many shades of darkness, punctuated by the occasional pulsating neon remark.

Raj directed his eyes upward to the moon and stars. He had always been fond of the heavens. There was something comforting about the moon's creamy glow, the visual warmth of it. He breathed deeply and tried to clear his mind.

Raj spied a nearby bathroom outside the unit's doorway and decided to wash up. He lowered his head toward the sink and was jolted awake by the water as it forced its way into every pore on his face. His brown skin tingled. He looked up at the mirror, and saw a familiar face smiling behind him.

"Hello, my friend," said Alex. "You look not so good. I hope you feel better than you look!"

He walked over to Raj and shook his hand while simultaneously clasping the younger, taller man's shoulder.

"They say my Irina is well and she can leave here later today. Perhaps you get good news too, yes?"

Raj nodded. He wasn't aware this stranger now considered himself a friend. It seemed presumptuous, but there were more important matters to attend to right now.

"Perhaps, Alex. Thanks. I'm happy for you," he said, forcing a wan smile born more out of politeness than sincerity.

He left the bathroom and returned to the unit, where he found Dr. Thompson standing, his hands interlocked in front of his waist, staring down at the bed. Dr. Thompson walked slowly over to Raj. Marc's lively eyes were darker than usual as he placed his hands in the pockets of his white coat. Raj felt his heart drop and his stomach churn.

"I'm sorry, we couldn't find you. It all happened so quickly," said Marc, "I, I don't even know what to say . . ."

"What do you mean?" Raj asked. "I was in the bathroom. I was only gone for a few minutes!"

It was then that he noticed the stillness of his parents' chests.

"They both coded...within a minute of each other. Cardiac arrest for your Dad, respiratory for your mom." Marc said. "Damnedest thing I've ever seen . . . We couldn't save them."

"It's, it's not possible," Raj sputtered.

"I'm so sorry." Marc offered a hug but stopped short as Raj stepped back.

"Is there anything you need right now," Marc asked. "Any priests or ministers or anything? Everything is just so sudden. I know it can be overwhelming. Anything you need, I'm here, OK, son?"

Rajesh shook his head. His body trembled. His dry, constricted throat gasped for air. He was a 26 year-old orphan. What was the antidote for that? Raj dabbed his face.

"Could I see them? One last time?"

The misty-eyed Dr. Thompson nodded and opened the door.

The nurses and doctors vanished as Raj reached the neighboring beds. He looked on the faces of death as he had never seen them before. Their glassy stares and cold skin were too much to bear. He turned away and stomped his foot. He buried his head in his hands. An older nurse came over and tried to guide Raj over to a corner, but his legs failed him and he crumpled to his knees by the nurses' station.

It seemed as though a hush swept over the unit. The nurses scurried away. Given the pain of the moment, Raj felt this was just as well. He had no desire to share his anguish. It was not theirs to have.

The irascible Mr. Cranston called out.

"Hey doc, I'm sorry. I'm . . ." Cranston shook his head and muttered to himself. "Poor bastard. Seems like a nice kid too."

Dr. Thompson helped Raj to his feet. "I know this is a horrible question and it makes me sick to ask it, but did your parents have any funeral arrangements or anything they ever talked about like that? Any family or friends I should call?"

Raj heard the sound of his voice but was not aware that it issued from his lips. "Cremation. They wanted to be cremated. Live on in a little urn I guess," he answered. "I'm an only child, so I guess the rest is on me."

Thompson nodded. "If you'd like, we'll have a social worker take care of that for you?"

Raj nodded and stumbled towards the back stairs. He sat down on one of the steps, oblivious to the musty, smoky odor, and cried softly as scores of busy hospital employees hurried past. He made several efforts to think, perhaps to move, but his grief left him in a state of catatonic emptiness.

Several hours went by with the young man sitting cemented to the stairwell, until at long last he was roused from his stupor by the harsh tones of the inimitable Dr. MacIntosh roasting the ears of another medical student. "Come on, you're supposed to be smart! Get your books out and read up, because you're presenting on this tomorrow morning!"

Dr. MacIntosh hurried down the stairs, nearly stumbling over Raj in the process. "Blast! What in creation?!" Dr.

MacIntosh prepared to launch in on a verbal tirade, but stopped. He leaned against the creaky metal handrail and looked Raj in the eye.

"I'm sorry, Dr. Patel," he said. "I cannot tell you how deeply sorry I am. Things like this aren't supposed to happen. Your parents were wonderful people, and I was blessed to meet them. I'm just . . . I'm real sorry."

Rajesh shifted his gaze to face his bearish mentor. "Huh? Oh thanks, Dr. Mac."

"You know what sometimes helps in situations like this?" Macintosh asked.

"Alcohol, drugs, screaming for days?" said Raj.

"Maybe those too, but no, I was thinking of something else," Macintosh replied. "People, relationships. Be with friends and family. Grief should never be a one-person process."

"Feels like that's inevitable," said Raj. "You forget that medical school is all consuming. It's not like I had time for friends or relationships. Ships passing in the night and all that. Social retardation's part of the deal. Besides, I had family. I didn't think I needed anyone else. I really felt like they'd be here forever."

"You don't have to be alone," Macintosh insisted. "Everybody needs someone. Everybody. Your patients need you, right? So why should you be any different? Don't forget that, OK? That's all I'm saying. If you need anything, and I mean anything at all, call me."

Macintosh walked away, leaving Raj alone with his grief and bewilderment.

Raj felt uncertainty swirling all around him. In the midst of it he determined that he must leave the hospital. The toxic cloud of misfortune threatened to suffocate him, and he needed air.

He rushed out the doors of the lobby and turned left into the cool air that was decorated with the crimson and orange hues of a setting sun. Raj had no preplanned destination, but his legs decided to turn left and continue for a few blocks. After a quick right turn and a few more blocks walking on automatic pilot, he stopped at a small park by the river.

The birds formed a small city along the river, an avian encampment marked by occasional squawking and fights over windblown bread crumbs. Raj retreated here when the stressful life of a medical student frayed his mind and body. The slow, soft rhythm of the water, the absurd strutting of the pigeons, and the glow of the setting sun were a fitting antidote to the clamor of the hospital.

Raj picked up a handful of loose gravel. He picked out a large pink stone and flipped it softly through the air, watching it land a few inches over the railing on the sparse mud of the riverbank. He selected another pebble, smaller but polished to perfection. He held it aloft and looked at the fading rays of the sun as they glinted off of it. He turned, heaved the stone with all the force he could muster. His eyes followed its arc as it screamed through the air before vanishing in a sundrenched patch of muddy brown water.

Chapter Four

Raj entered the chamber of the crematorium. His parents' lifeless bodies, devoid of expression, were dressed and ready to be processed. It was surreal to view them in their clothes, knowing that the shells encased by the attire were empty.

A thirtyish man in a herringbone jacket, black tie and white shirt approached. His floppy blonde bowl cut bounced as he approached.

"Hello, my name is Owen. "Do you have any questions before we get started?"

Raj shook his head.

"Would you like to say anything to your loved ones before I close the lids?"

It seemed the most appropriate thing to do. But what was there to say? Speak the truth, he decided. But truth was complicated and insufficient.

"I love you mother and father. I know I've taken you for granted, and I didn't show the gratitude and respect you deserve. I'm sorry. May I be the man you thought I was," he whispered. "I will always miss you."

Owen closed the black coffins. The smell of death was masked by sandalwood oil. The corpses were ready for their final voyage.

"As the designated family member, you may flip the switch," Owen explained.

The phrase evoked the judicial system's ultimate punishment. Flip the switch. He cringed. His parents didn't deserve punishment. If anyone did, it was he, for his blithe self-indulgence. And now he was being asked to do this, and he couldn't refuse. Perhaps he was the one being punished.

Tears welled up in his eyes. Without warning he was invaded by a sudden visual memory of his parents lying on their hospital beds, eyes swollen shut as the monitors stood vigil. He shook his head, bit his lower lip and inhaled, producing a hissing sound not unlike water boiling over onto a hot stove.

"May I have some time?" he asked. "This is all new to me, and it's a bit much."

"Certainly," said Owen. "I understand."

No you don't, Raj thought. Most often people who said that did so from a place of ultimate ignorance. After all, who truly knows another man's heart without feeling its every beat?

What was the fascination with all this? People live for decades fleeing life's extremes of nature only to end in a 1500-degree blast furnace that reduces them to dust. No different than any other carbonaceous ruin. What value was there in this ritual?

He turned on the switch and within minutes, his father's body was no more. The process was repeated for his mother.

"It'll take some time for the ashes to be cool enough to be released," Owen explained. "We also have to file paperwork with the state, which unfortunately holds things up. I'll try to expedite that. In the meantime, would you like to purchase one of our customized disposal urns? We have traditional options, earth-friendly biodegradable models?"

"My parents specified that they wanted their ashes to be placed in two silver urns," Raj explained. "These were used for my grandparents and great grandparents, to scatter the ashes into the Ganges."

"I see," said Owen. "Well in that case make sure to bring the urns with you when you return. Should be about forty-eight to seventy-two hours, best-case scenario."

Five days passed following the death of his parents and Raj wandered as though shrouded in a dense fog. He eschewed the daily rituals of food and hygiene. Sleep came in brief bouts of no more than an hour at a time, often punctured by unrecalled dreams that ended with a shudder and a scream. When he looked in the mirror, Raj saw eyes that showed the ravages of extended sleeplessness, streaked with red yet hollow and expressionless.

The memorial was to happen today at a local Hindu temple with a few family friends. Raj was reluctant to practice religious traditions, and his parents had given up their efforts to compel him when he was 13. One might say that forced piety was against his secular creed. The ceremony and superstition of religious ideology were too far removed from the scientific ideals that guided him.

From his third story balcony, Raj surveyed the neighborhood vista. He leaned forward and let the wind roll across his scalp.

Repulsed by the coldness of logic, Raj fantasized that the wind might carry him to a different time as he stared towards the rooftop of the ugly red brick office building across the street. He remembered stories of magic carpets that his mother read to him as a boy. The idea of being whisked away to a happier place and time seemed so bewitching when he was four years old on his mother's lap. But the real world was not populated by magic carpets or lamp-massaging genies. In their place stood death and pain. He blinked the tears out of his eyes and the image of his happy boyhood dissolved. He turned, picked up a tennis ball and flung it against his bedroom wall. What emotion remained within his enervated body and mind was a cesspool of anger: at his parents for leaving him, at the world for propagating its fairy tales and myths of happiness, at his colleagues for pretending to know his pain.

The basic premise of a memorial service infuriated Raj. It was all well and good to remember the great contributions people had made in their lives, but why the false wisdom, the sagacious-sounding words about souls and moving on to a better place? Did these people really expect him to believe? He had seen it before at the funerals of family friends, a horde of people eating and spouting platitudes that were supposed to be comforting but sounded rehearsed and insincere. It was a psychotic carnival, this post-mortem song and dance. He wished to send this circus of death away, but its time had arrived, and he was a required participant.

Raj forced himself to shower and shave. It would be difficult to rationalize not doing so in the face of the others who would inspect him. The mere thought of all those sad, pitying glances made Raj queasy. And there would be questions, especially medical questions. He was a doctor, after all. It was natural that people would want an explanation. But he had no answers. Not for this.

He stumbled over to the bathroom, pausing to inspect himself in the mirror. The smoothly shaven head now sprouted a coarse, fuzzy growth that dwindled toward the apex of his scalp. The darkness of his hollow eyes was matched by dusky stubble that clung to his normally unencumbered face.

41

He berated himself for his unkempt appearance, applying a generous helping of shaving cream to his face. He couldn't let those people see him like this. Though he no longer felt like a medical professional, he needed to look like one. He smirked at the observation, his lip curling to the left as his nostrils flared with indignation.

Raj stepped into the shower. The erratic spray trickled, spurted, then pulsed out in pressurized torrents, before finally easing into a steady hot rain. The warmth and wetness offered their aid in scrubbing away recent history. He closed his eyes and let the insistent multitude of droplets pound him, allowing them to dance and frolic in their chaotic frenzy upon his dark skin.

Water was a trusted friend, whether it was the artificial rain of a shower or the roaring, salty blanket of an ocean wave. Aqueous environments were safe and supportive places where one could be vulnerable yet protected. "Sogginess is next to godliness," he used to joke after running through sprinklers or summer thunderstorms. He smiled at the memory, but the water soon grew cold, signaling the end of this particular hydrotherapy session.

Raj dried himself and entered his bedroom to change. It was time to face the voyeurs. He knew they would dissect and judge his reactions. He preferred to think of himself as oblivious to public scrutiny, but today was different. This time, he was scared and confused. It would have been preferable to be blind for a day, immune to the pitying eyes of onlookers. He wished to vanish from the scene, but as the only child it was his duty to carry the morbid burden of public grief.

He scoffed at the absurdity of social conventions. The original traditions were long gone anyway, replaced by Americanized surrogates. Why cling to cultural remnants? But this wasn't about him, he reminded himself. As strongly as he might wish to retreat, the service was to commemorate his parents. Their sacrifice deserved much more than memories.

He slipped on a dark gray shirt and hurriedly looped a black tie around his neck. He headed to his closet and pulled his black suit jacket off the rack, then slowly draped it over his shoulders, placing his arms into the sleeves of the jacket in a deliberate, measured manner. After a quick view of his reflection in the mirror, he checked the time.

It was two o'clock. He needed to be at the temple in an hour. His listlessness irritated him. Punctuality was a point of emphasis in the Patel family, and how would it look to the others if he were late?

At the bottom of the three flights of stairs, Raj flung open the rusty fire exit door and squinted into the glare from the mid-afternoon sun. He rushed past the newspaper kiosk, the Chinese laundry, and the corner delicatessen. He lengthened his stride, which became smoother and more purposeful. He stared straight ahead, averting his eyes from those who crossed his path.

After several blocks, he reached the train station. Raj dug through the pockets of his infrequently used formal pants and found his wallet. He bought his ticket, and searched for the proper platform. The long-accumulated smells of stale cigarettes, spilled beer, and dried urine mixed to form the unique subway odor that he had grown to accept as a feature of big-city life.

He found a seat on one of the concrete slabs that passed for benches and his eyes watched a candy wrapper dancing in the warm gusts of wind, floating up and down until a sudden lull sent the waxy paper tumbling to the ground.

Other passengers trickled in at a steady pace, and by the time the train arrived five minutes later, the platform was almost full. Raj heard the unmistakable clatter of the approaching train and watched it crawl to a stop. Busy throngs of humanity spilled out onto the platform like mindless swarms of manic ants, followed through the open doors by Raj and his fellow commuters.

Raj found a seat in the corner where he could melt into the walls of the train. He turned his head to the right and looked out the window. Scores of concrete blocks passed before his eyes, with an occasional glance at urban decay interspersed. It was a gloomy vista, one toward which he would not normally have gravitated. But given his current state, the monotony numbed his troubled mind.

The passengers stuffed the train to capacity. Raj was forced to lean into the wall to avoid contact with the outsized backpack of a woman who had shoehorned herself into the corner of the train car. Life had a way of pushing one into a corner in so many ways, he thought.

As he emerged into the fresh air and warm sunshine Raj hustled across the street to the safety of the opposite sidewalk as oncoming traffic whistled past. The temple was a modest edifice, hardly identifiable as a place of worship. A faded wooden sign with peeling gold letters announcing "New India Hindu Temple" provided the only hint of the building's sacred purpose.

Raj entered the temple and was greeted by the priest, an old man with a few remaining strands of hair that had long since turned white. He smiled gently as he shuffled forward, stoop-shouldered to greet Raj. "Vikas Ramaswami. Now that you are here, is there anything you need before we begin?"

Raj shook his head.

"It is good to meet you," Ramaswami said. "I wish we had done so under happier circumstances. Your parents were wonderful people. It will be easy to remember them fondly, and hard to say goodbye."

The white-haired priest patted Raj on the shoulder. "It is OK. The body decays, but the souls live on. Your parents' virtues will outlive their bodies. Their spirits will be taken care of, and they will take care of you as well."

"Thank you, sir," Raj addressed the priest in a soft, child-like voice. But it was a wooden, inauthentic nicety, issued out of force of habit and obligation. His emotions formed a stew, a thick mixture he could not easily separate. Gratitude was not one of the identifiable flavors.

About a half hour passed in slow motion, as Raj paced through the small temple, hands knotted behind his back. Occasionally he stopped to watch the urban scenery through the large picture window on the west side of the church, noticing the laughing children running along the sidewalk, the panhandler with his dilapidated shopping cart and crimson, sun-fissured face, the commuters starting their daily voyage home.

Finally, the first of the guests arrived. Leading the way was Mr. Deepak Chatterjee, the avuncular figure who opened many doors in the business community for the Patels. Chatterjee was an almost spherical man who jiggled when he laughed, which was a common occurrence. Despite his age, he maintained a youthful glow. Raj had not seen Chatterjee in four or five years, but still maintained an affinity for the little fat man, who he knew as Uncle Deepak.

"Good to see you, Rajesh." Chatterjee offered his meaty right hand and vigorously shook the hand of the much younger Raj. "I am sorry for your loss. Tragic, tragic." Chatterjee shook his head and moved to a bench in the temple.

Next in line was Richard Thomas. The fiftyish businessman became acquainted with the Patels through his silk import business and love for all things Indian. His blond hair and blue eyes seemed out of place in the temple, but Richard had studied Hinduism for many years, lived in India doing missionary work, and even married an Indian woman (though they soon divorced). He was a frequent guest both at the Patels' shop and their home, where he bathed Mrs. Patel in compliments about her wonderful cooking.

"Meena, you are the best," he would often say as he was helping himself to extra food and addressing Mr. Patel. "Ganesh, you are a lucky man. Guard this woman with your life, I tell you."

The dapper Thomas approached Raj with uncharacteristic solemnity. His normally jovial face was creased with sadness.

"Rajesh, I am so sorry. I will miss them too," he said as he dabbed his eyes with a monogrammed handkerchief.

Raj thanked Thomas for his sentiments and moved on to greet the next guests. He thought to himself how strange it was that these people he had not seen nor heard from in years suddenly came out at the time of a funeral. Sometimes it seemed the dead had more friends than the living.

The door to the temple opened and a large, rough-looking man entered. Raj heard him before he saw the face. The loud, thumping footsteps stated that this could be none other than Mr. Sunil Gupta, hotel manager and purveyor of large feasts.

Raj surveyed the burly gentleman, whose muscular frame and clumsy gait belied his intellectual and professional sophistication. Gupta graduated with honors from a prestigious I.I.T in Mumbai before emigrating to the U.S. In short order he took over a small motel chain and turned it into a pot of gold. When they became friendly with the Patels, Raj had a nearby aunt and uncle. The Guptas served sumptuous feasts every Diwali with signature dishes from numerous Indian provinces and a minimum of three types of dessert. Raj could almost taste the explosive fire of Kamala's lamb vindaloo, and the nutty sweetness of her rich, buttery desserts.

Gupta halted in front of Raj. He clasped his hands in front of him.

"Rajesh," said Gupta, in his rich, smooth baritone. Raj admired the quality of the man's voice, which was as smooth as his gait was ungainly. "It is a shame. Such a shame. I will miss our dinners together. I will miss everything about them."

Kamala followed behind her husband, echoing his sentiments. "Yes, yes. Very terrible. You need something, call us, OK?"

Raj now walked slowly to his seat, closest to the priest. He felt his knees tremble as he sat down, and noticed his hands shaking. He clenched his fists together and crossed his arms, then relaxed them and let his hands fall to his sides.

The priest was ready to begin the ceremony. He clasped his hands in front of him and began to speak.

"We are here today to honor the memory of Ganesh and Meena Patel, our beloved friends."

The priest chanted a prayer in Hindi. All in attendance bowed their heads. Raj did not hear or comprehend the content of the priest's words, absorbing only the singsong intonation. He felt as though he were watching the scene from a corner of the rafters: it seemed distant and indistinct.

After performing a brief ritual, Ramaswami turned to Raj and nodded for him to say a few words. Raj felt his legs falter beneath him as he rose to begin his monologue.

"My parents were generous people," Raj began. "Selfless, industrious. They asked nothing and gave everything. Few among us are worthy of them, least of all me. I thank you for coming. They would appreciate it."

It was all he could manage. His eyes welled up and he could speak no longer.

Thomas, Chatterjee, and others followed suit, reminiscing about the Patels in the reverential terms that family and friends reserve for their departed.

When the last guests had spoken and expressed their condolences, Ramaswami approached Raj and addressed him in a gentle but grave manner.

"It is very important that the souls begin their journey properly, young man. You must take their ashes to the river and scatter them so the souls will be free. All souls deserve liberty."

Raj nodded.

"I understand," he said, though in truth he was lost and baffled.

The guests left the temple, but Raj could not. His legs collapsed and he staggered to his knees. Ramaswami stood by and bore silent witness as Raj prostrated himself and began to convulse with body-shaking tears.

Ramaswami pursed his lips, folded his hands into a pyramidal tent, and addressed Raj.

"Perhaps you would like some time alone? Stay as long as you like," he said before disappearing from view.

Raj spent an hour at the crematorium lost in thought with the urns at his feet. In the containers was the final connection to his past. He took a few deep breaths and gathered up the containers. He wandered towards the exit, nearly stumbling over a zigzag crack in the floor along the way.

Raj rode the train home with an empty stare on his face and an urn in either hand. As the crowd milled around him he stared at the floor, an endless sea of feet. There were large feet in grimy work boots and dainty women's feet in heels, shod for the evening, office workers in polished wingtips, and many nondescript pedal pairs belonging to equally undistinguished people.

When Raj heard the conductor's voice calling out his stop, he rose and clutched the urns tight to his body. He waited for his fellow travelers to disembark before sliding through the train's doors at the last possible instant. He forced his unwilling limbs up the steps, his head down, shoulders bent forward.

When Raj arrived at his apartment he fumbled for his keys and opened the lock. Propping the door open with one foot, he reached down and scooped up the two silver containers that held all that remained of his family. As the door closed behind him, he ambled over to a flimsy teak coffee table and set the ashes where the sun's last rays still shone.

Heavy-lidded, he stumbled to his bedroom and removed his jacket. He flung it disdainfully into a corner. His shoes suffered a similar fate, bouncing off the bedroom wall with a thud. Raj calmed down as he slipped off his tie and stripped down to his underwear. Exhausted, he fell asleep sprawled sideways on the queen-sized mattress.

Raj lay in his bed for three full days, arising only to relieve himself. Despite not eating, his stomach felt full. The rest of his being was empty, and the void dwarfed any physical needs within his body.

Sedation was the only reliable sanctuary in a treacherous world but it remained elusive despite his exhaustion. All he could see in his dreams was the scene from the unit, with his parents' bodies lying motionless and a relentless beeping sound keeping time like a metronome in the background. If that wasn't disturbing enough, at times the bodies vanished, and all he could see were his parents' heads, their mouths open in an inaudible scream.

When Raj finally roused himself from the bed, he realized he must do something with his parents' ashes. They sat bottled up on his coffee table and the priest had specifically instructed him to scatter the ashes within a day.

"Fuck the priest," Raj muttered. "Where was his wonderful higher power when my parents were clinging to life in ICU? Where was it when the car crashed?"

He picked up a tennis ball, tossed it into the air above him, then snatched it out of the air and hurled it into the kitchen. The ball careened off a wall and ricocheted into a drainer full of pots and pans. The priest's opinions were immaterial, but what of his parents and their wishes? They weren't orthodox Hindus but were clear about their burial wishes. In the absence of their beloved Ganges, the East River was their preferred resting place. He must get up, go to the river and let the ashes float down the warm breeze into the cushion of murky water below. In the wake of a less than dutiful life, surely he could do this one thing. He sighed and headed to the bathroom to shower.

Raj washed off the three-day accumulation of grime and odor and threw on a pair of sweatpants and a t-shirt. He laced up his well-worn Nikes, and snatched the pair of urns, clutching them in his arms. He slid out of the apartment, letting the door close behind him without bothering to lock it. Down the stairs he rushed, past a trail of his elderly neighbors who entered the building in search of shelter from the midday sun.

His gait was rapid and purposeful, unwavering until he reached the water's edge. Raj set the urns down on a nearby bench and paused to catch his breath. The breeze brought with it the noise of the river lapping at its banks and the smells of hot dogs and soft pretzels wafting through the air.

It was time to do his duty. He knew his parents' bodies were gone, and that the process was symbolic and alien to his thinking, but it must be done.

He removed the solid silver tops of the urns and set them on either side of him as he stood by the river. He waited for the first gust of wind and pitched his mother's ashes out towards the brown, steadily flowing water. He dropped the container at his feet and heard it rattle as the ash particles danced in the sun, finally alighting on the water.

The ashes of his father soon followed. At times the sun's rays hit the dust in such a way that Raj could have sworn the embers were still burning. He followed the path of the particles, watching as they drifted downstream and dropped out of sight into the dark waters.

Now all trace of family was gone. His parents left nothing in their wake, because they had given all they had for him in life. Raj stared at the empty containers. He bent down to pick them up, then reconsidered and left the vessels lying by the river. Emptied of all remains, they were of no use to him anymore. He bowed his head and shuffled away from the water's edge, unmoored from his past and adrift in his present.

Chapter Five

A firm knock came at the apartment door. Raj tried to ignore it, but the thumping continued. He made his way to the door, hoping the offending individual might be someone he could easily dismiss.

Raj opened the door and saw Gupta at the threshold bearing gifts.

"Just some brinjal pickle, bharta, and lemon rice, Raj," he said. "You must eat. You are too skinny. Your mother would not be happy with me if I didn't keep on you about this."

"Thank you, would you like to come in?"

Raj knew he was obligated to offer hospitality. He could fake his way through a conversation with Gupta. They drank Darjeeling tea with shortbread cookies.

"You know the Gita tells us that the Embodied one never really dies. 'Certain is death for the born, and certain is birth for the dead. Therefore over the inevitable thou shouldst not grieve," said Gupta. "Not my words, but ancient scripture."

"Wasn't aware of that," said Raj. "Guess you learn something new every day."

"Rajesh, you really need to get out of the house," Gupta said, rubbing his graying temples. "Come with us to temple, maybe meet someone. Your parents would like that."

"I'm not ready," said Raj. He squirmed in his chair. "I need time."

"You don't know that until you try. Take it from me. I have seen many years and strange things in life. You never know just what may come out of all this," said Gupta.

Raj detested the "silver lining" school of thought. He had bitten his tongue long enough.

"Please leave me alone," he said. "I can't buy that right now."

"No, no it's true," Gupta insisted.

"Get out," said Raj.

Gupta shifted in his seat.

Raj gestured to the door.

"I meant what I said. Get out!"

He glared as Gupta hurried out the door.

Didn't people understand? The grieving heart doesn't read a textbook.

Three weeks had passed since the death of his parents. Raj spent the time as an inert recluse. The department head stopped by a couple of times, but Raj sent him away without any promise to return. Sometimes Gail or Chatterjee tried to pry him out of his doldrums, but Raj dismissed them as well. It would be better for them if they gave up on him. After a while, the visits ceased.

Outside, the floral blooms in a kaleidoscope of hues provided a cozy and inviting vista but Raj only noticed for snippets of time. He hid behind self-made barriers of window shades and curtains. When he wanted light, he flipped on the television and watched the talking marionettes discussing the day's issues with ever-present smiles on their faces. Floods, murders, famine, and disease could not dislodge a hair on these ridiculous caricatures. He shook his head and turned off the news.

What was the point of pain? Maybe the sadness he felt was some form of retribution. There was the time he'd punched a kid in the nose and allowed someone else to take the fall. There were girlfriends he had cheated on and left because they bored him, or innumerable venial deceptions he'd practiced. Yes, he'd done some reprehensible things, but why would his parents pay for his transgressions? Still, he felt a need to make amends, and he had no idea how.

For several days Raj wished that the night would swallow him into its vast black belly, so he might never have to face the light of day again. But every morning, the sun's rays peeked in through the half-inch space under his curtains and Raj saw his wish denied. The past month taught him that hope was a fool's concept. Having garnered this knowledge, the pursuit of life's goals seemed empty.

Today the burden of grief assumed a heavier weight. Something must be done. Waiting for recovery served no purpose. Action was imperative. Could the wreckage of his heart be fixed, salvaged and made functional again? No, any efforts in that direction were doomed to futility. The only sensible option was to make a final end of the sadness and confusion.

Raj sighed and headed to the bathroom where he opened the door to his medicine cabinet.

Acetaminophen, diphenhydramine, ibuprofen. Oh, and the contraband Dexedrine he'd used when studying. These would form a good Last Supper. He took the four half-full pill bottles to the kitchen and looked for a suitable liquid accompaniment.

"Ah, champagne from New Year's."

Raj hardly ever drank, but had hosted a party last year at his apartment. The unfinished liquor bottle beckoned, and Raj was grateful for its presence.

He uncorked the bottle and sucked down a long drink from it. He opened the pill containers and swallowed the tablets in generous quantities.

"A handful of you, and you, and you," he addressed the pills. "Time for another drink."

He guzzled a long draft from the bottle followed by another round of pills. The world was fading away, and the sensation was not unpleasant. In all, Raj finished half the bottle of champagne and ingested approximately two dozen of each pill. Consciousness slipped away, and he slumped to the floor, falling with his head by the doorway and his body in the kitchen, his arms splayed wide apart.

The building superintendent, Mr. Augie Vitelli, had vowed weeks ago to fix the leaky faucets in the third-floor apartment. As Raj lay motionless, he heard the superintendent's familiar voice.

"Here to do those repairs you wanted," Vitelli said.

Raj could not muster a response. Though he was still conscious, his brain felt muddled, as if all of the detritus of his life were swirling around, blocking entry or exit of all coherence.

Vitelli knocked again, louder this time.

"I need to come in and do the work now," he heard Vitelli say. Raj heard the key turn and the door open, and then felt muffled pain as the corner of it struck his shoulder.

"Damned doors," he heard Vitelli mutter as he tried to force the door open.

"Holy Mary, Mother of God!" Vitelli screamed. "Hey, somebody help. Help! Call 911!"

Raj heard a clamor ensuing from the hallway, a variety of sounds and words that made little sense to his waning consciousness.

Within minutes, the paramedics arrived on scene, charging up the grimy concrete staircase, instructing the neighbors to disperse and stand clear. Some did so. Others, possessed by the perverse attraction of tragedy, looked on in the manner of drivers who slow to a crawl at the scene of a wreck.

Through half-shut eyes, Raj saw a grizzled, wiry paramedic with piercing grayish eyes.

"Airway appears to be clear, shallow breathing, has a pulse, but not responsive, let's get him in an ambulance. Let's move him, guys," he barked. The team worked with cool, detached efficiency, and within two minutes Raj Patel was loaded onto a stretcher and sent on his way to the ambulance that waited at the sidewalk below.

The ambulance doors closed. Two men watched over Raj, monitoring his vitals. He overheard snippets of their conversation.

"Geez, what do you think happened here, Jack?"

"Ah, who knows? Smells like he has some booze in him or something. Maybe he just fell and got knocked out when he was drunk. Happens all the damn time with these alkies. Good reason not to drink, Geno."

"Yep, you know me. My body's a temple! Why's he twitching and tachycardic, though?" Geno asked. He stared at his unresponsive patient, squinted and cocked his head to the side. "I dunno why, but he looks familiar. I think I seen him before, Jack."

"Geno, you're always seeing things," Jack scoffed. "You ain't never seen this guy before. Don't overthink it, I always say. Probably seen a lot of people that looked like him though. Hard to tell 'em apart sometimes."

"Yeah, you're probably right."

The ambulance screeched to a halt, a signal that Raj had reached his immediate destination. The jarring of the vehicle awakened Raj. He let out a faint groan and opened his eyes, though he remained in a stupor. Jack and Geno jumped into motion, pulling the stretcher out and wheeling him into the emergency room.

The emergency room doctor, a rail-thin, middle-aged, raptor-like woman with a pearl necklace, stared at the paramedics and barked her questions.

"OK, guys, short and sweet. What do we have?"

Geno stuttered and stumbled over the details of the case. His colleague Jack came to his rescue. "Found down, unresponsive, tachycardic at a rate of 145, woke up a little but still delirious. Possible head trauma, possible overdose."

The doctor nodded and dismissed the paramedics. She pointed to a patient care tech.

"Get this man in a room. And do it now!"

"Dr. Beakman," came the word from one of the techs, "we've got a room for your patient. Everything's set up the way you like it."

Before the last words were uttered Dr. Beakman flung open the door to the ER room and barked more orders. "OK guys, you know the drill, C-spine films, CT scan, fingerstick blood sugar, amp of D50, Narcan, get a u.tox, BAL, acetaminophen and salicylate levels."

The team flew into action as Raj floated in an intermediate state of consciousness. He saw people peering down at him, bright lights, and everything seemed out of focus. He heard the speech of people uttering medical phrases.

"It's OK," a voice addressed him. "We've got it all under control. We'll take care of you. Just stay still and calm."

Raj struggled to get up. He yanked at the restraints attached to his arms, but they refused to give way. Soon he felt a needle delivering a shot into his IV line, and he slipped back to sleep.

Raj heard Dr. Beakman above the hum of the ER as she read his test results aloud. "Hmm. Alcohol's .13, doesn't seem like a lot, but who knows how long this guy's been down. Blood sugar's normal. C-spine's cleared, CT looked normal. What the hell am I missing here? Oh shit. That acetaminophen level is high. And amphetamines, that's interesting. We're gonna need to give him Mucomyst and monitor. But there must be something else here."

She turned and hurried into the room where Raj lay in a tranquil haze.

"I'm Dr. Beakman," she introduced herself. "I've come to find out what's going on with you."

Raj opened his eyes, surveyed the room and recoiled from the doctor. It seemed unsafe to trust her. He groaned as his elbow thumped against a wall.

"It's OK. Can you tell me your name?" Dr Beakman asked.

Raj only managed a blank stare.

"Your name," Dr. Beakman said again in a loud, slow tone, as though to clarify her point by turning up the amplitude.

"Patel, Raj Patel," Raj whispered. He had no idea who this lady was, or why she was asking these questions, but considered it possible that he was in hell. By logical extension, she would be Satan.

"OK, now we're getting somewhere. Tell me where you are." Raj surveyed the room, began to tremble, and looked fearfully at the doctor. If she was a doctor, this could be a hospital, but if not, where was he? He shook his head.

"You don't know. OK that's not so good, but not unexpected. Tell me what day of the week it is," Beakman asked.

He wracked his brain but no answer was forthcoming, so he shrugged his shoulders and pulled the sheets up over him. The doctor approached and looked at his eyes, then pried open his mouth.

"Hmm. Looks really dry," she muttered to herself. "Dry as a bone, mad as a hatter. Mr. Patel, did you take any Benadryl today? I need to know. You could be experiencing what we call anticholinergic delirium."

Raj glanced down at the floor. Dr. Beakman, apparently having obtained what she needed, stalked off. She hurried to the nurses' station and spoke in a low but audible tone.

"Guys, get psych down here, and bring the patient in room three out to the hallway so we can watch him. I'm strongly suspecting an intentional OD here. The sooner they get him out of here, the better."

Raj lay motionless in the hallway, his darting eyes seeing blurred forms that flashed by in a whirl of color and motion. His thoughts blended into a soupy mixture, pureed together so as to be almost unrecognizable. He had surrendered to sleep when a loud knock on the wall behind him jarred him awake.

"I'm sorry to startle you, sir." A bright-eyed, petite, strawberry-blonde woman peered in. "Are you Rajesh Patel?"

Raj groaned and nodded.

"I'll take that as a yes," she smiled. She walked over to a chair that sat by the far wall in the nurses' station and pulled it over to the bedside. "My name's Dr. Morgan Meyerstein. I am one of the psychiatrists that work here, and Dr. Beakman asked me to speak with you. Is that OK? I apologize for the less than comfortable surroundings. I wish we had some place more private and comfortable to chat, but we'll have to make do with what we have."

Dressed in a long beige skirt and a cream-colored floral print silk blouse, with long, wavy hair, Dr. Meyerstein did not resemble any psychiatrist Raj had ever met in med school. He became more certain that this alleged hospital held some sinister alternate identity.

"I know it has to be hard talking to someone you just met," Meyerstein said. "But perhaps you'd be able to fill me in on what happened. I'd appreciate it if you could."

Raj realized that his throat was parched.

"Thirsty," he grunted.

"You want a cup of water? I'll be right back with some, then we can talk OK?" She looked at Raj, who nodded, and vanished to fill a pitcher.

When she returned, Raj gulped down an icy cup of water and began to feel somewhat better. It appeared that this shrink was here to help. There were so many gaps in his mind. Perhaps she could fill in the blanks for him.

"Thanks. Where am I?" asked Raj.

Dr. Meyerstein smiled and answered. "You're in the hospital, St. Ignatius Hospital emergency room to be exact. Clearly you're having some problems remembering things. Tell me what you do remember leading up to coming here."

Raj paused and frowned. He sat up, pushed himself up further against his pillow and surveyed the scene. It did indeed appear he was in an emergency room, not too dissimilar from his own hospital ER. Nurses, orderlies, and techs buzzed hither and yon, gurneys rolled by, and the episodic barking of orders and beeping of machines gave the environment a feel of controlled chaos.

"I remember . . . I was at home, in my apartment. I was very tired. I took some pills, and I think I had some stuff to drink as well," he said.

"OK, good start," said Meyerstein. "Do you remember what you took?"

"I . . . Tylenol and some other stuff . . ." Raj said in a tone that was as much question as answer.

"The medics found some Benadryl and ibuprofen there. Also some Dexedrine. Were those the other things you took?"

"Could be, seems familiar. I guess I'm still a bit confused. Sorry I'm not much help to you." Raj slumped back on the gurney.

"The confusion is probably a result of your overdose. Benadryl in particular can do that. The fog will clear but it may take a couple of days. Can you give me a picture of what was going on in your life before you took the pills? Maybe that will help us piece this together," suggested the psychiatrist.

Raj frowned again and tears escaped the corners of his eyes. He spilled his story with only dim awareness of the words he uttered.

"Not long ago, it seems like yesterday even though it wasn't, my parents died in a car crash. It was my fault. And now I'm all alone. I am worn out. I just want the hurt to stop, doctor. Can you make it stop?"

Dr. Meyerstein leaned forward and touched the railing of the bed.

"I only wish I could, Mr. Patel. I am very sorry about your parents' deaths. It sounds like life has been almost unbearable for you since they left. But I promise to do what I can."

A tear rolled down his cheek. He looked down at the floor and began to sob. Dr. Meyerstein walked to the nurses' station and returned with a box of tissues. She offered the box to Raj, who took them and blotted away the tears.

"I know this must be excruciating for you to talk about," said Dr. Meyerstein. "But I really need to know, when you took those pills, were you trying to die?"

"I don't know. That's the truth, although I'm sure you don't believe me," said Raj. His gaze wandered across the hallway in front of him. "The time when I took the pills is still kind of fuzzy, and I don't remember my intentions."

Dr. Meyerstein paused and looked at her patient, raising her left hand to her chin and tapping her long violet nail tips against her lips. She crossed her legs, tilted her head and waited. Several minutes passed before the she decided to break the silence.

"The thoughts. You don't remember what they were. But perhaps you could tell me how you feel right now about still being alive? Sometimes our emotions tell us more than thoughts."

Raj shrugged. "I don't know. I'm exhausted. I just wish it would all stop."

"Does that mean you'd do something to stop your pain?" asked Dr. Meyerstein.

"You mean like suicide?" said Raj. "To be completely honest, I have no idea. I am so confused, so messed up right now. Life makes no sense."

"So given that confusion, and given that it sure looks like you did some stuff that was pretty dangerous, would you be opposed to coming in to our acute psychiatric unit?" Dr. Meyerstein's eyes scanned the young man's face.

He sat up unsteadily on the gurney, bracing his weight on his elbows as he leaned backward. He searched her eyes through his blurred vision. They seemed honest and kind.

"Well, let me ask you, doctor, are you the one who will be treating me?" he asked.

Meyerstein smiled.

"Well, as it happens, yes. I hope that's a good thing?"

He might be beyond all assistance. But if anyone could help it would be her. Did he want to be saved? He scanned the piece of paper that was placed in his lap and signed it where the doctor had made a large "X". Dr. Meyerstein smiled and took the paper.

"I'll come in," he said, signing the paper. He hoped the choice was not one he would later regret.

"You've made the right decision. There is light at the end of the tunnel, and we'll help you find it. I will see you in the morning," she said.

Chapter Six

Raj awoke with a start. A tall, moon-faced patient care tech stared down from above. The androgynous figure wore white hospital scrubs.

"Mr. Patel? They're ready for you up on the unit. I've come to take you there. Just a couple of minutes ride on the elevator, and we'll be there before you know it," the orderly quipped in an oddly cheerful voice.

Raj regretted his decision. But it was too late to change his mind as he and the stretcher were loaded onto a patient transport elevator. In a matter of seconds he was wheeled up to the locked doors. Raj scanned the interview room in which he sat. The sterile white walls, undisturbed by windows, gave away no secrets about this place. It felt small and constrictive, not the tranquil and nurturing environment Raj had hoped for.

He had been sitting in the room for no more than five minutes when an obese, expressionless woman walked in armed with a clipboard, stethoscope, and neon-green pen.

"Hi, I'm Cecilia, I'm one of the night nurses. I'll help you settle in," she said in a slow, Southern-tinged drawl. "First I'll just have to ask you some questions, and then we'll get your vitals, and after that I'll help you to your room. Any questions?"

Raj shook his head.

"Good, let's get started," said Cecilia. "What is your name? And how old are you?"

Raj went through a litany of such inquiries, many of them repetitions of previous ones. He wished the fat woman would just shut up. The sound of her voice and motion of her jaws irritated him. As he answered, he consoled himself with the thought that in a short time she would go home and would be someone else's problem.

In what seemed no more than an hour, the necessary preparations had been made. Cecilia arose to guide Raj to his room. He followed her cue, wobbling on weakened knees as he stood.

"Careful, now," cautioned Cecilia. "We don't want you to fall down and crack that precious head. Hold onto my arm. I'll take you to your room."

Raj noticed that the hallway was narrow enough that he could touch both walls. Given his disturbed equilibrium, he was grateful for this fact. Patient rooms branched off both sides, surrounding a glass-enclosed center island where the techs, nurses and doctors took refuge and conversed in tones inaudible to the patients. The staff watched from their glass cage. He felt their eyes upon him as he ambled to his room.

Cecilia whispered as they paused outside his room. "You have a roommate. His name is Carlos. Sometimes he gets a little excited, but he's harmless. If there are any problems, come up and knock on the window to get one of us. That's your bed," she said, indicating a narrow but adequate hospital-issue bed adjacent the door.

Raj let go of Cecilia's arm and shuffled to the bed. How had life come to this? He was so estranged from home, from warmth, and even from himself. The sterile, impersonal echoes of a hospital environment that had been familiar were now forbidding. Even the familiar touches of the scuffed white floors and nurses' station seemed alien to him now. But it was too late now. Though he now doubted his willingness to be here, the events of the last day had sapped his last droplets of resistance, and his eyes closed tightly as soon as he pulled the flimsy blankets over him.

The night passed with disturbing haste. But what rest Raj obtained was much appreciated. He was awakened by a knock on the doorframe. Through his still sleepy eyes, Raj noticed a woman with skin the color of caramel pudding carrying test tubes on a rack.

"Hello," she said with a smile that clashed with the darkness outside. "I'm Jill from the lab. You must be Mr. Patel. The doctors ordered some tests so I'll need your arm if that's OK."

Raj slowly exposed his left arm and was roused out of his stupor by the pop of a needle into his arm. Recent events were starting to make sense now. The emotions that were drowned in his delirious haze of the previous day now came flooding back.

Jill soon finished with the morning blood draw and left Raj in peace for a few minutes. The intrusion of a morning visitor had caused the room's other occupant to stir. He flung off the covers, and turned his disheveled head toward Raj, the interloper.

Carlos sat up on the edge of the bed and raised his arms over his head. "I am Tarzan! TARZAN! King of the jungle! Lord and master of all the beasts!" He thumped his chest and issued a full-throated facsimile of the Ape-man's yell.

Though perhaps not sufficient to awaken the Amazon rainforest, Carlos' antics stirred the morning nurses moving and aroused some of the patients in the manner of morning reveille. A lanky male nurse with a blonde mustache entered the room.

"What's going on in here?" he barked with a glare at Carlos.

"I am Tarzan!" exclaimed Carlos, flashing a gap-toothed grin. "Where is my Jane? I have a banana for her."

The male nurse lowered his voice.

"No Jane right now. No bananas, Carlos, the jungle is sleeping right now. We need to be quiet OK?"

Carlos nodded and mimicked the nurse's tone.

"Quiet OK. OK. No banana. We have no banana. But you and me, Bob, we know the truth, eh?" he winked at the nurse, who turned away, shaking his head as he entered the hallway. Carlos decided to follow behind, cruising along with short, shuffling steps.

Raj had lost his parents and now, judging by his surroundings, his mind. He tried to kill himself to end all the pain and couldn't even do that right, despite all his medical knowledge. Life's paths were littered with so many mistakes. Words not said and actions not taken. These recent weeks were a cruel joke, a bad horror video. And there was no rewind button.

His dark musings were interrupted by the arrival of a cart loaded with the hospital's attempt at breakfast. The male nurse, noting that Raj was now awake, beckoned him. Raj obeyed, walking silently alongside the tall man to the dining area at the end of the hallway. The nurse pulled a tray off the cart and set it down on a gray plastic table, whose misaligned legs creaked in complaint. He pulled out a chair and motioned to Raj.

"I'm Bob. I brought you breakfast. You'll feel better if you eat," he said. "It's not much, but it does taste better when it's hot."

Raj slumped back in his seat and picked up his plastic fork. He glanced at the amorphous piles on his tray. In one corner was a small mound of eggs, blessed with the consistency of gelatin and the odor of sweaty socks. In the opposite corner sat a bowl of fruit salad consisting of a few slices of orange, some grapes, and two chunks of melon. In the center of the tray sat a hot bowl of something that resembled boiling glue. Raj guessed that it must be cream of wheat.

Raj speared a chunk of melon, twirled it on the end of his fork, and tentatively ate half of it. It was adequate, preferable to the eggs and gooey liquid that populated the rest of the tray. But eating was not a priority, so he pushed the rest of his tray away and leaned his chair back against the wall of the dining area.

Raj heard muffled footsteps approaching from the hallway. A gaunt, hollow-cheeked woman with cracked skin and bandaged wrists entered the room. She forced a smile that highlighted her pale, chapped lips and eroded teeth. Beneath sagging yellowed skin, her collarbones and wrists protruded. She sat down across from Raj and flashed a smile. He felt a twinge of pain and guilt seeing this miserable living skeleton. As he spied the bandages on her wrists, he imagined that this woman knew a life much harder than his own.

"What's your name?" She shook hands with Raj, who felt the thin bones of her fingers beneath her clammy skin. "I'm Lynette. You're new on the unit, huh?"

Raj nodded. "Yeah I'm a newbie. Name's Raj."

"It's a strange place sometimes, but they'll help you if you let them," Lynette said. "May not always have the answers, but they mean well."

He shifted in his chair, reflecting that these good intentions changed nothing about reality and its arbitrary cruelty.

"You been here a while?" Raj asked.

"Only 3 days this time, but it's my fourth time here," Lynette replied. She flashed a wry, yellow-toothed smile. "Just can't seem to get rid of my depression, and the meth sure don't help with that."

"Don't I know it," said Raj. In truth, he had little understanding of Lynette. Her life must be different than his, but maybe there was some wisdom in her words.

"Know what I used to do before I got like this?" Lynette asked, gesturing at her skeletal body. "Take a guess."

"Mmm. I don't know, receptionist?" Raj asked.

"Heh, guess again," she said.

"Teacher?" Raj was not sure what the point of this exercise was, but he was willing to play along.

"Close," Lynette answered. "I was a professor of English at a small community college. Poetry's my thing. Whitman, Hughes, Dickinson, Edna St. Vincent Millay. So much beauty can be found in language and books. Nothing too poetic about the life in here though, huh?"

Or was it too poetic? Stark misery and sadness were the essence of much verse, at least as far as Raj was aware.

Lynette finished the full contents of her tray, drank her juice, and excused herself.

"Maybe I'll see you in group. Take care," she said.

It was something to think about, the respective journeys people travelled to wind up here. Professors, doctors, who knew who else might be here and what stories they had to tell? And yet Raj found himself unmoved. Some might say that it was wrong to be so cold, so callous. But he lacked the energy and interest to attend to the woes of others.

Raj wandered the white halls with the feeling of a child tossed into a new school. Even among this collection of suffering outcasts, he did not belong. Assimilation was pointless. He shuffled back to his room and sat on the edge of the bed, gazing with an unfocused stare at the white wall ahead of him.

Thus Raj sat for a period of time that stretched far beyond his awareness. He rarely blinked, a motionless statue whose hands lay pinned to his thighs by invisible weights, feet magnetized to the floor. While patients milled about in the hall, Raj harbored only a peripheral awareness of them, and likewise they appeared oblivious to him.

Raj heard a female voice addressing him. He did not look up but went along with her hand that lifted him off the bed and guided him down the hallway. He did so without thought or question, shuffling along with the rhythm of the hand's vibration. They reached an interview room and the door opened.

He stood by the door and heard some more voices. This time the sounds were connected to faces and bodies. The faces and bodies murmured, and as he became more conscious, Raj began to feel cold. It was as though his hospital gown had been torn off and replaced with a layer of ice. He imagined himself as a piece of sculpture. These critics were present to deconstruct him visually, verbally, and physically. He looked back at the door, but his legs would not carry him out.

"How are you feeling this morning, Mr. Patel?" A gentle voice melted the ice, turning it into a blanket of warm water. Raj turned his head toward the sound, and saw Dr. Meyerstein leaning through the doorway of the hospital room. "The overdose cocktail you took was a pretty strong one. Are you feeling any clearer yet?"

Raj looked at the doctor, shifted in his black plastic chair, and looked down at the floor. It was a checkered pattern of white and pale green, pockmarked with the remnants of coffee stains and ground-in dirt.

"Oh, how rude of me," said Dr. Meyerstein. "You may remember me. I'm Dr. Meyerstein. But I just realized you know hardly anyone in this room. Let me introduce them to you."

There were four others in the room, two of them male nurses, one a female nurse, and one a male social worker. Raj did not pay attention to their names. He only briefly glanced at their faces before returning his gaze to the floor.

"And would you prefer to be called Mr. Patel or Rajesh, what do you go by?" asked Dr. Meyerstein.

He shrugged.

"Raj," he answered in a scratchy whisper.

"Well then, OK Raj. How did you sleep last night? Not too loud and disturbing in here I hope?" asked the doctor.

He shrugged, began to tap his right foot rapidly, and stared at the floor ahead of him.

The doctor turned to her compatriots and whispered something. She turned back towards Raj and attempted again to break through his stone wall of silence.

"By now, the effects of the medications should have cleared. I was wondering if you'd remembered any more about what happened? Why did you take the pills? Perhaps knowing this might help us to help you."

Raj raised his head and scanned the faces of the staff for clues.

"Can't say," he replied, squirming in his chair. If they knew conclusively that he had attempted to kill himself, they would use it against him. He hadn't figured out how just yet, but he knew it was best to admit as little as possible.

The social worker spoke next, in a gravelly bass voice that evoked the sound of distant thunder.

"Can't say, or don't want to say?"

The questioning eyes assaulted him and he looked away. His mind was clearing now and that wasn't entirely welcome. Lucidity brought with it memories of his dead parents, gray and motionless under white sheets, bodies and faces distended beyond recognition. He buried his head in his hands, stared at a brown stain on the floor, and began to rock back and forth in his chair. The urge to flee arose within him but he was too anxious and too weak to move from the chair. Instead he trembled, rocked, and wished that somehow he would wake up in a different, better place.

The female nurse knelt on the ground to make eye contact with Raj. "Are you OK?"

Raj nodded and averted his eyes toward the empty wall to his left. His body tightened and stretched to the brink of snapping.

"Make it stop!" he screamed, his mouth telescoping to its maximum width.

The nurses looked on and surrounded him at a distance.

"Stop, stop, stop, stop stop," he repeated numerous times in progressively softer tones.

Dr. Meyerstein signaled the nurses to back away and conferred with them before approaching Raj.

"What you're going through now, whatever is in your head and heart, I hope you can find it in you to let me help you," she entreated. "That's what I'm here for. You have a team here for you. Help us help you. It may not feel possible, but it is."

Raj remained in his seat, rocking in a slow, repetitive tempo. After a minute he raised his gaze to meet that of the doctor. She looked sincere enough to trust.

"Have you ever thought you had it all, only to find it was nothing but a dream, an illusion?" he asked Dr. Meyerstein. His voice stabilized and stiffened. "That's what I feel like now. I believed I knew what was real, what was important. But now I know nothing, and I question everything. What happens when your dreams become nightmares? This is where I am right now."

"That's a very sad and desperate place you're inhabiting," said Meyerstein with pursed lips and solemn eyes.

"This may sound weird, but I didn't even really know it was possible to feel this empty," said Raj more quietly. "Nothing too bad had ever happened in my life. And when it happened to others, I refused to feel anything. I had this great education, this fancy medical degree. All it gave me was insulation from reality. I was blind to life, ignorant by choice."

"You're a doctor?" asked Meyerstein. "And yet you didn't ask to be addressed that way. Why not?"

"What good is it? Two capital letters, but did they save my family? When it mattered most, I was completely impotent! I've renounced medicine. I just hope for your sake you don't see how useless it all is."

His shoulders shook and he dissolved into a storm of tears. He tried to choke back the plaintive cries to no avail, and soon the nurses gathered around again.

"I think we've put you through enough for one day," Meyerstein said. "You can go back to your room now if you'd like."

Dr. Meyerstein motioned for the nurses to help Raj back to his room. Raj looked around him, lost and bewildered, as a nurse escorted him back to his bed.

Raj watched as the staff went on with their examination and treatment of the other patients, but he could hear their discussions of his case echoing down the hall.

"They say his Mom and Dad died suddenly, first week of his residency. Car accident when they were coming to see him. I guess he just couldn't handle the grief," said Gerry to the nursing staff.

"Yeah, that's what I heard too," said Bob, the junior-most nurse on the unit. "Tragic. Some people just aren't built to withstand those kinds of breaks, I guess. Mmm. Tuna on wheat. Nobody knows tuna salad like my wife, I tell you. Hey, speaking of food, you know Raj didn't touch his breakfast or lunch. Want me to find out what's up?"

"Dunno Bob," said Meyerstein. "Could be that he's just too sad to be hungry, but it pays to check how long he's been like this. If it goes on much longer, we'll need to monitor his labs. Check electrolytes and prealbumin at least. That'll give us a baseline."

Raj heard loud footsteps approaching. Bob knocked on the door and approached. "Can I come in?" he asked. "We need to chat."

With the aid of modern medicine Carlos was fast asleep and Raj sat motionless on the edge of his bed, staring toward the room's small window in an apparent trance. His eyes gave no sign of any mental activity.

The nurse tapped Raj on the shoulder. Raj rotated his head towards the nurse and stared in his general direction.

"Hi, I'm Bob, remember me from this morning?" Hearing no answer, the nurse continued. "Well, it's not important anyway. But I noticed you're not eating anything. We get worried when people stop eating. How long has it been since you've eaten?"

Raj looked toward the ceiling, narrowed his eyes and pretended to recall his last meal. He shook his head and shrugged his shoulders.

"Been a while, huh? Well, I'll tell you what," said Bob, "you think of anything you might like to eat, anything at all, and we'll see if we can get it for you, OK? Special order from the cafeteria, if that's what it takes."

Raj nodded and looked away. Bob ambled away from the room to check on the ward's other denizens. It offered Raj a chance to be alone in silence, a dubious blessing.

The ritual continued for 12 more days. The staff repeated their entreaties to engage Raj. He admired their persistence, but felt they were wasting their energy on him. In his free-floating state of emptiness, no group of strangers could provide him a safe harbor. Stripped of dreams and purpose, he fancied himself a colorless, empty shell whose fate no longer mattered, even to himself. He no longer identified as a doctor or a child of immigrants. Instead he was just another drone in the giant hive of humanity. Though he used to believe he was special, Raj now experienced the deadening numbness of being an ordinary fool. Why wouldn't they let him fade away? That was the last remnant of self-determination he possessed.

In the meantime, Carlos was let out to play in the metropolitan jungle and a nervous little man named Tim replaced him. With fine whiskers, frightened eyes, and frequent facial twitches, Tim bore a striking resemblance to a mouse. He stood no more than five feet in stature and spent most of the day scurrying away from human contact. This meant that Raj rarely had a roommate when he chose to sleep, for Tim fled in a panic to the hallway or the dining room, only venturing back into his bed after Raj had been asleep for a few hours.

On the morning of the twelfth day Raj was led once more into the interview room. But something was notably different. The first clue came from Dr. Meyerstein's voice.

"Look, Raj, you're not eating, you're not participating in your treatment, and frankly, I'm really worried," she said with a note of panic in her voice. "I don't know if you realize how serious shape you're in, but please, let us help you. We can only help us as much as you allow us to. And we really want to help. You deserve it. Please believe that."

Raj sat and stared straight at the doctor's blue eyes. Although he appreciated her compassion, he wondered why she cared. In the end it should be his choice to live or fade away. Who was she to say otherwise? Who was anyone?

Dr. Meyerstein continued.

"Because you have not been eating or drinking, you have become dehydrated, and we will need to give you IV fluids to get some nourishment in you. It might also help you feel better all-around. And we're going to need you to start taking that medication for depression, OK?"

Raj assumed his familiar posture, looking down and away from Meyerstein, indicating his attention only with a brief shrug. After a few more futile inquiries, Dr. Meyerstein let Raj return to his room.

"Raj," Dr. Meyerstein called out. She pulled up a chair and sat by the bedside, lowering her head to establish eye contact. "Listen, there's something I need to explain. Nod if you're hearing me."

Raj nodded, then looked away, glancing over the doctor's shoulder when she tried to make eye contact.

"As you probably know, it's our job to get you feeling better," she said. "We're a team here, and you're the most important part of that team. You've accomplished a lot in your life. This is just one more hill to climb. Might it be steep and rough? Absolutely, but if you're willing to get on board, I believe in you. Are you with me?"

"I guess I have to be," Raj said. "Since I'm still alive, I've got no other choice."

"Maybe some people see a death on their own terms as self-determination," Dr. Meyerstein replied. "But that is not my jurisdiction. I'm no existential philosopher. My sole mission here is to get you back into life. I'm not sure what's going on with you because it seems like there's a lot of emotion that you're carrying alone. I do not pretend to know exactly what that's like. But what I do know is this: you tried to kill yourself, you need treatment, and we can't force it on you in this hospital. That's the law. So I'm going to send you to County Hospital, and if they judge you to be a potential danger to yourself because of the depression, they can force you to undergo treatment. I hate to do this, but I don't see any other option. As much as you may not believe this, you deserve to live, to grow, to flourish."

Raj heard the words, but refrained from expressing his opinion.

"You get what I'm saying, Raj?" Meyerstein asked.

"You're going to make me live, when there's no point." he replied. He shook his head. "What happened to autonomy? Go ahead, send me, for all the good that'll do."

Chapter Seven

Irina and her father sat on the steps of an abandoned brownstone. She drew a deep breath and gave thanks for the ability to do so. Many people might not think about their lung capacity, but due to multiple hospitalizations and ER visits, Irina was vigilant about the days when inhalation started to feel like a challenge.

"Father," she said. "When will this America be what we wished for? Will our dreams ever come true?"

Alex took a shaggy gray blanket and draped it over Irina's shoulders.

"Dreams do not follow a schedule," he said. "At least this is what I think. If they did, why would we treasure them so much?"

Irina nestled her head on her father's shoulders and looked up at the sky.

"I suppose you are right," she said. "It is just that in Russia, at least I was the pretty one. At least I had that. Here, I am nobody."

Alex squeezed Irina to his chest.

"Do not ever say that you are nobody," he said. "You are Irina Petrova, the child of Olga and myself. You are loved. And you are beautiful."

Irina sat up and faced her father.

"Of course you say that," she said. "And I love you for it. But you are my father. You have to say these things. That is what fathers do. Maybe I just want to be loved by someone who does not have to. Is this wrong?"

Alex shook his head and stroked Irina's cheek. "Hardly," he said. "And in time, you will find your place next to that person. And your voice will be heard. And the crowds will stand and clap. It will happen. Have faith."

"Faith?" said Irina. "Did faith stop mother from dying? Did it keep those men from treating me like Satan's toy? What good has faith ever done?"

She stood up and spat in a nearby garbage can.

Alex walked over and put has hands on her shoulders. He bent down and looked into her eyes.

"I am sorry I upset you," he said. "All I want is to give you comfort. It is why I thought we would do better here. Maybe you are right. Maybe I was a fool to think that we could run from a problem to a dream."

Irina held her father close.

"There are no easy answers," she said. "This is what makes me sad and angry."

A lone tear ran down her left cheek. She wiped it away with the sleeve of her soiled overcoat.

"Ach, all this yearning and crying," she said. "May happiness be just around the corner."

"I would drink to that," said Alex. "But we have no beer or vodka, and such things do not keep us warm outside. Come."

They walked back to the steps. A burly, hirsute figure approached.

"This is my stoop," he said. He crumpled an empty beer can and threw it in the direction of Alex and Irina. "I'm asking you politely to git."

Alex rose to respond but Irina yanked his coat, pulling him back to the step. She stood and nodded at the hairy man.

"We had no idea that we were intruding," she said. "We are sorry, and will be on our way."

She and her father picked up their duffel bags and walked away.

"Give me yours," Alex said, taking the full dark green bag from Irina. "We may have to walk for some time before we find a suitable place."

"You know I can carry a bag, father," said Irina. "Especially this evening, when I am breathing well."

"Yes, the hospital did a good job with you this time," said Alex.

Irina looked off at the stars on the horizon.

"I am thankful for those doctors," she said. "Especially the one in the emergency room. There was something about him."

"You liked him, eh?" said Alex, nudging Irina with his elbow.

"Well I just didn't get to thank him," she said. A grin crawled across her face. "Not properly anyway."

"Well I see your ability to dream is alive and well," said Alex.

Irina punched her father in the arm.

"Hey, give me a shower and a sundress," she said. "Then we'll see who's dreaming."

"You are hoping he will be?" said Alex. "I wish for your sake that you are right. He seems like a good man. But remember the past. We must be cautious before we give our heart."

Irina stopped and looked at her father. "Why must I persist in remembering?" she asked. "I just want to move ahead. I do not want to have to feel the wind of my past blowing on my burn marks and my scars. Don't I deserve to forget?"

Alex paused and stared into the distance. "There are things we all wish to forget. But who gets to say what we deserve? All we can say is what we desire, and we can hope to fill our hearts and souls. But I know what you did not deserve, and that is in the past. Now we have new challenges."

As they walked, Irina stopped next to a tall, sleek office building. Its high profile would shelter them from rain and wind. Out here on the street, geometry mattered, as it was often the difference between safety and vulnerability.

"Shall we tuck in here?" Irina asked. "I do not see anybody here to push us out, and we can be warm here."

"As you wish, my dear," said Alex. "We are weary and must rest. Dreams cannot be realized with an exhausted body."

They sat down and spread out two blankets, then lay next to one another and wrapped a larger blanket around them. Alex's girth made him a good heat source, but Irina also found herself cramped into a corner in their makeshift shelter. In these last few months she had come to accept constriction as a necessary part of street life. In some ways she welcomed it. The squeezing pressure meant she was not alone.

"Father," she said. "Do you think we will one day have our own place? Like in Russia?"

"If I have my way, it will be better than Russia," he said. "Only we must be patient. And when the chance comes, we seize it in our hands and never let go."

"I am sorry to pressure you so much," said Irina. "You must also have wishes, yes? What do you want?"

Alex smoothed Irina's hair. "What any father wants," he said. "Or what any father should want. I want happiness for my child. Beyond that, anything that happens to me is of no importance."

Irina turned toward her father and propped herself up on her elbow.

"You don't want to have a shop, or another special job, like before?" she asked. "I know you took pride in your work. I'd like to see you happy, too."

Alex chuckled.

"Do not worry. I am a man of many talents. Maybe small ones, but still, I will find a way." He pointed to his duffel bag. "I have many tricks in this dirty old bag."

"Rest well, father," said Irina.

"You too," said Alex. "May you have only good dreams of a brighter future."

Chapter Eight

The ride to County Hospital was cold and frightening. Raj looked back and forth at the two large paramedics accompanying him. They stared straight ahead, quiet and impassive. The claustrophobic silence made Raj wish to jump out of the moving vehicle.

But though his mind wished to flee, he was incapable of moving his extremities. So there he lay, a jumbled brain trapped in an enfeebled body. It was a merciful occurrence when the ambulance came to a stop at its destination and the doors opened to reveal daylight.

Raj was moved to the psychiatric unit of County Hospital, a large brick building that stood apart from the main medical facilities. In his days as a medical student, he heard colorful tales of the psychiatric unit here. Some said this was the best place to get a full flavor of an inpatient ward. He never dreamed he would be forced to taste it like this.

As he shuffled forward, flanked by two large psychiatric technicians who looked as though they may be retired football players, Raj looked at the others with whom he would be sharing this surreal experience. He saw patients with yellowed skin, track marks on their arms, and swollen bellies. There were overweight middle-aged women who stooped and shuffled, their glassy eyes staring forward, and agitated young men with clenched fists and skin stretched tight as a drum across their jaws as they paced the length of the floor . There was even a man with a long ponytail who shot imaginary arrows into the sky every few seconds.

What Raj noticed most of all as he entered the receiving room for his interview was the constant but non-rhythmic drone of ambient noise. Silence would not be obtained here, as echoes lingered in the hallways at a low level but sometimes rose to a cacophonic intensity. It was like being stuck in a stadium full of cabdrivers, each honking with no rhythm or purpose. Was the noise external, or did some of it arise from within his foggy mind? As he recognized his confusion, Raj grew alarmed. Whose reality had he been thrust into?

A tall, brown-haired woman with a small lower jaw and long front teeth approached. Her face reminded him of a chipmunk. She said he would have to wait until tomorrow to meet the chief psychiatrist. He imagined her voice coming out in rodent-like squeaks and laughed, unaware of the chipmunk's attention.

"Chipmunk," he blurted, giggling.

The nurse looked askance at Raj and he quieted down, realizing that he had verbalized his thought. Was this what it was like to lose one's mind? He scanned the room and picked at his cuticles, tossing the small shards of flesh on the floor beside him. A second nurse poked her head into the room and beckoned to the chipmunk. They whispered and nodded, and the second nurse rushed off.

The chipmunk spoke, and Raj caught some of the words.

"Well . . . gotta get settled . . . show you . . . room." It was telegraphic, but clear enough to rouse Raj from his seat.

She led him through a locked door onto a bright white hallway. They turned left through the open door, and Raj glanced at his Spartan abode.

"Into my cell," he murmured.

The room was small and spare and in spite of the white walls, everything looked drab and grey. A pentagon-shaped restroom occupied the far corner of the room. Two narrow beds were the only furnishings in the gloomy space. Raj shuddered and sat down gingerly on the edge of the near bed as the chipmunk disappeared without a trace.

From the bathroom emerged a gaunt, bearded figure with long, flowing brown hair that receded somewhat in front. Raj silently nicknamed the man Hippie Jesus. The bearded man lay down on his bed, turned sideways and appraised Raj with a questioning look. Hippie Jesus turned away after a few seconds but glanced over every few minutes as if to monitor the young interloper's movements and intentions.

"Don't say much, do you?" the shaggy stranger asked Raj. "Well, let me tell you, trust no one here! I have been here three times, and I learned that. Don't believe them, they're all in on it. Who knows, maybe you're one of them too." His eyes widened as he waved his bony index finger high in the air.

Raj turned towards his roommate and stared. Interaction seemed a fruitless idea. Mercifully, the longhaired man paused and sank back into his bed, allowing Raj an opportunity to do the same. He swathed himself in the cover sheets, swaddled like an infant in search of security.

Sleep refused to enter the dark night and Raj spent the time on his back staring at the ceiling, arms crossed like an Egyptian mummy. Tonight the myriad thought fragments that formerly kept him company were lost. In their place was a vast, deep cavern. Raj felt himself falling and spinning, with no sign of an imminent floor. And it was the landing he feared. Raj got up from his bed and paced back and forth, retracing his steps a multitude of times in the hallway. The specter of anxiety clung to him, an invisible shadow that mirrored every movement.

"Go away, go away, go away," he chanted internally. But he could only silence the refrain for a moment, and soon a nurse came and escorted Raj to his bed. He felt a quick stabbing sensation in his shoulder, and soon the shadow was gone, erased by chemical tranquility.

The morning was initiated with breakfast that seemed eerily familiar. It was the same less than delectable fare he had been offered in the first hospital. But today the questionable appearance of the food was outweighed by his hunger. He ate the first bite of fruit, then a second, and soon vacuumed all the food off his tray.

"You best watch out for those eggs, man. They're poisoned," warned Hippie Jesus, whispering the last word with ominous emphasis. "I don't eat 'em. Who knows where they're from? They're sure as hell not organic, probably not even real eggs. No, sir, I won't eat this crap. They need to feed us like we're real people, am I right? I mean, they say I'm bipolar, that I'm delusional, bat-shit crazy. But years ago, it would have seemed crazy some of the shit that happens now, am I right? Maybe these folks just lack imagination. Got no vision. Maybe I'm a prophet. But nobody listens to Tiresias, am I right?"

Raj was too hungry to consider the origins of his food and considered asking the longhaired man for his eggs but thought better of it. It was at this point that a loud voice cracked through the air.

"Hello, my friends." Raj turned to locate the source of the stentorian greeting. He was surprised to find that they belonged to a gaunt, short man with square-rimmed spectacles and a shock of gray hair that defied gravity.

"I am Dr. Hofheinz," the diminutive man introduced himself. Raj could hear a Germanic tinge to this voice, which, though exuberant, also grated on the ears.

"Raj, I see you are eating our wonderful food. I am glad you have found your appetite," Dr. Hofheinz smiled, his light green eyes twinkling. "Being here has a way of doing that to people."

"Come with me," motioned the doctor, gesticulating, then bounding out of the room. When Raj was slow to follow, the doctor re-entered the room. "Come, come, we must talk," he insisted.

Raj trailed Dr. Hofheinz down the hallway to an empty room. The doctor pulled up a high-backed plastic chair and motioned for Raj to sit in it. He slid another chair over in front of himself and sat down, placing his elbows on his knees and resting his chin on his interlocked hands.

"So, first let me explain something. You are here because Dr. Meyerstein considered you a potential danger to yourself and weren't willing to accept treatment. Now, we can do this the easy way and work together, or we can let the court decide whether to compel treatment. That usually takes several days, maybe even a couple of weeks, and a mental health hearing that involves lawyers and a judge. But if you let us help you, maybe we can skip that whole ceremony. Understand, my friend?"

"I guess," said Raj.

"Good enough," said Dr. Hofheinz. "Now that we know the ground rules, tell me your story. How'd this all start?"

For several minutes, he explained his situation and answered Hofheinz's questions until there was nothing left to say.

This repeated intrusion of strangers into his thoughts and feelings felt unnecessary and voyeuristic. Liberty and autonomy should count for something in this world. Why couldn't they just leave him alone?

"I am curious, Raj. What's different today, now, from when you took all those pills?"

"Don't know," answered Raj. "Maybe nothing. Maybe everything."

"Come on, my friend, you must have some thoughts on the matter," insisted Hofheinz. "I know you must be an intelligent man. For God's sake you're a doctor. An ER physician I understand? You're probably smarter than me and you've sure had plenty of time to think. Am I to believe that you haven't thought about how today is different?"

"It's not. I have no friends, and now no family, nothing to care about. Maybe nothing you do will ever make it any better," said Raj. He glared at Hofheinz. "You're wasting your time on me."

Hofheinz sighed, the outline of his thin shoulders protruding through his polyester shirt as he did so. He paused to clear his throat before beginning anew.

"Perhaps you are right. It could be that we can change nothing and this is just one big existential dilemma. But one thing I know. If you were feeling miserable and suicidal then, and nothing's changed, well something's got to be done. And we have to do it. This means medication, and a lot more thinking. I know it sounds strange to you now, maybe even abhorrent, but we're here to be your life support, even if that's not what you want. So think about how we can help you."

"Looks like I'll have plenty of time for that here," said Raj.

Hofheinz directed a dour glance toward Raj, then stood up.

"Well, I think this interview is over. But we still have a lot of work to do, you and me, OK? Like it or not, we're a team."

Before Raj could issue a response, Hofheinz bounded off to see another of his many patients. Raj arose in slow motion and walked over to his room, pondering the last words the doctor had said.

What had the doctor meant by a lot of work to do? And the 'we' part. As if Raj had a say in this, had control of his emotions? The bastard seemed to think misery was a choice or something.

Raj ventured into the large common atrium that stood between four hallways full of patient rooms. It was the only area of warm light in this constrictive, dark environment, and he craved the sun's rays. A few humble ficus plants in heavy ceramic containers craned their bodies toward the light. When the sunrays streamed through the glass they illuminated floating dust particles in the air, imbuing the room with a near-celestial quality.

As Raj arrived in the atrium, he saw Hofheinz attempting to engage in a rational discourse with one of his patients, a leathery-faced man with multiple neck tattoos and steely blue eyes.

As he watched Hofheinz and the patient gesticulate at one another, Raj remembered his own encounters on the other side of the doctor-patient relationship. To what end had he tried to prescribe medicines, to save others from the processes of death and disease that inevitably won out? For a time it made him feel important, worthy of the esteem his parents and patients heaped upon him. But now he saw that the adulation and respect of others were meaningless. And without medicine, what would he do if he were compelled to endure the future?

The routine continued for seven days. Raj ate and drank with regularity. His strength and vitality improved but they still lagged behind their usual levels. He offered perfunctory answers to Hofheinz's questions but preferred to isolate himself from the others. He ventured out into the atrium only when it was relatively empty.

Though he was polite to the staff, Raj declined the medications they offered, reasoning that his illness was of an existential nature that could not be solved by mere pharmacology. He would not bend before the pressure of those who pretended to know him and care about him.

As he pondered the futility of treatment, Raj heard the voice of his doctor addressing him.

"So, Raj," Hofheinz began. He sounded irritated. "I guess you are wondering what is the purpose of all these people here? Do you think this is a game?"

Raj shook his head and feigned ignorance.

"I guess I have no idea, Doc."

Raj remained silent. He looked away and smirked, anticipating harsh words or some sort of punishment.

"It's like I told you, Raj, we can only help you if you work with us," Hofheinz explained in a tone that sounded rehearsed and insincere. "You see, I am powerless if you refuse help. I need you to trust me."

Raj allowed his tongue free access to his thoughts.

"You say I need to trust you, Dr. Hofheinz. Why should I? How do I know I can? To you I'm just another crazy guy. As far as I know, you don't care."

Only when he saw the startled looks on the nurses' faces did Raj realize the impact of his words. This didn't bode well for him. He looked away from the occupants of the room and began to pick at his fingernails.

"Well Raj," said Dr. Hofheinz, "I was hoping we could work together. But it looks like we will need to have a court decide whether you need treatment or not. And I have to tell you, I am confident they will see a need."

Hofheinz terminated the meeting and Raj was escorted back to his room. His shaggy and garrulous roommate was out in the atrium, which gave the Raj a long time to ponder the events of the last half-hour.

The longer he stayed here, the clearer it became that County Hospital was unsuitable to anything other than stagnation. Sooner or later, he needed to get out, and the earlier he could manage it, the better. What should he do? It was evident that whatever he did or said could be twisted against him. He needed to get back to the real world. There life was empty, but at least it was his own.

It took Raj a full day to decide how to obtain the information he needed. It was evident that the staff was now his adversary. He needed the advice of someone savvy, objective, and less than completely scrupulous. There must be no shortage of patients who fit the bill, but the trick was to find the proper one, a true veteran of the system.

He tried talking with Horace, the bombastic Jesus-resembling roommate who had grown quieter and more coherent now. It turned out that Horace was a chemical engineer before bipolar disorder struck.

"So what the hell are the rules of the game here?" Raj asked his roommate.

"Damned if I know," said Horace. "They'll tell you a lot of self-serving mumbo-jumbo, but I think the truth is they just let you go when they get tired of you." He tucked his pillow underneath his head, yawned, and soon was snoring loudly.

There were others as well who appeared familiar with the workings of the unit, but some were too intimidating to approach. After much deliberation Raj decided to pick the brain of one of the repeat customers who frequented the atrium. Joshua McGee was a well-preserved man in his mid fifties, with a long, equine face and a lean, muscular body to match. His tousled brown hair even fell over his shoulders in mane-like fashion and blew freely on the patio in the afternoon breezes.

Joshua often engaged other patients in conversation and appeared none too unhappy about being hospitalized. He told colorful stories of his many previous hospitalizations and was familiar with most of the regular nursing staff. As he talked and laughed, he looked like a "normal" person.

Raj walked up to Joshua, startling the older man from an apparent reverie as he introduced himself.

McGee chuckled and smiled, revealing a small gap where one of his upper front teeth had been. The gap gave him a disarming, folksy quality that he often used to charm the staff into giving him special extra privileges.

"So you do talk," said McGee in an effeminate tone. "Well, my name's Joshua. Not Josh, Josh-you-ah mind you. Like in the Bible. How you doing?"

"Not so great," admitted Raj. "But I know I want to get out of here and it seems everything I do just puts me further in the hole."

"Ah, a rookie." McGee smiled. "See, these people, they can be fooled, just like anybody else. You tell 'em you're depressed and wanting to kill yourself, they're gonna keep you. You just have to know how they think." McGee tapped his right temple with his index finger for emphasis.

Raj frowned. "You actually want to stay here?" he asked. "What on earth for?"

"Not all of us fit out there," said Joshua. "Life can be kinda brutal for a gay man in the projects. Out there I really do want to kill myself sometimes. But not between these walls. It's safer in here. Ain't nobody gonna beat me with a bat or burn me. And in here there are even some folks who understand me, if you know what I'm sayin'."

"Fair enough. Never really thought about that," Raj admitted. "Well, if I wanted to stay here, I suppose your advice would help, but I've got the opposite problem. I want out of here, the sooner the better."

McGee tapped his head again. "You gotta know the drill. You here voluntary or involuntary?"

Raj looked around to make sure nobody was listening. This felt like the kind of information he ought not to share, but what did he have to lose?

"Involuntary," he admitted.

McGee narrowed his eyes. After a brief silence, his expression brightened and he looked at Raj with a raised index finger.

"Well, I think I know what would work," he began. "Now mind you, I don't choose to do this, 'cause I kinda like it here. But I've seen others work it well. Basically, what you have to remember is that they don't judge you by nothing but your words and your action. You gotta sell them on a new you. Act like you're different. Born again. It's all theater. Understand?"

Raj nodded.

"You have to take your meds and pretend you're feeling better," McGee continued. "Then you tell 'em you've realized how much you need these meds and you'll stay on 'em. Attend the groups and talk, let them see and hear you. Make yourself visible. See, these folks, they're busy, and they would prefer to get you the hell outta here. So if you act well, they'll believe you are well. It's all about convincing them you've seen the light."

"It's that easy? Just take the meds for a short time, then act happier?" Raj stared at McGee. "Hofheinz will never buy it."

"Didn't say it was easy," Joshua corrected him. "Trick is to make it convincing. But you seem like a smart guy. I bet you can pull it off. And Hofhound, he's got an ego the size of this whole city and then some! Flattery will get you everywhere with him! Just kiss his ass, tell him how grateful you are to him and how the meds he's prescribing are magic and he laps it up like a cat does milk." McGee laughed at his own colorful imagery.

It made sense. But how could it really be that easy to get out? And why hadn't Raj, with his incisive mind, figured this out sooner?

"Thanks, Joshua. I'm Raj, by the way," he said to McGee as he left to head back to his room. The two men shook hands, and Raj felt less afraid, knowing that there was a road out of the kingdom of lost souls.

The day after his meeting with the staff, Raj began his mission to convince them of his changed heart and mind. He launched into testimonial mode for fourteen days. Raj took his pills, conversed with the nurses and Dr. Hofheinz, and praised them for their patience and professionalism.

"At first, I didn't trust you, but I realize now what's best for me, and I know you know what you're doing. Thank you so much for sticking with me." He repeated these words and other similar phrases like sacred mantras that would soon deliver him from confinement.

Hofheinz accosted Raj in his room on day fifteen with more than his usual quota of energy.

"Good news, Raj, the hearing date is today. Your court appointed lawyer has been going over your case, and you'll get to say your piece as well. Then the judge will decide what needs to happen from here."

Raj was confused. How could court be a good thing? Wasn't this what he had been seeking to avoid by playing the model patient role? He was hoping to forestall it. But Joshua's words echoed in his head: "these people, they can be fooled." The trick was figuring out what they wanted to hear. Sell the epiphany.

Hofheinz left and was soon followed by an odd-looking young man with thin, wire-rimmed circular framed glasses, a slight limp, thinning brown hair and a bowtie. The bowtied gentleman appeared to be no more than five years older than Raj, who was not encouraged by the thought that this was his appointed advocate.

"Hi, Tony Ghirardelli, I'll be your lawyer." The attorney's thick Brooklyn accent clashed with his appearance. "I've been looking at your case, and I think we can get you out of here if that's what you want?"

"Isn't that what everybody wants?" Raj asked.

Ghirardelli chuckled. "You'd be surprised. But anyway, here's what I'm seeing here. The reason you got transferred here in the first place is that you made a suicide attempt and appeared to be unwilling to be involved in your own treatment. But the last couple of weeks you've taken the meds voluntarily and the notes have shown some improvement. Plus, you're eating, which means you're not in medical danger anymore. All you need to do is keep up a good appearance in court and you'll be good to go. But be prepared, sometimes the judge will ask you questions directly. So you'll need to be able to show that you really are feeling good enough to leave and that you don't need further treatment to be enforced on you."

Raj nodded. Ghirardelli might look underwhelming, but his words suggested he would be competent enough. Release from confinement could not be far away. The thought made him question so-called freedom. He decided that it was the lesser of two evils. If he were to fade away, he'd much prefer to do it while alone, far from this madness.

In a few hours, Raj was summoned to appear at his hearing. Ghirardelli walked with him through the doors of the unit. They boarded an elevator that deposited them in the hospital's administrative wing. Opposite the elevator doors stood a moderate-sized conference room that would serve as "court" for the day. Raj entered the room first, followed by Mr. Ghirardelli. They strolled to the back of the room and sat at the end of a long, ovoid table.

In the front of the room stood an elevated platform with a rickety desk for the judge and another that served as the "witness stand". To call this a courtroom required a liberal definition of the word, but the room served its purpose.

The judge was the next to make his appearance. Judge Lawrence O'Rourke was a venerable civil judge who would be handling this case. O'Rourke's fleshy, dangling jowls, intense glare and perpetual scowl gave him the look of an irritated bulldog.

"Tony, where's your counterpart?" barked O'Rourke.

Ghirardelli shrugged. "Don't know, your honor. Thankfully I am not my opposing counsel's keeper."

O'Rourke chortled. "Well, we've still got a few minutes, so let's wait for her."

As he finished his sentence, a tall, slim woman in a black business suit strode hurriedly into the room. It was Carmen Rodriguez, the opposing counsel. Her frizzy black hair stood up in tight coils. The ends waved as she walked, like sea grass in a light breeze.

"Nice to see you, your honor," she said to the judge as she took a seat at the middle of the table.

A court reporter entered quietly and sat in the front right corner of the room. Judge O'Rourke looked around the room and pulled up his chair at the head of the table.

"OK, court is now in session in the matter of the County vs. Rajesh Patel. I'm Judge O'Rourke for those who don't know me. And we are here to decide the need for involuntary treatment. So, will the county attorney please begin?"

"Your honor," Rodriguez began slowly. "I will attempt today to show you that Rajesh Patel was a danger to himself and remains so at the present time. You will hear the testimony of two doctors and a paramedic. The city takes the position that without involuntary treatment, Mr. Patel would not engage in treatment and will cause himself bodily harm."

"Thank you," replied the judge. "You may sit down. Mr. Ghirardelli?"

"Your Honor, we do not dispute the fact that Rajesh Patel was a danger to himself two weeks ago. But the law stipulates that he must be an imminent danger to himself or others. We will attempt to prove that Mr. Patel is not currently a danger to himself or anyone else, and that treatment should therefore be on a strictly voluntary basis," said Ghirardelli.

The hearing began with testimony from Dr. Meyerstein, Dr. Hofheinz, and one of the paramedics. Raj was surprised by the alacrity with which the proceedings moved forward.

After a recess for the judge to consider the evidence before him, O'Rourke turned to Raj and addressed him in a grave tone.

"Young man, we have been discussing you for a while now. I would like to hear your thoughts on the matter. Mr. Ghirardelli, perhaps you'd like to begin?"

"Thank you, Your Honor," replied Ghirardelli.

Raj sat uneasily in the chair, watching the other faces in the small makeshift courtroom. Ghirardelli approached him and smiled.

"So, Mr. Patel," he began, "tell us how you're feeling now."

Raj cleared his dry throat and began to speak. Though he was averse to speaking any significant untruth, this seemed like a suitable time to make an exception. For the moment, he had to be a salesman.

"Well, I'm feeling a lot better now. I don't have any desire to die. And although Dr. Meyerstein and Dr. Hofheinz have been great, I know that I don't want to go through this again, which I know I would if I tried to kill myself again. This place is not for me. I just want to get back to trying to get on with life. I've realized that I have to, and I want to."

"But Mr. Patel," Ghirardelli asked in anticipation of his opposing counsel's question, "you did try to kill yourself, so why should we believe you're not a threat to yourself now?"

"I was really hurting, dying inside from grief," said Raj. "But I've learned that some people, like the doctors, really care about me, and that's helped me to heal. I am still sad, but I know now that death is not the answer. Like Dr. Meyerstein said, a lot can change in a couple of weeks. Life goes on. It has to proceed. I have a strong mind, a strong body. I'll find my way. I'll do it for myself, for the legacy of my parents. And I'll be forever thankful to the doctors and staff here."

Raj was excused, and Judge O'Rourke announced that he would need to deliberate for a few minutes before reaching a final decision.

Following the brief recess, all parties returned to the courtroom and O'Rourke issued a sonorous, guttural rumble that signaled his readiness to announce a decision. Raj felt two invisible boulders pressing down upon him as he hung on the judge's words.

"Today, we've heard some very edifying testimony," O'Rourke said in a solemn tone that was very much congruent with his stern facial appearance. "It is clear to me that Mr. Patel was, at the time of his initial admission to the hospital, very much in need of treatment. If he did not get the aforementioned treatment, at that time he would have been in danger of self-harm. However, it is also apparent that Mr. Patel's condition is now much different, and that he now does not meet the standard for continued involuntary treatment. The system has worked as it should, and now he is not an acute danger to himself or anyone else. In accordance with state law, I therefore rule that Mr. Patel cannot be compelled to receive treatment at this time. Mr. Patel, it will be up to you if you stay or leave. This hearing is now officially over. Thank you, all."

Raj breathed a deep sigh of relief. The weight was lifted and he stood straight and tall. As Raj returned to the unit, he encountered a tall female nurse with radiant ebony skin who smiled and inquired about the hearing.

"Well Yvette, apparently I get to choose now, so I'm leaving. Thanks for all you've done though," Raj said. "Oh, and could I get a bag to carry my medications and stuff?"

The nurse scurried away to gather his belongings and provide him with a bag and his discharge medications. She came back with a thin white plastic bag, but informed Raj that his medications would not be ready for another two hours.

The nurse left and Raj sat on the edge of his bed, meditating on the future. The treatment team might be right. Maybe medication could help erase the pain. It seemed unlikely, but his training told him to believe in the power of medical science. Of course those same practitioners of medicine who had indoctrinated him in their secret ways had failed him. Could he return to work among them? The thought of doing so repulsed him. He knew he couldn't function as a doctor right now, probably not ever. Life after the hospital would require a new identity.

He was handed his wallet by a doughy, pale young psych tech, and after a few brief handshakes, Raj climbed into a cab and was headed home. "1128 West 32nd," he heard himself say to the cab driver. He sighed with relief. "Ah, never thought I'd be so happy to say those words."

"Been a while since you were home, huh?" the cabbie inquired in a gruff yet amiable tone, glancing into the rearview mirror to face his passenger.

"You could say that," replied Raj. "Sometimes a few weeks feel like forever." He turned his body to face the window to his right, watching the tree-lined city blocks fly past.

The cab deposited Raj at his appointed destination. He slid out of the torn leather seat. He ascended the steps, which he preferred to the slow and balky elevator.

As he searched for the proper keys and tried the lock, Raj heard a voice and felt a firm grip on his left arm. "Hey, buddy, you can't go in there!" the voice barked.

Raj jumped, startled by the strident voice and the command it uttered. "Mr. Vitelli. This is my apartment. What gives?"

He spied a large suitcase sitting by the door.

Vitelli averted his eyes and adjusted his glasses.

"Was your apartment," Vitelli corrected.

"But I've been sick for a while, in the hospital," Raj protested, staring at the white door frame. "You can't penalize me for that, can you?"

Vitelli shrugged.

"C'mon Mr. V. I just need a week to get situated," Raj pleaded. "I've been a good tenant. Surely you can get them to give me that?"

"I'm not the landlord, I don't make the rules. If it were up to me, you'd stay. I like you, kid. But no rent for a month past the due date means you're out. Those are the rules. Can't have freeloaders, you know. I gathered as much of your stuff as I could in a suitcase. The rest was thrown away. Lock's been changed. Good luck, son."

Of course, the rent was due the week he went in the hospital, but in his determination not to live, he ignored it. What could he do now?

"All my stuff is in there. Could I at least go in and see what I can salvage?" asked Raj.

"I really shouldn't let you," grumbled Vitelli, "but what the hell. Let's go."

Vitelli unlocked the apartment and Raj looked around. It was empty. His cell phone, wallet, and suitcase comprised the sum total of his possessions.

"See? Come on, it's time to get out of here," Vitelli chided. The two men descended the staircase.

"What happened to all the rest of it?" Raj asked. "My books, my family pictures, my medical equipment?"

"Movers," said Vitelli. "Had to get the place ready for the next tenants. Sorry if there's stuff missing. I did the best I could."

Vitelli departed without any further explanation. Raj meandered along the street clutching his black Samsonite. The consternation that haunted his days at the hospital presented itself once again.

Raj checked his cell phone. There were five messages from the hospital. The last was left two weeks ago. He reviewed them with a growing suspicion that the final piece of his old life was about to be stripped away. The last call sealed it:

"We are sorry to inform you that due to hospital HR policy your unexcused absence for greater than 14 days will result in immediate termination. If you wish to reapply for admission to next year's first year class, you must do so by this coming December. Readmission will be considered on a case-by-case basis."

No place to live, and now no job. The doors to the past were now fully shut. The letters behind his name brought pride to his parents, but now they were no more useful than an appendix or a coccyx. He could try to get back to the hospital and plead his case, but he thought about what they'd said in HR orientation regarding "probationary periods" and "right to work". This was so unfair, but he knew the hospital could do this. It was in his contract and he had no recourse. He could appeal and beg for mercy, but how could he face the supervisors, explain to them that he had fallen apart? Nobody wanted a broken healer.

Raj abhorred an unexpected change in plan, and this was an extreme case. His parents' shop and house were mortgaged to the hilt when they were alive. Bankrupt as the business was now, those relics were worth nothing to him. The mortgages were convenient when he needed to pay tuition without loans. He was supposed to pay his parents back with his physician's salary. But now all plans were shattered, and the store carried painful grief within its walls that may as well be buried.

Raj felt a searing pain behind his eyes. The throbbing pressure presaged a migraine. In a state of virtual unconsciousness, he meandered eastward before coming to rest on a park bench.

The bench, though rickety and cracked, was a welcome sight. Raj slumped backward on it. He wished that life would allow him a firm foothold on the earth beneath him but instead he felt himself somersaulting through space. He clenched his eyelids tighter, then opened them and perched his bag between his knees. He opened the suitcase and examined its contents. There were plenty of clothes, his toothbrush and toothpaste. Tucked between two windbreakers was a picture. It was a black and white portrait of his parents from their wedding day. Though they were gone and left him little to hold on to, he took some solace in seeing their faces filled with hope and promise.

He remembered his mother's entreaties to him. "Rajesh, why do you have to be so stubborn?"

Why indeed? Maybe it was his foolish insistence on pursuing the illusion of independence. His obstinate refusal to take medication kept him in that hellhole for an extra long time. Now his denial of assistance placed him on a park bench with few possessions and fewer prospects.

PART TWO

Chapter Nine

Irina walked past the pizzeria, turning behind the kitchen door exit. This was usually a good place to find leftovers. Sometimes this consisted of a crust of bread, whereas on other occasions the restaurants may leave pounds of uneaten food. Today the chef saw her and dismissed her with a wave. "Nothing to see here," he said.

She walked back to her father, shoulders drooping. "I'm getting tired of this," she said. "And it's all my fault. My stupid, blind ambition."

"Hush," said Alex. "You have dreams. So do we all. It is not wrong to dream. And one day they come true."

The sound of shouting came from far away, followed by a loud thud. "That sounds bad," said Irina. "We must see what we can do."

Alex held her back. "Let these things take care of themselves," he said. "These scuffles are not our affair."

Irina shook loose of her father's grasp and ran toward the origin of the sound. Two blocks north she saw a man lying on his back on the sidewalk. Another man was shuffling off down the road with a suitcase under his arm. Irina turned her attention from the man with the luggage to the other man who lay motionless with his arms spread apart. His eyes were swollen shut, but she recognized him from somewhere. She noticed that his chest wasn't moving and put her cheek to his lips. He wasn't breathing.

She thought back to the basic lifesaving training she had taken in high school, as required by the teachers. At the time she assumed she would never need to use it. But now she needed to remember. How was she to do this? The man needed a hospital, but there wasn't time. His life was in her hands.

She felt for a pulse. There wasn't one. She pushed on his chest with as much force as her small frame could muster.

Two breaths, she reminded herself after completing a round of fifteen chest compressions. She placed her mouth around the man's and blew into it. On the second breath, he opened his eyes and began breathing.

She'd done it. Was this better than the applause of a large crowd? For the moment, it felt as though it was.

Raj opened his eyes to find himself supine on the sidewalk. His formerly annoying headache was now a monster. He was having difficulty seeing out of his right eye. As he grasped his face he realized that the eyelid was swollen shut. A warm trickle of blood ran down his hand.

"Where am I?" he whispered. He shook his head and the pain rippled outward. He obeyed its demands and lay quietly. "Am I dead?"

"Shh… just dazed" a soft, Eastern European-accented female voice responded to his inquiries. Raj looked up to see a fine-boned, delicate face, with thin, pouty lips and concerned eyes peering at him. The young woman's soft but unkempt red hair brushed against his shoulder.

"You are alive, doctor," she said. A smile creased her lips. "I am very thankful for this."

"What happened?" he asked. "Did you find me?"

"Someone beat you up," she said. "He ran off with your bag. When I come, you are not breathing, not moving. But I help you, breathe for you, and you wake up." She wiped away the blood with a rag. "Maybe when we get you clean we find that bag."

"Who are you? Do I know you?" Raj asked.

The young lady smiled and shook her head. Her untamed hair framed high cheekbones. Even as his head throbbed, Raj was drawn to the pale face with a narrow, short nose and those delicate lips. Her eyes were vulpine blue yet warm and inviting.

"My name is Irina. And yes, we have met. But do not worry about this. First you must rest. My father, Alex, he has called for help. You are hurt. You must go to hospital."

Raj moaned.

"Oh, not the hospital. I don't want to go."

Irina smiled again and chided Raj.

"You men are all the same. Stubborn. You hush, and I take care of you."

An emergency medical crew arrived within a few minutes as Raj lay supine at Irina's feet.

"So what happened here?" asked one of the EMTs.

"Last thing I know, I was sitting on that bench after I got evicted. I don't know what happened. She saw though," he said, motioning to Irina. "Maybe she can give you a full picture."

"Somebody hit him, a big man, then they ran away when I ran after them," Irina explained. "It was I that called you."

The paramedics listened, then turned their eyes to the grimy young man with his blood-flecked face. They checked his vision and asked him the day, date, and time. Raj answered all of their questions.

The second EMT, a boyish, freckled man, frowned as he examined Raj.

"Man, the guy did a number on your eye. I think we should take you to the ER, make sure you don't have serious damage."

Raj shook his head.

"I know you have your job to do guys, protocols and all, but no thanks. I'm perfectly competent to make my own decisions. If I'm still having problems in a couple of days, I'll come in."

The freckle-faced man shrugged his shoulders.

"Suit yourself." He turned to his partner.

"Competence? Sheesh! Let's get out of here," Raj heard the man say to his partner as they walked away. "Just not worth talking sense to these bums."

Raj found that the fog within his head was clearing, in spite of the painful swelling around his eye. As the haze dissipated, reality hit with the force of a category-5 storm.

"Apartment's gone. Wallet's gone. Job's gone. Phone's gone. Even my damn clothes are gone! What the hell am I going to do?" he murmured.

"Welcome to our world, a world without papers or walls!" said a loud, familiar voice. "I think we've met before. Alex Petrov. Do you remember my lovely daughter?"

"Alex?" Raj asked. "I know you?"

A memory of the round red face floated up. His mind did still work. That was something to be thankful for.

"Alex, from the hospital, yes! I do remember you. Nice to see you."

A familiar face provided unexpected comfort, and Raj gave thanks for his two new acquaintances. He had no material possessions, but he still had his life, thanks to their intervention. Twice now, death had rejected him. Was it time to return to life?

The three formed an odd-looking assortment: bald-headed, dark-skinned Raj, plump and pink-skinned Alex, and petite pale Irina with her sea of red ringlets. Alex led them to a secluded alley by a nearby abandoned building.

"You stay here. I be right back," whispered Alex.

Petrov disappeared around the corner for a few minutes while Irina and Raj rested in the alley.

"Like I'm gonna go anywhere," said Raj. "I have nowhere to go. No job, no family, no home. No ID. Not even clothes. Can't get my ID because my social security card was in the wallet. Damn, what a mess." Tears flowed down his face but Raj, conscious of Irina's company, brushed them away. "How rude of me, you saved my life and I didn't even thank you. You don't need to hear my sob story."

Irina smiled.

"Men. It is OK to be sad," she consoled her new friend. "I know what makes proud man cry."

Alex reappeared soon, his face more flushed than before. "Good news. We can get in shelter today. I told them three. They say they have room. Must be a good day."

Raj shook his head.

"You want us to go to the shelter? I don't know if I can live in a shelter. I'd rather stay out here. Thanks for your help, but I don't want to bother you."

Alex chuckled. "You are like me when I first got here. 'Shelter? No, I no live in shelter.' Raj, out here, we cannot choose. You like sleeping on the street better than sleeping on bed?"

"I don't know. But I prefer to find my own way if you don't mind."

"OK, but please, be careful," said Irina. She touched his cheek. "Nobody deserves these bruises."

Chapter Ten

Life's reconstruction begins at the studs. Raj realized how much of life's simple privileges he had taken for granted. He recalled the warmth of a plush blanket on soft sheets, the satisfaction of a full belly, and the nurturing touch of loving parents. All of these were basic features of his comfortable past life, his right to which he now questioned.

He had never been penniless, but effectively he was now, lacking any access to his accounts or any identification that would convince a bank to reissue his ATM card. When Raj entered the bank and explained his situation, the teller politely dismissed him, explaining that there was nothing she could do. Was it his disheveled appearance, the bruises on his face, or the desperation in his voice? Whatever the case, the world was not interested in restoring to him his former comforts of life. If this were how life was to be, he was in for a series of radical adjustments.

Raj scanned the street. He had no idea how to approach this new challenge of daily subsistence. But he would have to find a way or suffer an unknown slow death.

He needed to find shelter from the sun's harsh glare. That was obvious enough. What else? Proximity to a safe public space would be a good idea. That way the day's earlier debacle would not be repeated.

Food was another basic need. Maybe he'd try to put that off till later, but his stomach demanded satisfaction, and the smell of kebabs in the air wasn't helping. He didn't have money, so the options would be limited. He would need to beg, scavenge, or even steal. Survival was a full-time job, and it might require humiliating oneself.

There was a library a few blocks away. That would be a suitable sanctuary. He was at home amid the towering stacks of books, some of them placed so high as to require a ladder. It made him wonder what forbidden truths they contained that would be stowed so far from easy access. He set up shop around the corner from the old red brick building.

Once he was situated, it was time to get to work.

"Excuse me miss, can you spare any change?"

A young, blonde woman with a yellow silk scarf turned to look, then recoiled and hurried away. She tried to hide her revulsion, but Raj saw a message that didn't need to be spoken.

He was disgusting.

That was an eye opener, but he had to persist. Twenty, thirty strangers passed him by, maybe more. All shook their heads and scuttled away without words. Wasn't he at least worthy of the words "I'm sorry?"

His parents said no child should ever have to go to sleep hungry. They were mindful of their own experiences with childhood deprivation. As the afternoon light faded to darkness, Raj remembered this. It was fortunate that they did not have to witness his predicament. As much his ego was bruised and aching, the pain they would feel was much worse.

"Forgive me father and mother, I am sorry for dishonoring you," he spoke aloud, addressing the heavens above as he walked to find a sheltered overhang outside the library's rear entrance. It had the requisite qualities of security and privacy. For tonight that would have to suffice.

It had been years since Raj slept on such a hard surface during his fifth grade camping trip in the Adirondacks. An extensive knowledge of surgical anatomy was no help in finding a comfortable position for his body. His eyes closed and he dozed off for brief periods but was intermittently jolted awake by the abrasive nature of the sidewalk and the distorted dream images of his parents' corpses.

The arrival of morning came as a relief. Raj was more equipped to handle the daylight than the intangible challenges of night. But hunger's siren call could no longer be ignored.

The convenience store three blocks over would meet his needs. He shuddered as he considered what he would need to do. He imagined his father standing over him, waving an index finger and shouting.

"Stealing! You are stealing? You have no respect for law? What kind of son have I raised? Shameful, shameful!"

Raj took a few deep breaths and strolled into the store. The owner was a short brown man with a thick black mustache, black hair and a blue and white striped polo shirt. Averting his face to avoid eye contact, Raj kept his eyes trained on the various items: chips, candy, sandwiches, alcohol, soda, water and cigarettes. He palmed a couple of candy bars and slid them into his pockets, then went to the refrigerated section to get a jug of water. He monitored the shopkeeper, who headed to the back storeroom. Raj watched him disappear behind the main display area. Time to go.

He turned and ran as fast as his undernourished limbs could propel him. The water jug sloshed as he ran. Lacking his customary physical endurance, Raj relied on adrenaline to carry him. He heard the shop owner yell after him, "I saw that.

Don't you come back in my store!" but the sound disappeared behind him within seconds. When he peeked over his shoulder, he saw nobody in his wake.

Raj slowed to a walk, made his way back to the library and chose a spot that was well hidden from the main drag. He sat down, cracked open the water and took a long gulp of it. The candy bars were a chocolate-caramel-nougat mixture. He'd chosen them from the picture on the wrapper. These weren't the most nutritious items he'd ever eaten, but they might have been the most satisfying.

As good as it felt to sate his appetite, Raj knew that thievery was not a sustainable practice. Eventually he would be caught, and then what? Arrested, maybe worse.

As he pondered his dilemma he heard two familiar voices.

"Hey, look who it is!" said a light, lilting voice.

"Mr. Independent," said a deep, louder voice that then proceeded to laugh.

Raj glanced up. Irina and Alex walked towards him.

"How was your night?" Alex asked.

Raj shook his head.

"Not good."

"It is hard out here alone," said Irina. "Have you eaten?"

Raj flashed the empty candy wrappers and his jug of water.

"Where did you get that?" Alex asked.

Raj remained silent.

"Did you steal that stuff?" Alex asked. "Is very dangerous. These stores, some owners have guns."

"They shoot people like us, those who have no homes, who nobody will miss," said Irina. "To them, we are pests, like rats or roaches. Tell me you didn't do that?"

Raj did not answer and looked away.

"Oh my god!" Irina and Alex exclaimed in unison.

"You're coming with us," they said.

He was in no position to resist. It took strength and savvy to live out here, and alone he had insufficient quantities of both. Reluctantly, he agreed to follow his newfound companions.

"OK, you're right. I 'm no expert out here. I need your help."

Alex, Irina and Raj maintained a steady pace through the late afternoon sun. A smoggy haze blurred the sky and softened the sun's impact, but breathing was a different matter. Irina and Raj labored to catch their breath, straggling a few steps behind Alex.

"Come on. We must be quick if we want space," said Alex. Raj marveled at Alex's vigor. It was admirable yet bizarre. Did Alex have no idea how hopeless life could be, or was he insistent on persevering in the face of futility?

After a few blocks, Raj, Irina and Alex arrived at the Casa Esperanza Hospitality House. The paint peeled from the white block letters engraved on a large green sign above the doorway, and the door creaked on its loose hinges as they opened it. Inside, a waiting room with cracked, faded tile floors held about fifteen or so others who sought a place to stay for the night. A family of six adults sat huddled on a concrete bench, while the others, single men and women, occupied the few plastic chairs available.

Alex walked over to the far corner of the room, where a middle-aged, nondescript gentleman in a faded denim shirt and thick glasses sat behind a counter, apparently reading something. Alex cleared his throat and the man in the denim shirt looked up.

"Excuse me, sir. We are three, needing shelter for the night." He gestured toward Raj and Irina. "I was here earlier. Can you still help?"

The man in the denim shirt glanced at Alex with a look of annoyance, then sighed. "Well, lemme check. You guys are numbers 18, 19, and 20. Yeah. You got the last three spots today. You got TB cards?"

"My daughter and I, we have. But my friend, he was robbed. They took his wallet. He has no card."

The man squinted at Raj from behind bifocal lenses.

"Well, sure looks like someone did a number on his face," he said. "What the hell, I believe you. Wait here in the waiting room. We open up the beds in a half hour, and we'll have food ready in an hour and a half."

The trio waited for the main shelter area to open, standing in silent anticipation. Even Alex didn't say much, limiting his commentary to a short piece of advice.

"You just stay with us, do what we do, you be OK," he instructed Raj.

Raj was too bewildered to object. He could not afford to be wary of these strangers. Blind trust felt dangerous, but the world was tossing him like a rubber dinghy in a hurricane. In such circumstances, he gave thanks for lifebuoys that came from unlikely places.

When the doors to the main floor opened, the waiting crowd trickled in. Each found their way to a bed, depositing their belongings on or beside their mattress. Alex led the way to a corner, where Irina deposited a small plastic bag with a few clothes and other assorted personal items next to a bed abutting the wall. Alex then took his small backpack and opened it. He took half his clothing and deposited it on one bed, while the bag itself went on a third bed farthest from the wall.

Alex motioned Raj to the middle bed and the clothes on it.

"This is yours. Clothes too. Let's sit down and rest, wait for dinner. I am hungry tonight," he exclaimed.

"Papa, you are always hungry. You eat a whale, you are still hungry," scolded Irina with a playful grin.

"Just 22 years old and she talks to me like this," said Alex to Raj. "This generation. No respect."

The comment spurred Raj to remember his parents' emphasis on reverence for one's elders. He strived to make them proud, and to preserve the honor and dignity of the family on their behalf even though he questioned the validity of the culture they championed. Those concepts felt so distant from reality.

"Is tough, I know," Alex said, patting Raj on the shoulder. "But you will get used to it. A man is more than his clothes, his house, more even than his life. You will learn."

A male voice proclaimed that dinner was ready. The shelter's bedraggled denizens lined up on cue, eager to fill their plates and their bellies with some form of warm food. Unlike the paunchy Alex, most of the others were haggard folk who bore the signs of chronic malnutrition.

Alex, Irina, and Raj took their places in line, picked up trays, and asked the food servers for what they wanted. Tonight's fare consisted of chicken noodle soup, meatloaf, mashed potatoes, and carrots. Raj fancied that the same cooks who made hospital food must moonlight here. Not a pleasant memory.

Despite his misgivings, Raj ate well. He partook of all the food, which was plentiful if not savory. He was bruised and in need of a shower, but a thick curtain of fatigue overshadowed his aches and his soiled skin. Within a few minutes after dinner, Raj washed his face, wincing as the water ran over his bruised eye. He then laid his aching body on the old single bed and shut his eyes, wishing for a moment's peace.

Alex and Irina whispered as Raj lay on his bed. Despite their efforts, Raj could catch snippets of their conversation.

"Poor man," he heard Irina say. "What should we do with him, Papa? I think he needs us."

"We do what is right," responded Alex in a hushed yet definitive tone. "We help . . . we do what we can for him. He has helped us. It is only right that we help him."

Raj pondered his companions as from his supine position. Why did Alex, who had so little, feel compelled to share with Raj? Did he want something? It didn't seem as though Alex was a manipulator. There were no signs of any hidden agenda. But if not, what could motivate a man with nearly nothing to share everything?

The thoughts swirled around his head, sucking Raj into sleep's dark realm adorned with vivid dreams and surreal imagery. Despite his body's exhaustion, Raj tossed and turned throughout the night, his nightmares waking him every hour. With Alex on his left side and Irina to his right, Raj tried his best to rest his body but instead he rolled and tossed. Though he was tired and bewildered, Raj could not ignore the attraction he felt to the girl who had breathed life into him. It was more than gratitude. No, this was the sort of romantic yearning he avoided as a medical student, blinded to the beauties of life by his career-focused tunnel vision. But here as he lay in a drafty room, he could not avoid seeing her and could not ignore the tingling on his skin that came from the sweetness of soft her breath when she turned towards him. Amid the memories of his parents' swollen, bloody faces that rose and fell from his consciousness, it was her breathing that calmed him, finally allowing him enough peace to stay asleep.

As the light cracked through the windows, a gentle nudge startled the young man to a state of bleary-eyed wakefulness. He looked around and heard Alex speaking in his general direction.

"Get up, sleepyhead."

Raj opened his eyes and observed the men and women lining up. Steam rose behind the breakfast counter, but there was no particular odor to indicate the presence of food. The hard mattress took its toll on his spine, and he groaned as he stretched his weary, sore joints.

"Come on," Irina coaxed. "You need some food in you. It will make you feel better."

"Yes, food is good," Alex said.

"Except when you are always eating and getting fat, Papa," Irina playfully scolded her father. Alex chuckled as Raj approached the line with his newfound comrades.

Raj assessed the pasty white material that bubbled in vats from which the food was served. He was surprised and dismayed at what passed for breakfast.

"You'll get used to it," Irina said to Raj.

"God, I hope not!" Raj grumbled.

Raj carried his bowl of lumpy gruel to a long table. He began to comprehend the chilling reality of his new life. He sat in soiled clothing, his bruises still raw and painful, with a group of anonymous men and women. In years past he had heard, spoken, and thought of "the homeless", "the poor", "the disenfranchised" as abstract concepts. Now, in one fell swoop, he embodied all of the above.

Raj hung his head and stared at the insipid porridge. At Irina's insistence he forced himself to eat it. After they finished their meals in silence, Raj looked up at Alex and Irina.

"So, what are we doing today?" he asked.

"Well, we'll go get jobs, find an apartment and live happily ever after," Alex deadpanned, dissolving into a cackle of laughter with Irina soon thereafter.

"Oh, you are so new to this," Alex said with a grin. "You will soon realize nothing happens quickly out here. We do what we can. We do what we must. We survive. That is our day. We live by the day, by the hour, sometimes even by the minute."

A sunburned man with a Yankees' cap and a crooked nose capped by a hairy red mole rang a large bell. The normal commotion of breakfast subsided.

"Everybody finish up breakfast. You'll have an hour after for you to do whatever. After that, everybody needs to be out for the day."

Raj turned to Alex. "They can do this, just kick us out like that?"

Alex nodded. "Is not so bad. They open up again in the evenings, and hopefully we get back in time to get a spot. In the day, we search for day jobs, or food. Then if we are lucky, they have place to sleep for us. If not, we manage."

"You're tough people," Raj said to Alex with a sigh. "I don't see how you do it. A day has been almost more than I could stand. I don't know what I'd have done without you."

"You are getting soft now my friend," Alex teased. "Like delicate woman!"

Raj laughed. It was the first time he had done so in weeks, and except for the stretching of his bruised facial muscles, it felt good.

"Hey Papa, he laughs!" Irina joked, her almond-shaped eyes twinkling.

"It is good to see you not always so sad," she said to Raj. "Your smile is beautiful."

After breakfast, Raj washed himself and changed into the borrowed clothing. It was dirty and ragged but it would have to suffice. When he returned from the bathroom, Alex and Irina were packed up and ready to go.

They left the shelter and walked for several blocks. Raj was struck by the way passing pedestrians veered away from them, laughed or averted their gazes from the shabbily clad wanderers. He recalled to himself with pangs of guilt the way he used to do the same things. He yearned to be seen as a real person. Once he was a reputable man who walked with a swagger and held his dream-filled head high. But now the dreams had perished, and without them he was nobody.

Chapter Eleven

Raj and his new companions walked dozens of city blocks beneath the oppressive summer sun, whose rays glimmered off the nearby pavement. They stopped outside a red brick warehouse, its exterior festooned with various styles of graffiti. Dozens of men and women stood in line outside. Raj watched them pacing and milling about, craning their necks for a better view of the warehouse entrance.

"What are we doing here?" he whispered to Alex. "And what are all these other people doing?"

"Well, this is how we get money. We work day jobs, when we can get them. And all these others, they are here for same reason," Alex answered. "When you have no money, any job is good job."

After a few minutes of waiting, the crowd hushed as a warehouse door opened. A tall, wiry man with leathery skin and black, beady eyes stared out at the prospective day laborers.

"OK folks," he boomed in a Texas-flavored drawl. "Y'all need work, and I need some help today. I need five people to help load and unload trucks. Now don't go gettin' all excited. Only got room for a few of you."

The tawny, weathered supervisor sauntered through the motley crew of potential workers. He stopped to look at Raj.

"Boy, somebody did some work on you. You oughtta get that looked at by a doctor." He passed by and indicated his choices, five burly young men who stood on the periphery of the group. "You fellas come with me. All the rest of you have a nice day."

Raj had been hoping for something more. He stared at the ground in front of him as they walked away. Was this his future fate, to be dismissed as insufficient? Survival would be so much easier if only he could rediscover a relevant place in the world.

Alex motioned for Irina and Raj to follow him. They turned east past a row of burnt out buildings festooned with eclectic styles of graffiti. After several blocks, they came to a small park. The park bench was unoccupied and shaded by a thick, tall elm. Raj and Irina sat down on the bench, while Alex perched on the ground with his back resting against the bough of the sturdy tree.

"Looks like no work today," said Irina. She sighed and slouched against the back of the bench. "All this time, nothing to do."

"Nonsense," scoffed Alex. "In Russia, when times were hard and we have no job, we talk. Doesn't put food in the belly, but it is comforting."

"Sounds like a plan to me," said Raj. "I don't know much about life in Russia. Tell me about it. Nothing like a good story to pass the time."

"Ah, Russia. We had some good times there." But actually, you know, I was not born in Russia. I come from family in Kiev. That is in Ukraine. We move to Moscow when I was very small, just less than two. My mother used to tell me about the trip. We went mostly by train. I was scared of them, she told me. They were big, crowded, and noisy."

The tales sparked a glow of excitement in Alex's face. The bags and wrinkles softened and he rubbed his hands together, as though conjuring up an obscure magic spell.

"All that noise can be scary," said Raj. "Never liked the subway much myself as a kid. I still don't."

"Ah, yes," Alex chuckled. "But anyway, we move for my father. He was a butcher, and very good. All the important people bought their meat from him. My father would be cleaning up, and these stylish women would walk in. I remember most their shiny, black shoes. I hear click, click on the floor. My father would stop what he was doing and bring special meat out of a small room in the back. Beef, pork, lamb, whatever these people wanted. Sometimes more than the rest of the customers bought for a month. And after they were done, the ladies would simply walk away. No 'thank you', nothing. But I knew my father must be the best butcher in town, because these ladies always came back."

"Grandfather was quite a man," Irina added. She nestled her chin on her hands, leaned forward, and smiled.

"Yes, he was," Alex agreed. "Little skinny man, thinner than you, Raj, and much shorter. He hunched when he walked. But he is strong. He cut meat with the force of a giant. 'It is all in the arm and the head' he would say. And he always knew exactly where to cut. He was like your surgeons. I loved his shop, and as soon as I could help out, I did. I went to school in the day, and cut meat at night. But Papa always wanted me to find something else. 'One day, you'll know something better than the smell of blood' he always said. But I do not care about the smell, the blood. I was with Papa." Alex emphasized his last words with a loud clap of his hands. His eyes clouded with a misty suggestion of tears.

Raj felt the grief as though it were his own. The pathos of Alex's words was undeniable. Raj was reminded of his own childhood memories, tagging along at his father's heels in the shop, playing hide and seek in the storeroom amid the smell of turmeric and ginger.

"Yes, sometimes that's all a child wants," said Raj. "So, what happened to your father?"

"He died many years ago, when I was 18." Alex glanced skyward. The mist turned to a shower arising in Alex's eyes, the droplets falling to the ground beneath for a minute before the storm passed. "I was in the university, studying to be a lawyer. He was so proud of me. But his heart gave out, and he died. My mother is alone. I must return home to take care of her. I took over the shop. I did the best I could, but I was not my father. I shall never be."

"I think you underestimate yourself," Raj observed. "From what I see you are a very good dad, a man who cares and never gives up."

"Papa is too humble," Irina added. "His father was his hero. Papa is mine."

Alex sighed and wiped away a stray tear that had escaped his left eye. The jolly round man seemed to have retracted into himself, his face twisted with angst and pain. But Irina's gentle words lifted the pall over his features again and he cleared his throat and laughed.

"You are kind Irina," he said. "My mother and I, we had some good times. I had no brothers or sisters, so I was all she had, and she was such a kind, gentle person. I think Irina has the same soul. My mother told me my future is in USA. Still, I stay. We struggled, mother and I, for twelve years. But it was a happy struggle. Happier when I met Olga, Irina's mother. She is the one who gave Irina her voice, her graceful walk. Olga was a dancer. When I meet her, she is just twenty, so shy, so beautiful. She came into our store with her mother, and

I told mama, 'I will marry that angel'. Mama laughed, but she told me, 'If you must, go get her.' And as I walked to the shop, I passed the little ballet studio and stopped outside every morning. For a month I stood there watching, not knowing what to say, and finally, she noticed me."

"Very fairy-tale romance," said Raj. He glanced at Irina and wondered if they might one day share a similar story. In his mind, their bodies mingled in the morning light, but he tried to dismiss the thought. Such fantasies were premature and impractical. "It must have been magical."

"Yes, my mother was very beautiful," Irina said. As she smiled, Raj thought he could see her conjuring the sweet images of childhood. "My father tells many tales, but this time, he does not make up stories. She was tall and thin, and when she walked, you would swear you were looking at a queen or a princess, right off the pages of a storybook."

Alex nodded.

"It is no wonder that her first words to me were, 'Aren't you the butcher? What are you doing standing here?'" he said. "But for some reason, maybe heaven, maybe something else, she smiled at me. I told her I had been watching her performance. She gave me ticket to her next recital, and I watched this woman move like she walks on air, like she is not human, but from up there. And maybe she was because that could be the only reason someone like her would fall for someone like me. After the show, and we talk, until early in the morning. Soon, we spend all the days together, and a year later, I keep my promise. I marry that woman. And a year after that, Irina came, always sick, but always happy."

"Sounds like those were some good times for you," said Raj. "Hard, but good."

"Is life," Alex replied with a sigh. "Olga and Irina and I had each other. She said it was all we need. We made it day to day, and the store gave us just enough to live on. We were tired at the end of each day, but it was the kind of fatigue that let you know you had lived an honest day. Love and work. That is what we had."

"Some say love and work is what it's all about," said Raj. "That's what Freud thought, anyway."

"This is what I believe," Irina observed. "I hope one day I find a love like what father had."

"Some day you will," Alex replied. "One never knows when he will come."

Alex smiled and winked at Irina.

"Maybe sooner than you think," said Raj, imagining what it might be like to taste her delicate lips.

"How is it that you and Irina are here, and Olga is not?" asked Raj. "You say 'had' and 'was' a lot when speaking of her?"

"Olga is the reason we are here," said Alex. "It was clear very early that Irina had great talent in music. Must be from her mother. She has the voice of a bird and the soul of an angel. But we knew that she could not make it in music in Russia. Olga gave up her dance. But she wants big things for Irina. She say, 'We must go to America, for our future, for Irina'. When Irina is nine, Olga is pregnant with our second child. But something goes wrong, and I she is bleeding horribly. She turns very pale like ghost. All I can do is stand and watch. God is taking my wife, my baby, but nothing can be done. And soon it is just me and Irina. I do not even have time to cry."

Alex paused, his face contorted with the pain of prolonged payment. For a moment it appeared the weight of his emotion would break his ample back. This must be what drove Alex to be so generous to him. He, too, knew the sadness of loss, of impotence in the face of tragedy but unlike many men, Alex found a way to turn his pain into compassion. Raj considered himself blessed to have encountered these unlikely benefactors.

"Papa, it is all right. We have each other," said Irina, soothing her Alex father as if he were a starving infant. Her voice unfolded the angular furrows of sorrow that had emerged in Alex's face. Soon the old man's smooth, round features returned once again.

"My friend, perhaps I talk too much. I am sorry if I bore you," said Alex.

"Oh no, quite the contrary," said Raj. "Your story is many things, but never boring. I feel now like I know you. I'd like to hear more."

"Well there isn't all that much more," replied Alex with a wry smile. "For five years, Irina and I live in Moscow. I worked at the shop. She went to school and helped me when she could. But every night, I go to sleep, knowing the promise I had made to Olga, to let Irina follow her dreams, to come to America. Finally, a man comes into my store. He tells me he wants butcher to set up a store in America. I come to New York with Irina on boat, with many others, to work in his store. I slice meat and sell it by the pound. We eat little, and living with ten others is hard. But we manage. Then only a year after we move here, the place closed down, and I know nobody. I cannot find job because I am not here legally. We must leave apartment. For last three years, this is our life. Sometimes we get jobs for day or two, or sometimes Irina's songs earn us money for food. We have no insurance when Irina get sick, like at the hospital. And for a poor immigrant in New York there is no place to live, besides the street or shelters. Life. It is hard to figure."

"I know what you mean," said Raj. "My parents were everything to me, but it wasn't till they were gone that I realized it. We understand each other, I guess."

Irina turned her gentle eyes toward Raj.

"Tell us about yourself, your family," she said. "You know our story. We would like to know yours."

Her hospitable eyes and gentle voice were the perfect invitation for Raj to lower his guard. He relaxed enough to begin exposing a self that once soared with confidence but now labored beneath the weight of doubt and guilt.

"We share much in common, Alex," said Raj. "My parents were also immigrants and shopkeepers. They worked hard to make a good life for me, like you do for Irina, even though they knew they would never be fully accepted here. 'We give the Americans chicken curry,' my dad used to say, 'and they give us chicken shit. Trust us. Trust family. Nobody else will give you anything."

He sighed and re-crossed his legs. "My father in particular had dreams for me. He had special respect for doctors, so that's what I strived to be. I studied hard to get good grades. I wanted to please them. I felt like I owed it to him and my mother. Sometimes Father would come home from the store at midnight, and I'd hear him as he came in. He would fall asleep on this old rocking chair we had. I was small, so I was supposed to be asleep, but sometimes I sneaked out to the top of the stairs. I sat on the top step, watching him sleep."

"Curious little fellow, eh?" said Alex.

"Yes, that I was," Raj agreed with a hint of a smile. "Whenever dinner was being prepared, I always had to know what it was. So I would pull chairs and footstools and tables over to the stove so I could see and smell what was cooking. And it was always good. Sometimes I can still smell the spices in my mind, turmeric, coriander, ginger, garlic."

"This I know so well," said Alex. "The smell of my mother's borscht, I still know it now, even after all these years. The nose has a wonderful memory."

"Yes, it's true," Raj agreed. "And my nose would get me to stand up on the chair, peering over the stove until my mother scolded me. 'Get down from there. You will hurt yourself, silly boy.' But then she'd give me a taste of what was cooking, so all was good. That's how she was. If you lived anywhere within sight of my house, my mother would bring you food, watch you eat it, and chat with you. Vicarious pleasure was my mom's thing."

"That is how good mothers are," Irina observed. "They are givers of happiness. Givers of themselves."

"That she was," said Raj. "I remember my friends would complain about their parents, and I always wondered why I had no problems with mine. My parents just wanted a better life for me than what they had growing up. And when I graduated from high school and college, it seemed they had swelled to the bursting point with pride in me. So when I graduated from medical school and saw them in the crowd, I felt like finally I had given them back something for all they had done for me."

His respiration slowed and lightened. It was good to speak about this and expel the grief.

"I remember I handed them the diploma, and my mother ran her hands over every corner of it, as though it were some golden treasure. To her it was. So now I am a doctor, but it means nothing without them. That's why I walked away from it. Dreams without their dreamers have no meaning."

He tried to suppress his tears without success, and the salty stream ran down his cheeks. He felt as though he were suffocating. Irina extracted out a soiled handkerchief from her pocket and held it out to Raj.

"Thank you," he said, dabbing at the persistent teardrops. "My parents got in a car accident on the way to see me, to celebrate with me. They were in the same unit as you. But they never made it out. I told them, before it happened, that I was too busy. Can you believe it? They shouldn't have been on the road. I should have gone . . ." his voice cracked and trailed off. He wiped his eyes, wiping them with the backs of his grimy hands.

"Oh, we did not mean to make you hurt," said Irina. "It's OK."

Raj looked away, fighting off the sadness that he was sure was emblazoned on his face, raising his hand as if to parry Irina's words.

"It is all right," said Raj in a loud but shaky voice. "Sometimes the pain forces its way out. This is the way the body tortures us, but also how it heals. Maybe that isn't so bad. It helps to have you here to listen. I took my family for granted. And now they're gone. You are the closest thing I have to family now. And I will not make the same mistake twice."

"That word can mean many things," said Alex. "But yes, we are now like family."

Alex rummaged in his faded, dusty bag and pulled out an antique harmonica. Irina glanced her father, who nodded. Irina nodded back, and began to sing in Russian while Alex played an accompaniment.

The mournful soprano tones pierced the late afternoon air, and some of the early commuters paused to hear the haunting voice crying out from the depths of her pure Russian soul. Men and women turned to watch from a distance before proceeding into their respective buses, trains, or taxis. The lyrics were foreign, but their meaning cut across language barriers. Even an uninterested bystander could not help but feel the mournful sentiment of a funereal lament.

Raj sat transfixed, appreciating the elegance of Irina and her voice while simultaneously reminiscing over his recent pain. As Irina ended with a lingering, soft half note, Raj bowed his head and murmured his thanks.

But there was little time left to think, to feel, and to cry. The impromptu concert had attracted the eyes and ears of the local police, and soon a man in blue, his wide frame straining the capacity of his uniform, approached the trio.

"Sorry to do this, people, but this is a park, not a house, and you guys need to move along, OK?" The officer delivered his words in a polite, almost deferential manner, and it was almost enough for Raj to believe the sincerity of the officer's statement.

"Thank you, officer," said Alex. "It's OK, we understand our time is up."

Chapter Twelve

For the next month, Raj, Irina, and Alex wandered the streets and alleyways of New York. They traversed four to five miles each day by foot and slept in the shelter of trees, building overhangs, and subway stations. Without the scheduled meals provided by soup kitchens and homeless shelters, survival depended on spare morsels left behind by others. These meager tidbits helped stave off complete exhaustion, but Irina grew pale and fatigued. As her strength waned, her spirits suffered, though she attempted to hide her discomfort behind an unwavering smile.

"Well, it is time," Alex pronounced on a cloudy and cool morning. He stretched and yawned.

"Time for what?" asked Raj and Irina in unison.

"We see if they have job for us today. We need money to eat. We cannot let Irina and you starve. Me, I have plenty!" He grinned and patted his ample belly.

They walked to a construction site where a group of men were busy digging ditches. Others waited hopefully. The foreman, an angular man with beady green eyes and a thin red mustache, motioned to Alex and Raj.

"You two, you want to help out? I'll give you guys 20 bucks each for the job today."

"What do you . . ." Raj began to ask a question but was silenced by the raised right hand of his friend.

"We take it," said Alex. After a brief meeting with Irina, Alex returned and the two men followed the foreman back behind a dilapidated brick building where piles of dirt abutted the beginnings of ditches.

"Your job is simple, folks. Start digging, and keep digging. Lunch is in five hours."

The foreman walked away and Raj turned to his companion. Alex wielded his shovel with force and skill, hauling away piles of dirt and debris while Raj struggled to break through the rocky soil.

"Work, is good thing," Alex proclaimed as he shoveled.

"I guess," Raj grunted as he pitched a shovelful of dirt over his shoulder and onto the pile that stood on the ledge above him. "You know they're not giving us a fair deal. 20 bucks is a rip-off.

"Fair, unfair" Alex shrugged. "You Americans care too much about this. Life is not fair. Something is better than nothing. Every morsel is precious. This is all I know."

The two dug silently, their shovels hitting earth and small rocks in dual percussive rhythm. Sienna-colored dirt speckled the their skin and clothes, sticking to their bodies as the sweat poured off their brows.

The foreman returned to check on his new charges.

"Not bad for day labor," he observed. "You guys work hard. Now keep going."

The foreman walked away, again leaving Raj and Alex to their own devices.

"Bastard," Raj muttered. "Not bad for day labor. What the fuck did that mean? He should be grateful at that pay rate."

Alex leaned on his shovel and laughed.

"Grateful? Him?" he said. "You have much to learn about this world, Raj. We are desperate. He has everything. It is we who must be grateful for chance to show our worth. But you are probably right, he is probably bastard, and I doubt even his mother loves him."

As day wore into early evening, the foreman returned to tell Alex and Raj that the site would be closing for the day. They could return tomorrow and he would see if their assistance would be necessary.

Irina arose from a bench on the street opposite the construction site and walked slowly over to Alex and Raj. Her stooped posture and made her seem older, enfeebled by the strain of living outside.

"We have a little money," Raj told Irina. "We can buy food today. Your father works so hard, they ought to pay him double, but no matter. Tonight we eat well."

They walked around a corner to a convenience store. Irina took their money and headed into the store. Raj tried to follow behind her, but Alex held him back.

"They see you and me, they say 'get out of store, you bums'. They see her charming face and they say, 'poor girl'. If we want food, she must buy it. She is our face, because only she can open their hearts."

Irina soon emerged with bread, fruit, cold cuts, and a gallon jug of water. "I still have 10 dollars left Papa," she said.

"Keep it, Irina. Maybe we eat well tomorrow too," Alex suggested.

The modest feast did wonders to restore their energy and optimism. The most pressing question was where they would sleep this evening. Showers began as a cooling mist, comforting as it kissed the skin. But shelter became an urgent need as the rain intensified. With the deepening of evening shadows the raindrops hit harder, pounding away like an untrained five-year old on a piano.

It was too late to consider the homeless shelters, so the wandered in search of a place that would afford they shelter from the storm. Raj pointed to some abandoned buildings, but Alex shook his head.

"Could be crack house. Dangerous. Better we sleep on street. At least there we can see what comes our way." They walked until Alex found an alley next to a restaurant. A large concrete pipe rested against the restaurant. It was easily big enough to accommodate two people lengthwise.

"This will do," Alex decided. "Raj, you and I take turns. One sleeps, one watches. Irina, you take far end."

"What about me, papa?" Irina asked.

"Hush, child, we cannot have you getting sick again", Alex chided her. He placed a checkered wool blanket around her shoulders. "You sleep and let us keep things safe."

"I'll take the first shift on watch," said Raj. "You should rest, Alex."

The city buzzed with the electricity of urban summer. People bustled past the alley unaware of the three huddled bodies in the alley. Raj watched them laughing and joking with one another. He listened as their shoes beat a rhythmic cadence on the sidewalk. Young hipsters and their chic dates slipped into and out of the restaurant's door, sometimes stopping for a quick kiss or flirtatious glance.

Raj was again reminded of his invisibility. He recalled his childhood fascination with disappearing, hiding, and otherwise vanishing from view. At the time it seemed magical, but the reality of anonymous isolation was not at all romantic or exciting. It was colorless, desolate and lonely.

The raindrops' rattling assault on the ceramic rooftops eased to a gentle sprinkle. Raj slipped off his damp shirt and placed it on the pipe, letting the dewy mist kiss his dirty skin. He was adjusting to his sweaty, malodorous life, but it still disturbed him. His parents prized personal cleanliness, and the filth that covered him reminded him of all that had been lost from his distant past.

The young man's musings were soon disrupted. Alex tapped him on the shoulder, and Raj jumped, startled by the unexpected touch.

"Lesson number one of living on the street: always watch your back," Alex whispered. "Anyway, your turn to sleep."

Raj took his shirt, stained with sweat and clay and moistened by the summer rain, and folded it into a makeshift pillow. He placed it into the pipe and slid himself in afterward. The enclosure was just long enough for him to feel Irina's long hair brushing against his face as he positioned his back and shoulders strategically on the pipe's concave surface. She stirred and opened her eyes.

"Shh, it's just me," he whispered to Irina, who closed her eyes and went back to sleep. The proximity to her and the touch of her hair were made his skin awaken as his heart quickened. As his body yearned for her, it was hard for him to calm his mind, unsettled as it was by the intoxicating influence of desire. It was only when the heavy black blanket of exhaustion engulfed him that Raj was able to fall asleep till the dawning of the sun.

The summer months faded and autumn's frosty evening chills provided a foreshadowing of the hardships that lay ahead. The frenetic city slowed its pace just a step, bracing for a rough winter. Shelter vacancies grew scarce as the climate cooled. The makeshift heat of an exhaust vent, a train station, or an abandoned building was only slightly more plentiful. In times like this, they relied on one another for the bodily warmth that made outdoor evenings survivable.

Raj, Alex and Irina roamed the streets in search of survival's building blocks. To sustain their bodies they picked at the scraps and leftovers thrown away by local bakeries and restaurants. They rummaged in dumpsters for bedding and blankets. To earn money, they searched day labor sites but were rebuffed more often than not. The daily struggle left Raj full of nothing but doubt. Now that he wanted to survive, he questioned his ability to do so. He tried to think his way out of the dilemma his life had become, but his thoughts traced a repeated circular path of regret and confusion.

As Raj contemplated his past, Alex tapped him on the shoulder.

"Raj, we must go. This place, it is not good for Irina."

Raj detected a hint of desperation in his friend's voice. The tone alarmed him, accustomed as he was to the jocularity of his traveling companion. If a man who had survived five years on the street was worried, this could only mean that times were about to get harder.

"You have a plan?" Raj inquired. "It's one thing to say we need to get out of here, another to do it."

Alex tapped his head. His somber face reanimated with an impish grin.

"The train, Raj. I believe it is our friend. It takes us away from cold and snow," he said.

"Ugh. Maybe so, if we had any money," Raj said, staring away from Alex into the evening lights. "But we don't, so I'd say we're stuck."

"Money is not problem," Alex explained. "All it takes is little hop, skip, and jump, and we are on train."

"Jumping the turnstiles? That's your plan? Great, then we can spend winter in jail. I guess it's warmer there at least."

"Hah, "Alex scoffed. He grasped Raj by both shoulders. "We have done it before, and we can do it again! Besides, they don't care enough to send you to jail. They just yell and say 'bad boy, don't do it again'."

"I suppose it's worth a shot," said Raj. And so the seeds were planted. In the meantime, the trio continued to search the streets for refuge in the form of basements, doorways, or sheltered overhangs.

While Alex set off to find shelter, Raj and Irina went together to scavenge behind the local restaurants and convenience stores, searching for the goods that many businesses threw away in alleyways and atop large dumpsters. The idea of eating possibly expired food repulsed Raj in days of plenty, but now the compulsive force of hunger opened his mind to meals that would once have seemed inedible.

"Let's try Lenny's," Irina suggested. "They always have meat and bread left out, and they don't usually care who takes it."

"Sounds like a plan," said Raj. They walked toward the Jewish delicatessen, a favorite neighborhood haunt for college students and the hipsters who gentrified the neighborhood one storefront at a time. Raj felt a twinge of envy as he thought of these people, drinking coffee and gorging themselves on oversized corned beef sandwiches in the comfort of leather-backed booths.

As they approached their destination, Irina burst into a coughing spell that stopped her where she stood. Her shoulders rose and fell with each gasp of breath and she doubled over at the waist. She looked unsteady and about to pass out when Raj caught her, leaning her against his chest.

"We've got to get you to the hospital," he said. "Your lungs sound terrible. And it could get worse."

"No," she said. "I'll manage."

"Nonsense," said Raj. He scanned the street. There were no clinics or hospitals nearby. They'd have to settle for the next best thing. "At least we need to get you some medicine."

He picked her up in his arms, and carried her down the street to a small pharmacy.

"Please, we need some help," he shouted. "It's urgent."

The pharmacist, a stern-looking man whose gray hair was parted in the middle, heard Irina's wheezing and hurried to the counter.

"How can I help you?" he asked.

"She's having an asthma exacerbation," said Raj. "She needs an albuterol inhaler, but she's out, and we have no money. Please, could you spare us something? Also budesonide if you've got it. We'll pay you back."

The pharmacist's severe features softened into a sympathetic smile. "I can see she's in trouble. I'll see what I can do," he said.

In a few seconds the pharmacist returned with two containers.

"Here's the albuterol inhaler," he said. "And I got you the budesonide as well. It's on the house."

Irina took two puffs off the inhaler as soon as they got outside, and within minutes her coughing had receded, though she still looked pale and tired.

"Thank you," she said to Raj. She kissed him on the cheek and grinned. "I've been meaning to do that for a while. Now seemed as good a time as any. You just saved my life, again."

"It's the least I could do," said Raj. He felt a flush rising in his body as the kiss melted his defenses. "You're the woman who brought me back to life, so I owed it to you. Besides, I just did what I'm trained to do. And it was my pleasure to help."

He grinned and placed his long arm around her shoulder, holding her up as they walked back to meet Alex.

After several days of watching his daughter's distress, Alex had made a decision. It was time to move swiftly, he insisted. In the gloaming of a brisk late autumn day, Alex detailed his plan.

"Today we must go. This New York cold is no good. Is first of December, good time to leave. Train station is crowded, we sneak through, and then we go south. Like birds, we find warm skies," he said.

Alex was correct in at least one statement: the rush of urban holiday shoppers was well underway, crowding all forms of mass transportation. Three hapless people amid a throng of human chaos would be as inconspicuous as teardrops in a thunderstorm. Irina and Raj listened as Alex continued.

"As the sun starts to go down today and the people head home from work, we will go to station, jump over turnstiles. That's where you come in, Raj. You help us find a train that's headed south. We keep going, switching trains until we get to warm place."

"Or they catch us," Raj muttered.

"You worry too much." Alex gave Raj a slap on the shoulder. "We get on train, you leave rest to me."

Alex, Irina, and Raj slipped onto the train as though unseen. In a sense they were. Wherever they sat, the others in the train avoided their gazes, instead staring through them or over their shoulders.

The crowded, smelly train cars used to repulse Raj, but life on the streets immunized his nose to all but the most sickening odors. In contrast to the stench of the train, its climate-controlled temperature was a welcome change. Irina's breathing slowed to a normal rate in the warmer air. Her coughing became quieter and less strident. She smiled at her father, and he pressed her hands between his large, ruddy palms. Raj admired Alex's nurturing paternal style. It reminded him of his own parents' concern for him and gave a hint of comfort and safety that could not otherwise be found on the streets.

"Last stop, all passengers please exit," said the muffled voice of the conductor, its timbre distorted by the antiquated public address equipment.

The three travelling companions filed out of the crowded train silently, searching the schedules for the next train to continue the next leg of their journey. Raj checked the large clock hanging on the station wall.

"Almost eight o'clock, Alex. What do you want to do?" he asked Alex.

"Well, we could sleep here," Alex said. "But no, let us find next train. We sleep after that."

The three comrades climbed the stairs and crossed a walkway over the tracks, then descended onto another platform. Though many people stood awaiting the next train, the benches were almost deserted, save for an old, stoop-shouldered Indian woman. She wore a sari that peeked out under her beige winter coat, her hair bound up in a bun. Through silver-rimmed glasses, she glanced at the newcomers. After a few seconds of appraisal, the old lady grasped the ivory-inlaid handle of her wooden cane tightly and shuffled away a few paces, sitting with her back to the wall and eyeing the strangers suspiciously.

After several minutes, a few other passengers stood waiting on the platform and the train could be heard rumbling slowly toward the station. Seconds later the doors parted.

The old lady stepped into the train and dropped her purse, a small, turquoise imitation leather model. Raj bent to pick it up and turned to offer the purse back to her.

But she moved with feline agility when it came to her money.

"Give me that," she railed at Raj, tearing the purse out of his hands and brandishing the cane in front of her. "I knew you were trouble. Budhu! Go! Get lost!"

Alex grabbed Raj and Irina and hustled them through several cars in the train before they finally stopped and stood silently for a short interval. After several minutes, it became apparent that nobody had followed them and any immediate threat of arrest had passed. A few passengers disembarked and Alex and Irina sat down. Raj remained standing, bewildered by his recent brush with the feisty old lady.

Alex could contain his amusement no longer and began laughing.

"What was that word she called you?" he asked.

"It means thug, or ruffian," said Raj. He shook his head and smirked.

"You, a thug?" said Irina. She snorted and giggled. "That's a good one!"

"For smart guy, Raj, you are dumb ass sometimes," said Alex.

"What?" said Raj. "It's not funny. I just tried to be polite. No good deed goes unpunished, I guess."

"What got into you, Raj?" Irina asked. "Did you actually think this lady will say, 'Oh what a nice man, he is giving me my money?' He is prince! Of course she thinks you are a thief. We look like beggars and thieves. Remember that the next time you want to act like a hero! To rest of world, it does not matter what is in our heart. Only how we look."

Painful as it was to hear, Irina's statement rang true. How many times had he looked askance at ill-groomed, malodorous men in train stations? And now, to all appearances, that's what he'd become: a smelly hooligan.

"I suppose you're right. That was pretty dumb," Raj conceded. "I need to get used to my new identity."

The train rolled onward in its rhythmic staccato clatter. The noise of the rails was hypnotic and soothing, and Alex and Irina both fell asleep. Raj stayed awake, keeping watch as he perched his elbows on his knees. Never a hefty man, he now felt the contours of his bones pressing at his skin. The uncertainty of homelessness stretched him on the inside, as though the struggles of his vagabond life pulled him in opposite directions from the ends of his body. A tangled beard hung from his chin and his hair, formerly shaven, clung to his scalp in short, mossy patches. A disheveled appearance used to perturb him, but now his anonymity served as an optimal disguise for shame.

The train emptied its innards a little at each successive stop. Raj stared at the patterns made by the ground-in dirt on the floor, then fixated on a web made of chewing gum that clung with admirable tenacity to the far corner of the car. A fitting metaphor for life, he reflected.

Chapter Thirteen

"I guess we're here," said Raj.

"Where's here?" Irina yawned, opened her eyes, and stretched her arms.

"Judging from the schedule and the map, we're in Washington, DC," said Raj.

"Capitol of America," said Alex. "Is great place, full of history."

"For better and worse," said Raj. He recalled the historical stories of slavery, the Trail of Tears, and the Japanese internment camps. Doubtless the District of Columbia was the site of many proud moments, but it also spawned much ugliness for those who looked or sounded different from those who made laws. "Should we go further south or stop here?"

They decided to stay at least overnight in the city, which meant shelter was the top priority. This was a slightly more daunting task than navigating the familiar neighborhoods of New York. Raj had stayed in Washington before, but in starkly different circumstances. For all of their survival skills, Alex and Irina had no knowledge of these city streets and were almost as lost as Raj.

"We're here, so what do we do for shelter?" asked Raj.

"What we always do," Alex replied. "Find it or make it."

Raj continued to worry about Irina, who was coughing harder. A roof, temporary though it may be, would be preferable to the vicissitudes of street life.

Irina walked down the street, pausing to catch her breath at signs or landmarks of interest.

"Where should we stay?" she asked.

"Hard to say," said Alex. "If we go to wrong place, the immigration is problem. Or the police. Or junkies. I wish I knew this city. But we will figure it out."

They walked further down the street but after half a block, Alex and Raj noticed that Irina was lagging behind.

Her coughing beat a persistent rhythm now, and her breath was drained by the fits that shook her body. The spell persisted until Irina stumbled, barely catching herself on a nearby brick wall. Raj and Alex rushed over and picked her up, supporting her shoulders.

"She needs X-rays, a nebulizer, maybe antibiotics," said Raj. "The inhalers are just not cutting it anymore."

"That's it. You heard the doctor," said Alex. "We go to hospital."

Raj heard the honorific title and it sparked a twinge of sadness. He was reminded of a life once lived, now alien and irretrievable.

"It's OK, papa, really," Irina objected, but her stooped posture and feeble voice belied her true condition.

The three wanderers strode into a brisk wind. Alex and Raj carried Irina together, allowing her to preserve what little breath remained in her failing lungs.

They tried to flag down passing strangers, but the on-lookers walked by as if blind to Irina's condition, confirming Raj's sense of invisibility. Finally, another burst of coughing startled a passer-by.

"Does she need help?" the man asked. On closer inspection, Raj noticed a white clerical collar beneath the long black coat.

"She needs urgent medical attention, Father," Raj explained. "But we're new here, and we don't know where the nearest hospital is."

"There's a twenty-four hour urgent care clinic just four blocks that way," the priest said in an Irish brogue, pointing east. Tell 'em Father Michael sent you."

"Thank you very much, Father," Alex replied.

"Glad I could help," said the priest as he strolled away into the brisk morning air. He turned around and called out, "If you need anything, our church, St. Mary's, is always open, a couple of blocks down from the clinic."

Alex, Irina and Raj hastened over to the walk-in clinic. Though it was only 10 o'clock, the waiting room was full. Irina looked at her father.

"Maybe we should go. We'll never get seen," she said. But Alex would not be dissuaded.

"We are here, and you need to be seen, and you will be seen," he said, wagging his finger in the air as she collapsed into another coughing spell. "Besides, what kind of father lets his daughter suffer like this? Already I wait too long! Listen to our friend. He says you need doctor, and he knows best."

Raj nodded his assent.

"At least it's warm in here," he said. "That will help you breathe easier until you get treated. Cold air is hard on the lungs."

After an hour or so, the receptionist, a stout woman with a deep frown carved into her smooth olive complexion, called them to her counter.

With a hasty wave she beckoned them. "What seems to be the problem?"

Raj took over. His medical training taught him to be confident in these situations and his allegiance to Alex and Irina spurred him to do all he could to help.

"She's been coughing, progressively worse for the last three weeks. The last couple of days she doesn't seem to be breathing very well, and she has a chronic history of lung problems, asthma especially," Raj said to the receptionist. "Father Michael said this was a place she could be seen and helped."

"Father Michael, huh?" the receptionist smiled. Her severe expression softened and the light reflected in her hazel eyes. "Good man. Wait here, and we'll try to get her in as soon as we can."

"Soon" was a relative term, as it often is in the medical profession. They waited quietly amid a sea of men, women, and children who showed signs of everything from psychosis to frostbite. Shortly after the old-fashioned clock on the wall passed the two o'clock hour, Irina was called back.

"Can my father and my friend come with me?" she asked.

The triage nurse, a wiry brunette with jaws that looked like a bear trap, scanned Irina's travelling companions.

"I guess, it's up to you," she said, motioning for Alex and Raj to follow.

After a few minutes of anxious silence, a doctor entered the humble examining room. He was a dark, pudgy, soft-looking man, equipped with the flat nose of a pug and a crest of black hair rimming his brown, otherwise hairless head. He smiled, eyes twinkling yet solemn as he entered the room, clasping his hands in front of him as he inquired about Irina.

"I am Dr. Galvez, and you must be Irina," said the benign looking physician, offering his hand. "What can I do for you today?"

At this point, Irina's thin body began to shake under the influence of continuous harsh coughing. Dr. Galvez nodded and turned to Alex.

"You are the young lady's father?" he inquired of Alex, who nodded. "So how long has this been going on?"

"A couple of weeks, but it seems to be getting worse," said Alex.

"She has a history of asthma as well, Dr. Galvez, including an ICU stay," Raj chimed in. "She's been having dyspnea, increased accessory muscle involvement in her breathing. We're worried that she might be decompensating."

"And who are you?" Galvez inquired, raising an eyebrow. "You seem to be well-versed in medical terminology."

Raj hesitated before speaking. He looked down and away from the doctor. It felt shameful to admit his former profession, perhaps because of his current predicament.

"I'm just a close friend," he said. "We travel together."

Dr. Galvez looked at the three strangers with a bemused expression and pulled out a stethoscope from the pocket of his white lab coat. He began to listen to Irina's lungs, grimacing as though exerting extra mental effort.

After completing the examination, Dr. Galvez addressed Irina in a grave tone.

"My friend, you have let this go on for a long time. I am glad that you have people who care enough about you to get you some help. Your breath sounds are not normal, and I think you could use an X-ray to see what is wrong with you. I suspect pneumonia."

"Doctor," Irina began in a hoarse tone. "You are kind and I appreciate it. But I do not want to go to the hospital. It scares me. Besides, we have no home, no papers, and no money."

"Nobody wants to go to the hospital, but sometimes it's necessary," said Galvez. "I can try to treat you with some medicine as an outpatient if you wish. But where are you going to go? The street is no place for anyone, much less someone who can't breathe."

"You're right, Doctor," said Raj. "But the truth is, we have nowhere to go. We're hoping to maybe find a shelter, but we're new to DC. My friends and I don't know much about this city; it's only thanks to Father Michael that we found our way here."

Galvez nodded and rubbed his chin with a leathery left hand. He remained silent for a few seconds before speaking.

"OK friends, here's what I'll do," he began. "Irina, you and your friends all will need TB tests and chest X-rays to get into the shelters around town. So we'll get you all X-rayed, and depending on what the results show, we'll get you whatever medicine is appropriate. I can keep you out of the hospital for now. But if things get worse, I mean even a little bit, I want to see you back here."

Irina nodded. Dr. Galvez disappeared to set up the X-rays for Irina, Alex and Raj. In a few minutes they were all whisked off to separate rooms before reconvening in the small examining room.

Galvez reappeared two hours later with three X-rays in hand.

"Alex, your X-ray is clear. Here's a note saying you have had a clear chest X-ray. Do not lose this note. Raj, same thing for you, clean bill of health."

He stopped before Irina and regarded her with a very solemn expression.

"The good news is, it doesn't look like you have TB, which is the main thing shelters are afraid of," he said. "Unfortunately, Irina, you have a case of pneumonia. I can give you this medicine which will keep your asthma from getting worse, and some antibiotics to fight the infection, but if things get worse, you'll need to come in to the hospital, understand?"

They left the clinic and braced for the angry winter wind, still concerned about Irina but also reassured.

"The doctor, he was very nice. Is a good doctor," Alex commented as they walked slowly into the wind gusts. "I bet you would have been like him, Raj."

Raj admired the doctors in clinics like this. They were modern-day knights, saving those who had no resources and little support. Once upon a time he wished to be a member of this order. People revered their missionary devotion. Now the dream of being a medical savior seemed to belong to another lifetime, maybe even another person.

"I don't know," said Raj. "I think I mostly wanted to be a doctor because of the status. People still look up to the profession, you know? No, I'm not like him. I think he's a better doctor than me, probably a better man. Anyway, that was in another lifetime. That version of me is dead."

"Sorry, I just thought . . ." Alex looked at his young traveling companion with a wounded expression. "I shouldn't have brought it up, my friend."

"Thanks, Alex, I just don't like to look at who I was," Raj explained. "The dreams of my past are not something I like to talk about. Besides, looking back won't move us forward. So where are we going to stay?"

It was, as usual, the most urgent of questions. And with no idea of the city's layout, the three travelers may as well have been travelling in a maze. A windswept labyrinth of glass and brick appeared before them.

Irina, motivated by her frail lungs and educated by the hardships of street living, proposed the first strategy to find a safe place to stay. It was with great surprise that the Raj heard her speak up. He had expected she would save all possible breath to fight her illness.

"Papa, Raj, I have an idea," she said in a raspy voice. "You know how Father Michael helped us, right? What if we could find his church, maybe ask them if they could help us out?"

"What do we know about this priest?" Alex dismissed the suggestion. "How can we trust him? We're homeless, but we're not desperate."

"What's the deal?" asked Raj. "I'd say we are desperate. It's late, Irina's badly off, and she's only getting worse. Even if we find a shelter, they may not take us with her coughing like she is."

"You are right," said Alex. "They may think she spreads disease. It is just that in Russia, the church is not to be trusted. I suspect them because they are corrupt. Just like the government. Only out for their own benefit, for money and power. Nothing they offer is for free."

"Please papa," Irina said. "We have no time for pride."

"We don't know the city," said Raj. "We don't know where any shelters are, but if we can find a church, sometimes they have shelters associated with them. We don't have to ask them for anything other than directions. And he did invite us. We must take help where we can find it."

Alex squinted at Raj.

"You agree?" he asked. "Oh well, maybe this old man is not thinking straight."

They wandered eastward, searching for a telltale spire or anything that might suggest a religious establishment. The wind blew harder with each successive block, whipping them onward from behind. The two men stood behind Irina, who hunched down in front to hide her diminutive frame from the frosty gusts.

As they gazed at the opposite side of the street, a humble grey stone building caught the attention of Raj.

"Wait," he called out to his companions. "Look at that."

They looked at the stone archway with its engraved lettering. A humble stained-glass rendition of the Virgin Mary sat

atop the point of the doorway's arch. "St. Mary's," Raj muttered. "Stained glass, fancy lettering, the name, might just be
the place. What do you guys think?"

"I think we check it out and get warm!" said Alex, smiling.

The three exhausted travelers hurried across the street as
fast as their weary legs could carry them. They knocked at the
door and awaited an answer. None came, so Raj turned the
doorknob and pushed the thick door open. As they wandered
inside, the sound of organ music swelled, then stopped. They
proceeded up the creaky center aisle, and were greeted by a
voice emanating from the balcony above, in the vicinity of the
organ.

"Hello, how may I help you?" said the voice, at once familiar and strange. A quick succession of footsteps followed
and a grey-haired man emerged from the staircase leading
down from the organ to the front of the church.

"Good day my friends," said the man. As he approached
closer, Raj recognized the man's face.

"Father Michael?" he said, lips parting in a smile.

"We meet again, my friends!" replied the Irish cleric with
hands folded and just a slight hint of a brogue. "So did you
get to the clinic?"

"Yes, we did, Father, thank you," Irina responded with a
smile. "They were very nice there."

"Ah, well good, good," Father Michael replied with a paternal smile. "So what brings you here right now? And what
are your names? So silly of me, we haven't even been properly
introduced!"

"Alex Petrov," the old man interjected. "This is my daughter
Irina, and our friend Raj Patel."

Father Michael gave vigorous handshakes, greeting his
visitors with the air of a politician on the campaign trail.

"It is a pleasure to meet you all," he said.

"Well, I . . . now that we've thanked you, maybe we should go," sputtered Alex.

"You need help. That's why you're here, and that's what I do. It is God's will," Father Michael explained. Three rows of wrinkles creased his previously untroubled forehead. "What can I do?"

Raj, impatient with the exchange of pleasantries, got straight to the purpose of their visit. "The fact is, Father, we're down and out. We came down here on our way south from New York so Irina could get well. Now, we need a place to stay, at least while she's stabilizing. We have no money, no jobs, and no familiarity with the city. We need a shelter and some food. We decided to come to a church because we thought that might be where to find what we're looking for. Can you help us?"

Father Michael's eyes never moved from Raj as he spoke his short, impassioned plea for help.

"Thank you for being clear with me, Raj," Father Michael said. "Your dilemma is all too common nowadays. We are a disoriented, disenchanted, disenfranchised world. Unfortunately, my small church doesn't have a shelter associated with it, and the nearest one I know of is 12 blocks from here. But I do have an idea. I used to live in this place, but the room is vacant now. I rent a small apartment west of here. It's closer to some of the other places I work, but that's neither here nor there. What matters to you is the rectory is yours if you want it. It's a big room, clean, and the shower and toilet are in working order. There's only one bed though. You could take your chances on the shelter, but I don't even know if they'll have beds open when you get there. They get pretty busy this time of year."

"You'd really let us stay here, in your own place?" asked Raj. "What's the catch?"

"There is not always a catch, my son," Father Michael answered. "And anyway, this is God's house, not mine. We're all renting on this earth, am I right?"

The line sounded rehearsed, but the priest's expression looked authentic. They'd be foolish to walk away from Father Michael's offer.

Raj turned to his friends. "Alex, Irina, what do you think?" he asked.

"If we live here, we should give something," said Alex. "It would not be right to take the Father's gifts otherwise, and it would make us all feel better."

"Alex, the chance to help you is gift enough," the priest replied. "But if you insist, I am sure I can think of some things for you to do. Come, the room's upstairs, I'll show you there."

Raj had never seen churches as a source for salvation. The concept ran counter to his reverence for objective scientific reality. Religion's practical applications in the world were often worse than even Marx described. But here he was, and at the moment their arrival seemed providential.

The room was typical of an early 20th century rectory. Its hardwood floors creaked and groaned in various places. The formerly white walls were darkened by years of wear and long periods of disuse. The small, attached bathroom featured no shower but a usable claw-foot tub. The furnishings were appropriately spare, highlighted by a small gilt figure of Jesus on the cross hanging above the doorway and a large but peeling canvas of the Virgin Mary on the west wall. The sun streamed in through two large, dust-streaked windows.

The one problem with the room was that there was only one bed, a folding cot that Father Michael used when he was too tired to make the trek back home to his apartment. All in all, however, the travelers agreed this was the best lodging they had experienced in weeks, if not longer. For once, they did not look behind them for the nearest police officer or petty criminal. Instead, they made themselves at home. While Alex and Raj made pillows from their clothing, Irina lay down on the bed, and fell asleep within minutes.

Raj lay awake in the old church. He breathed more easily than he had for weeks. The invisible corset of anxiety that constricted his entire being was slowly loosening. As he lay still on the floor, he reflected that rest was not merely a physical entity. It was a state of emotional security, an absence of spiritual agitation. Could he find that tranquility here, on the floor of a rectory? The thought lingered in his mind like the sweet aftertaste of his favorite mango kulfi. He smiled as he closed his eyes and wrapped his arms around the makeshift pillow.

The stillness of sleep was broken the next morning by a knock at the door.

"Hello, friends, it's me!" said the cheerful voice of Father Michael.

Raj awoke and rubbed his eyes.

"Oh, hello Father," he sputtered, "uh, what time is it?"

He walked to the door and opened it to let the priest enter.

"It is eight o'clock, my friends. I trust you slept well?" said Father Michael. "I thought you might need some things, so I brought some. I hope you don't mind."

By this time Irina and Alex had also arisen, and Alex greeted Father Michael with a smile and a handshake.

"Thank you, Father," Alex said. "We appreciate your help, you are so good to us. But you offer more than we deserve. How can we return the favor?"

"The work really is its own reward," Father Michael replied. "You see, in my younger years, before I went to seminary, I did my share of damage in the world."

Father Michael rolled up his left sleeve to reveal a Hell's Angels tattoo.

"I owe God, and I owe society. Without Him, who knows where I'd be? So the fact you are here, that I am able to help, this is a blessing to me. But if it would make you feel better, perhaps you could help me fix up the place. As you can see, it needs a little work, and also, I am handier with people than tools."

Irina stood up and smiled.

"We would be happy to assist you," she said to the priest. "We owe you at least that much."

"Believe me," said the priest, "you don't owe me a thing. Most people who I help out are not so grateful as you all. The Lord's work gives to those who do it as well as those who receive. But if you'd like to help, I can get some paint and some cleaning supplies, and let's go to work! But first things first."

Father Michael hurried off and disappeared for a few minutes, only to reappear with arms filled by a pair of large bags.

"I took the liberty of bringing some clothing and grooming supplies by. We had a drive recently and some of it was left, so here it is. There should be something in there for all of you. Also, I have some food in a couple bags downstairs," he explained as Alex and Raj rushed over to relieve him of his load.

"Oh, and there's some spare bedding down in the basement. I can get it if you like," he offered as Alex and Raj plodded up the stairs.

"Father, wait," said Raj, but the busy priest had already disappeared once again in search of spare mattresses.

"Hope I have that kind of energy when I'm old," said Raj. In his medical training he learned to associate age with senescence and decay. But the father was still vigorous and passionate despite his years.

"We old guys do OK," Alex responded with a hearty laugh. "But you are right, he is amazing."

In a matter of minutes, Father Michael appeared again, dragging a pair of air mattresses behind him.

"I hope these will do for now. I think I can round up some sheets, too," said Father Michael.

The three friends were soon settled in their new, temporary abode. Perhaps one day they would be able to move on. Until then the promise of warm beds, hot showers, and clean clothes offered hope for the immediate future.

The rest of the day was spent helping to clean and restore the church's drab interior. Alex and Raj sanded off chipped paint and applied new layers to some ailing areas of the church walls. Irina cleaned away the cobwebs and dust that dulled the floor and pews, and Father Michael flitted about like a manic hummingbird, aiding his new friends and providing ample food and water.

By evening, the interior of the old building looked clean, proud, and distinctive. Though lacking the pomp and flash of some of its wealthier relatives, St. Mary's now-clean interior radiated hope and providence.

The building's new tenants, spattered with paint and covered in dust, may have appeared less respectable than the church, but Raj did not mind at all. He scanned his surroundings with satisfaction.

In recent months he had few occasions to feel accomplished. He wanted to feel useful and productive. This was a start. It wasn't much, but he and his friends had done something with their own hearts and hands and they had done it together. His moment of quiet contemplation was interrupted by the thump of a meaty hand on his shoulder.

"It looks good, no?" Alex nodded and gestured at the painted walls. "Is good to do work and see it standing there before you. It makes a man feel honest and useful."

. Raj scanned Alex's round, red face, now tinged in droplets of clear sweat.

"You know, you're right Alex. Work is a good thing. I wonder if maybe Father Michael could tell us where we can find something more permanent. I guess maybe it's not so bad, taking this help he gives us."

"You mean, get jobs?" asked Alex. "We know this is not easy. We try, but it does not work. But maybe you are right. Maybe we need help. We are much alike, my friend."

Raj agreed with Alex. The two of them were stubborn and principled. Now clad in equally drab and humble trappings, their spirits were recognizably identical as well.

Father Michael approached once again. Accompanying him was an elderly lady who wore black plastic-rimmed glasses and a white hat. She was humbly dressed in a long gray wool coat that covered a faded pink-and-white checkered dress. Her snow-colored hair spilled out from beneath the hat. She stooped as she walked, leaning on a cane fashioned of dark-stained wood, with a silver-inlaid handle. Every few steps she stopped to lean on the cane as she caught her breath.

"This is Alice Mitchell," Father Michael declared with a gesture toward the distinguished lady. "She is one of my most faithful parishioners. She's always said a little TLC could make this church look brand new, so I thought I'd show her what you've done."

"It's very nice," she commented. "A church should be humble, but bright and clean, and that's just how it looks now. Been a while since it looked this clean. And I gather you are responsible for this?"

"We did our best, Ms. Mitchell," Raj answered, averting his gaze toward the floor. He felt as though he were in school, going over his homework with an exacting teacher and awaiting criticism.

Alice pulled Father Michael aside for a moment. Raj heard snippets of their conversation and divined that Ms. Mitchell harbored certain reservations about him and his friends.

"Yes, I know they did a good job . . . do you really think you can trust them . . . you can never tell with these sort of people . . . just be careful, Father," he heard Alice say in brief snatches.

The faithful parishioner and the priest returned from their brief audience, and Ms. Mitchell spoke again.

"Father Michael says that you are people of good character, and I think he would know, being a man of God. I was thinking perhaps I could give you some money, to help you get on your feet, or something."

"We do not do this for money, Ms. Mitchell," Alex answered. "We do this out of thanks. We do this because it is right. And doing what is right is worth most of all, I think."

Ms. Mitchell's eyes opened wide. She nodded and glanced at each of the three strangers for a moment.

"OK, so it's not money you're after, but there must be something I can do for you helping my dear friend, Father Michael."

At this point, Father Michael interrupted.

"Alice, these people have expressed to me a wish to work, to do something productive. I know you are connected with a number of places, perhaps they might be able to secure jobs of some sort?"

"Well, I do have some friends and family in the restaurant business. Do you think that you all would like that kind of work?" the old lady inquired.

"Would be great," Alex burst out with a broad smile.

"Alex here is an experienced butcher in New York and Russia," Raj explained to Ms. Mitchell.

"Ah, you could be quite an asset then," she said, smiling at Alex.

"How about you, young man?" she asked Raj.

He hesitated before responding, shifting his weight back and forth. His former vocation seemed so long ago and far away. He preferred to consider it a closed compartment, sealed forever.

"I'm willing to do whatever you ask me. I'm skilled with computers, and I'm very trainable and eager to learn," he said. If anything good had come of his brief medical career, it was the development of this ability to think on his feet.

"And you, young lady?" Ms. Mitchell asked Irina.

"I am not sure what I can do, but I wish to help," Irina said meekly.

"You are too modest, my dear," Alex protested on his daughter's behalf. "She is a marvelous singer, and a pretty good cook!"

"Hmm, you certainly are charming, my dear," Ms. Mitchell commented to Irina, smiling. "We'll find something for you to do, too. I'll be back in two days, with some information on jobs. Until then, good day, and God bless you all," she proclaimed as she turned to leave the church.

"Thank you," the three called out as Ms. Mitchell approached the door. She paused as she pushed it halfway open.

"Yes, you're welcome. But don't thank me until I've got you your jobs," she quipped with a wink and a nod as the door closed behind her.

Chapter Fourteen

The day arrived for Alex, Irina, and Raj to report for work at Cranchione's Old-World Italian Trattoria. It was a neighborhood eatery run by Ms. Mitchell's long-time acquaintance. This was all they knew upon arriving at the establishment, which announced itself to the world in understated cursive lettering on an oval-shaped sign whose hinges creaked in the wind. Ms. Mitchell greeted them at the door, along with an old man with tightly drawn skin and an aquiline nose.

"This is Joe, the owner of the restaurant. Joe, these are Alex, Irina, and Raj. They're the friends of Father Michael I was telling you about," said Mrs. Mitchell.

Irina forced herself to smile. Though her lungs felt clearer now, she was uncertain about this apparent stroke of good fortune. Joe approached and shook her hand, clasping her on the shoulder. She shivered. It had become a reflex to recoil at the unexpected touch of a man's hand. She wondered why Raj didn't evoke that reaction. For some reason, her body trusted him.

"Well, nice to meet y'all, any friends of the Father are friends of mine," Joe said. "Now that we've got the introductions all done, we'll figure out what you're all doing, and I'll get you some uniforms."

He rushed off to the back of the restaurant and came back with three uniforms. Alex and Raj were handed light green T-shirts trimmed in white, red pants and baseball caps reading "Mangia" in red script. Irina, meanwhile, was given a waitress' light green blouse and white flared skirt.

Irina went to the bathroom to change. As she peeled off her old clothes and slipped the skirt over her slender hips, she remembered the last version of a work uniform that she had worn. This garb felt safer. Beneath the costume she could hide her scars and show nothing more than the surface of her skin. But what if things changed? Her early adult years told her that change was a constant, and the thought caused dull ache within her belly.

She exited the restroom to reconvene with Alex and Raj. Joe inquired as they paced the length of the small but busy eatery.

"Alex, Mrs. Mitchell tells me you've done some butcher's work in your time?" Joe asked.

"Is true, Joe," said Alex. He rubbed his hands together and smiled.

"Well, you and your buddy here will start as dishwashers, but I'll ask you to show me some work and if you're any good, I might move you up to prep work soon."

He approached Irina and pointed. "You, Irina, will bus tables. That means cleaning off all the dirty glasses, plates, and all that good stuff. Do well, you might get to be a regular wait-ress, and you keep your tips, got it?"

He made it sound like honest work. She hoped he wasn't lying. A life of simplicity, security and transparency was almost as seductive now as fame and attention had been years ago.

Within minutes, Irina and her friends set to work, stum-bling unguided through their initial day in the restaurant.

The kitchen, redolent of garlic and preserved meats, grabbed hold her senses instantly. Its dark brown tile and dim light combined with pungent smells and formidable heat to give the kitchen the air of a culinary swamp.

As Irina went in and out of the kitchen, she saw Alex and Raj crouched over their respective sinks, feverishly washing and drying various dishes and pieces of cutlery with nary a break in the action. It was good to see father working again. She knew the value he placed on work and the ability to provide for her. In turn she wished to see him smile, fueled by the fulfillment that comes at the end of a day's labors.

Joe hovered over the shoulders of his new employees, answering questions and explaining procedures. Raj was getting used to the old man's interruptions but was still surprised when Joe walked up behind him.

"I know you from somewhere, Raj," said Joe. "I never forget a face. I'll figure it out, but just remember I got my eye on you."

Raj felt his heart skip a beat. The tone of the old man's words offended him, but he kept silent and continued washing dishes. What now? He breathed a sigh of relief as Joe trudged off into the main serving area of the restaurant. The thought of his new boss watching him like a hawk made his hands tremble as he scrubbed the dinner plates and utensils.

In time the routine of work grew comfortable. Predictability and simplicity were not to be underestimated. Raj may not have understood that years ago, but he did now. His former desires for prestige and acclaim had evaporated and were replaced by a new appreciation of more mundane labor.

But he remained reluctant to trust in the kindness of man and fortune alike. He was grateful for the ample meals and adequate pay Joe provided, but could not shake Joe's words: "I'm watching you."

After two weeks a strange occurrence shed new light on the events of the first day. It began when a short, stocky blonde man walked into the restaurant in an expensive-looking blue suit.

The blue-suited gentleman accosted Irina, who startled as he placed his hand on her shoulder.

"Sorry if I scared you," he said. "Is Cranston here?"

"I . . . I am not sure. Let me find out, sir. I will only be a minute," said Irina with an uneasy smile.

She hurried into the kitchen and whispered to Raj.

"There is a man out there. He scares me. He is asking for a Mr. Cranston. But I don't know a Mr. Cranston. What should I do?"

"Hmm," said Raj, rubbing his chin as he contemplated the proper course of action. "Let's ask Joe."

Joe soon entered the kitchen and Raj and Irina began bombarding him with information and questions. Joe raised his hand to halt the barrage.

"Whoa, whoa, slow it down guys," he commanded. "Now what's going on?"

"There is a man in a blue suit out there. He asks for Mr. Cranston. I told him I would find out if he was here," said Irina. "He seemed kind of scary."

"Mr. Cranston?" Joe laughed. "Well, last time I checked, that's me! I think I know who this guy is. Blue suit, blonde hair you say? That sounds like the health inspector. Don't worry, I'll take care of him. His bark is worse than his bite."

As his boss hurried off to meet with the inspector, Raj searched his memory.

"Cranston, I remember that name from somewhere," he thought. "If I could just remember where."

As the synapses of his brain made rapid connections, the circumstances of their encounter hit Raj like a thunderclap. He remembered the beaked nose and the insistent barking. "Get me some water!"

"Oh my God! No, it can't be," he said to himself, unaware that he had stopped working to stare out the door through which Cranston had exited.

He flashed back to the urban ICU, with its incessant beeping monitors, ubiquitous tubes, and stern-faced medical staff. The bruised faces of his lifeless parents returned to his mind in full color.

"Ahh!" he cried out, dropping a knife onto his shoe and startling those around him. Alex shook Raj by his shoulders, jarring him back into reality.

"Raj, what's wrong?"

"It's Cranston, I . . . I know where I've seen him before," Raj replied.

"Oh, that's it?" said Alex. "Well, back to work for me."

The rest of the day proceeded without incident. This was fortunate for Raj, whose concentration was minimal now that his mind swam in a river of memories.

As the three walked back toward their lodging, Irina peered at Raj.

"You don't look well my friend," she commented. "Did something happen in there?"

"Yes, yes you could say that," Raj replied.

"You look like you'd seen a ghost," said Alex.

"I guess I did," said Raj. Alex and Irina looked on with evident puzzlement, then stared at each other, shrugged their shoulders, and continued walking.

They tromped back to the church, up the stairs, and into the old wooden room. Finally, Raj broke the silence.

"Why does the past never die?" he whispered, his voice quivering as the words trickled out. Unbeknownst to him, his question was heard by his two comrades. They stopped and surrounded him.

"What are you talking about?" Irina asked, rushing over and placing her hands on his cheeks. Her eyes darted back and forth, as though reading a map.

Raj grasped her hands within his own.

"Do you remember, in New York, when you were in the hospital? My parents died in that hospital," he said.

"I know, I know," said Irina. But Raj was in no mood for consolation.

"Shh. This is hard enough to explain. Please hear me out. You see, in that hospital, there was a bitter, demanding, crabby guy. A patient. That guy was Cranston. And the moment I realized where I'd seen him before, it was like the whole scene came back to me. I could see it, hear it, even smell it. That damned hospital room will not leave me alone, ever. It really is like seeing a ghost or being haunted by one anyway. I'm not even sure I can go back there, to the restaurant."

"Do not decide in a hurry, my friend," Alex advised. "You are in pain. A man in pain is never wise. Sleep, and make your decisions in the morning."

As he listened, Raj realized that his body needed rest and so did his memory. If only he could pacify his mind.

"To sleep, perchance to dream," he murmured to himself.

And sleep arrived, but only with the unwanted company of vivid, unpleasant images of distorted faces with tubes protruding from them. In the nightmares he heard screams superimposed on the rhythmic electronic beeping of some anonymous machine. He saw himself shouting for help as sundry white-clad men and women walked past. Over and over, he reached for them, only to see them disappear. All that remained were screams in the emptiness. He woke to a rapid heartbeat and sheets saturated in sweat, relieved to leave the night behind him, but fearful of its return.

The aftermath of his disturbing night left Raj shaken and exhausted. Though he feared the return of his uninvited visions, Raj decided to return to work. The restaurant and Mr. Cranston were good to him, and he could not let his employer down. If there was one principle he had internalized from a young age, it was the value of a strong work ethic. He could not dishonor that lesson or the beloved parents who had instilled it.

He walked to work, wearing a scowl of determination to mask his fear. He needed to tell Cranston. He couldn't say why it was necessary, but it was. And as luck would have it, the crusty owner of Cranchione's Italian restaurant greeted him as he walked in through the rickety door.

"Joe, can I talk to you?" Raj heard his words but was only vaguely aware that they originated from his own mouth.

"What about?" Cranston scowled.

"I think I know where we know each other from," said Raj. Cranston's eyebrows rose.

"So shoot."

"Do you remember the hospital in New York? You kept asking for a glass of water." Raj searched Cranston's face but saw no sign of recognition. "You probably don't remember. Maybe I shouldn't be bothering you."

"No, no it's OK," said Cranston. "Today's kind of a slow day anyway. Wait! I've been in a New York hospital only once. Had my bypass there. I think it's coming back to me."

"My parents were in there the same time as you," said Raj.

"But wait, it can't be," said Cranston, tapping his chin with his index finger. "I remember a guy who looked like you; parents were in the unit. Answered my question when everyone else was ignoring me. But I seem to remember he was a doctor?"

Raj sighed and stared at his boss. Cranston narrowed his eyes, as if calling the scene to mind from the recesses of his memory.

"Oh my Lord. That was you, the kid whose folks died in there, who collapsed in the middle of the unit. That was you! But how . . . why . . . here?"

"That was me, and it's been a long, downhill road ever since, Mr. Cranston," Raj answered. "You could say I lost myself, and I'm in the process of finding who I am. And what you've offered is a vital part of that. I was drowning out there, and you and this place have saved me. I want you to know I'm grateful, and I won't let you down."

"You're a good man," Cranston replied. "I'm fortunate to have you. And happy you're here. I know you're overqualified, so I hope I can find something more your speed."

"That would be great. "Regardless, I'm happy to be here."

Raj walked out into the cold air and inhaled a long, slow breath. After the kitchen's stifling heat, the jolt of wintry air entering his lungs made him feel as if he were aroused from an extended torpor. And contrary to his prior fears, the awakening was accompanied by a lightening of his pain.

As he brushed the crystals of frozen sweat from his face, Raj watched his breath evaporate in a steamy trail. Each breath seemed lighter, more natural.

He did not anticipate that spilling these secrets to a stranger. And yet Cranston offered no judgment, no resistance. Raj was a mere employee, but the boss never once told him to shut up or looked at him with disgust. People were full of surprises. All his years studying the human body taught him so little about matters of the heart. How could he explain that?

"Ah, why ask why?" Raj answered himself aloud. The icy winds buffeted his cheeks. He clutched his arms tightly around his thin body, rubbing his shoulders as he headed back to the kitchen.

"You OK to stay?" Cranston asked.

Raj nodded. "I'm good, thanks," he replied with a quick smile.

Now that the mystery was solved, Raj accelerated into the remainder of his day. He had underestimated the amount of debris that filled his cranium and slowed his progress. The clutter allowed so little advancement of his thoughts. Memories poured back in rapid succession: his parents' lifeless bodies lying bloody and motionless as incessant beeping played in the background, the burning of their corpses, the weeks spent avoiding life's painful responsibilities. He cursed himself for his inertia. So much time he had spent merely existing. Would his parents approve of this? In truth, he didn't know. And to his surprise, the feeling of uncertainty no longer frightened him. He drew a deep breath and scrubbed the stubborn crust from a pan, encouraged by the visible sheen of the metal.

Raj, Irina, and Alex meandered toward the church. Constant proximity facilitated a tight bond between them. This allowed

Raj to share his intimate thoughts in ways he never dared before.

"Alex, my comrade," he said. "Do you think a man can be dead inside, but still be alive?"

Alex stopped and squinted at his young friend. He cocked his head like a dog that has heard a favorite word. "A man? Do you mean yourself? I don't know everything about you, my friend. But I think a man can be like frozen lake. In my country, winters are cold. And water freezes, for many meters. And it seems like the ice will never melt. Sometimes I am that lake too. But you know, there is always a little stream of water, under all that thick ice. And life continues in that cold stream. And then spring comes, and the water is free. A man can be frozen too, but some day, he will be free. He will melt and flow forward into the rivers of life."

Raj nodded and pondered the old man's words for a second. "You're sure you were a butcher, not a poet or philosopher or something?" he asked with a wry smile.

Alex guffawed, further strengthening his resemblance to the mythical "St. Nick".

"I have many layers my friend!" he proclaimed with a twinkle in his eyes. "Like big Russian onion!"

"Round and smelling like a restaurant?" Irina needled her father before scurrying away, eyes full of mischief.

"Come here, you!" Alex bellowed at his daughter, running to envelop her face and shoulders in tight, laughing embrace. The three then shared a hearty, contagious spell of mirth, intoxicated by the type of carefree giddiness that binds families together.

Weeks passed in a comfortable tedium. Raj no longer wanted for life's necessities, but the tenuous nature of life's stability remained etched in his consciousness. With the blessing of Father Michael, he and his friends saved a portion of their collective earnings in hopes of amassing a down payment on an apartment. The rest of their money went toward daily necessities such as food, clothing, and Irina's asthma medications.

Despite their improved fortunes, Father Michael refused to accept any money from his three pilgrims. Even the work they did in maintaining the church grounds was a product of their own gratitude, rather than his requests.

"God does not sell His love. Goodness and charity are their own reward," Father Michael reiterated.

At work, Raj watched as Alex and Irina were given more responsibility. Cranston told them how lucky he felt to have such dependable employees.

Alex, with his knowledge of the butcher's craft, assisted the chefs. He appeared to relish the more active rhythm of slicing and chopping meats to exact thicknesses. Raj watched as Alex practiced his craft like an artist, a veritable Giacometti of roasts and chops. Sometimes Cranston took Alex with him to the various meat suppliers to provide an expert's eye and assure quality control of Cranchione's renowned veal.

Irina waited tables. Her efficiency and charming manner endeared her to the customers. Even the most demanding clientele had nary a complaint about her and often requested her on repeat visits to the neighborhood eatery. On Friday and Saturday evenings she provided vocal concerts for the customers. Word of her talents spread and crowds sometimes swelled out the door.

As his friends advanced, Raj remained mired in the soapy drudgery of a dishwasher's life. The daily routine and dignity of hard labor afforded him a sense of pride. It was work he might have considered mindless in the past, but as he scrubbed plates and forks he felt honest and virtuous in a way that didn't accompany medical work. Raj gave thanks for the comfortable and secure routine of work, but the prickle of an under-stimulated intellect irritated him. Cranston had promised that the life of a dishwasher would be temporary but thus far Raj saw no sign of change. He had no desire to return to the often-tragic world of hospital work, but he wished to contribute more with his mind, not just his hands.

When Raj arrived at work this winter day with his comrades, a thin white coating of fresh snow blanketed the ground. He gave thanks for the warmth of the restaurant, watching his frosty breath trail away as he crossed the door's threshold. He removed his black down jacket and gloves and rubbed his hands together.

"Raj," Cranston called. "Let's go to my office."

Raj felt an unpleasant stirring within him. Perhaps it was his upbringing or his medical training, but he harbored a conditioned visceral fear of being summoned to offices. The recent past had taught Raj to brace for misfortune. He wasn't even sure what Cranston's office looked like, but he pictured it as a small place with old leather furniture, vintage pictures of Italian-American heroes like Sinatra and DeNiro, and the odor of old cigars. As for the goings-on, Raj suspected that this was a place where unpleasant tidings lay in store. Could it be that he was being fired? If so, where would he go? The questions and fears accelerated, spinning in his head like a caged rodent's wheel.

Cranston gestured to Raj to follow him. He opened an unobtrusive forest green door and motioned Raj inside.

Raj looked around him. He had not been entirely mistaken about the office. The smoky odor was noticeably and fortuitously absent, but a young Sinatra, Joe DiMaggio, and DeNiro in "Taxi Driver" all festooned the walls. Behind a gray metal desk sat a tattered brown office chair. Across the desk, a pair of ugly beige folding Chesterfield armchairs flanked the doorway.

"Have a seat," Cranston directed Raj, showing an ambiguous smile as he settled into his armchair. "Well, I guess you have no idea why I called you here today, and I suppose I should have told you."

"Uh, no I really have no clue," Raj responded. His throat and chest tightened with dread.

"Well, just so you know, nothing bad," Cranston commenced. "In fact, you may find this very good news, but it is a serious matter. You see, as you know, I'm not getting any younger, and I'm realizing I need some help running this place. You're very educated, and you work hard and it seems a waste to have you limited to kitchen duty. How would you like to help me out with the books and monitoring some of the day-to-day operations, supplies, stuff like that? Kind of my assistant manager."

"Well, yes, that sounds . . . great!" Raj stuttered. "I've been wanting to do more, to wake up my brain."

"Understand, I don't give this job lightly," the old man admonished Raj. "There's a lot of trust involved here. I think I can trust you. Can I?"

"You can, sir," Raj answered with a solemn countenance.

"Good, you start today, welcome aboard!" said Cranston with a smile. "First task is to do inventory. I'll show you how I like it done, come on."

"OK, let's go!" said Raj. "But you know, now that we're working together, I just have one question for you."

"What?" asked Cranston with one upraised eye brow.

"Well, it's about the name of the restaurant. It says 'old world Italian'. How does a guy named Cranston become 'old-world Italian'?" he inquired.

"Good one," said Cranston. "You see, when my family came over here, our name was Cranchione. Good Italian name. But they knew things weren't so good for Italians back then, so they changed it to Cranston. So now I got the best of both worlds, I figure."

"Sounds like it," Raj concurred as the two walked along the perimeter of the restaurant's dining area. "Old-world Italian lineage, and a name that doesn't stick out."

The two men spent the lion's share of the day together, detailing the restaurant's various supplies and financial records. Cranston's organizational schemes were unconventional, but Raj was an eager student of the intricacies of restaurant management.

"You seem to know what I want you to do," said Cranston. "You ever done anything like this before?"

"My parents used to run a little import/export shop, so I know a bit about inventory and ordering, bookkeeping, that stuff," Raj explained. "They were not so wise about the business end, so I'm sure I have a lot to learn, but you know how it is, you grow up around something and stuff rubs off."

"I do know how that is," Cranston agreed. "That's how I came by this line of work myself. Always wanted to be an actor, but the restaurant business is what we do in my family."

Cranston showed Raj the computers and logbooks. These were not the complex vital statistics and laboratory data of a hospital ward, but numbers and technology reminded him of the responsibility he once enjoyed.

"I can update this for you," said Raj. "There are better programs for tracking inventory and other data. I was a computer science major in college, so sprucing this up shouldn't be hard."

"I'll be grateful if you could help this place run better. Computer science and medicine, and you're working here?"

said Cranston. He shook his head. "I guess it's true when they say God works in mysterious ways."

Raj pondered the statement. It was hard to give credence to a higher power, but he conceded that if there were a Supreme Being, its methods were beyond all explanation. This was what made it futile to find justification for the tragedies of days past. He followed behind Cranston, listening to explanations of storage techniques, health codes, and purchasing practices. It was satisfying to feel his mind assimilating new information.

Closing time drew near and Cranston granted his new charge an early reprieve from his duties. Raj sat down at a deserted booth, a glass of water stationed by his left hand as he reclined against the maroon upholstery. It had been some time since his mind was valued, and the new role suited his pride.

As he waited for Alex and Irina to get ready for the walk home, Raj permitted himself a smile of contentment. He was beginning to believe the clouds of bad luck might be moving on.

As the three friends meandered back to the church, Irina waxed philosophical about their relative good fortune.

"It is not much, this life," Irina mused. "But it is so much more than what we have had. Maybe soon we will move to our own place. Maybe I go back to school, or sing on the big stage. Papa, do you think it will happen?"

"Why not, my dear?" Alex proclaimed in agreement. "Why not, indeed. Dreams are a country where all are welcome. Of course, maybe our friend here does not need such dreams. He is big fancy man now! I hope he doesn't forget us little people!"

Raj Patel paused and looked at his friend's serious face, disturbed by the apparent barb until a torrent of laughter bubbled forth from Alex. He and Irina soon joined in, and together they strolled back to the church, their spirits lifted from the spontaneous outburst of communal happiness.

Chapter Fifteen

The holidays arrived and St. Mary's teemed with strange faces making an effort to expiate their sins. Raj watched admiringly as Father Michael buzzed through the days meeting with parishioners, community organizers and even complete strangers.

"I tell you my friends, if everyone worshipped the way they do the last week of the year, I would never sleep," said Father Michael. "I suppose it's fortunate for me they're not always this pious!"

Raj listened as Irina enlivened Christmas with her renditions of modern and traditional Christmas carols. Despite his secular leanings, he loved his childhood Christmas carols. As he heard Irina singing "Ave Maria," Raj recalled the days when Christmas and New Year's Eve meant special treats and festivities. He remembered bounding down the stairs of his house and tearing into an armful of presents. Every New Year's Eve was spent with a pot of spiced apple cider, waiting for the ball to drop on the television. Though his parents stayed true to their Hindu faith, they adopted a few Christian traditions of their new country for his benefit.

Even as he admired the delicate beauty of Irina and her voice, Raj struggled to feel warmed by the Yuletide spirit.

Father Michael encouraged Raj to join in the celebrations, but he declined. As snow fell and bells jingled, he viewed the proceedings with a detached feeling, as though the concerts and parades were part of some bizarre cinematic production.

"Do you ever feel like this isn't real, like it's a big show we're watching that just goes on outside of us?" Raj asked Father Michael one evening. "I don't know. I'm really trying to get back into life, to throw myself into it, but it seems so bizarre and absurd sometimes."

"I think I know what you mean," Father Michael assented. "And the fact is, I feel that way too sometimes. I suspect everyone does. The pace of this world can be dizzying. Sometimes you just want to step off and watch the merry-go-round twirl by itself for a while to figure out what it all means."

"You know, for all they did, I feel like my family never prepared me for the life I have now," said Raj.

"It's a tough job that parents have," Father Michael answered. "To protect and prepare. Sometimes these duties conflict with one another. Maybe that's why I never opted for marriage and children myself."

"I never thought of what they did as protection."

"But maybe that's what it was. They kept me sheltered and insulated from suffering, from hardship. But in some ways that's not appropriate. Now I'm still learning how to build myself up. Nobody gave me a blueprint for this, least of all them. It's hard to say I resent them for that, but I guess maybe it's possible?"

"I'm no therapist," said Father Michael. "But I know this: life's actions and feelings are not simple. It's rare to feel just one way. You have to allow the ambivalent emotions to coexist within you. And I suspect you have the blueprint. You just have to learn how to read it."

"Maybe you're right," Raj rubbed his forehead. "Could be it's all this searching for definite answers and explanations that's the problem. Thanks for giving me food for thought. I'm sure you have lots to do, so I'll let you go."

Despite his admiration for Father Michael, Raj dreamed of leaving the church to live with Irina and Alex as a family. Helping hands were not to be forgotten, but independence was still a cardinal feature of manhood. Fewer obligations would leave him feeling, he imagined. And as willing as Father Michael was to provide for them, one never could be sure when luck or charity would run out.

It was in this spirit of cautious gratitude that Raj and his friends retired for the night of January 5th, unconcerned about what lay in store in the forthcoming days.

The morning of January 6th began in much the same way as any other eastern winter morning. Irina dressed slowly, watching wax paper wrappers dance on the wind that whistled outside the church windows, rattling the tired wooden frames. As Alex slept, she stared at the clouds that loomed overhead, threatening to release a snowstorm.

Raj had left the church early to get started on midweek inventory duties. Meanwhile, Father Michael arrived at the church somewhat later than usual this blustery morning. Irina heard him addressing two men.

"Welcome my friends," the priest said. "How can I help you? Are you new to the church? I haven't had the pleasure of meeting you before!"

"We're from ICE, Father. We've been given some information that some churches in this area might be harboring illegal aliens," a stranger said in a monotone.

Irina stood and moved toward the door of the room to hear the conversation more clearly.

"You think I might have some knowledge of this?" Father Michael asked. "My friends, I respect the laws of our nation. I am a good, loyal American citizen."

"Spare us, Father," the second man said. "The robe and the accent can't hide you, Father. If you know anything, we'll find out. Consider this a friendly reminder. Next time won't be friendly."

A knock came at the door of the rectory. Irina opened it to see Father Michael. She was relieved that he was unaccompanied, but concerned when she saw his furrowed brow and ashen face.

"You don't look well," said Irina. "Do you need to sit down?"

"Some people were just here," Father Michael sputtered. He paced across the room, waving his hands in the air. "They know. I don't know how but they asked questions. They asked me if I knew about any illegal immigrants being hidden at neighborhood churches. They asked and I said nothing, but they knew."

"Yes, I heard two men," said Irina. "They are immigration, yes? But are they interested in us? Why?"

Father Michael nodded.

"What he's saying is that the immigration, they know we are here," said Alex. "To them, all of us who do not have papers are not welcome. It makes no difference if we are criminals or children. If they catch us, they deport us and Father Michael may get in trouble."

"Going back is not an option," said Irina. Her knees shook as she remembered Tolya and his henchmen. "We would not survive."

"Please, I don't want you to leave for me," said Father Michael. "I will harbor you as long as you need. If I get arrested, so be it. I've done time before for doing the Lord's work. I just think you should know they have been asking about you, that you should be careful."

"You have been more than good to us. Now it is time that we are good to you," said Alex. "We cannot have you get in trouble over us. You have others to take care of. We will find some place. We will survive."

Alex and Irina rushed through the packing process, shoving their belongings into bags and dispensing with anything they deemed unnecessary. When all was ready, Irina paused to write a note to Raj.

Father Michael watched as Irina put down the pen and left the note on the windowsill where a thin rim of snow frosted the outside of the glass. As she placed it down, Irina began to cry and a few of her tears spilled onto the precisely folded sheet.

Raj toiled away at the inventory and other mundane chores of restaurant management, unaware for the majority of the morning that his comrades had failed to report for duty. It was only after the noon hour that Cranston, his face flushed with anger, tapped Raj on the shoulder.

"Where are your friends?" he asked. He approached Raj and stood chest to chest with him. "They just leave me here? I have a goddamn restaurant to run here! What the hell is going on?"

Cranston addressed two patrons as they stared at him.

"Excuse me," he said, his lips forming a tight smile. "Carry on with your meal, please."

The two men retreated to the office. The door slammed shut with a sonorous thud. Cranston placed his hand on his hip and glared across the desk at Patel.

"What's the deal, Raj?" Cranston asked. "My best waitress, my expert deli guy, just gone, like that? And who's going to sing on Friday and Saturday now? Something's happened. They're never this late. They're not gonna show today."

He paced the length of the small office, hands interlocked behind his back.

"We have to get to the bottom of this, and we have to get some help," Cranston muttered. "And it's gotta be quick. And Raj, I really hope you're not thinking of bolting like your friends. I trusted you. You don't want to mess with that."

"Joe, I . . ."

Cranston stormed out of the office muttering obscenities. An unsettled feeling churned the pit of Raj's stomach. He understood Joe's frustration, but why the threats? And why were Alex and Irina absent? Something must have happened, and as he pondered the possibilities a fear of loneliness took hold. He was a preschooler abandoned in a foreign country: scared, confused, and far from competent.

Raj returned to the church with this heavy burden on his mind. His preoccupation diverted his focus and he almost stepped in front of a taxicab as he started across an intersection. The angry honking and profane gestures aroused Raj from his fog, but clarity of thought evaded him.

He trudged through the church doors and up the stairs, his shoes slapping against the thick wood. Raj opened the door to his room, and his fears were confirmed. His two friends left few traces of their existence, having vanished with most of their clothes and personal effects. Raj was alone again and angry at his fate.

Raj found the letter and mouthed its words.

Dear Raj,

Immigration came today. Father and I must go
before they find us. It hurts me to leave you like this, but
one day we will be together again. We will be family.
Love,
Irina.

He clenched his jaw and opened the window, staring into
the busy street outside. It seemed that everyone who came into
his life only did so in anticipation of leaving. Did love always de-
part before its petals reached their full splendor? Irina and Alex
breathed him back to life and awoke his heart, but now fate left
him alone again. As some minutes passed he tried to grasp at a
faint glimmer of hope. After all, his friends were probably still in
town and not dead or completely gone. Irina said that one day
they would be united again. He must hold on to that promise.

Raj fell onto his bed, staring at the ceiling with his hands
folded behind his head. His mind flashed back to his initial
meeting with the vagabonds who had become his family. The
circumstances of their initial encounter were less than ideal,
but he nonetheless remembered it with fondness. Soon sorrow
returned in the company of guilt, as he grieved the loss of those
who had helped him without asking anything in return. Would
he see them again? He needed to. Debts of gratitude should not
remain unsettled, and words of love must not remain unspoken.

The night descended, but Raj barely noticed the darkening skies. Instead, he spent most of his time ruminating
about life and its various injustices. How could people who
had never met Alex and Irina be so eager to ruin their lives?
And what about him, not to mention the crusty Joe Cranston?
He spent the bulk of the night hatching and abandoning a

variety of plans to "make things right" before surrendering to sleep for a few brief minutes before sunrise.

The next morning Cranston met Raj at the door. As Raj removed his coat Cranston peppered him with questions.

"Did you find out anything?" he asked. "I'd sure like to know where they went. Are they coming back? What happened?"

"Wait, wait. One question at a time, Joe," said Raj, raising his hand to request the old man's silence. "Here's what I know. Irina left a note. She says that ICE came around to the church where we were staying. I don't know why immigration came, but it spooked them, and they left. I don't know if they'll be back, when they'll be back or even where they went."

"Goddamn ICE bastards!" Cranston exclaimed, slamming his fist onto a nearby table. "They tried to jail my grandfather. Said he was without papers. 'WOP' they called us back then. And do you have any idea how many people I've lost to those guys? Hell, I don't mind them rooting out drug dealers and thieves, but why the hell do they have to mess with honest folk? The damn government, I'll never understand it!"

"I'm sorry," Raj sputtered. "If it's any consolation, I know how you feel, and then some. Alex and Irina were family, and now I don't know if I'll ever see them again."

Cranston's scowl softened. He sighed and put a hand on Raj's shoulder. "Ah, don't be sorry. Not your fault those suits downtown have no damn clue. Guess we'll just have to move on, try and survive. First order of business, I need to replace what we've lost. Hope they come back, but you never can count on that in this business."

The myriad responsibilities of restaurant management allowed Raj little time for grief or anger. He and Cranston patched together staffing for the next few weeks, often toiling well past closing time. The personnel challenges added to the usual variety of organizational chores, but the restaurant continued to flourish.

When not preoccupied with the tasks of restaurant management, Raj was left in the company of his thoughts and memories. If there was a benefit to the hours of newfound solitude spent in the spare room of the church, it was that he had ample time to consider his future. He was grateful to have a job and a roof over his head, but the ghost of his parents' dreams lingered. Would they have wanted him toiling away in a restaurant for the rest of his life? Had they sacrificed their time, energy, and money for this? He remembered his father's frequent advice: "Always remember, you were put on this earth to make it better. Don't sit still. If you stay in one place, the world will push you backward. It's up to you to step forward and keep going." He should be doing more to make that happen.

It was with these thoughts in mind that Raj decided to approach Cranston one brisk winter morning to discuss his future.

"Joe," he greeted his boss. "You know I have been doing some thinking."

Joe looked up from throwing trash in the dumpster. "What about?"

"Well, you know I like this job, Joe," said Raj. "But the fact is, I don't want this to be all I ever do. I was thinking about what you told me that day. You know how you said you always wanted to be an actor? Did you ever wish you pursued that path?"

The old man shrugged his shoulders. He scowled his disapproval.

"I've had those thoughts, sure," Cranston admitted. "Guess everybody has second thoughts. Although with a mug like mine I doubt I would have gotten far. But why do you bring this up, are you thinking of leaving me too now?"

"No, not anytime soon, that's for sure," Raj said. "It's just I've been thinking about things since Irina and Alex had to leave. The world is full of people who are never seen or heard. This is who Alex and Irina are, who I was for a while. And you know what? I'm sick of the world trampling on people who can't fight back. So I'm going to fight for them. I'm going to apply to law school. It's taken me a while, but I've figured it out. This is my calling. I can speak for people who have no voice. This is my dream."

"That's very inspiring," Cranston replied. "But what about your job here? I need you, you're my right-hand man!"

A pang of guilt struck. The old man tossed him a lifeline when he needed it most, and Raj didn't wish to be ungrateful to him. In younger years Raj scoffed at loyalty to strangers, but these recent months had changed his mind.

"Well, it's up to you, of course," said Raj. "What I'd like to do is come in early, then leave for night classes; I could come in after class and finish up whatever you needed help with. But it's up to you. If you can't have me be away, I'd forget about school, I guess."

"Ah, hell!" said Cranston. "I know as well as anyone else that you're capable of a lot more than this job. I need you, but I'm not going to stand in your way. I'm behind you. Go to school. Just get your work done here too."

"Thank you!" Raj exclaimed, embracing the surprised Mr. Cranston. "I will make sure you won't regret saying yes."

"One more thing," Cranston interrupted.

"What's that?" said Raj.

"If you're going to be a lawyer, be the best damn lawyer you can, son," said Cranston. He came closer and raised his index finger for emphasis. "Do big things. Make an old man proud and follow your dreams as far as they can lead you."

As Mr. Cranston turned to walk away, Raj breathed a deep sigh of relief and gratitude. He recalled Dr. Meyerstein and her exhortations about his right to live and grow.

She was right, he decided. For so long he had floated like a chunk of driftwood on the capricious currents of fate. Living must be an active voyage. He would take the rudder and choose a direction. Navigating uncharted waters was never easy. But he had to try.

Chapter Sixteen

Irina and Alex sat under an overhang, staring out at the Potomac. The February winds blew in off the river, bringing an icy dampness with them.

Irina softly crooned a portion of Johnny Cash's "Hurt". She closed her eyes and swayed to the rhythm of her inner metronome, then threw her arms open wide as she belted out the final lines. When she finished, she smoothed the ground around her and looked at her father.

"One day, I want to sing these songs for crowds," she said. "I want to hear applause. Is it wrong? Will it ever happen?"

"It is not wrong," said Alex. "Far from it. You have talent that deserves to be shared. We must believe, but also we must wait."

"I miss what we had, Papa," said Irina.

"I know," said Alex. "But is there any purpose in looking back? It is difficult enough to survive, to get you medicine, to eat and stay safe."

"But our days are full of nothing," Irina said. "Here we sit. I am useless. I do not like it, and neither do you."

"You are not useless. Not to your father or the world," said Alex. "But I think what you really miss is something more. Or someone."

"You know my thoughts and my heart," said Irina. She blushed and looked down. Not like those boys in Russia. Not like Anatoly . . ."

"Do not mention that dog Tolya," said Alex. "He does not deserve a name. It is shameful what he do to you. He tries to own and sell you like a cow or a tractor. I am glad you stabbed him. Do not feel guilty. We do not have roof but we have our freedom."

His hands shook and he rocked back and forth.

"I was so blind, my dear, so stupid," he said. "I thought rich man must have nice son. He cast a spell on me with his pretty words and fancy clothes. My mistakes cost you innocence. It is my fault. I can never forgive myself this."

"All can be deceived," said Irina. "I, too, was drawn by the pretty things. I thought they saw me, appreciated me. I thought they do things for me, for us. Their eyes and tongues deceived me. But I do not want to be a fool again. I don't forget this man I love, who does not know the love I hold for him."

"Nobody says you must forget Raj," said Alex. "I agree with you that he is special. But if we return to the church, we may be deported. And if that happens, we will never see each other again. He is a good man, and I want you to be together. But it cannot happen now. Not with our lives and safety threatened. We must be invisible, at least for the moment."

"I know, Papa," Irina agreed. "But sometimes, I get sick of being invisible. I just wish someone would see me besides you. One has to be seen to be loved."

"You are," said Alex , throwing his left arm around Irina's shoulders. "And you will be."

"Even with everything?" she asked. "Even with my story, with this?"

She pointed to the numerical tattoo that read "5306" branded just below her left armpit. It was Anatoly's symbol of ownership. How could she explain the number? Since she first moved to America she had never done so, always opting to hide the shame of her past mistake. Who was she? At one time, she wanted to sing and speak for a generation, to bring pleasure and inspiration through her voice. Now that dream was withering on the vine of its origin, and she awaited the birth of a new one.

Late March brought spring sunshine to thaw the icy streets in the nation's capitol. Raj had gained admittance to a small, unheralded law school with a flexible curriculum that allowed him to attend most of his classes at night and online. The demands of work dictated that he had only a limited time in which to chase his new dreams, but fortunately night classes agreed with his diurnal rhythms. Sleep was a scarce commodity, but that was acceptable for now.

The restaurant business remained busy and profitable. Cranston was pleased by the steady flow of customers and cash. He relied on Raj in every aspect of the restaurant's management and Raj met every demand without complaint. His acumen and diligence allowed the boss latitude for relaxation. Cranston still worked long hours but no longer needed to micromanage every leaky faucet and lost dime.

The rectory was silent and empty without Alex and Irina. Every morning, Raj woke up and peered out the window, hoping to see his friends. But these expectations met with daily disappointment, and he began to resign himself to their absence. He saved enough money to make a first month's payment on a modest one-bedroom apartment two blocks from the restaurant, and now was as good a time as any to declare independence.

Autonomy had its perks, but as he stared at the dull gray walls, Raj dreamed of Irina. Throughout their time together, he was drawn to her quiet strength and compassionate soul. And there was something bewitching about the sparkle in her eyes and the wildness of her reddish hair that beckoned him to explore further. Despite his feelings he had remained silent. He thought he did so out of respect for Alex, but now he realized he was afraid of romantic love, a quantity in which he had never dealt. And now, when he wished to unburden his heart, she was gone and regret was his sole bedmate.

Though he did not see her, Raj wrote to Irina each morning before he left for work. It was a way to keep her close, if only in his heart and mind. Every day he penned a few lines, folded the paper and put the note in a stamped envelope addressed to Irina and Alex at "General Delivery". He knew the missives would collect dust in the post office, but they represented hope. And that was something worth keeping on life support. She taught him that.

Today he deliberated over the page. What to say that he hadn't already?

Dear Irina,

The days are still cold and the restaurant seems less alive without you. I miss you, and wish you were there for me to tell you just how much. If ever I see you again, I'll make sure you know. Though I am not a man of faith or prayer, I find myself wishing and praying for you to come back. Love is difficult to recognize sometimes, but now I know I've heard her voice and seen her scarlet hair, and she is you.

Love,

Raj

At the restaurant, the Juan and Benito Garcia had stepped in to fill the roles of Alex and Irina. Older sibling Juan Garcia was quiet and granite-jawed. A veteran of three years in the Federal prison system, his face had a hardened appearance that aged him far beyond his twenty-eight years. His brother Benito was a stark contrast, a jovial, curly-haired waiter who chatted and laughed with the restaurant's patrons as though they were his cousins.

Raj took a liking to Juan, the solemn older brother who scrubbed dishes with the grim determination of an undertaker. Raj greeted him each morning when he came in to work. On occasion they engaged in casual conversation, but most often Juan preferred to focus on work.

Today was an unusual day, as it was Juan who sought out Raj.

"Boss," he called to Raj. "Can I ask you something?"

"Sure," said Raj. "And you know you don't have to call me boss. That's Joe. For me, Raj will do just fine."

Juan kneaded his fingers together and wiped them on his apron. He glanced towards the office. Raj guessed that the normally stone-faced Juan had a sensitive matter to discuss. He motioned for Juan to join him in the office.

"What's up?" Raj asked. "You seem a bit nervous."

"Well, I don't know if you can help me, man," Juan explained. "But I heard the last people here before me and my bro, that they were illegal and they were your friends. Well, my brother and I, we're not illegal, but we want to become real Americans, you know? Living the dream and all. And I was just kind of wondering, man, can you maybe help us with our high school equivalency exam?"

"Oh, that's it?" Raj answered, relieved. "Well sure, I'd be happy to. I kind of could use the company anyway."

For the next two weeks he walked to a small roach-infested studio apartment where Juan and Benito lived amidst peeling wallpaper. The pipes groaned like a dog aroused from sleep. Despite the apartment's state of disrepair, it was larger than the one-bedroom where Raj lived, and the hearty laughter of the brothers made it feel warmer than his lonely walls. American history, English, and algebra were the order of the day, but for Raj the most welcomed aspect of these lessons was an opportunity to feel like an expert. It had been a long time since he'd thought of himself as such.

Between the study sessions, Benito told colorful tales of his friends and relatives in Oaxaca and Jalisco. One could almost smell the vanilla fields and hear the boisterous laughter.

"Oh, the music and *muchachas*," Benito said with a twinkle in his eye. "Sometimes I miss those days. My nose can still remember the smell of fresh fields and mole. You just don't get that here."

Underneath their superficial color and vibrancy, Benito's spoke of loneliness and deprivation. The brothers came to the States with their father and lived in squalor for most of their childhood. Things went from bad to worse when their father died, an innocent bystander in a bodega robbery.

"He sacrificed his life for us," Juan said, his voice cracking under the weight of the memory. "For him, we must rise in this world."

"Man, I can't even imagine what that would feel like," said Raj. "I felt like an orphan losing my parents in my twenties. To have it happen when you were kids, how did you survive?"

"Guess we did what we had to, like anyone else, you know?" Juan answered. He sighed and slumped back against the wall. "I worked at a convenience store, then I started supplementing."

"Supplementing?" Raj asked. "Do I want to know?"

"I sold drugs, all kinds, and I'm not proud of it," Juan answered. "Got me sent away, and that got my bro here into foster care. Thank God he's a people person. Helped him survive. But I did my time, I learned my lesson and now I'm straight. Ain't no shame in that. Now we together, right Lil' B?"

"Amen, *hermano*," Benito replied. "This place isn't much, and we're scraping by, but we'll make it. We're moving up. I can feel it."

The Garcia brothers welcomed Raj into their meager dwelling to teach them about the sanitized American history and academic skills they had not yet learned. For Raj, the lessons were a way to sharpen his mind and assuage his loneliness. He had not been blessed with the company of siblings and never wanted them but now he wished for a bond as tight as these two enjoyed.

By the time their sessions ended, the streets were vacant. Raj hurried home to the church, huddling inside his jacket against the breeze of a chilly spring night. He avoided contact with others. In frigid darkness, nothing good would arise from bumping into strangers.

One night he departed the brothers' decrepit apartment later than usual. On most evenings the blustery wind and pungent scents of urban winter sufficed to keep Raj alert and until he arrived at home. Tonight was different and he yawned, shutting his eyes for a moment as he strolled down the sidewalk. He breathed deeply, opened his eyes, and collided with a small, lithe figure in an ivory-toned winter coat.

"I'm so sorry," he said. The slim strawberry-blonde woman retrieved the contents of her bag that had scattered beneath the fluorescent light of a streetlamp.

"It's OK," she said.

"Here, let me help," said Raj.

He kneeled down to gather up papers and other scraps that threatened to float away in the light but persistent breeze.

"I should have been watching where I was going. The least I can do is help you clean up," he said.

"Really, I'm fine," she insisted.

She glanced up and Raj found himself face-to-face with his past.

"I know you!" he blurted.

"I don't think so," she said.

"Wait, you're Dr. Meyerstein, right?" said Raj. "Doctor Morgan Meyerstein! I need to thank you. You saved my life when I didn't know it was worth saving."

The doctor glanced at the ground in front of her and blushed.

"You've found me out," she said. "You do look familiar, though I'm not sure from where. I see a lot of patients, and I'm not exactly used to encountering them in the darkness. I am glad to have been of help, though. Listen, I really must go, but if you do ever need my services, I have some cards somewhere here."

"These?" Raj asked. He swept a few red-lettered business cards off the ground by the lamppost. "Thanks, I'll take one. Never know when I'll need your help again."

He looked at the card as he walked away. The crimson lettering, long and elegantly curved like the doctor herself, showed dimly in the combination of moonlight and flickering old street lamps. Raj considered the merits of seeing the doctor again.

It would be nice to have someone with whom to discuss life's insanity. But therapy was only realistic for the wealthy or the indolent. It was a luxury that would have to wait in the absence of surplus time and money.

His weary feet carried him home to his empty room. The silent chamber was more desolate than usual tonight. Raj was used to keeping his own company, but there was something to be said for companionship and a wise, sympathetic ear. Who would be there to hear his complaints, or share in his successes? His thoughts turned to the spritely Irina and her jovial father. Did they miss him? He suspected that they held his image in their memories, but fleeing from ICE might make reminiscence a decadent indulgence they could not afford.

Left to a solitary life, all colors faded to a drab grayscale. Before a person's value could be appreciated, their footprints vanished like a windblown sand mandala. Raj flopped backwards onto his bed, his crossed hands supporting his head as he stared upward at the ceiling and the doorway with its small crucifix hanging above the doorframe. He continued gazing upward, eyes unflinching, until the darkness overcame him.

Though sleep descended within seconds, its arrival brought disturbing dreams that forbade a restful slumber. Heads of different shapes and colors appeared, stretching and shrinking, eyes protruding and disappearing as their mouths opened in recurrent screams. The contorted faces reappeared over and over, lingering for a minute even after he woke up and attempted to clear his head. The process of fighting off these distressing images left him more exhausted than he was when he retired for the night.

Several days passed, and each night the dreams recurred: screaming, crimson-hued heads, shaped like three-dimensional Picasso paintings. Their bodies vanished in his foggy dreamscape, and the sounds they issued made no sense. There was a panicked quality to the voices, but they echoed loudly in an incomprehensible idiom. He woke in the middle of each night with clammy skin and a palpitating heart. It took hours for his mind and body to approach a resting state.

"You look like hell, my man," Benito greeted Raj.

Raj looked in a mirror that hung by one of the tables. The dark circles around his eyes combined with his long, wiry frame to give him a skeletal appearance. He winced as he saw the truth of Benito's statement.

Raj withdrew the business card from his wallet and fiddled with its edges, smoothing them out where the leather compartments had bent the corners. The demons were back. But now he could not allow himself to surrender. The time had come to enlist some help from an expert.

"Meet your once and future patient."

With that, Raj buried the card in his pocket. He went to the bathroom and splashed water on his face, lingering to allow the icy chill to open his pores and his consciousness. He tore off a jagged brown paper towel and wiped the residual droplets of water from his forehead and chin. With a deep sigh, he opened the door and walked over to the office to begin his day.

Raj completed a diverse array of tasks, wandering through them in a state of detachment. It was as if there were a palpable yet invisible haze surrounding him, one he could not penetrate with any of his sense. He experienced the sensation of watching himself from the corner of the room, his mind estranged from his body.

Without warning, the faces reappeared. He couldn't hear their screams as he did in his dreams, but the images were unmistakable: disembodied, distorted heads with the veins bulging out, wide-eyed with mouths stretched open in terror. He closed his eyes, squishing his lids shut to push out the visions, but they returned uninvited a few minutes later.

This could not continue. Raj picked up his phone. He fumbled with it as he tried to dial the number, but after a few tries the seven digits were entered properly.

"Hello." He spoke to an androgynous answering-machine message. "It's me, Raj Patel. I'm having some problems and could use your help. The sooner, the better."

Chapter Seventeen

The Tuesday morning air was crisp but comfortable. Raj pressed the buzzer outside the small brick building. He announced his name and the door unlocked, allowing him entry to a narrow stairwell. He climbed slowly, as the rails seemed unstable and the ceiling unusually low. It was an odd location for an office, tucked away in a residential neighborhood. The only clue to the nature of the office was a small black plaque with white lettering on the doorway: "Morgan Meyerstein, MD".

Raj hesitated, sighed, and tapped on the door. He rapped softly once and then knocked louder. Dr. Meyerstein peered around the edge of the door.

"Please, come in Mr. Patel, "she said, motioning him to enter. "Would you prefer that I address you as Doctor, Mr. Patel or something else?"

"Please just call me Raj," he said. "I'm no doctor anymore, Mr. Patel was my Dad, and, he's not here anymore, so I'd prefer to avoid the bad memories."

He fidgeted and stared at the floor as he stood in the doorway. Meyerstein waited in silence, a benign expression gracing her face. Raj wondered if she knew how hard it was to seek help, to exfoliate one's emotions in full view of another.

"Perhaps I'd better go," he said.

"I can only imagine the reasons for your reticence," said Dr. Meyerstein. "But maybe you'd like to sit down for a little bit before you make that decision? You called me for a reason. We're here together, and I sense that you're a thoughtful man, so let's see if we can sit and talk and think this out, shall we?"

Raj shuffled over to a dark brown leather armchair that sat next to a small coffee table. He looked at the table, which contained a neatly stacked pile of magazines and a bowl of peppermint candies.

"Help yourself to some of those mints if you'd like."

"Thank you," said Raj, grabbing a handful of candy. He unwrapped one and popped it in his mouth. He turned his gaze across the room towards Dr. Meyerstein.

The doctor sat behind a large white oak desk, her legs crossed underneath it, one foot tapping the air.

"I can see this is hard for you. Perhaps we could start by you telling me what prompted you to seek my assistance."

Raj took a deep breath and cleared his throat.

"Well, as you know, the death of my parents was an earth-shattering event for me," Raj began. "And since then the last few months had been a whirlwind, but I was starting to get back on my feet. The depression, the suicidal thoughts are gone. I had some focus in my life. I'd started climbing back up the mountain. But now I'm having dreams, and I'm afraid they'll pull me right back down to where I was when I saw you in New York."

"Tell me more about these dreams."

"Well, you'll think they sound crazy, "said Raj. "I don't know."

"Why would I think dreams are crazy?" Dr. Meyerstein asked. "After all, they're a major foundation of our field, and I've heard a lot of unusual things in this office. I'd venture to say that nothing shocks me. So please share."

"I don't know," said Raj.

"I think the dreams feel crazy to you," Dr. Meyerstein said. "But maybe they're not an unexpected reaction. Maybe your cerebral cortex is just trying to send you a message. The human brain is funny like that. So, let's try and decode that message, together, OK?"

"Yeah, I think you're right," Raj agreed, staring into the kind, calm eyes of Dr. Meyerstein. Her offer reassured him, and he leaned back into the armchair. He pressed his neck into the soft leather. It cradled his tight muscles as his eyes looked back and forth between the ceiling and the doctor.

"Well, anyway, the last few nights have been torture," he said. "Every night, it seems, I get these really strange thoughts and gruesome images. Sometimes I'm not sure where the waking thoughts end and the dreams begin, you know what I mean? Anyway, in the dreams, I see these heads . . . see why I think this is weird?"

"Please, continue," Dr. Meyerstein replied. "I know it's disturbing, but sometimes the fact that it disturbs you is the signal that this is the stuff that needs to come out."

"Ok. Well, these heads, in the dreams, are never connected to any bodies. Or at least I never actually see bodies. All I see are these heads. They look like they're being tortured, screaming. Sometimes, in the dream I can hear them."

"Sounds very disturbing," Dr. Meyerstein said. She took her silver pen and jotted notes on a pad of yellow paper.

"Disturbing?" Raj moved forward in his seat and leaned toward the doctor. "No, more like terrifying. It's like this totally consuming dread, and then I wake up and I'm even scared to go back to sleep again."

"They sound extremely powerful," said Dr. Meyerstein. "And they occur all of a sudden, without warning?" She touched the pen to her lips and furrowed her brow.

"Yes, they come and go at will," said Raj. "So much so that they've been keeping me from any sort of rest. Then recently, the heads started appearing to me when I was awake! You can see how that would freak me out, right? How can this not be crazy?"

"You seem awfully concerned with my opinion," Dr. Meyerstein commented.

"Well you're the trained professional," said Raj. "You're supposed to know what the hell is going on here."

"Are you crazy?" Dr. Meyerstein repeated the question. "I don't know. I don't even really know what 'crazy' means. In my opinion it's a word created by people who fear what they don't comprehend. I think crazy's in the eye of the beholder. Maybe you could help me understand what it means to you, what you're afraid of. The context of thoughts and dreams is everything."

"I'm afraid of losing my damn mind!" Raj slammed his fist on his leg. He felt tears beginning to emerge but choked them back. He reached out to grab a candy. "You know, I graduated from medical school. For a brief period, barely a minute, I was a doctor, I had all the answers, or so I thought. I was so sure of myself. And now . . . now I can't even be sure what horrors my brain is going to churn out from day to day, or even hour to hour. I can't trust my own mind, the rational part of me I've always treasured most. Do you know what that's like, Dr. Meyerstein?"

Meyerstein let the question linger for a few minutes. A ponderous silence pervaded the room. Raj watched the doctor cross and uncross her legs. He hoped she understood, but then again, he wouldn't wish upon her the pain and confusion he felt.

"I'm not sure anybody could know the pain you're in the way you do," Meyerstein said. "I believe everyone suffers on some level. Pain is a universal human condition. To live is to hurt, but everyone's suffering is different, even if nobody is fully unique. My pain and my scars are different from yours. But I am here for you. For this time, in this place, understanding your ache is all that matters. We have to know it before we can heal it."

"You're right, I suppose," Raj agreed. "I want somebody to understand. For a while, you see, I had that. But now, I don't know. Maybe I'm just lonely." He shook his head and glanced at the floor, wondering if he was being self-indulgent by inflicting his petty problems on a doctor who must have bigger fish to fry.

"Your words minimize your feelings," said Dr. Meyerstein. 'Just lonely'. Your face says loneliness is not trivial to you, but your mouth says otherwise. I suppose I'm wondering why you feel the need to pretend."

"Maybe you're right," Raj admitted. "If I had to guess, maybe I don't fully trust you. Well, not necessarily you, but relationships in general. It's not easy, just laying this all out before you. It's like being naked or something. Perhaps I'm afraid to let you see what's inside. Because then what will become of me?"

"It's scary to trust someone," Dr. Meyerstein reflected the words back to Raj. "Especially for people who are highly rational, trust is not the most intuitive process. If you found it effortless, you wouldn't be here."

"Scary?" Raj responded, deliberating over the word. "You know I never used to fear anything when I was young. Even a couple of years ago I really didn't know the true meaning of fear. My biggest concern was a subpar test grade. My parents kept me insulated from the bigger dangers of life. There were no violent movies or video games. No teenage dating, no sleepovers. They even kept me from watching the news, fearing it would scar me forever. Lacking fear, I did what I set out to do and I took pride in being steadfast and unshakeable. But now I am intimately familiar with terror. I feel its shadow following me every single day. Makes me stare over my shoulder, makes my stomach turn, keeps me awake at night. So maybe I am scared of you, too. Maybe I am scared of what you'll reveal to me about myself."

The doctor's expression remained unchanged. She maintained silent eye contact, as if waiting for Raj to unburden himself more fully.

"It's just, these visions–they're so twisted!" Raj began again after another pause. "I guess if you can help me get the demons out of my head, I have to trust you. Sounds like I need an exorcist, not a therapist, huh?" Raj chuckled and glanced at Dr. Meyerstein, who sat listening, pen in hand, eyes focused directly on him.

"So what do you think? Am I crazy, possessed, or what? And more importantly, can you help me?" He squirmed in his seat, wishing to compress himself into it and disappear.

"I'm not here to judge you," Dr. Meyerstein replied. "But I do agree with you, the most important question is whether I can help you, which I can. We can approach your problems using medications, therapy, or both. I recommend the combined approach, but that's for you to decide, and I hope you'll let me try. I want to help. It's why I do what I do."

"You helped me before, maybe you can again," sighed Raj. "But there is the small problem of money. I work, but I don't have insurance."

"Money is a problem for a lot of patients," Dr. Meyerstein admitted. "Seeing a psychiatrist is not a cheap undertaking. I'll tell you what we can do. "I'll reduce my fee based on what you make. This would, however, depend on you having some source of income."

"Well, I do have a job," said Raj. "It's not much, but it does offer steady pay."

"Good enough," Dr. Meyerstein replied with a smile. "Basically, I'll charge you a tenth of your weekly income as a price per session. If your income rises, you might be expected to pay more, and if you get fired you will only be expected to pay twenty-five dollars per session for the duration of your unemployment. I'll ask you to bring in a pay stub from your work to the next week's session, and after that we'll be on the honor system, OK?"

"Sure, that'll work," Raj replied. "I'm making about four-fifty a week, so I could pay forty-five an hour. Thank you."

Raj spoke some more, explaining his recent past and the odd sequence of events in it. Soon the fifty-minute "hour" was up. He paid the doctor and stood up from his seat.

Dr. Meyerstein handed Raj Patel a prescription. "This is for clonidine. It may not be the newest or fanciest drug out there, but it's inexpensive and often effective for dampening symptoms such as nightmares. Call me if you're having any side effects, like dizziness or excess sedation, OK?"

Raj nodded.

"I'll give this a try," he said. "Any improvement would be a relief."

Raj stuffed the prescription in his pocket as he rose to leave. As he walked toward the doorway he turned to look at Meyerstein.

"Just one last question," said Raj. "Why are you being so nice to me?"

"Maybe we can discuss that question next time," Dr. Meyerstein replied with a cordial but cryptic smile.

Irina sat with her father in a cobblestoned alley. He wrapped his arm around her shoulder and she leaned into him, watching the waning summer twilight that glinted off the Potomac.

"I feel like singing," she said. "This weather, it makes me feel good. I do not have trouble breathing. The trees, the grass, and this wind off the river . . . it is all so beautiful. And yet, I feel something is missing."

"When you feel like this, it is exactly why you should sing," said Alex. "Nothing cleans the heart like music. That's what your mother used to say."

Irina tossed her hair back, straightened her shoulders and launched into "Somewhere Over the Rainbow." As the words poured out, she imagined herself in the gentle arms of Raj, watching willow trees swaying in a gentle wind. The lyrics gave her hope that one day she would share her love with him. Theirs was a flower that needed to bloom. And she needed to smell its ambrosial fragrance.

"Sing another one." Alex applauded as Irina concluded the song. "In Russian this time. Our mother tongue never sounds as good as when you sing it."

"How about 'Katyusha'?"

"Ah, very good."

Irina had just finished the first verse when the melody was interrupted by a tall man dressed in black. He wore his hat pulled down over his eyes. "You got the time?" he asked.

"I have no watch, but it is about 8:00," said Irina. "Have a nice evening."

The man turned as if to walk away, then spun around and marched toward Irina.

"You! You are a Russian whore!" he yelled. "I heard your accent. I bet you two are illegal."

Alex stepped in between the tall man and his daughter.

"You do not insult my daughter like this," he said, placing his hands on the tall man's chest. "Please apologize to her."

"I apologize to no one," the man said. He pulled out a long black stick and hit Alex on the side of the head. Alex fell to the ground, groaning. Irina shuddered and backed away. She wanted to scream but no sound came..

"At least you can be useful. You're going to make me some money." The man licked his lips and grabbed at Irina, ripping her blouse to expose the tattoo under her armpit and the scars on her back. "Ah, I see you're familiar with the business. Better still."

As Irina turned to run, Alex lurched to his feet and tackled the tall man.

"Run, get out of here!" he said.

Irina froze for an instant but fear took over and she fled at top speed past the dumpster and around the corner. She entered an abandoned building that bordered the alley and hid in an empty room. She tried to quiet her ragged breath as she watched through a cracked window as her father and the man wrestled. She heard her father pleading for his life, and then came a horrible sound.

It was a single explosion that tore through the quiet night and might just as well have pierced Irina's heart. She saw her father fall backward to the ground, splayed like Jesus on the cross. The tall man lingered for a second. He bent over and picked something up, illuminated by the streetlight as he walked past the dumpster, then back again.

"I'll find you!" he yelled. "You can't hide." But she did and after what seemed an interminable quantity of time he left. Irina waited for several minutes to make sure he didn't return before running to her father's side. By then Alex lay still, his eyes fixed in a vacant stare, surrounded by a pool of blood.

Irina fell on top of her father and wailed. She couldn't help feeling that her past had taken its revenge on the one she loved most, and the guilt constricted her chest worse than any asthma attack.

Winter yielded to spring, which then gave way to the sultry air of urban summer and Raj fell back to his routine. The hideous dreams departed, but he still visited Dr. Meyerstein three times a month to unburden himself of nagging worries and lingering sorrows.

Raj had entered his second year of law school. Legal studies received the same assiduous preparation that medicine once did, with similar results. Though managerial duties at the restaurant placed time at a premium, his diligence and memory allowed him to excel.

Raj lived on an austere budget but despite the ongoing need for fiscal discretion he felt secure. His apartment, equidistant from school and work, was a humble nest. Dr. Meyerstein's weekly sessions and the occasional sleep aid left his mind sufficiently rested to follow its waking dreams. His life was moved forward and upward as it had years ago.

The one painful thorn that penetrated his otherwise comfortable interior was an awareness of isolation. He had the company of the Garcias, but the relationship lacked the depth of attachment he had only known with Alex and Irina. Alex was a friend like none he ever knew, and Irina was the woman he was meant to love. This was clear now. The realization left a hollow yet tender spot, an area of emotional phantom pain. His industrious nature saved him from morbid rumination, but at night a vortex of loneliness tried to suck him downward.

One day, Raj awoke an hour earlier than normal to squeeze in some reading time. He pored over a hardcover copy of his introductory "Primer on Legal Ethics" that he purchased used at a small local bookstore. Even at this early hour, the air was thick and stale. The small fan on the sill of his open window fought a futile battle, and sweat dripped off his forehead onto the bottom of the page. Raj attempted to concentrate on the words and integrate their complex meanings. He could usually rely on an ability to devour written words with aplomb, but the summertime humidity dissolved his concentration. He sighed in frustration, closed the book and flipped it, backhanded, onto a TV tray that served as his makeshift desk.

Raj headed to the tepid water of his shower to wash away the early morning droplets of sweat and prepare himself for work. As he lathered his body with soap and then watched the bubbles swirl to their demise in the drain, he imagined the ways in which Alex and Irina had been swept away from their life. Raj was rendered powerless and immobile as the thought swept through him. He visualized himself standing on a pier, watching as people came swimming into shore and floated off, carried away by riptides. He needed to jump in, to save Alex and Irina, but how?

Raj stepped out of the shower, shook the thoughts from his head, and gave his skin a thorough wipe-down with a striped terrycloth towel. He dressed quickly and stared into the mirror for an instant.

He reflected on the oddities of fate as he buttoned his white poplin shirt. Years ago, this strange and often painful journey would have been too horrific for him to imagine, and yet he now felt the ground settling beneath him. But philosophy was a vice for which he couldn't spare the time. Right now, he needed to hurry.

He set out into the steamy morning with his books tucked under his arm, half-jogging towards the subway station. The milling throngs rushed out to their myriad jobs, and Raj could see them all. He viewed the milling crowds differently now than he did in New York. Bankers in tailored suits jostled for position on the same platform as menial laborers in stained blue overalls. The irony was lost on most, but Raj noticed it. The plurality of styles pleased him. A subway platform was the one place where all men truly were created equal.

Raj opened his book and made another brief foray into the field of legal ethics as he sat on the train and awaited his stop. The subject was dry but the opportunity to read and think and memorize facts was a comfortable process. The sound of a garbled announcement roused him from his state of intense concentration. He'd reached his destination.

He tucked the book away and rushed up the stairs of the springing up the steps two at a time with his long legs. Soon he was back at the street level. He turned right and briskly half-jogged the remaining block and a half to the restaurant.

Raj put the books down on an empty shelf in his office and picked up a folder full of papers. He shuffled through the uneven stack of papers on the desk in search of a calculator. It was his job to figure out what supplies the restaurant was in need of and how much money would be required to pay for them. He figured out pricing and promotion strategies to keep the place in the black. Joe still managed payroll and personnel decisions, but seemed happy to delegate other responsibilities to Raj.

The job provided Raj with ample challenges and opportunities, but it was a mere rest stop on a greater journey. Law would be his chosen destiny, just as medicine was his parents' dream. Most often he spent his lunch break sipping coffee while squinting at a law book or daydreaming about the life of the esteemed legal scholar he wished to be.

He walked around the restaurant, inspecting glasses for cracks, checking on various food supplies, and calculating how much money would be needed this week to fill the public's seemingly constant appetite for tomato sauce, cheese, fresh bread, and the best cheesecake in the city. As he scrawled notations to himself in a pocket-sized, spiral-bound notepad, he felt a tap on the shoulder.

"Hey Raj, I need to talk to you." It was Cranston. The channel down the middle of his chin looked deeper, as did the lines that ran laterally like rolling waves across his red-tinted forehead. His eyes were darker than normal. "Let's go to the office."

They hurried toward the small office. Raj took large, loping strides, while the old man shuffled as fast as his age and soreness would allow. Raj arrived at the door first and opened it for Cranston. Cranston sat down and motioned Raj to do the same.

"I got a call today," he began with a solemn expression, smoothing the gray hair on his forehead with one hand. "It was from Father Michael."

"Oh, I hope everything is OK?" Raj responded.

"Well, I'm not sure, but he did specifically request that you stop by the church as soon as you can," said Cranston, his hands trembling. "He said something about Irina being back and needing to speak to you. He didn't say anything more than that, but it sounded really urgent. I hope nothing's happened to that girl. I really like her. Such a sweetheart."

Raj left the office without saying another word. Besieged by intense discomfort that rose and fell in the pit of his stomach, he spent the remaining three hours of his workday with a split mind. Somehow, he managed to address the day's requirements, but most of his awareness drifted to fear and speculation.

Why did Cranston only mention Irina? Had something happened to Alex? Why was Cranston so nervous? There were many questions, and no clear answers. The only thing Raj knew was that Father Michael's message must be important.

Listen to your body. That's would his mom used to say, like some sort of guru. Despite his scientific leanings it was advice he followed. In situations like this, his body functioned as a sophisticated barometer. Today, it forecast ominous news.

Chapter Eighteen

Raj loped through the evening crowds, retracing the path he had travelled many times before to the church. He ran most of the way, fueled by urgent foreboding as he weaved his way past couples enjoying a leisurely evening and families with laughing adolescent children. It seemed like a decade that that he had been absent from the worn but charitable walls of St. Mary's, though logic told him that he had only been away for two and a half years.

Raj perspired lightly and breathed heavily as he grasped the wrought iron door handle to the old church. As he opened the door, Father Michael jogged down the center aisle to meet him.

"Hello, Raj," said Father Michael. "It's been a while, too long if you ask me. I hope you are doing well, my friend?"

The two men walked to the rearmost pew in the church and sat down. Father Michael's demeanor changed. The corners of his eyes sank and his face assumed a solemn cast. He cleared his throat twice before speaking.

"You're probably wondering why I called you down here," Father Michael began. "I wish I could say this was just a social call. But alas, it's not. Even at my age it's still hard to do this, so let me just tell you. This morning I found Irina in here shaking, frightened, and in tears. She said somebody killed Alex."

"Killed? No!" Raj yelled, jumping up from the pew before sitting down again, trembling with rage. "How did it happen? And Irina, is she badly hurt?"

"She's hurt," said Father Michael. "Lots of bruises. But her most grievous injuries are a broken heart and a spirit that's in critical condition. This worries me most of all."

Raj paced the length of the center aisle. "I don't understand," he said. "Alex was a good man with no enemies. Who would do this to him? How does your God let this happen?"

Father Michael gave the young man a box of tissues. The two men sat together as Raj stared at the floor. Raj felt his jaws clench with vise-like tension as Father Michael grasped his shoulder.

"I have asked myself the same question, more often than you know. All I can say is that sometimes people do evil things," said Father Michael. The priest's eyes clouded with a thin mist of tears. "Parishioners often ask me to explain why this evil happens. And truthfully, I can't. It is appalling, maddening, and depressing, all at once. Maybe even God can't stop the evil that men perpetrate. All I know is that we can't give up. There's a young lady up there with a beautiful soul and a pure heart that needs us. Needs you. You are angry, yes, and you have every right to be. But you know what? Sometimes two wounded souls can be each other's best medicine. Think about it. If you'd like, I'll leave you here to have some time and space alone. Irina's upstairs if you feel up to talking with her. And I'd suggest you do."

Raj nodded, his gaze still fixed on the floor. He balled his fists up and pounded them into his knees. The memories of Alex and his infectious good humor returned. Even in his grief, Raj could not suppress a wry grin at the old man's charm and optimism. But in seconds the fond remembrance blended with guilt, his all-too-familiar companion. He should have kept in contact with Alex and Irina. He should have looked for them. Even though his efforts may have proven futile, he reproached himself for not trying harder. How dare he live his life without consideration of their struggles? Once again, Raj beheld his self-absorption, and the sight disgusted him.

"I let you down, Alex. It's my fault," Raj murmured. Tears clouded his eyes as he gazed aloft at the church roof. "Please forgive me my absence in your time of need. From this day forward, I will redeem myself to you. And to Irina."

He wiped the salty trails of expired tears from his cheeks and prepared to face a grief-stricken Irina. Now was the time to live for someone else. He knew there were no proper words to say, but he felt compelled to be there. This was about her. She needed support, and he would provide it. The goal may prove difficult to achieve, but failure was not an acceptable option.

Raj marched up the stairs and knocked at the door. It opened and Irina appeared. She was not the same spirited woman he remembered. Instead his eyes beheld a shivering young girl, her delicate features marred by large bruises around her left eye and lower jaw. Her fine red hair was blood-streaked and disheveled.

"Dear God," Raj exclaimed. "We need to get you to the hospital. Your bruises look bad. You could have some internal injuries."

"No," said Irina. "They will find me there. Either immigration or the man who killed Papa. Here is where I am safe. Only with you. Please."

With that, Irina collapsed into his arms. Her body convulsed with tears. They stood in the doorway for several minutes, saying nothing. Every few seconds the sobs ceased, only to be followed by a new wave of tears. Raj felt her delicate ribs shaking in his strong but gentle embrace. He kept his sinewy arms wrapped around her and brushed the hair out of her face with his fingertips, wiping the tears off Irina's cheeks in an effort to soothe her.

Raj was bewildered to see Irina so unraveled. For all her physical frailty Irina always maintained an upbeat, even playful composure in the face of adversity. In their time together, he'd never seen her cry. To see her tranquility shattered made him sad and angry. There must be something he could say to stem the tide of grief. But adequate words eluded him, so he stood silent and motionless.

"Come in," Irina whispered as she wandered across the room. Raj entered the room and gently shut the door behind him. He stood a few feet inside the doorway, while Irina walked to the window and propped it open. She leaned against the worn wood trim of the window, peering at the dormant street below. Raj moved closer and pulled up a chair.

"Would you like to sit down?" he asked. There was no script, no instruction manual for such situations. Perhaps being present was all he could do. "Come, sit."

Irina waved the chair away, and Raj sat down in it. He kept his eyes trained on Irina. Her shallow breathing, shivers of fear, and recurrent bursts of tears pointed to acute trauma and distress.

"Irina, where does it hurt?" Raj inquired. He smoothed her tousled hair. "What did they do to you?"

Irina simply shook her head side to side, repeatedly, as if to deny reality.

"I'm here. I'm here. Is there anything I can do, Irina?" Raj asked. "Surely there must be something."

Irina shook her head again.

"It's all my fault," she said. "We wouldn't be in this country if it weren't for me. Papa wouldn't have fought back if it wasn't for me. Where I go, I bring trouble. It has been so since my teens."

"Nonsense," said Raj. "You're blameless here. A parent will always protect their child."

"I'm not the sweet girl my father said I was," Irina said, her eyes filled with tears. As she sniffled and raised her head, her lips trembled. "He speaks of me that way, but I put him through hell once I hit sixteen. Running around with boys, drinking too much vodka, running away. Papa would never say so, but it was my problems that made us come here. I am damaged. Impure. And that is why father is dead."

She hid her face in her hands and shuddered from head to toe. Raj reached out a hand and touched her arm, rubbing it until she was able to calm down.

"Shh," he said. "It's going to be OK."

"But it's not, don't you see?" Irina said. "Back in Russia, I got involved with some bad people, dangerous people. Especially this guy named Anatoly. He was charming, but it turned out he was just wealthy criminal. That's where this tattoo came from."

She pointed to the stark black numbers,"5306", imprinted on the skin below her armpit like a serial number.

"This mark means he owned me, that I was nothing more than a number. I deserve shame because I allowed it. I let him use me because he promised me fame. He told me I was going to be a star, but he turned me into a prostitute," she said. She rocked back and forth on her knees, her hands pulling at her hair. "Until one night I stabbed him with Papa's knife and ran. Papa brought me to New York to get away from all that, to save me from those people, but now he's gone. Gone!"

She slammed her fists into the ground. "This is all my fault! I hurt a man, maybe even killed him. I can't help feeling that because of this, Papa is dead. What is the word in English? Karma?"

"Our pasts are behind us," said Raj. "They may be littered with mistakes and regrets. There is much we cannot change. We are all more than just our virtues and achievements. Your father taught me that. But we can make the present and the future better with each other. I need you too. And this was not your fault. You can't blame yourself for the deeds of evil men. Never blame yourself for needing to survive."

"Don't leave, Raj," she whispered. "Just don't leave."

Constancy was one thing he could promise. "I won't. Not ever."

He gazed down at the red-haired face that leaned against his knees and the frail arms that clung tightly to his legs. Her breathing had become more regular, but her arms and legs trembled and her eyes were glassy as they stared straight ahead. He held her hands in his as she lay in shocked silence. He watched every micro-expression, waiting for the next wave of shadows that were sure to descend. He expected that her mind wouldn't allow her body to rest, and he wasn't sure he could trust it to protect her from the horrors of her past. After an hour of anxious waiting, he sat back as her body relaxed and her eyes closed. He laid her featherweight frame gently on the bed. She stirred only briefly and fell back into a deep slumber while Raj smoothed the blankets and sheets around her.

As Irina slept, Raj kept a silent vigil. What transpired that fateful night? He wanted to believe that all problems could be solved. But who dared to do this to his friends and why? Someone must be held accountable. The quest for answers started at his doorstep.

Dr. Meyerstein peered across the desk. "What is happening?" she asked. "You look very troubled today."

"It's so . . . I don't know how to explain this." Raj began. He pressed his palms together, rocking them back and forth repeatedly. "Sometimes life reminds you that you're just one person, that you can't really do much for others, you know what I mean?"

"Perhaps the feeling you are experiencing is one of help-lessness?" she suggested. "Are you having other symptoms of depression as well? Guilt, hopelessness?"

"No, just the helplessness," Raj muttered. "More accu-rately I guess I'd call it powerlessness. I hate it! I wish there were a pill for this kind of impotence. Your medicines helped me sleep, and you have helped me feel sane. I don't over-think so much, and I've regained my equilibrium. I know what to do for myself. But now I want to do something for Irina and for Alex. I owe them so much, and all I can do is sit here, blith-ering to my shrink. What kind of man does that?"

"Blithering?" the doctor objected. "You think that's what you're doing?"

"Well isn't it?" Raj replied. He felt his voice rise in a cre-scendo of rage, sadness and confusion. "It feels unmanly. I need to help out and all I can do is worry about myself. I should have been there. Maybe I could have stopped it. But I was preoccupied with living my own life. And now, all I can do is watch. I don't know how to help."

He glanced at Dr. Meyerstein.

"I should have been there instead of worrying about my-self and my own petty problems while my best friends in the world needed me most. I don't know if I'm the man my parents would want me to be. But I do know for certain I'm not who I want to be."

"You are angry and bitter at yourself. And now you're punishing yourself." Dr. Meyerstein commented. "Does the punishment feel good?"

"Of course not," Raj retorted. "But the fact is, I deserve to be punished."

"Do you? More likely you wouldn't feel 'right' if you didn't feel lousy," said Dr. Meyerstein. "Sometimes guilt feels comfortable, even when it shouldn't."

"Sounds kind of strange, huh?" Raj said. He unwrapped a peppermint candy and sucked it. "But this is kind of the story of life, or at least my last few years."

"How do you mean?" Dr. Meyerstein asked.

"It's just like my parents," he said. "All those years I needed them, they were there. And I just took what they offered, not for any other reason than that it was what I wanted. It was convenient to take. I wasn't truly grateful. But in the end, when they needed me, I couldn't even bear to watch. I couldn't help. Do you know I never kept the urns? Just left them, by the river. Abandoned and alone. And now I guess I did it again. All this I, I, I. Narcissism, I guess you'd call it."

"You make yourself sound like quite the black-hearted devil," Dr. Meyerstein observed. "And yet you say Irina came to you? How do you account for that? Why would she turn to someone who doesn't deserve her?"

"Maybe she was desperate. Maybe I am her only option. Who knows?" Raj shrugged. "I don't know that it was so much a choice as . . . well, I guess it was in a way. You know she thinks she's unworthy of me, all because of her past, and that kills me, because if anything it's the opposite. Maybe because she feels so bad about herself, I'm all she thinks she deserves.

But I'm so afraid I'll disappoint her too. She's been through too much already. I can't fail her. I can't!"

"You feel obligated," said Dr. Meyerstein. "And feeling guilty makes you responsible for all that happens to those around you?"

"Yes, but obligated doesn't even begin to cover it," Raj explained. "Obligation is a part, but also love. I love her, more than anyone before. In fact, I don't think I knew what love was, now that I feel this. And if anything were to happen to Irina, I couldn't bear the sight of myself in the mirror every morning." He opened a bottle of water and took a long sip.

"I've got to figure out what to do. I guess what I want to know now is how to help. I feel I should be trying to solve the murder, but also taking care of Irina. And I don't fully know how to do either, let alone both. It's all so confusing," said Raj.

"Love, guilt: these are very confusing, particularly when they occur together," Dr. Meyerstein agreed. She propped her elbows on her desk and pointed at Raj with her pen. "But I believe you underestimate yourself. You are very capable."

"I don't know," said Raj. "I feel like all the answers have gone away."

"And that's why I'm here," said Dr. Meyerstein. She moved her chair out from behind the desk, sat down, and peered at him. "Together, we can help you rediscover the things you always knew. You'll move forward, you'll see."

"I guess that's a good place to end, because we're all out of time for today."

"Thank you, it's been a help," said Raj, swinging open the door to exit the office. He turned the knob to close the door and vanished down the stairs with two large strides, leaving the doctor behind him.

Raj awoke to the sound of screaming. At first he thought it might be coming from his own throat. Upon shaking off the blankets and his drowsiness, he realized that the voice belonged to Irina.

It had been a week since she moved in with Raj. He had gone to a thrift store and bought for himself a small but serviceable cot. Irina slept on the bed a few inches away. Often, in those first few nights, he heard her tossing, turning, whimpering. Every night he felt her pushing, flailing, as if fighting off an invisible enemy. In the daytime he tried to gently pry into her nightmares, but she persisted in closing the door to his inquiries. Devoid of any meaningful interventions, Raj sat and worried.

"Please, please . . . STOP!"

Her cries were alarming every night, but never had he heard a sound so heart-rending as this. It was a full-throated aria of pain, outrage, and grief. The usually mellifluous tones of Irina's voice were bent like fine glass in a red-hot furnace.

Raj walked over to the bed and knelt next to Irina. He brushed her hair from her face and she startled, gasping and groaning until she recognized his face.

"Oh, Raj, did I wake you again?" she whispered. "I am sorry."

"Shh, you don't need to apologize," he said, cradling her head in his arms as he gazed down on her face. Though the swelling had gone down and the scars were fading, Irina's face lacked animation. In place of her customary wide grin, her lips now tightened into uncharacteristic solemnity. When would she feel better? He hoped ishe would heal soon, but knew that the rhythm of a wounded heart is ponderous and painful. "It's the dreams, isn't it? Something horrible happens, and the devil gets in your dreams. Go back to sleep, Irina."

"Hold me?" Irina asked. "Maybe you can keep the devil away."

Raj slid into bed. She nestled into him, using his chest as a pillow. His arms encircled her, lightly, as though he feared a firmer grasp might cause her to shatter. He stared at the ceiling, watching the shadow of her slender arms move ever so slightly with each breath. He stroked her right arm with his fingertips and kissed her on the forehead and neck. His skin tingled with anticipation, and he yearned to do much more, but he reminded himself that now was not the time to think of his own desires.

Because he could not sleep, Raj pondered the future. He asked himself how he could exorcise the evil spirits that had scarred Irina. Love and laudable intentions might not suffice to heal these wounds. His mind and intuition said Father Michael was right when he had spoken of wounded souls providing salvation for one another. It might just be true that interdependence would be a mutual cure for life's tragedies.

Soon the weight of the humid night air overcame him and he fell asleep, his arm around Irina, her breath on his cheek. Fortunately for Raj, the torment of Irina's dream world was not visited upon him. He spent the rest of the night in peace, undisturbed by the pressure and uncertainty that dominated his waking thoughts.

In the morning, Raj awoke to the unmistakable whistle of a teakettle. He peered out of a half-open left eye toward the small stove. Irina, still clad in her pale yellow nightgown, leaned over the teapot.

"Good morning," she said with a smile. It was a tired-looking grin, accompanied by circles under her eyes, but Raj was heartened to see Irina's lightness returning. "I know I woke you up last night. Wanted to give you something to help you wake up. I hope you feel like tea?"

Raj rubbed his eyes, yawned, and stretched. It amazed him that Irina could think of others with all she had been through.

"You are a saint, Irina, you know that?" he said, sauntering toward her as she held a waiting cup in her outstretched hand. "After all has happened, you still keep kindness alive. Despite all the pain in your heart."

"The pain will go away," said Irina. "It must, or I go mad."

"What are they like, these dreams of yours?" he asked.

He took the cup, set it down on the table behind him, and embraced Irina, clasping her slender body tightly to his. He felt her heart beat, first quickly, then more slowly as she relaxed into his chest. He ran his fingers through her red ringlets.

"It's like I'm there again," she said. She grasped his hands and squeezed them. "The man attacks me. I run. They fight. I hear the shot. It vibrates in the air. And then all I see is blood, a big pool of it, spreading toward me, and I wake up. It is too horrible to think about."

She buried her head in his shoulder and shook it, as if to deny reality.

"You are strong," said Raj. "And you have me. I will listen. And when the dreams come, know that I am here for you, OK? You will never face them alone."

Irina nodded and turned to face him. She draped her arms over his shoulders and kissed his cheek.

"For that I am grateful," she said. "You have no idea how much so."

He massaged her neck and shoulders. She stretched herself, cat-like, under his touch.

"How's the tea?" she asked.

"Good," said Raj, sipping slowly. "You know, tea was a tradition in my family, a part of every day. Every afternoon, when I came home from school, there my mother would be with a cup of tea, drinking it slowly, enjoying every last drop. And my Dad was the same way. He would come home from closing up the shop, at night, and always my mother had a cup waiting for him."

"Mm. Sounds nice," said Irina. "That was how we were, Papa and I. We did not have much, but every day, after he finished work, we sat and talked over a hot cup of tea. It makes even Russian winter seem OK sometimes. But now, he is not here."

She began to cry again. This time the tears came with no sound, welling up in a steady stream and dribbling down her cheeks.

"We'll share tea together every morning," Raj promised, wiping Irina's cheeks and cupping her delicate chin on his right index finger. He stared into her eyes, wanting to spill his amorous feelings in their entirety. But sentimental words were alien to him, so instead he pledged, "From here on, we'll share everything."

Irina threw her arms around his neck and squeezed his body tightly against hers. She broke into a sudden thunderstorm of sobs that ended as quickly as it began. She loosened her grip on his neck and leaned her head back to stare up at him.

They sat by the window, sipping tea as fluffy clouds floated overhead, pierced by sunlight that smiled on the cherry trees outside.

"I have a favor to ask of you," she said. "I know you've already done so much and I hesitate to ask but . . ."

"Whatever you need."

"Take me back to work with you, Raj," she pleaded. "I need something to do, something to distract my heart."

Raj sighed. He rubbed his temple in the slow rhythm he used when pondering important matters. Her request surprised him and he had more than a few misgivings. Was Irina ready for the noise and clamor? How would she handle the inevitable questions? But on the other hand, she was the woman he loved and he had pledged to help in any way he could.

"Sure, why not?" It will be nice to see more of you. I worry about you when I'm away at the restaurant or studying. This way, I'll know you're OK. Let's go."

Irina smiled. Her white, slightly jagged teeth shone in the light. She jumped up and kissed Raj on the lips, then laughed and scurried toward the bathroom.

"Thanks, you're the best," she called to Raj. "I'll be right out. I need to get changed and ready!"

In a matter of a few minutes, both Raj and Irina made themselves presentable for work. A shower, some fresh clothes, a comb and a smile had restored some sparkle to her appearance. Though life had battered her, Raj saw that she would never allow herself to be beaten.

"You look great," he commented as they headed out the door and down the dark stairwell of his humble apartment building. He kissed her on the cheek. "Let's go. I'm sure Joe will be glad to see you again."

Chapter Nineteen

At the restaurant, Irina's return was greeted by Cranston with tears and an embrace. She was installed as a dishwasher, laboring in the bowels of the kitchen. Cranston explained that he would have preferred to install Irina back into her familiar role as a waitress, but he felt obligated to Benito, who had put in yeoman's work as a server. Cranston apologized for "demoting" Irina but explained that he saw no alternative.

"I am just happy to be back, Mr. Cranston," Irina said. "This job is a blessing. When my body is busy, my mind can rest."

Irina's thanks were sincere. She needed a diversion, but the job provided more than that. When she scrubbed flecks of tomato sauce, cheese and other residue off the heavy plates, she could concentrate on the steam of the kitchen and the bubbly texture of soapsuds on her hands. Even the sink's fusty odor was cathartic. It allowed her to ground herself in physical reality alone. For a few hours each day, memories and nightmares were denied access.

The day stretched onward in hot and sticky monotony. After the restaurant closed Irina spent the night waiting at the nearby university library while Raj consumed an enormous thermos full of coffee to keep him awake through the obtuse jargon of his classes. The warmth and comfort of the old chairs and the proximity of the man she loved let her slumber comfortably here.

Irina wasn't sure how long she had slept when Raj grasped her shoulder. He woke her as gently as he could, but she startled as she sensed his fingertips. She calmed down when she saw his familiar face. With a yawn and a stretch, she arose from the couch, kissed Raj on the lips, and slipped her arms around him, resting her head on his chest.

"I missed you," she whispered. "I am glad you are back."

"I'm glad to be back," Raj answered. He stroked Irina's hair, brushing a few rebellious strands away from her eyes. He wrapped his arm around her waist and pressed his lips to hers. Irina savored the way that their bodies lingered in soft contact for a few moments. "And I won't ever leave."

"Irina? I am Dr. Meyerstein," the psychiatrist introduced herself. "Make yourself comfortable. Help yourself to some candy if you like."

"Thank you, I haven't been eating so well," Irina responded. She took a few chocolate candies from the doctor's ample confectionery supply. "I'm not sure why Raj wanted me to see you, but he speaks well of you, and I trust him very much. He worries about me."

"Well, perhaps you can tell me what's been going on recently and together we'll figure out how I can help," Dr. Meyerstein offered. "I know this is difficult."

"How recently?" Irina asked. "Well, maybe I could just kind of tell you my life story from the beginning. Maybe that would help?"

"If that is easiest for you, by all means," Dr Meyerstein agreed with a nod.

Irina cleared her throat and shifted her hips in her chair. Speaking of father's death was difficult, but she knew she must do it. The painful feelings and images within her needed to be released.

"Well, I come from Russia," she began. "I, Irina Petrova, was born in Moscow. My father was a butcher. My mother, she was beautiful, like you. She was a dancer. She could have been a star, but she gave it up to raise me. I remember that she used to sing to me, teach me about music and flowers and animals."

"She used to sing this one song. Irina began to sing in Russian, a sweet, rich lilting melody that built to an expansive, sweeping, operatic finish. Her voice filled the office with the sweetest sounds it had held in years. She finished a verse. "I don't know the words in English, but it was so beautiful. It always used to put me to sleep."

"It sounds like you love your mother very much," Dr. Meyerstein observed. "And you sing extremely well."

"I did love her. I do love her. But then when I am just nine years old, she is pregnant with my little brother. She falls sick, and she and the baby both died. My father and I were left alone."

"I'm sorry," Dr. Meyerstein replied. "That most have been horrible."

"It is very sad when this happens," Irina averted her eyes from the doctor's and glanced out the window. "But I recover, because I have Papa. I helped him in his shop, going to school during the day. We laughed and cried. We were always together. But you see, my father made this promise to my mother, and he is an honest and honorable man."

"A promise? Tell me about it."

"Well, like I was saying, Mama gave up her dreams to be a mother," said Irina. She smoothed her skirt and scooted forward in her chair. "But she taught me to sing, and many people felt I am good singer. She said she wished some day I would have the chance to be a famous singer. This became her new dream. So she made Papa promise that if anything ever happened he would bring me to America to sing for the world. Even after Mama died, Papa and I stayed in Moscow for several years. I was not a good child toward the end of those years. Started hanging around with people who had money and charm, but no souls. You know the type? Maybe you wouldn't, but they're dangerous."

"It sounds like they deceived you," said Dr. Meyerstein, frowning.

"Worse," Irina said. "I thought I was lucky that handsome and rich men would pay attention. They tell me I am beautiful, I am talented. They make big promises that smell like roses, taste like honey. They got me singing jobs, at clubs. I thought they gave me what I wanted, what I needed. I felt important, and I let their words blind me to their nature. It was only later that I learned their honey was laced with poison."

"It is easy to be fooled when one is young," said Dr. Meyerstein. "Why do you blame yourself?"

"I was stupid. I blame myself for this. But then things got worse. Those men sold me, made me do . . . shameful things," Irina said, turning her eyes toward the floor. She inspected the cracks, wondering how many other patients had sat here before her. "Most of all selling my body to rich men with filthy desires. I still have scars from this. They are in my mind and on my body. I knew that I was being used, like a chair or a shovel, and I could not survive that way. So one night I hid a knife in my stocking. And I stabbed that man and ran. To this day, I do not know if he lives. That was it for us in Russia, so father took all his money and paid a man to bring us to New York. Without that, who knows where I'd be?"

"Your father sounds like a man of principle and courage," said Dr. Meyerstein. "But you, too, are brave. Not everyone could do what you did."

"I don't know that I am brave," said Irina. "I think what I did was more from desperation than from bravery. I agree with you about my father, though. He was a big man, with big, warm heart. He was always happy, unless something is wrong with his family. Then he worries, even cries like a big baby. Almost six years we spend here in America. But Papa does not have good luck. We live on the streets of New York. That is where I meet Raj. New York weather was not good for me. So we come here. Life starts to get better when we meet this priest, Father Michael. He lets the three of us stay in his church, helps us find work. It was nice. But then the immigration came to the church, and they made threats to Father Michael because we are not in this country legally, Papa and I. So we run back to the street."

Irina's stared at the floor. She felt the weight of large nascent teardrops on her long eyelashes.

"That must have been hard on the two of you," Dr. Meyerstein speculated. She rubbed her chin and her eyes narrowed. "To be ripped away from a promising life."

"It was, but it was the right thing to do," Irina murmured, still staring at the floor. "We managed, survived but then it happened."

"It?" Dr. Meyerstein repeated.

"My father . . ." Irina exploded into a torrent of sobs. She glanced up at the doctor, feeling the rise by a righteous anger that vibrated in her throat.

"The bastard killed Papa." She spat the words through clenched teeth. "For no reason. And yet it feels like there was a reason. I was that reason. It was my fault."

"What makes you take this guilt upon yourself?" Meyerstein asked. "It must be awful to carry such a heavy burden."

"That man, the killer, when he heard my voice, he called me 'Russian whore' over and over," she said, her voice dwindling. "Like he could see who I am inside. He even mentioned that he could make money off me. We came here to get away from that, and now there are times that it feels like that's what I am, all I am, a whore. Maybe it is my punishment for stabbing a man, my sentence for doing harm to another. He killed my father, and all I did was watch."

She paused to wipe her tears and catch her breath. She crouched forward in her chair.

"Sometimes I wish it was me," she said. She clasped her hands together tightly. "Instead my father paid for my sins."

Irina's lips trembled as rocked back and forth on the edge of her chair.

"Irina," said the doctor. "I know it is hard for you to remember this and to talk about it. I can't even imagine what you're going through. But I know I can help you get through this. I'm here for you, OK? We'll do it together. We won't let him win."

Irina did not look up, but stopped her rocking on the chair's edge, and slid back a few inches.

"Thank you, you are very kind," she said. At last she straightened up in the chair and brushed the hair out of her eyes. "Would it be all right if I came again this time next week?"

"If that works for you, sure," Dr. Meyerstein replied. "Actually, our hour is up. I look forward to seeing you."

Irina laid the money down in a neat pile on the doctor's desk and walked slowly toward the door. She exited and proceeded down the stairway out into the brisk morning breeze.

The session was an enervating experience, and Irina's legs wobbled beneath her. The biting gusts of wind brought back memories of late fall in Moscow, with its punishing cold.

Irina engrossed herself in the internal newsreel of childhood memories that people create when adult life requires a diversion. She walked to the train station and rode without sound or movement, staring out the window as if watching a series of still-life photographs passing in front of her eyes. Her mind removed her from the cityscape and the changing scenery outside the window.

To Irina the restaurant was a cocoon, complete with warmth and the security of her preferred mate. The young man who once appeared to her unconscious with a battered, blood-streaked face was now her knight and the only person to whom she felt connected. In his presence, she was safe. Recent events reminded her that safety was far from absolute. The innocent bliss of childhood and parental proximity was gone. But Raj shielded her from the cloud of fear that followed her in solitude. He might not comprehend how much she valued the gentle refuge of his company, but her gratitude extended beyond words.

Irina devoted her full attention to the job. She only stopped to peek out of the kitchen to check on Raj and reassure her of his continued presence. She compelled her hands and shoulders to scrub with the force of a carpenter sanding endless layers of wood. Only when the last dish was washed, the last droplets wiped clean did Irina permit herself to wipe her face, which glistened with a mixture of sweat and steam. She removed her hair net and liberated her unruly curls, allowing them to cascade over her shoulders.

"Let's go home," she said to Raj. "I'm tired."

"I've still got a few things to do here, but it shouldn't be long," said Raj without looking up from the inventory he was doing.

"Go, I'll take care of this," came the sharp voice of Mr. Cranston. He shuffled toward Raj, leaning on a broom he used to sweep the dining area.

"Really, I'll be fine. I may not know much about women, young man, but I've lived long enough to know she needs you. Go, and be with her," he said, patting Raj on the shoulder.

"Thanks, Joe," Raj said, grabbing his belongings with one arm and Irina's slight shoulders with the other. They leaned their heads on one another and headed for the door.

"You take care, hear!" Cranston shouted as the door swung closed behind them.

As the crisp wind kicked up a variety of wrappers and other trash off the sidewalks, Irina huddled closer to Raj, nestling her head against his neck. She looked up at him and smiled. He noticed and returned the affectionate glance.

"What is it?" he asked. "Is something wrong?"

"Mmm, no," Irina said, still glancing upward at Raj. "I was just thinking how grateful I am that you are in my world. You even gave up Dr. Meyerstein for me, didn't you?"

"Well, uh, yes." said Raj. "It was the right thing to do. I'm happy to do it."

"Shh," Irina whispered. She beckoned Raj to bend down. "I want to give you something in return."

She grasped him around his shoulders and pulled him to her, then pressed her lips softly against his. She imagined that she felt a hunger and thirst of loneliness in the pressure of his lips. She wished to inhale every musky scent, to merge with him in the most primal of human dances, one in which she sensed he was still inexperienced. But she was sure that if they listened to the drumbeat of their mutually desperate affection, it would guide them together in synchrony.

"You know what, Irina, there's so much more in here," Raj said, tapping his left chest with his right palm. "And from now on, it all belongs to you."

He reached down and lifted Irina off the ground with a tight embrace, then set her down and bent down to kiss her. Their lips touched lightly at first. After a series of tentative explorations, they sought each other out with fervor, each one consuming the intoxicating nectar of affections fermented in involuntary abeyance. Irina wanted to feel whole again, and Raj was the only one she trusted to fill her empty spaces.

The two returned towards the apartment with the un-hurried steps of those whose hearts are full. They marked the journey with furtive glances, intertwined hands and all manner of nonverbal love expressions. In a matter of a few moments Irina felt the pain of her physical wounds fading beneath the flushed urgency of desire.

The would-be lovers hurried up the stairs into the room. Their steps were hurried in the manner of two long-con-fined soulmates eager to liberate themselves together. Irina jumped up onto Raj, wrapping her legs around his waist and her arms around his neck. Nothing she could say could fully express her need for him, but she trusted her actions to speak for her.

In lieu of words, Irina led Raj to the bed and pushed him down on the mattress. She pounced on him, tossed her head back, and laughed, as she hadn't been able to in weeks.

"I love you," she whispered, sitting astride Raj and rubbing his shoulders and chest as she kissed his neck. Raj felt the softness of her hair and skin as their hands and bodies merged. Her breathing, so soft and delicate, took on a more sensual quality as their naked flesh intermingled. He grasped her slender hips with his fingertips and then rubbed his hands across the small of her back as he merged with her. They rose and fell upon one another like thunder and rain, and after about an hour of unbridled pleasure, Raj succumbed to a tranquil slumber.

Irina was not as fortunate. Her hopes for satisfaction were not realized that night. She had wished for this moment of closeness and intimacy for many days, and her body enjoyed the display of passion. But her mind was a different story. The excavation of old memories had begun to build a maze of confusion.

As Raj lay beside her, lost in oblivion, Irina stared at the ceiling and trembled. An image materialized above her, shadowy but familiar and terrifying. In a matter of seconds, it sprang to life, descending toward the bed. Irina tried to shrink into the mattress, but it was no use. The shape was that of an elongated man, with rough hands, holding a stick of some sort. She could not see his face – a light source blocked her view. She hid her face in her hands, huddling into the corner of the bed, trying to disappear into the nightstand.

"No!" she screamed aloud. "Please don't hurt me. Don't hurt us. Please."

Irina whimpered and wailed. Raj woke up and tried to hold her. She pushed him away, throwing his arms aside with unnatural strength. Her fists flailed as she awoke with a start. She sat on the side of the bed, rocking and covering her face.

Raj slid over to the side of the bed and touched Irina on the shoulder. She threw her arms around him, every muscle fiber in her small body twitching and shaking.

"I'm sorry, Irina," Raj murmured, tears rising in his eyes and spilling down his cheeks. "I am so sorry. We will get through this together. It will be OK. I promise."

"It will be OK," he repeated. "I will not let him harm you. Not ever again."

She wished she could believe him.

Chapter Twenty

"Thank you for seeing me doctor," Irina murmured, her eyes fixed on a distant spot in the corner of the room.

"That's my job, and I'm happy to do it," Dr. Meyerstein replied. "So what's been going on?"

"I made love with Raj," Irina replied. She felt a smile move across her lips, then vanish within seconds. She squirmed in her chair.

"Go on," said the doctor. "I know these topics are often difficult, but I'm here to listen."

"Well, it was wonderful," Irina said. "I felt safe, healthy, like I was alive again, you know? But then, I don't know, it slipped away."

She frowned and shifted in her chair.

"Are you saying something happened, after you made love?" Dr. Meyerstein asked.

"He came to me," Irina answered. "I tried to escape, but I couldn't. He just kept coming closer and closer and I am so scared."

"This is common. Intimacy stirs many emotions, not always how we'd like it to. You are safe here Irina," Dr. Meyerstein assured Irina. "Tell me what he's like. It's OK."

"I mean . . . he . . . the killer," said Irina. "I hear his words: 'Russian whore'. Taunting me. It is too hard! I see him coming for me, running after me, but I will not let the man get me."

"He can't get to you in here, it's OK," said Dr. Meyerstein. But it was no use. Irina was exhausted and collapsed against the chair.

"This thing, this trauma, it drains the life from me," Irina said. "It takes all I have."

"It's a struggle for you to get through the day," said Dr. Meyerstein.

"Yes, it is a struggle," said Irina, her voice rising to its usual volume again. "But it is more than that. After that night, I want to make love again. I want the felling of being alive, connected. I want this more than anything. But I can't. I am too scared. And Raj, he does not know what to do or what to think. I think he believes it is his fault."

"This 'thing' as you call it, is keeping you from what you want most," Dr. Meyerstein said. She pressed her palms together as if in prayer. "This troubles you. Do you feel bad about yourself?"

"Yes, and I don't know how to tell Raj about it," Irina said, gesticulating with her delicate hands, which waved like a maestro's baton. "I come to you because you know about these things. But I do not know if even you can help me. I do not know if anyone can. This guilt is my burden. Only I can carry it and only I will know when to put it down."

"You feel very much alone right now," said the doctor. "Trauma is like that. It is hard to be you right now. But you are not alone. We'll work together every week, for as long as you need. This is terrible, but it is also temporary. The human spirit is very resilient. You are very resilient. You are more than your fears, more than the demons that visit at night. Believe that."

Irina nodded. Her eyes wandered through the room, looking for some comfort on the wall before her. She dabbed at the tears that escaped containment and seemed more bitter than usual.

"Thank you," said Irina after a brief silence. "You know it is times like this I miss mother and Papa most. But sometimes you remind me of mother. She was very kind, and her voice always made me feel better, just like yours."

Another lull ensued, and Irina stared at the wall again. She took a sip of water from a Styrofoam cup.

"Does it ever get better? Can you make it go away?" Irina pleaded, her eyes widening as she cast a plaintive glance at the doctor. "Will this ghost ever leave me alone?"

"You sound doubtful," Dr. Meyerstein replied. "And I can see why. It's hard for you to believe you can beat this. Many of my patients feel that way at the start. But it does get better. One day you will see yourself as the survivor you are. I can give you some medicine to help you sleep. Perhaps we can start with that. Therapy works better when we are rested."

"I hope so," Irina responded with a deep sigh, reaching out to grab the prescription. In a few seconds her shaking stopped and she secured slid the paper into her purse. "We work together. I will get better. I must. Please."

With that entreaty, their time was up, and Irina vanished, leaving only a neatly arranged stack of five-dollar bills.

When Irina finally arrived at the restaurant, even her bright uniform could not hide the facial signs of a troubled night. Mr. Cranston tapped her on the shoulder as she arrived, and Irina jumped.

"I'm sorry if I scared you," Cranston apologized. "Hey, you really don't look so good today. Is everything OK? If you need to, take the day off, Irina."

Irina shook her head and declined the offer.

"No, thank you Mr. Cranston," she said. "I will be fine. Just tired. Really, I am glad to be here. It is good to be busy. It keeps my mind from going into darkness."

"Suit yourself," Cranston replied. "But remember my offer, OK?"

Cranston ambled away. His gait was slow and his shoulders stooped. He seemed older every day. The thought sent pangs of sadness through her heart as she imagined her father, deprived of his own old age.

She pictured Alex telling stories, becoming hunched and slow in his gait, but always smiling. She was certain he would have aged with the same passionate zest with which he had lived his entire life. The bullets changed everything, ending the future with indiscriminate cruelty. Some evenings she still heard the gunshots' sonic ripples and saw the image of her father's glassy-eyed body ringed in an ever-expanding pool of crimson.

The thoughts stirred rage within her and she stomped off to the kitchen. Irina assaulted the surface of every plate, glass, and piece of cutlery, scrubbing and scraping without mercy. She imagined every speck of tomato sauce as a fleck of dried blood, and her frail forearms scrubbed harder. The thin tendons running from each finger pushed their way to the skin's surface as her hands strained to wipe it all away: not only dirt but the twin devils of horror and pain. Her face folded itself into a fixed stare, her lips drawn back into a snarl.

Irina was still scrubbing when the kitchen closed up and Raj massaged her shoulder. She continued for a minute while he waited. At last Raj broke the silence and roused Irina from her angry trance.

"Irina, Irina my love," Raj called out. She remained fixated on the dishes. Finally he tapped her right arm gently, and she placed her scrubbing brush back in the sink. "Darling, it's time to go home. You and I both need rest. Let's go."

Irina nodded and slid her arms into the coat that Raj held by her shoulders. She leaned against him and placed her head on his chest as they walked out of the restaurant into the night air.

"I'm sorry," said Irina.

"For what?" Raj asked. "You say those words so often, but I don't understand why you would feel the need. There is nothing you should feel guilty for."

"I guess it's just for the way I've been lately," she replied with a deep sigh. "I wanted for us to make love, but . . ."

"That's OK," Raj said, caressing the back of her neck. "We will have all the time in the world. And trust me, you have nothing to apologize for."

"That makes me feel good," Irina said. "You see, something happened that night. I don't remember it all, but there is one part I can't forget. This man, he had a stick, and he held it to my throat. I heard him, I smelled him. He tried to grab at me, and I fall down. But Papa, he yells at the man, and then I hear a popping sound, so loud. I can't forget that sound. I think it will stay with me as long as I live. And then I hear the man running, and I turn around. Papa is lying there. And there is blood . . . blood everywhere."

Raj covered her head and shoulders in his arms as she cried. The quiet air was fractured by Irina's piercing wail. Her body shook like the limbs of a sapling in a hurricane. Raj stood without speaking, cradling her slender frame with his long arms until the shaking stopped. When the storm passed, Irina looked up at him and wiped her eyes, sniffling.

"Thank you, my love."

They walked home in silence. Irina leaned against her lover's wiry but strong frame. She was almost limp, like a baby drained of its last tear before slumber.

Once inside the apartment, Raj lifted Irina onto the bed. He brushed her silky hair back from her face, stroked her cheeks for a minute and kissed her lips and forehead. Exhausted by her most recent flashback, Irina soon fell asleep. But Raj could not allow himself to do so.

He had long suspected that someone had attempted some unspeakable act towards the woman he had grown to love more than anyone. Now he had an even clearer idea. Whether it was the explicit statement of the act, or perhaps the mental image he had of a wide-eyed, trembling Irina shrinking away from her assailant, he was now a bubbling cauldron of righteous fury.

As he sat and seethed by the bedside, the meaning of justice was difficult to define. Law school taught him that the term varied in different contexts. Retribution was in order for Alex, for Irina, and for his own sanity. He had ample time to consider this through the hours of night. As dawn arrived he saw Irina's eyes open wide when she sensed his presence.

"You're up already, Raj? You didn't sleep, did you? Come back to bed and lie with me a little while," she beckoned. "I miss you when I'm sleeping. I'm so lucky to have you."

"We have each other," Raj answered, crawling into bed next to Irina. He caressed the sinuous curvature of her hip as she lay on her side. "And I'm pretty sure I'm the fortunate one."

"Maybe misfortune is always with us." Irina said. "And only sometimes it knocks us down. If I didn't have you, I think it would have killed me. And maybe I would have deserved it."

Raj leaned in and kissed Irina's neck, smoothing her hair. "You can't believe that. It isn't true. Nothing you've done, now or ever, merits this."

"You did not know me when I was younger," she said. "Before Papa stopped me, I was willing to join this rich man who was asking me to steal from other wealthy men. It is strange even to think of it. Anatoly convinced me nobody would get hurt, that it was just money, and I was so taken by his gifts and attention. Blinded by greed and selfishness. How father found out, I'll never know. We never spoke of it. But if he hadn't given me the knife that day for protection and arranged for transport out of the country, who knows where I'd be?"

Shiny rivulets streamed down her cheeks, glistening in the morning sun.

"Don't do this to yourself. You were young," Raj said. "That's why they took advantage of you. Men like that, they know how to get into your head. It is not your fault."

"It is, for being stupid." she insisted. "And if I had not been, how different would life have been?"

"We can't think that way," Raj ran his fingertips over her back, massaging the C-shaped outline of a scar that bordered Irina's right shoulder blade. "We all make mistakes. Some can't be erased, but maybe they allow us to become who we are. You are more than you think you are. Every day, you are my teacher. You show me how to endure, to be compassionate. You are the reason I survive. And I think you're perfect. Tattoo, scars, and all."

Raj and Irina strolled home in the light of street lamps and traffic signals. They leaned on one another with the trusting comfort of love that doesn't require speech. After climbing the stairs to the apartment, they sat down, arms entwined, on the bed.

Raj turned to Irina and looked into her eyes.

"You look like there is something you want to say." Irina commented. "What is it?"

"Just thinking," Raj said.

"About what?" asked Irina, leaning over to plant a firm, lingering kiss on his lips.

"About us, our future, our life," Raj answered, wrapping his arms around Irina. "I think I know what we need to do. In a strange way, I think maybe I have since I first saw you. But I denied it."

"Really?" asked Irina. "What is that?"

He slid off the bed and knelt in front of Irina, grasping both of her palms in his.

"Marry me Irina. This way there will be no fear, no loneliness for us anymore. We will make things right in our lives, in our lives, past and future. We will be happy together."

Irina jumped up and clasped her hands over her mouth in surprise. She cried and threw her arms around Raj.

"I've wished for this day to come. I told Papa, and he told me it would, that one day I would cry the tears of greatest happiness," she said. The excitement faded, and a brooding expression replaced it on her face. "But Papa is not here. And I am broken. I want to do this. But now is not the time for this. We shall do it later, when I am whole. I'm sorry. Are you upset?"

Raj felt disappointed. This was not the response he'd hoped for. But he couldn't argue with her logic. Irina needed to heal, to focus on herself. He could help her do that.

"I could never be upset with you," he said. "And marriage or not, wherever you are is where I want to be."

PART THREE

Chapter Twenty-One

Raj sat in the empty studio. Irina liked the minimalist lighting, cozy acoustics, and inexpensive rent, so she practiced here twice a week. For Raj it was an opportunity to see her vibrancy and inspiration in its most natural habitat. She sang her most recent composition, a slow, bluesy number.

> "*I carve my name in sand*
> *The wind blows it away*
> *Unsteadily I stand*
> *Remembering that day*
>
> *I left you in a church*
> *I left you with your tears*
> *A broken sapling birch*
> *Bent over by the years*"

Her mature voice balanced boldness with delicacy. Raj recalled Alex's description of Olga. As he watched and listened he knew what it was to be in the presence of ethereal grace. So many individuals aspired to wealth or status. He'd fallen prey to that craving in younger years. But how many people could move hearts and souls with the sound of their voice? That was a true art, a gift to be treasured. He was grateful to have learned this lesson from her.

Their life as a couple allowed a modicum of comfort. Raj practiced immigration law. He enjoyed the opportunity to help new immigrants realize their dreams of becoming "real Americans." The pay was not what he could have gotten in a high-powered firm, but he made enough for them to live well. He was always home by six o'clock to eat dinner with Irina and their daughter Lena.

Irina sang in small establishments on weekends. During the week she helped at their daughter's school. She was a multidimensional woman, balancing past, present and future with ease. Even her body asserted its independence, buoyed by the full curves of motherhood and a greater ruddiness of her cheeks.

Raj sat and listened. He should appreciate his good fortune. The realization of his luck escaped him for so long, but now he knew the blessings of love, parenthood, and a career that helped others.

Irina wrapped up the song. She sipped a glass of water, sighing with satisfaction as the cool liquid quenched her dry throat.

"That was amazing," Raj commented. "Your voice isn't just back. It's even better than ever."

"I hope so," said Irina. "Tomorrow's Saturday, and I have to sing at Lounge Cat. Good pay means high expectations, you know."

"You'll knock 'em dead," said Raj. "I've seen you enough times to know that."

"It's good to have believers," said Irina. "It helps me have faith in myself."

"As well you should," said Raj.

"Yeah, maybe you're right," said Irina with a bright smile. "Let's head home. Lena will be missing us and I'm sure the sitter is ready to leave."

"Mama, mama, look!"

The energetic hazel-eyed child careened around the living room with the joy peculiar to five year olds. Lena danced, skipped, and displayed the same buoyant smile that Raj remembered wearing as a young child. Fatherhood was both more challenging and more gratifying than Raj imagined. And Irina's gentle, unflappable demeanor was the perfect foil for their fearless daughter.

"Shh, Lena, don't yell so loud," Raj admonished the girl. "Your mother is trying to sleep. She has a concert tonight."

"No, she isn't Daddy," said Lena. "See for yourself. She's awake."

Lena grabbed her father by the hand and yanked him with all the strength in her small frame. She marched to the tan leather couch.

"Look," she pointed at her mother. "She's awake. Eyes open and everything!"

Raj and Lena paused for a second. Though Irina was not asleep, her eyes appeared glazed, and her hands shook as she stared at the local newspaper. Raj walked over to her and peered over her shoulder. Nothing seemed out of the ordinary. The daily accounts of violence, corruption and tragedy dotted the pages in their usual pattern.

On closer inspection, one small headline caught his eye. He read the headline's large, bold typeface.

"Murderer Strikes Russian Immigrant Again," the bold letters screamed. The ensuing lines suggested that there was a link to a series of brutal assaults and murders over the past 5 years, but the killer had never been found. Raj scanned Irina's pale face, speckled with drops of perspiration. The paper tore in her clenched hands, and the noise stirred her back to full consciousness.

Irina's reaction could only mean one thing. The article had summoned an evil spirit from her past. He walked over to the couch and placed his arms around Irina, kissing her lightly on the cheek. She trembled and shook her head. For six years, Raj had attempted to uncover the truth about the fateful day that Alex was murdered. He was left running in circles, but one never attains an elegant solution without asking the proper question. Now he had a face to go with the story. It made the quest for justice more urgent and more real.

"I'm sorry, my love," he said. "So sorry about this."

"Mommy, would you like some water?" asked Lena from behind her father's knees.

Irina smiled, but Raj knew this expression was feigned. It was the best she could do at the moment, as she was trying her best to hide her fear and sadness for Lena's sake.

"Lena, why don't you go upstairs and Daddy will be with you in a minute, OK?" he said.

Lena trundled upstairs without any arguments. She paused for a second to peer between the slats of the wooden railing before continuing up to her room. Raj turned to Irina.

"That's him, isn't it?" he said. "I'll kill him. I'll . . ."

"No," Irina's eyes flashed as she tossed the paper aside and waved her hands in the air. "No. I want no talk of such things. It is him. But killing this man? Violence helps no one. My father, he is still dead. Who has that helped? I still have bad dreams sometimes. This man, killing him changes nothing."

"Let me do something," Raj pleaded. He paced the width of the living room. "It's not right, what he did. I want Lena to grow up knowing people can't just hurt other people and get away with it. I want her to know there is justice in this world and that there are people who will fight for it. I want her to see how to stand up for the people you love."

Irina rose to her feet and stood face to face with Raj.

"Enough crazy talk," she said. She grasped his hands and held them tight. "For years, I am able to live, to move on even though that man killed my father. I survived. You know how I did that? Did I forget? No, my heart can never do that. But I gave up on justice. That is not ours to have. It is a crazy dream. It is not yours to give, even now that you are fancy lawyer. We are a family, not a court, not police."

"I'm sorry, you are right," said Raj. "It's just I get so angry at him for hurting you and your father. This outrage comes from love. I want to erase the problem, make it like it never happened."

As he embraced Irina, a tear spilled from his eye, splashing onto her bare shoulder. She looked at him and wiped his eyes with her gracile fingers.

"I know, Raj, I know," she said. "Lena is waiting. Better go up and tuck her in."

He jogged up the stairs. Now in his thirties, Raj still retained the lithe gait of the athlete he was more than a decade ago. He arrived at Lena's room and opened the door. She was busy drawing an intricate picture with her colored markers.

Raj sat next to his daughter and peered over her shoulder. He saw the multicolored stick figures with their primitive facial features and smiled.

"What are you drawing?" he asked Lena, who was hard at work on her current opus. Her joyful face turned solemn when she drew. She looked back at him and smiled, then looked down at the paper again and resumed her work.

"It's a picture of us," Lena answered. "I'm going to give it to Mommy, to make her happy."

She paused for a moment. Her stubby fingers placed caps on all the markers and set them on her bedspread.

"Daddy, why is Mommy sad?" she asked her father, her eyes widening as she awaited the answer.

"What makes you think she's sad?" said Raj.

"I don't know," Lena said with a shrug and a sigh. "Her face just looked sad. Her lips were all frowny. And it looked like she was going to cry. She never looks that way. It scared me. And it sort of makes me want to cry too."

Raj lifted Lena and put her on his knee. He placed his arm around her and bent down so his face was nearly touching hers.

"You know how in stories, sometimes there are bad people? Like the big, bad wolf? Or the wicked witch?" Raj asked. Lena nodded. "Well, sometimes there are bad people in real life too. And these bad people sometimes do things that hurt good people. Your mommy met a bad person like that a few years ago, and he was very mean to her and to your grandfather. So sometimes she remembers him, and it makes her scared and sad."

Lena frowned and stared at her father.

"Did the paper make her remember the bad man?" Lena asked. "That's why she was sad?"

"Yes, that's right," said Raj, patting Lena on the back. "You're a smart one, Lena. Nothing escapes you."

"I don't like the bad man," Lena declared. "I think I hate him. I hate anyone who is mean to Mommy."

"It's OK not to like him, Lena. In fact, you know how I always say 'hate' is a bad word? Well it's OK to hate this man.

He deserves it." Raj said. "I don't know him, but I'm pretty sure I hate him too."

Lena looked up at her father again and gave him a quick kiss on the cheek. She giggled and smiled, but then her expression turned serious again.

"What is it, Lena?" Raj asked, noting the sudden change in her expression.

"Daddy, in stories, the bad man gets punished," she said. "Will you get the bad man? Will he get punished?"

Raj nodded and tousled Lena's hair.

"Yes, I'll get him," said Raj. He uttered the words to reassure his daughter, but the message was meant for his own ears as well. Though Irina said she didn't want revenge, Raj couldn't help believing that justice would ease her pain. And maybe if he repeated his mantra often enough, it would turn out to be true.

Raj kissed Lena on the cheek and tucked her into her bed, nestling the butterfly-festooned covers around her. He shut the door and trotted to the top of the stairs. Raj bent over and peered down toward the couch. He expected to find Irina asleep on it but failed to see her lean silhouette anywhere in the living room area.

He tiptoed to the room and found the lights turned off. In the course of their relationship, Raj learned that Irina could startle violently from even the soundest slumber. It often appeared as though she awoke to fend off an unseen attacker. Her sleep had improved after Lena's first year of life, but in light of the recent news, Raj was careful to make no sound.

He slid onto the floor and sat up alongside the bed. In case of unexpected guests in her dreams, he would be there. Irina needed an uninterrupted respite from the jarring news. At least one of them should rest tonight. But Raj could not permit himself the liberty. Not right now, with the man who killed Alex still at large. The time had arrived to formulate a plan of attack.

"Thanks for meeting me, Dr. Meyerstein," Raj groaned as he nestled his achy lower back into the leather chair. "I know you have lots of patients with problems worse than mine."

"I'm happy to help," said the doctor. "And I'm curious why you feel the need to minimize the importance of your own issues. You've known me well enough for long enough to know I'm always here for you."

Raj shrugged and shook his head.

"I guess I feel guilty about what I'm going to be telling you," Raj replied. "I feel like I'm sneaking around."

"So you didn't tell Irina you were coming?" asked the doctor. "You make it sound the way someone would if they were being unfaithful, cheating."

"Oh, no I told her," Raj reacted. "I just didn't tell her what I was going to discuss."

"OK, it seems you're dancing around the topic, so let me ask you, what is the secret that's making you so nervous?" said Meyerstein. "Maybe you feel the need to hide this from your wife, and I'm curious about that. Although, as always, you know I'll keep those motives confidential."

"You know how Irina was traumatized by the man who killed her father?" said Raj. "Well, I decided to do a little digging and help the police bring this guy down."

"And Irina?" the doctor prompted her anxious patient. "Where does she fit in?"

"She's not fully opposed to it," Raj explained. "But she doesn't want me to pursue revenge, and I don't think she believes in justice after what happened. Quite likely she worries about me putting myself in danger. But I can't justify sitting on the sidelines. I can't just be a spectator anymore. I've got to do something. The way I see it, I've been waiting for life to happen, and that has to stop."

"Why now?" Meyerstein asked. "And why this?"

"Sounds like you don't approve either, Doctor," said Raj.

"No, I really don't have an opinion one way or the other," said the doctor. "This is not an issue that's for me to judge. I'm just trying to get a handle on your thought process. Something important is spurring you into action, and I'm curious to understand what it is."

"Honestly, I don't know why now, or why this," said Raj. "But I do know that my wife cries in her sleep and I imagine that murderous asshole sleeping like a baby. I know my wife has no father. I know what that's like. My child will never know her grandpa. And there's not a damned thing I can do about that."

His voice cracked and he fought back tears, ripping a handful of tissues from the box that balanced on the arm of his chair. He balled them up, pressed the wad against his eyes and waited as the cotton absorbed all stray moisture from his cheek. The thunderstorm of sadness ended as quickly as it began, and after a few moments the doctor coaxed Raj to speak.

"You mentioned her father, and you have often mentioned your own," Meyerstein said. "Is that what this is really about?"

"I wasn't there for them," said Raj. "I wasn't there for Alex. And I need to make up for it. I need to atone for my absence by being active, not just present. Showing up is not enough. I need to show my wife and my daughter that I will protect them now. Because back then, I didn't."

"And what constitutes atonement, in your mind?" Dr. Meyerstein asked.

"Justice, and maybe vengeance," he said. He sat forward in his chair and raised his voice. "And that means making sure this man is caught. I was taught to stand up for what's right, no matter the consequence."

"Your parents had high standards for you," said Dr. Meyerstein.

"No higher than they had in their own lives," said Raj. He squeezed the wad of tissues in his hand and tore at the ends of it with his thumb and forefinger. "My Dad taught me to live for justice, and if need be to die for it. He taught me that as long as you live according to your principles, you can look at yourself in the mirror and be proud. My mother taught me to be kind and giving. That's how you make the world better. Otherwise you're just existing."

"Is that what you feel you're doing now? 'Just existing'?" asked the doctor. "That sounds like a dramatic exaggeration."

"If I just sit and watch, then yes, that would be a pointless existence," said Raj. "If I work to do something to bring him down, make him pay, then I'm living with a purpose. The purpose I ought to have, regardless of my parents' wishes or anything else."

He stared hard at Dr. Meyerstein, searching her face for some sign of approval or reproach. If she had an opinion, her expression gave nothing away.

"You're not quite certain if I've lost my mind," he concluded after his facial survey. "You think maybe I'll do something crazy?"

"I've said nothing of the sort," Dr Meyerstein corrected her patient. "You are a good, rational, and compassionate man. But your bringing that up makes me think you are second-guessing your own actions. What is it that seems out of line to you?"

"If it is truly the right thing to do, as I am so sure it is in my heart, then my motives are proper," said Raj. He deliberated over his words as he crossed his legs. "I've never been sure that I was a good man. For a long time, I was convinced. I wasn't. I was good at appearing virtuous. But my motives were impure. The conflict weighed on me when you first saw me in the hospital. But if what I want to do is truly righteous, then I should be able to explain it to Irina. Instead, I am holding back, because I fear she wouldn't approve. I have to do what's right, but on the other hand she's the one who suffered most from this."

"So how do you resolve this conflict?" Meyerstein asked. "You're a good problem solver. One doesn't get through a life like yours without being good at finding answers."

"I was once, wasn't I?" Raj observed. He felt the muscles of his jaw relax into a smile.

"You are," Meyerstein objected. "Present tense."

"Thanks for the vote of confidence," said Raj. "I think I will do this. I'll tell Irina that I have to do this to honor the memory of my own parents, as well as Alex."

"And if she's upset?" Meyerstein responded.

"At heart, she wants this all to go away, but she knows it can't and won't until the killer's caught," Raj concluded. "She will disagree, but she has never been one to try and hold me back. We love each other, and she always pushes me forward, like my own personal tailwind."

"It's nice to have a tailwind," the doctor observed.

"In my case, I've had many, yourself included doctor," Raj mused. "Maybe now it's my turn to push the plane."

What was the most efficient way to unmask a killer? The press had dredged up information. That meant that there were clues to be had, but the idea of sifting through police files was daunting. Despite his facility with legal matters and online information collection, Raj knew little of criminal investigative procedure. The killer had eluded authorities for years, in spite of their superior manpower and technology. A solo quest for justice was impractical.

How had the District of Columbia metropolitan police department been unable to find Alex's killer? Raj wondered if they cared about the murder of a homeless immigrant. He remembered what it felt like to be invisible. It was his motivation to become an attorney for those the system chose to ignore.

In working with the legal system to obtain asylum and citizenship for his clients, Raj made passing acquaintances with a few policemen, the sort of meetings where one party uses another for a mutually agreed upon purpose before vanishing without a thought into the night. But he needed more. He required a policeman who would invest his heart into the case. It must be someone who knew what it was like to live on the margins of society, who would consider the death of a homeless man a matter of utmost importance.

Raj remembered his old compadre, Benito Garcia. Cranston, with whom he still talked on a monthly basis, had mentioned Garcia's graduation from the police academy. Benito had been on the force for 18 months now. This was the perfect place to start.

Newly assured that he had found a trustworthy partner, Raj was drew a deep breath and sighed. It no longer felt wrong to sleep, so he slid into bed, well aware of the energy he would need to undertake this mission.

The next morning, Raj dialed Benito's number and hoped for the best. To his pleasant surprise, the phone was answered on the first ring.

"Hello, Metropolitan Police Department. Officer Garcia here, what can I do for you?" Benito answered in a staccato tenor voice. Raj imagined that the pitch of his voice must elicit considerable ribbing in the testosterone-infused environment of a police precinct.

"Benito, amigo!" said Raj. "It's been too long since we've talked."

"Sure has," Benito agreed. "So what's up?"

"You remember Irina, from the restaurant." Raj felt his muscles tighten and rubbed the back of his neck as he spoke. "Remember how I told you about her Dad when she came back, and that story?"

"Yes," Benito replied. "Somebody beat her pretty bad, killed him, as I recall?"

"Yeah," said Raj. "Well, we're together now, and the other day she saw that article about the guy who's been terrorizing the Russian community. She thinks it may be the same guy who killed Alex."

"Hmm, for right now that's just a hunch," said Benito. "But if she's right then it's a vital piece of information. The area where those crimes happened is served by a different precinct than mine. I'll make some calls, see what I can do."

"Any help you can offer would be great," Raj pleaded. "This isn't just for me, it's for her, and for our daughter. If you get anything, call me at my office or on my cell, OK? Any time, day or night. I need to be part of the solution."

"I got you," said Benito. "Believe me, this is a big case. I'll take all the help I can get, and I'll keep you updated."

"Can we meet today?" asked Raj. "I think it would be helpful to go over what I know so far."

"Four o'clock?" Benito suggested.

"I'll be there," said Raj.

Raj entered the precinct office. He stopped at the black desk, a '70's style monstrosity that bore numerous scratches and stains. Behind it sat a young, pudgy receptionist whose thick black hair was drawn up into a bun. She glanced at Raj from beneath horn-rimmed glasses.

"Benito Garcia please," he said.

The receptionist smiled. "I'll go get him."

Garcia approached.

"Thanks Paula," he said. "And remember, the offer still stands to split my future lottery winnings if you want to go out Saturday!"

Paula rolled her eyes and walked back to the desk.

"You still have an eye for the ladies," said Raj.

"Some things never change," said Benito, smiling. The unblemished whiteness of Benito's teeth also hadn't changed. "Let's find a room to talk."

They entered a metallic gray room with a dust-smeared window and a metal table tinged with rust. The two friends sat down across from one another.

"So tell me what you've got," said Benito. "From the beginning."

"I guess the beginning of what I know is Irina's story," said Raj. "From what she's told me, she and her father were hanging out in an alley, by Foggy Bottom, smelling the breeze off the river and singing songs. Then this guy comes by, asks for the time. He's about to walk away, then he turns around and starts to attack her. He calls her "Russian whore", says he's going to use her to make him some money, and when Alex tries to protect her, the man beats him with a stick. Alex tells her to run away. She does, into a nearby building. She sees Alex and the man fight, and the man shoots Alex."

Benito placed his palms on the table and sighed.

"When I was a boy, I used to hang out with my uncle a lot," he said. "He knew a lot about nature. One thing he used to say was that every snake leaves its own trail. If you know the snake, you will find him and capture him. It's a lesson that works just as well out here in the city as it did in the desert. We need to determine what kind of guy this killer is, and then we can figure out his identity."

What made the killer tick? Maybe the information superhighway would provide answers. Ever since he touched his first keyboard, computers had made intuitive sense to Raj. The internet's dark spaces were full of clues. It was up to him to reveal them.

"You know I'm a whiz on computers," said Raj. "Plus being a lawyer gives me expanded access. Tell me what you can about what you've learned so far, and I promise I'll get you more."

They walked down the hall to a dimly lit, musty room not much larger than a broom closet. Benito pulled out a laptop and with a few keystrokes called up case notes on the series of murders.

"Katarina Stoichkova, age 29, Russian, occurred in the 31st precinct, unsolved," he read aloud. "Hmm, let's go back a year and see who else this guy got to. Ah, here's another one, maybe. Natalya Petrenko, age 22, perp killed the guy who was with her, beat her up pretty bad. I remember something about that case. Overall, looks like at least seven cases within a ten block radius over the past five years."

"So there's a geographic pattern?" Raj asked.

"Yes," said Benito. He furrowed his brow and tapped his chin with his index finger as he stared at the screen. "How could somebody not have seen a pattern here?"

"Maybe they didn't want to," said Raj. "But we do."

"Yes sir," said Benito. He rose and they shook hands. "And we will."

It was a quiet Saturday morning in the Patel household. Lena remained sound asleep as Raj and Irina sipped tea and digested the usual morning mixture of sugary cereal and splashy headlines.

"Oh, honey, I forgot to tell you something," said Raj. "You remember Benito, from the restaurant?"

"The young Mexican gentleman, sure I remember," Irina responded, raising her head and cocking an eyebrow toward her husband. "What about him?"

"Well, you know that he's a cop, right?" Raj asked. "I, uh, told him about your suspicions."

"Suspicions?" Irina's eyes flashed. "Firstly, I know that must be the same guy who attacked me. It is not suspicion! Second, I do not want to do anything more about this. No more! I forbid you to do anything more about this. Let . . . me . . . forget!"

Her lips trembled and her fingers blanched as she curled them into tight fists. Raj put down the newspaper and crouched next to her chair, his arm draped over her shoulders.

"No more," Irina repeated again, this time in a whisper. She folded up in his arms as Raj brushed her silky hair with his fingers.

"I think I am not feeling so good," said Irina. "I am going upstairs to lie down."

Raj was left to his paper and his thoughts. The latter interfered with his enjoyment of the former. He discarded the sports section. Even now, years after the event, he failed to comprehend the magnitude of what happened to Irina. It was probable that he never could. He reproached himself for once again failing to see outside of his own narrow field of vision. He remembered the Hippocratic oath, "Primum non nocere," first do no harm. And now he had hurt the one who mattered most.

She forbade him nothing, nor did she need to do so. For her to contravene him now meant that he needed to listen. If only he could keep Irina out of it. But no, the avalanche had started. The police would want to speak with her. Her memories were sure to be rekindled. Maybe he could convince the department that she wasn't up to it. He could try to help them find evidence that would make her involvement unnecessary.

He ruminated on his guilt until his error was fully digested. But as the sun painted the western sky, leaving salmon-colored trails across the horizon, a loud knock came at the door. In the absence of a response, the visitor rang the doorbell, which set off an elaborate, twenty second-long, off-key snippet of the "Star-Spangled Banner." Raj was no patriot and found the length of the ditty annoying, but Irina was fond of it, so the recording stayed.

Raj trudged to the door, and upon opening it found the smiling face of his friend, Benito. He startled slightly as he beheld his friend's unmistakable broad grin. Benito reached out to shake hands and slapped Raj on the back.

"My friend, it's good to see you," he said. "I see you are doing well for yourself. I always knew you would."

"Benito, uh, I don't know, um," Raj stammered. "Right now might not be such a good time."

"Where are your manners?" a voice admonished Raj from the staircase behind him. "Tell him to come in."

Raj was taken aback. Just this morning she chastised him for going to the police, yet now his wife stood fresh and beautiful as ever in a yellow sundress, welcoming the officer into her living room with a warm smile.

"I thought . . ." Raj began again, looking at Irina, who dismissed him with a wave of her hand and showed Benito to his place on the couch that sat behind an ovoid table.

"It is good to see you Benito," said Irina. Her eyes glimmered with the same gentle openness she showed Lena. "Would you like some tea? I have good tea."

"Well, actually this is more than just a social visit," said Benito. "I really came to talk to you, Irina, about your father, what happened to him."

"Ah, well if we are talking about these things, I will make some tea," Irina declared. "Because God knows, I will need it."

"This is not a topic she likes to discuss," Raj interrupted. "Couldn't we put this off to another time?"

"It's OK," said Irina. "Benito is here. He has a job to do. I might as well talk. I do not want to, but I have to sometime. One cannot run from nightmares forever. And if I can help you catch this man, it will be good for everyone. So what do you want to know? And why are you interested now?"

"Good questions," Benito agreed. He sipped his tea. "I guess I want to know what happened that day, and the reason is we think it might be the same guy who has done some similar crimes in the same area. We need your help to stop him."

"OK, I will tell you what I remember," said Irina. Her quiet monotone seemed to betray a Herculean effort at stifling what lay beneath it. "It happened one day in this one alley, three blocks from the train station with the funny name, Foggy Bottom. There was a parking lot behind the building, next to the alley. I was sitting on a blanket, in an alley near the street.

Papa was behind me, towards the parking lot. We were singing songs and laughing."

Her right leg started to shake, vibrating as if independent of the rest of her body. She cleared her throat, smoothed her skirt, and continued.

"This man walks by, then he comes back and stands in front of me. He asks Papa and I for the time. Papa tells him he has no watch. We say it is about eight. The man looks at Papa, and suddenly, he is angry. He tells us 'Get out of here.' Then he stands over me. He calls us names. 'Russian whore,' he keeps calling me, over and over. He tries to grab me and I see something flash in front of my face, something shiny, very bright. He puts this stick, a black stick, against my throat. Papa tries to pull him off, but the man is strong. He is very tall, maybe a full two meters, maybe more. Then, the stick is not there and they are fighting. I hear him shouting at Papa. I run and hide in a building. Then I hear two loud noises. 'Pop,pop' like that. I hear something fall, then I look and the man, standing over my father. And Papa, Papa is lying there. Just . . ."

Irina's eyes clouded with a film of tears. Raj knew these tears. He'd felt their weight and bitterness before. They were the bitter souvenirs of irreparable loss. She cried because Alex would never return. Though she professed to have accepted the finality of her loss, this raw wound was now provoked to bleed. But Irina was undeterred by sorrow. Though her voice wavered she continued to tell her story.

"He was lying on his back, in a pool of blood." Her voice rose and sharpened. "The man killed him like he was worse than a dog. That man. I did not want to be involved, but I am. I do not wish to remember, but I do. You must get him. He is evil and he must be stopped."

"Thank you very much for telling me this, Irina," said Benito. "I can't imagine how hard it must be to talk about it."

"I tell you, Benito, this whole thing, I could not have handled it without Raj," she said. She patted Raj on the hand. "And the psychiatrist, Dr. Meyerstein. If you want to know how bad it was for me, ask her. She can tell you everything."

"Thank you," Benito responded. "In the meantime, stay strong and take care of each other, my friends."

Chapter Twenty-Two

Raj knocked at the door to Dr. Meyerstein's office. She opened it, dressed in a white blouse and navy blue knee-length skirt.

"Come in," she said.

"This is my friend that I told you about on the phone, Officer Benito Garcia," said Raj. "He's the one doing the police work on the Russian murders."

"He's the brains. I'm the badge." Benito smiled.

"So, you said you think I can help in some way," Meyerstein said. "Tell me what you need to know, I'll tell you what I can."

"Thank you doctor," said Benito. "I am investigating a series of murders. And Irina she told me she used to be your patient and that I could talk to you."

Dr. Meyerstein interrupted. "Officer, you should really know better. It's a serious matter to violate patient-doctor confidentiality. I can't discuss the specifics of a case without a court order or specific written consent from the patient."

"I can help with that," Raj said. He handed the doctor a signed paper that indicated Irina's consent to release information. "I assure you, she knows what Officer Garcia is doing. She understands his purpose and agrees to it."

"Yes, she's the one who suggested I speak to you." said Benito. "But anyway, I guess I am looking for something else, something bigger. Irina gave us this testimony, and we have some other information. If I show you what I have, could you help us figure out what we might be missing? You wouldn't have to tell me what you guys talked about, but maybe knowing what you know and us knowing what we know, we could work together. What do you say?"

"Well, I'm no profiler," said Dr. Meyerstein. "But during our time together I have formulated an idea of who the perpetrator might be, in general terms. Show me what you have."

Benito shuffled through a file of papers and pulled out three pages of testimony and case notes. It was a sparse database but the doctor pored over it for several minutes before handing the papers back to him.

"I can give you some thoughts that come to mind," she offered. "Possibilities, but nothing specific."

"Please," said Raj. "Anything would help. At this point there are a lot of questions and very few answers."

"Ok," Meyerstein began, fiddling with a letter opener as she talked. "This guy, he's not a totally premeditated killer. He's wound pretty tight, though. He's not like some killers. This isn't about power, or some sort of sexual, thrill-seeking thing. Hate is what fuels him. But it's not the kind of thing that is fully planned. He has a trigger. In all likelihood it's something visceral that has been there since childhood. The impulsive nature makes me think maybe he has some problems with alcohol or drugs, but he's also been doing this for awhile, so he's smart enough to tie up loose ends. I don't think your killer has any conventional primary psychiatric diagnosis. He's probably got antisocial personality disorder, but so do a ton of criminals, so that doesn't help you."

She moved her chair forward and tapped her desk with her pen. "It's pretty evident this guy has an issue with foreigners in general, but Russians in particular. He's sensitized, waiting for them to stumble across his path. I think you're looking for a guy who is powerful physically and occupationally. And somebody Russian really angered him in the past. You know, I wouldn't be surprised if maybe he himself has a parent who is Russian and who really did something horrific to him. Whoever set this off, I'm thinking it happened a while ago, and he's been smoldering ever since."

"How do you think he's identifying the nationality of the victims?" Raj asked. "That's what I keep coming back to. It's like he has a predisposition, but then something triggers it."

"Triggers are usually sensory," Meyerstein explained. "Sight, sound, smell. These things remind one of certain persons or places. Maybe it's the language. It's not like you hear Russian that often, so if he did, and he knows it a bit, that could be enough. You know what they say, 'speak to a man in your language and you speak to his mind, speak to him in his language and you speak to his heart'. Maybe speaking to this guy's heart is a dangerous thing to do."

She shrugged and shook her head.

"I'm afraid I haven't been very helpful," she concluded. "But I'd be willing to run through some more stuff with you when you get it."

"Thanks doctor," said Raj as he arose to leave. "And you never know. You might have helped us a lot more than you think."

"I'm sorry I called at the last minute like this," Irina apologized. She held onto Raj's arm as she wiped her feet before entering the office. "But something new has come up. I brought Raj as well, for support. I hope this is all OK?"

"It is your appointment, your time. Feel free to talk about whatever is on your mind." Dr. Meyerstein responded. "Please, tell me about these new developments."

"Yes, tell her what you told me," Raj encouraged. "Don't worry, the two of us won't let anything happen to you."

"Since the story about that man hit the papers I have been having these strange experiences," said Irina. She deliberated over the words, arranging them like silverware at a dinner party. "I say experiences because I do not actually know how else to describe them."

"In these 'experiences', what happens?" Dr. Meyerstein inquired.

"It is weird, hard to explain," said Irina. She closed her eyes as her memories rose to mind. "They're not dreams, because I am fully awake. But it's as though I'm right there, in the alley again. Only this time, I see more."

She paused, opened her eyes and met Dr. Meyerstein's gaze, searching for reassurance.

"Am I going crazy?" she asked the doctor, who leaned forward to catch every soft-spoken word. "I am embarrassed to be this way in front of you. After all you have done for me."

"You are far from crazy," said the doctor. "These are what we call flashbacks. Often your mind tries to seal over parts of traumatic memories, but then they seep through. Your mind is trying to tell you something, but sometimes it does so in little bites, so as not to overwhelm you. It lets you in on frightening secrets just a little at a time. Sometimes memories come back because of the focus we are directing to what happened. I am glad you came to me for help."

Irina nodded.

"Thank you," she said. "It is nice to know you can help."

Irina paused and wiped her eyes, which had blurred with a misty film. She cleared her throat and stared at the doctor.

"He had some sort of badge. Or at least he does in these visions."

"So the flashbacks are visual," Dr. Meyerstein clarified. "What else did you see in the visions? Don't worry, it is safe to talk here. You are safe."

"He is dressed in all blue. He is very tall. And he is wearing a hat. Its brim is pulled down over his eyes." She shifted in her chair and covered her face with her hands. "I . . . that's it. I don't want to see any more."

Irina rocked back and forth, resting her head on her palms as her elbows dug into her frail knees. Raj grasped her hand and squeezed it.

"It's OK," Dr. Meyerstein called out to her patient, who seemed to be far away at the moment. "Remember the safe place we spoke of? Your father's shop?"

Irina's body shook but she managed to nod.

"Go there. Smell the air. Look around. Inhale, hold it . . . now exhale. Focus on your breathing and your body."

Irina struggled to follow the instructions. She shook her head, trying to rid it of the thoughts that bedeviled her.

"Ok. Now come back here, to the office," said the doctor. "You are safe now. Just breathe. Slowly."

After hyperventilating for a minute, Irina was able to do as the doctor requested. The room came back into focus and the vivid, fearful images receded.

"You made it," Dr. Meyerstein commented with an encouraging smile.

"You are right." Irina replied, slumping back against her chair with obvious exhaustion. "It is gone, wherever bad dreams go. At least for now."

"How does that feel?"

"It feels much better, like this thing that was inside does not live here anymore," said Irina. "But I am very tired. Like I just ran across all Siberia."

She looked at the doctor. "Do you think he was a policeman? mean, I was just thinking."

"Who knows?" said Dr. Meyerstein. "Memories are strange creatures."

Chapter Twenty-Three

"Do you think it's something?" Irina squeezed the juice from a lemon wedge into her tea.

"I think your memory is trying to sort things out," said Raj. "And in doing so, things get clearer."

"Should I tell Benito?" Irina looked at Raj for a signal of approval.

"I can do it if you want," he said.

"You think it's a clue?" she asked. "You think it will help catch the killer?"

Raj nodded. "I think what you saw will help us a lot."

Irina picked up the phone. "Then I'll tell him. My memory is my responsibility."

Her fingers shook as she dialed. It was vital that she share this information, but recounting the images in her mind would not be easy.

"Officer Garcia here," said Benito.

"Benito, it is Irina, I think I have something for you, but I need to know you will be careful with it," she said.

"OK, Irina, OK, take your time," he answered. "I'll be discreet with what I hear."

"Good," she said. "Benito, I think he was police. I've been remembering these things. He wore all blue, and something on his chest that could have been a badge. I needed to talk to you because I think I can trust you. If he is police, I don't know who or where he is. So that's why I need you to be careful. I don't want him to hurt you too."

"Don't worry about me," said Benito. "I'll get on this. It could be a big lead. But I do need to let my sergeant know. He's solid, a real straight arrow. And if you have anything else you remember, you contact me, OK? I am glad you called. Take care of yourself, OK?"

As Irina hung up the phone, Raj touched her hand. Though she had grown used to intimate contact with him, and often craved it, the phone call left her shaken and she jumped.

"I'm sorry I startled you," said Raj. He took her palm between his hands and squeezed it. She felt her heart and her breathing slow to their normal pace. "I'm so impressed at your strength. You'd have every right to walk away from all this, but you don't, even though I can see it's so painful. I can't help thinking, though, that I wish I never got you into this."

She forced a smile and took a deep breath. "Fate brought me into it. And one gets nowhere by ignoring fate. I do what is right, just like you and Papa."

Raj knelt behind her and enveloped her shoulders in his wiry arms as she leaned on him. There was a potent gentleness in his embrace that calmed the waves within her. She kissed him on the cheek and rose to walk toward the window, heartened by the sun that peeked through the curtains.

The day had passed into late evening. As Lena and Irina slept, Raj sat him his home office, rotating in his ergonomic leather-backed chair. Spinning was a nervous habit he used to stimulate his thoughts. He explained it as a self-soothing behavior. Occupational therapists would say it was something to do with the vestibular nervous system. The habit did not always work, but like most comforting rituals, it was one he did not wish to break.

Raj pondered the most efficient method of assembling a comprehensive data set. He knew from his computer science classes that the beginning of an algorithm often determines the end, so he must choose the right point of origin. As he plotted strategy, the phone rang. Raj let it ring a couple of times before indulging his curiosity.

"Hello. This is Raj. How can I help you?"

"Hey, Raj, it's Benito."

"Couldn't sleep either, huh?"

"No rest for the wicked," said Benito. "Listen, I was thinking some more about what the shrink said, and what Irina told me. But first, I need you to promise not to do anything stupid with this."

"You know me, Benito. I'm stubborn but not stupid," said Raj.

"Irina and the doctor think the guy we're looking for may be a cop, right?" Raj heard tension and excitement in Benito's voice. "And Meyerstein said he may have Russian ancestry, right? Maybe we need to focus on cops with Russian parents. Although I'm hoping this isn't a fellow officer. It just doesn't sit right to think of them killing in cold blood."

"I'll do a personnel search and cross-reference it with murders in the area," said Raj. "You do a deep dive into the specifics of the current case files. That way what one of us misses, the other might catch."

"Good idea," said Benito. "But how do you propose to get personnel records."

Raj dismissed the question with a wave. "I have my ways," he said. "Techie stuff, wouldn't want to bore you with it."

"Are you saying it's best I don't know your methods?"

"Perhaps." Raj smiled and stroked the stubble on his chin. "If we find that a suspect pool of cops, it'll narrow things down. But it also complicates your investigation. Look, I know how to ferret out information that might be too sensitive for you to uncover. Let me take care of this."

"Can I stop you? But please remember, this guy is very dangerous. Be careful."

"Believe me, I know what he can do," said Raj. "That's why I have to stop him. This guy took the life of my best friend, and not a day goes by that the memory doesn't torture Irina. But I'm not looking to die. I'm looking for justice. There's a big difference. I want to see this guy's face when he heads away in handcuffs. It won't bring Alex back, but maybe it will let Irina sleep at night. She deserves that."

"Just remember what I told you earlier," said Garcia. "Irina has already lost her parents. Don't make her a widow as well."

The reminder stung. But there was no going back.

"I know," he said. "Damn, you sound like my Mom. But don't worry, I'll be careful."

"Buena suerte, amigo," said Benito as he hung up.

Raj wanted to believe in good fortune, but knew luck to be a fickle ally. He could not wait for a break in the case. It was up to him to make one.

"No!" Irina shouted. She twitched and flailed, her eyes opening and darting to survey the dark room.

Raj stabilized her slender body at the waist, pressing his long, warm fingers against her skin. Her rapid, shallow breathing slowly normalized and she returned to somnolence, quivering like a cold baby bird. Raj suspected that the killer had visited her again in her dreams, the same ones she'd recounted before. Over the years she had recounted to him the vivid horror of her memory. It was horrible enough for him to imagine the scene. It was worse yet to view the toxic effects of a poisoned memory.

The government and media speak often of terrorists. But what Raj saw in Irina's nocturnal flailings seemed the most insidious sort of terror, injected as it was into what should be a day's most peaceful hours. Raj looked at the ceiling, his rage fermenting. As long as the woman he loved could not sleep, neither would he. If his parents had taught him one thing about relationships, it was that marriage is all about solidarity, so he sat beside her, ever vigilant.

Raj recalled his parents' wedding picture, a black and white portrait of two new immigrants devoted to hope and to each other. He remembered his father's frequent favorite Shakespearean quotation: "To thine own self be true". Dad didn't know that Polonius was a notorious hypocrite, but the philosophy was worth remembering.

As the words rang in his head, Raj gathered himself and walked to his desk. Within minutes of internet exploration, he found his way into MPD personnel records. Raj looked up all cops over six foot three. There were around 100. Of those, ten had excessive force complaints. Of those ten, five had internal affairs investigations for other matters as well. This subset made a good starting point. If Raj and Benito could map out where all the killings and attacks were and cross-reference them with where these five cops lived and worked, something would click.

Raj shook his head. Never in his younger life would he have imagined meddling in this cloak and dagger affair. Back then, life seemed normal and tranquil, but now he wondered if he ever understood the relative nature of normalcy.

Medical school brought him in contact with life's fragility on many occasions. At that time he was relieved to have avoided such life-changing moments. Though he witnessed them, he was not of them. Thus he never feared for his future. Not once did he consider the possibility that a tsunami could sweep him under. He admired people who fought through significant levels of adversity, never anticipating that he would confront such challenges.

Now Raj did not feel "admirable" or exemplary. Driven? Yes. Maybe even obsessed and compelled to make amends. He owed so much to Alex and Irina, the people who saved his life and inspired him to embrace it.

What did it mean to be true to himself? That depended on who he really was and who he wished to be. Right now, it meant being the person his parents believed they had raised, a man of action and principle. And there was no cause more urgent than obtaining justice for a fallen comrade.

As Raj sat at his desk writing notes on a scrap of yellow paper, Irina stirred and opened her eyes.

"It's three AM," she whispered. "You've been working since seven this morning. Come to bed."

"I'll be there soon," he said. But the questions in his mind would not be silent. With each one that he answered, another emerged. He felt like a child walking around an intricate corn maze at Halloween. Only when the sun peeked over the horizon did he permit himself to take a break.

Raj sat in the kitchen, enjoying his tea on a lazy Sunday morning. The local political intrigue and gossip never stopped.

Though he detested the sensational nature of mainstream news coverage, a good lawyer needed to be alert to trends in social culture.

Irina entered and stood behind him.

"Thank you for what you're doing," she said.

"I don't understand?" he said, looking up from the paper.

"The meetings, the phone calls, the data searches," she answered. "All the extra hours working after Lena and I are in bed. You've put so much into getting justice for Papa."

"It's not just for him," said Raj. He put away his paper and gazed at her. "This is for you, for us."

Irina smiled. She walked over to face Raj and straddled his lap, then pressed her lips against his, lingering in the sandalwood scent of his cologne. She rubbed his tight shoulders.

"Just remember to take care of yourself," she said. "I can't afford to have anything happen to you."

"I'll be safe," Raj answered. "I just want to see you happy and at peace."

Irina felt the knots in his muscles melt beneath her fingertips. She placed her right index finger on his lips.

"Being with you, seeing you stand with me, it makes me happy," she said. "I love you for it. And I want to help you. When this man is caught, then I can be at peace. I need to help."

"Do you think it's wise?" Raj asked. "That you're ready for this?"

"I do not know if I am ever ready for what happened," Irina answered. "Is anybody? But I know I cannot let you do this alone."

"We are a team," Raj answered, kissing Irina's hand.

"The best," she said with a quick smile.

"You'll let me know if things are getting too stressful?" Raj asked. "I'm your partner, and I love you, so I don't want you hurting yourself with all this."

"And I don't want you taking all the pain yourself," said Irina. She her soft palms over her husband's smooth head. "As much as anything, I need to do this to get stronger, to be who I used to be."

"You've never changed," said Raj. "You were just injured, inside and out. But you're still you. Though you feel your voice quiver, you are the same person who brings audiences to their feet with song. You are the same person who Lena and I love more than any other. Remember that."

"You sound like the doctor," said Irina.

"I guess she's taught me how to say what I feel," said Raj. "I hope that makes me a better man."

"We do this together, OK?" said Irina.

"To the end," Raj promised.

Raj puzzled over a new case that had been referred to him by the local Rwandan consulate. A young man whose family had been killed in ethnic conflict was looking for refuge in the city. All he wanted was to go to school away from gunfire and bloodshed. Raj shook his head. Why were such simple dreams so hard to realize?

Irina burst into her husband's office. "I hope I didn't interrupt anything too important."

"Of course not, dear. Just working on a TPS case," Raj replied with a smile. "It's complicated, but it can wait. You come first."

"There's something really important I have to tell you!" said Irina. She paced around the room with her arms crossed. Raj motioned her to sit.

"Relax," he said. "I always have time for you, so first take a deep breath. Join me for a cup of tea. I needed to take a break anyway."

Irina stirred her hot, unsweetened Ceylon tea as she spoke. The tendrils of steam curled up from the cup and danced in the air.

"I saw him," Irina explained, "I mean really saw him. His face, too."

"He?"

"The man who killed my father," Irina explained, thumping the arm of her chair with a closed fist. "He is tall, and a weird thing, he has one green eye, and one blue. And there was this weird white patch on his forehead, like horses have. What do you think?"

"I think you've hit the jackpot," said Raj. "There are certain genetic traits that are linked. In this case the first one you mentioned is called heterochromia. The second is piebaldism. They're both uncommon and related to abnormal melanin deposition, but they're known to occur together sometimes. Let me alert Benito of this. I think you just found the needle in a haystack."

"How so?" asked Irina.

"If our suspect's DNA shows that he has both of these conditions, and he's six-foot-seven, there's basically no chance it could be anyone else," said Raj.

"You know, all this time, I thought I just wanted to forget," said Irina. "I thought that if I could wipe my memory clean, erase that night, I would find peace. But now I realize, my memory is there for a reason. Maybe I should not forget. No, there are things that must be done first, before I can rest. I will face him. I will testify."

"That's a heavy burden you choose to carry," said Raj. "Why? What would be the reason for holding on? Surely doing so is painful."

"So is childbirth, but if my mother hadn't endured it, I wouldn't be here," Irina replied. "If I hadn't gone through it, we wouldn't have our wonderful Lena. Maybe holding the pain is what we do for family, for the world."

"I grant that sometimes we sacrifice for the good of others," said Raj. "But why choose to testify?"

"I thought it was best to leave the police to look for my father's killer," Irina said. "After all, it's their job, not mine. But you are putting so much into this, and you do it for me, for Lena, and for my father. And now this memory, it must be a message. But not like, 'voices talking to me' or spirits or ghosts kind of message," she said. "I'm distressed, not crazy."

"Crazy is a relative term anyway," said Raj. He held her hands between his, rubbing them to warm them up. "But I wasn't suspecting you of losing touch with reality. Your mind is very clear and strong."

"It is like there is this force, this urgency within me that tells me I must help."

"Help how?"

"The police," said Irina. "They don't have the killer yet. I will tell them what I remember. Like you said, it could be very important."

"Yes," said Raj. "But how does aiding the investigation help you? That's what I care about."

"I don't know what's in it for me," said Irina. "But I still feel like I have to do it."

"It seems almost as if you're asking permission to tell the police what you know," said Raj.

"Not permission, no," said Irina, "but definitely your opinion and advice."

"I think you know me well enough to know I'll never tell you to go against the wishes of your heart," said Raj. "I just ask this, make sure you're doing what you want and need, not just what you think you are supposed to do. Do not do this for anyone else, even me."

"Thanks," said Irina with a smile, her shoulders relaxing from their somewhat hunched posture. She walked around the desk and sat down on his lap. She ran her fingernails over his scalp with the light scratching movement he loved. "I will."

She stood up and walked away and he stared at her as she walked down the sidewalk, her head upright, shoulders thrown back in defiance of the winds of ill fortune that had blown her way. Her grace and strength melded together into a formidable alloy. He marveled at how the furnace of tragedy that normally would melt a person had only served to further shape and polish her.

Irina walked through the precinct doors. She adjusted her purse and approached a male receptionist whose beady eyes were intently focused on a computer screen.

"Officer Benito Garcia, please," said Irina.

"Benito, there's a pretty lady asking for you," the office assistant called out.

As expected, Benito came running.

"Irina. I wasn't expecting to see you. Not that you're not beautiful. That's not what I meant. Anyway, come, let's talk."

They walked down a dimly lit hallway and opened a heavy, dark brown door. Benito motioned to Irina to sit, and they settled down at a table in the spare gray interview room.

"There is something I must tell you," said Irina. "Raj thinks it may be very important."

"OK, let's hear it." said Benito.

"He has different colored eyes," she blurted. "One blue, one green. And there was this white patch on his forehead. Raj says it is genetic. This has to be something, right?"

"I'm no pathologist, but a genetic marker would narrow things down considerably. Let's see if it lines up with the DNA and forensics."

"I want to testify," said Irina. "I'm ready now. I want to help put him away."

Benito folded his arms and sighed.

"You have a whole lot of guts. And I respect that, but damn! This guy's killed a bunch of people. Why choose to face him again?"

"Yes, he has killed many," she answered. Her upper lip trembled. "And one of them was my father. That's why I have to face him. I can't let my fear hold me back. I'm doing this for Papa, for Raj, for Lena. And I'm doing it for me."

Chapter Twenty-Four

Raj and Irina sat on the park bench underneath a cherry tree. Lena cavorted on the nearby play structures, jumping and skipping. She sang ad-libbed approximate rhymes and laughed as though they were the stuff of first-rate comedy.

"That's true happiness," said Irina.

"I hope she can always feel that way," said Raj.

"Me too," Irina replied, "Even though I know she will be visited by sadness in her life. It happens to us all. But why must it be that way?"

"Maybe without our troubles, we wouldn't appreciate each other," said Raj, pressing Irina's hands between his own. "Bitterness is the taste that makes us value honey."

Irina leaned over and kissed him on the cheek.

"You always know what to say to cheer me up," she said.

"That's easy when I believe it," Raj answered. He squeezed her hand. "I've come to understand that it's the truth. Without misfortune, I would not have met you. I would never have been introduced to your heart and soul and body. And my life would be the poorer for your absence from it."

"Hopefully our daughter will be wise and well-spoken like her dad," said Irina.

"I don't know if I am wise, but wisdom is nothing without strength and compassion. Thankfully she has you to show her these."

Lena ran up to her parents. She was cupping something between her two tiny palms.

"Mommy, Daddy, look what I found!" she shouted. She uncovered her lower hand carefully. "A ladybug."

"Make the best wish you can," Irina said, squeezing Lena's shoulders. "And blow her away."

Lena closed her eyes and blew on her hand, propelling the red and black creature into the windy sky.

As the sunlight expired outside his office window, Raj shuffled papers from an immigration case file. He was under pressure to complete the asylum application for a young lesbian woman fleeing persecution in Uganda. Deportation would be a death sentence. How could love be wrong? That was what she had asked him. She was right. He had vowed not to let her down, but precedent and the winds of jurisprudence were blowing against him. His argument appealed to human compassion as much as it did to legal doctrine. Even judges had hearts, and sometimes those organs could be used to move them in the direction of righteousness. As he finished his brief, Raj leaned back in his chair.

The sound of a loud knock on the door startled Raj. He had no further appointments. He was hoping to go home and see Lena before she went to bed. Since the case had started, they spent less time together, and he reproached himself for not being more present in her life.

"Come in," said Raj.

Benito opened the door. He held a thin blue folder in his hand.

"I've got some very interesting information. I think I've got a possible guy. His name is Lieutenant Andrei Orlov. He was actually born in Moscow, moved to the US at age three, speaks Russian. He's six-seven so he meets the height description. And when I looked over deaths in the areas in which he's lived in the past fifteen years, I came up with a total of ten homicides involving Russians that happened within a ten block radius of his past residences. The area covers two neighboring precincts, which may be what kept people in the dark."

"You think the killer knew precinct lines? That's pretty sophisticated, but it would go with the theory of the killer being connected with law enforcement," said Raj. "How do we know that was intentional? Ten murders is a ton. But why would Orlov be our guy? I admit it's a lot of carnage, but maybe he's just a guy who lived in some bad neighborhoods."

"Maybe, but he has seven reprimands for excessive force, was under investigation a couple of times, and was briefly suspended for a drinking problem," Benito replied.

Raj rose from his chair and walked to the window. He gazed out at the hazy streetlights that made the night air seem animated. "What about Meyerstein's profile. Was it on the money?"

"Well, the one part I'm not so sure about is what she said about him being intelligent and chronically angry," said Benito. "This guy has only a high school diploma, and he used to have some misconduct issues but he's cleaned up his act over the last five years. So if he's losing control in one way, he's improving it professionally. It could still fit though."

Raj fiddled with a pen, tapping it against the window sill in a rhythm that sounded like dripping water.

"Do we have any forensics linking him to the scenes?"

Benito shook his head. "Not that I can see. But we haven't exactly been rounding up cops for DNA tests."

"Let's keep an open mind," said Raj. "That genetic abnormality will be huge. I'm sure of it. But until we've connected the dots, let's not run down the wrong alley."

Raj sat at an empty table in the back corner of the Rio Tinto internet café. Benito's suspect could be the culprit, but Raj was unconvinced. What if the murders went back further in time? As the data changed, new patterns may emerge. He decided to explore records of murders in Foggy Bottom and surrounding areas going back twenty years.

There were two more killings that fit the profile. The victims were Russian. Most were shot to death in the same general area. In total this killer had left twelve bodies behind him. This meant more tragedy, but also more evidence, which left Raj feeling both sad and hopeful.

He searched through the demographic information of the five officers he identified earlier from the pool of IAB complaints. Two lived far outside the city, and a third was only on the job for three years before committing suicide. But in addition to Orlov, there was someone else to consider. Raj saved all the information to a flash drive, which he backed up with encrypted paper notes. He erased all traces of the search and signed off.

Raj walked down the street and sat down on a bench outside a small church. He pulled out his cellphone and dialed Benito.

"Raj, pleasant surprise to hear from you so soon," said Benito. "What's going on?"

"I've got some info I think you're going to want," said Raj.

"Lay it on me, Raj," Benito replied.

"There are a couple of cops you might want to check out," Raj offered. "I believe one of them might be responsible for up to twelve murders going back twenty years, not including Irina's father."

"Based on what evidence?" asked Benito.

"Physical evidence is your department. I'm all about information, which I've got my ways of acquiring. We're working side-by-side on this." Raj said. "Internet data says that one of the guys has resided within ten blocks of twelve murdered Russians in the past twenty years, and the other also could be of interest."

"Twelve? OK, that's interesting. I'd only found ten, but I wasn't looking back that far," Benito conceded. "But I need more. And back to you getting personally involved, I think that's a bad idea. Dude killed a dozen people, man."

"Thirteen if you count Alex," said Raj. "But I might be able to give you more motive than Meyerstein did. And speaking of motives, I sure as hell have one to bring this guy down."

"Raj, this guy could be more dangerous than anyone I've dealt with, and I'm a cop," said Benito. "You're out of your league. Police work is a process. You have to trust the experts."

"Last time I 'trusted the process' I watched my parents die in a hospital," said Raj . "Not going to let that happen again. And, all due respect, you can't stop me from doing what I have to do."

Benito sighed. "OK, Raj, since you are too bull-headed to listen to me, let's move on to your info."

"The first suspect is your guy," said Raj. "Andrei Orlov. Born in Moscow. Dad was Russian. Moved here at age three. Anger issues, disciplinary problems, drinker. I agree he's worth looking at."

"OK, that's something," Benito agreed. "But we have him on our radar. We'll definitely look into him. What about this other guy?"

"He's got more of a back story," said Raj. "Name's Billy Volk. I thought about what the shrink said, and this guy fits the profile to a T. His dad was Russian, and left his mom, who was German, soon after they came here. Dad took up with a Russian prostitute, while mom worked in a laundromat to make ends meet. Billy was a smart kid, lived with mom until he graduated from high school. He went to college at George Washington on a basketball scholarship, went to law school for a year but dropped out, then went to the academy. Dad eventually was convicted of child sexual abuse and died in prison, mom died of an OD. So we have the picture of a tightly-wound, intelligent guy with mommy and daddy issues and a large axe to grind against Russians."

"Whoa!" Benito exclaimed. "That's a hell of a motive. You've done well. You have copies of all this?"

"And look at his picture." Raj pointed to a snapshot.

Benito squinted at the photo and nodded. "Mismatched eyes and a white patch of skin on the forehead. If Irina's right, this is our guy."

"Problem is, eyewitness testimony is notoriously unreliable. You know that, I know that, and the defense attorney does too. They'll question the accuracy of a traumatized victim's testimony. We need something that can't be questioned or ignored. A smoking gun." Raj paused and sipped his tea. "And there's another potential problem."

"What's that?" Benito's scowled.

"Volk hasn't worked as a cop in years."

"So what does he do now that he's not a cop?"

"He's an ICE agent, anti-trafficking task force," said Raj. "You think that could have anything to do with what he said to Irina? Calling her a whore, saying he could make some money off her?"

"Maybe," said Benito. "But it's a big assumption."

"I don't think it's a leap to think that he's dirty," said Raj. "Wouldn't a guy who's capable of serial murder be capable of trafficking? We need to dig deeper."

"It's a good lead," said Benito. "Now let us follow it up, and keep your digging away from any landmines. OK?"

Raj and Irina strolled hand in hand by the Potomac. The trees lining the path bent toward them, puppets of a persistent breeze. Raj watched as Lena skipped and danced ahead.

"I'm sorry I've been so busy," said Raj. He massaged Irina's shoulders as they walked. "I haven't been making enough time for you and Lena. Sometimes I get so focused on what I think I have to do that I don't see the bigger picture outside myself. I get tunnel vision."

Irina stopped and faced him. She stroked her fingers down his cheek, then stretched up and kissed him.

"It has been hard, it's true," she said. "I miss you when you're working late. The bed is colder and lonelier without you. But living with a broken heart is also hard. At least this way, we are doing something to move forward. And that makes me feel like I am taking my life back."

"That's a relief," said Raj. "I don't ever want to disappoint you. Or worse, hurt you. You've survived enough. I don't want to be another obstacle."

"Like Papa used to say about me, 'Small but mighty'. I guess I'm tougher than I thought." Irina smiled. "Look at the sunlight sparkling on the river."

"Beautiful," said Raj. "Like you."

She cradled his head in her hands and deposited a soft kiss on his lips, then let her fingertips slide down his chin.

"I'm starting to really appreciate these views again," said Irina. She walked with him toward a railing that bordered the river. "For a time, everything seemed less alive. Dull and gray. Now I see the color."

"Back to how it used to be, before this whole investigation mess?" Raj asked.

"No," said Irina. "But I can feel the load lightening. This mess was always there. Without you I did not dare to clean it up. And when it's gone, I will feel better. Then my soul will be able to sing like my voice."

"You know, back in my old medical life, I remember the burn unit," Raj reflected. "It's hard to forget some of the screams you'd hear there. And the scars you'd see. But sometimes the only way for people to heal was this thing we called debridement."

"What's that?" Irina asked.

"Basically they keep washing off and cutting out skin that's dead or healing," said Raj. "It always seemed so unfair to have to keep them suffering with all they'd been through. But I convinced myself that this was necessary pain. I hope it was."

"Mine is like that," Irina agreed. "Necessary pain. And I will heal. I will be free."

They halted by the river, savoring the sweet odors of the flora and the dancing rays of light that glittered on the copper-hued water.

Raj scrolled through his copies of the case files. What was he missing? The first four victims, all male shared other demographic similarity beyond their nationality. Volk was at every crime scene either as the first on the scene or the lead investigator. The subsequent crimes had no obvious association with him.

Had he gone from being the first responder to allowing others to find the bodies? It could be that he wanted to prove his superiority to his colleagues. Or maybe Volk was pushing the envelope in hopes of being caught. The evidence drew Raj toward Volk as the killer. But evidence was not always what it seemed. He reminded himself to stay open to the idea of Orlov or an as yet unknown assailant as an alternate suspect. He remembered what his undergraduate biostatistics professor used to say: "Target fixation is the enemy of validity."

Raj perused the autopsy results. All were victims of repeated blunt-force trauma, though for some reason one had been shot as well. All had defensive wounds on their right forearms and wrists, suggesting that the killer swung left-handed. It was also suggested in the reports that the assailant must have swung the object from a considerable height.

He needed physical evidence. Anything tangible would help.

"Plastic shards," he read. "Found in the scalp."

This was something. But the next cases didn't have plastic shards. Was this a mistake by a killer who learned to refine his methods as he went on? There might be other gaffes. Dr. Thompson's aphorisms about careless lapses echoed in his head. "Lawsuits are rarely about what you do. They're about what you don't do." In medicine Raj had been trained to fear these "errors of omission." Now such gaffes gave him hope, for if humans didn't make them, police would have an impossible job.

He looked at the evidence from the first and second murders, and his heart nearly skipped a beat. There was a faint trace of blood on one body that didn't belong to the victim and skin and blue fibers found underneath two of the nails of a second victim. There was a dark hair found on one victim's right hand. Something was amiss here. He looked at the signatures on all the autopsies. They were the same: "Aloysius McGonigle, MD". Benito wondered what had become of the medical examiner. He had the impression that the M.E. might know something about the case. How had skin and blood evidence not been tested? Was this just a glaring example of evidence slipping through the cracks or was it ignored on purpose?

It would be challenging to find the doctor after so many years, but not impossible. It was time to make some calls.

A firm knock came at the door. Raj was not expecting visitors at nine o'clock in the evening, but the lateness of the hour posed no trouble for him. He had learned to maximize his work time, balancing the investigation with his usual client services at the expense of sleep.

"It's late, my friend. Burning the midnight oil?" asked Benito.

"Yeah, kind of obsessed with this lately. Sleep can wait," said Raj.

"You got time to talk? I think I have something you could help with," said Benito.

"Sure, come in," Raj offered, motioning Benito to the kitchen. "Everybody's upstairs. So what is it you need?"

"I'm not sure what I've got, but maybe something," said Benito. "Can you find a Dr. Aloysius McGonigle?"

"The former medical examiner?" Raj asked. "I've been seeing his name on the first few files. What do you think he knows? You think he was pressured into ignoring the evidence?"

"Maybe, maybe not," Garcia said. "Either that or he's in cahoots with our murderer. One thing's for certain. Only he knows the answer. I got nothing on him since the case reports. No address, no phone records, no employment information. Nada."

"On it right away," said Raj.

Chapter Twenty-Five

Raj and Benito strolled toward the wooded Virginia lakefront. As they approached a short gray pier, Raj spied a diminutive gentleman with sallow, wrinkled skin in a frayed plaid shirt. The old man jumped to attention as they walked up the pier.

"Don't think I've ever seen you guys around here, friend. Fact is, I hardly ever see anyone out here," said the old man. "How can I help you?"

They walked to the dock's end and Benito flashed his badge. He reached down and helped the old man tie up his silver metal boat.

"Benito Garcia, MPD. This here is my friend Raj Patel. He used to be one of you."

"Former doctor, eh? Well, whatever the reason you're here, I do appreciate the help. These joints are not young and spry anymore. How did you find me?"

"Nowadays, with the internet and guys like my friend here, nobody's off the radar," said Benito.

"I'll give it to you straight," said Raj. "We need your expertise to solve some cold cases, doctor."

"Doctor, heh," said McGonigle. "Nobody's called me that in quite some time. Most folks call me Al these days. Still got my license, though. Used to be when they called me 'doctor' it was because they wanted something. So, what is it you fellas want?"

Benito pulled a sheaf of papers from a dog-eared green folder. He handed them to McGonigle and waited.

McGonigle's facce changed. He shook his head as he looked down toward the dock's planks and pillars.

"Ah, these cases. Never did sit right with me. You see, I saw the first two cases and suggested that we had a serial killer on our hands, I suggested that they pursue the cases as such."

"So, what happened?" Benito asked.

"The investigating officer, Volk, convinced his superiors that it wasn't worth going after a serial killer based on two cases," said McGonigle. He became more animated and waved his hands like rotors in the air. "Just a couple Russians, he said to me. It was weird, like he didn't want to solve the cases. Especially strange since he was usually gung-ho. Quite honestly, he scared me."

"So, what about the next two?" Benito asked. "Just dropped it?"

"I still believe to this day that all four had the same killer, but again, Volk convinced them it was just a coincidence," said the doctor, shaking his head. "Never could explain the hair, the plastic, the skin. It bothered me that it didn't match any known criminals, but I was told to drop it. I had enough of guys like him overruling me, and I figured maybe it was time to retire awhile afterwards. But it's been years. What brings you guys all the way out here after all this time?"

"We've been combing through some cold cases. Our information suggests he's struck several times since you retired," said Benito.

"One of those victims was my wife's father," Raj explained. "He was my friend, as well."

"So this is personal for you, young man," said McGonigle. McGonigle offered his shaky hand, and he clasped it, Raj felt the doctor's fragility in his thin bones and clammy, blue-veined skin. "You have my deepest sympathy and my undivided attention."

"For certain reasons, we've been very quiet on this. We believe the killer is, shall we say, 'connected'," said Benito.

"Connected?" McGonigle asked. His eyebrows rose, as did his voice. "A cop?"

Raj shook his head to indicate assent. "That or someone similar."

"Volk?" McGonigle hissed. "I knew something was wrong, but I didn't know what. The sociopathic bastard played me. Never liked him. Never trusted him. He always seemed to have his own agenda. He was smart as a whip, but ruthless. He was a lone wolf, and not in a good way."

"Interesting you would mention him," said Garcia. "He's one of our two prime suspects, along with another cop named Orlov. I'd make myself more scarce until we catch whoever this guy is," Benito warned. "If he figures out we're onto him, you'd be a loose end."

"Appreciate the warning," the old doctor replied. He pulled a business card out of his pocket. "I may be in my golden years, but I'm in no hurry to see them end."

McGonigle handed the card to Benito. It was yellowed around the edges, bearing the doctor's embossed name and credentials in bold italicized letters.

"If you need my help, young fella, I'm glad to offer it," said McGonigle. "After all, I kind of feel like this blood is on my hands. Maybe if I'd persisted, if I hadn't been so willing to take orders. I like to be clean. My mother used to say, 'There's no sure path to Heaven, but a clean life sure helps'. And this, well this is a stain I need to erase."

"I will definitely keep you in mind," Benito replied.

As they walked back to his car, Raj spoke.

"Plastic shards, fibers, skin. All well and good, but we still need more."

"If it's out there, we'll get it," said Benito. "Just a matter of time."

As Irina and Lena slept and a gentle wind blew the branches of trees in a swaying dance, Raj pored over his computer. He decided to scramble any trace of his IP address. The information he was looking for was sensitive, and if the killer got a whiff he would not hesitate to respond.

Once assured that he had masked his online identity, Raj attempted to access Orlov and Volk's bank accounts. His first two attempts were met with the dreaded phrase "Access Denied". It was time to engage some specialized software.

"I'm in," said Raj to the emptiness surrounding him.

How far back should he go? Too much data could make the picture unclear, smearing it like a forest seen from space. He would start with ten years.

Orlov was a mess. His accounts were in the red more often than not, often related to heavy gambling losses, rehab expenses, and alimony payments. This didn't seem to go with the picture of a smart, calculating individual.

Raj turned his attention to Volk. For a few years his income and expenditures were unremarkable. Volk got his paycheck, paid his rent and had few extra expenses. The one oddity was a sprinkling of payments to an an entity called "Lynx Inc.". A few clicks showed that Lynx was a local escort service. As much as Volk denounced prostitutes, he clearly enjoyed their company.

The next six years showed another recurring payment. This one came in to Volk's account on the same day of each month. At $10,000, the amount was enough to provide a comfortable nest egg for Volk, yet he did not seem the type to be interested in a lavish lifestyle. The amount increased to $15,000 when Volk joined ICE. That couldn't be a coincidence.

"Cherkasov Industries, let's see who you are," said Raj.

The answer was murky but intriguing. The company appeared to have many tentacles that spread widely into the real estate, transportation, and energy industries. The owners were nouveau-riche Muscovites who often made the society pages in European papers. Why did they need to get their hands dirty with an American immigration officer?

Perhaps the Cherkasovs were involved in international smuggling. If that were the case, Volk was a perfect conduit for their illicit commerce.

Café Lyon fell short of its pretentious name. The rustic establishment featured bitter coffee and uninspired baked goods. But the low quality of the menu was offset by the café's intimate environment. At the moment privacy trumped culinary virtue.

"Hey, Raj, thanks for meeting me here." said Benito. "Any progress?"

"I've been going through our two suspects' digital and financial footprints," said Raj. "And it looks like I found something. Orlov's spending almost all his checks at casinos and massage parlors. So he's impulsive, but he's living hand to mouth. He gets nothing but his salary. Volk, on the other hand, gets a monthly stipend from a company called Cherkasov Ltd.

It looks like a shell corporation with its fingers in everything from soup to nuts. I suspect there may be an organized crime component. But they've got a sprawling, tangled network, so I'll need you to make some inquiries."

"I can do that," said Benito, "While you're at it, I have another request if you're up for it."

"You name it." Raj answered. "I'm all in."

"Can you locate someone who's dropped off the grid and doesn't want to be found?" asked Benito.

"Of course I can." said Raj. He hoped he wasn't overreaching with his promise, but there was no turning back now. "I've told you. I can find any sort of information you need, simple or complex, why?"

"There's a name, a Natasha Semenova, who might be important to the case," said Benito.

"Girlfriend of one of the victims, may have seen the killer," said Raj. "I remember reading the file. She was a graduate student at George Washington, was supposed to give a statement, but never showed up."

"Yeah. Problem is, nobody knows where she is," said Benito. "She may have changed her name. If she's alive, it's possible she's not in the country at all."

"I see your dilemma," Raj observed. "You're looking for someone whose name you're not sure of, and you need someone with skills and discretion. This is right up my alley."

Raj paced the length of his office as he considered the accumulating data. A solution must be close at hand, but he still couldn't see it. Who was Natasha Semenova and what connected her to the case? Whatever the relationship may be, he sensed that Benito was closing in on some answers. Though this should have been a great comfort to him, it was not. He craved the completeness of comprehensive data, and there were too many holes here.

Raj grabbed a half-empty jar of peanut butter and dipped a plastic spoon into it. As he sucked the sticky brown paste off the white spoon he considered what the meaning of the case. It was about loyalty: to the legacy of his dead friend, to his wife, to his principles. Raj imagined the frightful apparitions that yanked Irina's body upright in the middle of the night. If he had been there with them, he could have stopped it. The pragmatist in him argued that they would be no closer to a resolution and both he and Irina would share the same torment. The internal debate did nothing to assuage his restlessness.

Raj pored over the data that streamed across the computer screen. It was evident that Benito was correct. There was no trace of Natasha Semenova in the US after the date of the murder. Had she vanished, or was she another victim? Raj considered her profession. He knew enough about academic research to recognize that scientists live and die by their publication history. What Social Security and the IRS couldn't tell him, PubMed and Ovid might.

Within a few hours his search proved fruitful. Natasha Semenova was now Natasha Volquez, living in Cuba and continuing her work on disorders of collagen synthesis. Her publication list was prolific. He felt happy for her that she had put the horrors of the past behind her and moved on. He wished the same for Irina, even if the process may take time.

He deliberated over the letters beneath his fingers. He needed Natasha to trust him. He was no wordsmith. How could he convince her to share information she would probably rather forget? The truth would have to do. If Natasha hesitated to divulge information on her own behalf, he hoped she could do it for those who shared her pain.

Greetings from Washington DC, N. I can only begin to imagine what this horrible man has done to your life. I can tell you what he has done to my wife's, and perhaps you will understand why I have become obsessed with bringing him down.

Alex, my wife's father, was a kind and gentle Ukrainian man. He saved me from a life of tragedy and insanity, quite literally. Unfortunately, when we were living in a church shelter, immigration came, and he and Irina had to leave in a hurry. While they were away, this man attacked Irina and Alex and killed Alex as Irina watched. I have forever felt responsible for not being there, for not doing something, and my wife has had nightmares and sees a therapist ever since reading an article about the man in the Post. It appears he has killed many others. Our daughter asks why Mommy cries. How does one explain this? I imagine perhaps you know what Irina experiences. If you have anything that could be of assistance, I'm begging you to help us.

Raj sat outside the high-rise apartment building. It was gray, drab and forbidding. If Volk did in fact live here, it seemed a suitable habitat for such a silent but voracious predator. Raj glanced up at the window of the apartment registered to Volk. It was time to shake the killer's tree and see what fell out. But how should he do this without being sucked into the whirlpool of death that surrounded Volk? He had decided to drop a note outside the officer's door. As he left the car he donned latex gloves and rummaged through a garbage can to find a magazine and a sheet of paper. He returned to the car and cut out letters, which he glued one by one on the paper: "WE KNOW".

If this didn't rattle Volk's cage, the voice-distorted message he left at Volk's ICE office should. Raj had not informed Benito of his freelancing. It would be better to ask forgiveness than permission. But now that the deed was done it was only fair that Benito should be brought up to date.

He called and explained how he had baited Volk.

"You what?!" Benito yelled. "Are you crazy? Are you suicidal?"

"I called him, but no way he traces it to me," said Raj. "With all the gadgetry I used to distort my voice and re-route the call and all. And don't ask how I did all that. Better you don't know."

"OK, I won't," Benito agreed. "But I've got another question. What the hell were you thinking? Messing with a killer? A serial killer, no less. I appreciate your planning and information gathering. The picture's getting clearer. But we can't go off-script on stuff like this. We have no idea what he'll do now."

"Well, you want to catch him, right?" Raj retorted. "I thought maybe we should smoke him out, get him off his game. Nothing ventured, nothing gained."

"Of course, but you're no cowboy," Benito admonished his friend. "This ain't the movies. Plus, I don't know how many times I've told you, it's dangerous. You've got a wife and kid to think about. Leave this to the professionals."

"Listen, between you, and me, I figure we can track this guy and maybe he'll lead us to the evidence you need," said Raj. He sipped Assam tea from an oversized mug. Its astringent character served to heighten his focus on difficult problems. "And with multiple people following him, we can make the pressure on him seem greater and less predictable."

"And what do you suppose he'll do under pressure," asked Benito. "Crack? Confess? Throw himself on the table and beg for mercy like some crime-show villain?"

"No," said Raj. "But one thing life has taught me. Pressure creates errors. No matter who you are, how smart or cunning, nobody thinks as well when the heat is on."

"You're right, but lay low, OK? We haven't officially eliminated Orlov," Benito ordered his friend. "You need to let us work the other aspects of the case and we just might find that mistake, whatever it may be."

"Fine, I'll be good and stay out of the way," Raj knew Benito needed the assurance, but was unsure that he could keep his promise.

Chapter Twenty-Six

Raj scanned the subject line of a mysterious e-mail. "Tragedy never dies," it read. His pulse quickened.

"It seems we have something very much in common. Both of us lost someone special to a very evil man. In my case, Slava was the love of my life. I have been running and hiding from the killer for several years, but upon hearing what he's done, I decided to contact you. Obviously, I am concerned that this might be a trick, so please tell me something more about you. N."

He inspected the e-mail. It was possible this might be a ruse to get him to reveal himself. In a few frenzied keystrokes he traced the IP address To Santo Domingo. N. must be Natasha. From Cuba it wouldn't be unreasonable for her to travel to Santo Domingo. He saw no evidence of masking or spoofing. The message was not a trap. Raj determined would e-mail "N." back. Just for safety's sake, though, do it from a library, university, or internet café, and wipe out all traces of this communication from his computer.

Raj jogged to a local community college. He sat in the computer lab at the library, sipping a Chai tea whose strong clove flavor remained uncorrupted by milk or sugar. The blustery eastern winds cut across courtyards and trees. Raj weighed his words before his fingers hit the keys. The wrong message could drive Natasha away.

He resolved to let his heart compose the message. This would be both the most effective way to enlist Natasha and also the most honest.

He gasped for air and his hands shook as he sent the e-mail. His heart palpitated for what seemed like a few minutes. He drew a few deep breaths, dabbed his eyes with a tissue, rose and ambled toward the door. The cold wind leaked through the frame of the door, jolting him fully awake from the anxiety-laden trance into which he had sunk while writing.

Dear Natasha,

Thank you for contacting me. I can only imagine how hard it was for you to do so. In light of the nature of this case, I understand your wariness. I'm an immigration lawyer by trade, but I'm helping to direct the police investigation. If you want to verify my identity, you can look me up online. I have a contact at the police department, Officer Benito Garcia, who is a personal friend, and very trustworthy. If you'd prefer to avoid the police contact, which I certainly understand, feel free to mail me at 69815 Cherry St., PO Box 9875, Washington DC 20211.

It was a bold move, fraught with risk and uncertainty. He sensed that Natasha had something very important to contribute, but she had absconded for a reason. There was no guarantee that she could be persuaded to return to the States. He imagined her enduring Irina's flashbacks and nightmare states. The idea made his head sag toward the ground. The wanton destruction of women's lives done by evil men lasted far too long. But maybe Natasha would change that. Could she be the bearer of consequence, the noose that would hang Volk? The thought pleased him and his head swung upward as he headed into the brisk wind. Vengeance should be the property of all survivors.

Raj and Irina walked along the sidewalk, past the trees that sent out their distinctive cherry blossom fragrance. They clasped their hands together and swung them in a lazy rhythm, walking in silence block after block.

"A penny for your thoughts," said Irina. "You're so mysterious."

"Just thinking about this case," said Raj. "We ran into this company called Cherkasov Ltd. I'm trying to figure out what it is."

Irina jerked her hand away. All vestiges of color drained from her cheeks.

"Cherkasov?" she asked. "Andrei Cherkasov? He is a monster. He says he is 'businessman', but he is just criminal with fancy toys."

"How do you know him?" asked Raj. "Is he one of Tolya's guys?"

"More like Tolya is one of his guys," said Irina. "Everyone at the club fears him. They give him anything he wants. He did this to me." She raised her right sleeve and pointed to a long, thin scar across that spanned three ribs. "And that was nothing compared to what he did to others."

Raj felt a hot wave of anger wash through him.

"What horrible things you've had to endure," he said, running his fingers through her hair. "He sounds like a very bad and very powerful man."

"He is," said Irina. "Any crime you can imagine, he has a hand in it. But trafficking is his specialty. Drugs, sex, farm slaves. He has connections everywhere. Even government officials are afraid of him. He makes his money on the blood and sweat of other people. And I was one of them. You think he is involved in father's killing?"

"Not directly," said Raj. "But from what you've told me before, the killer may be involved in trafficking. So there could be a link."

They turned and walked back toward the house, arms linked, eyes locked on one another.

"I can't let him do what was done to me," said Irina. "What if he's already doing it, here in DC? Maybe that's why the killer said what he did to me. I have to tell Benito. We have to stop him. I cannot undo what happened but I can prevent my past from becoming someone else's future."

The unassuming package was wrapped in brown paper with a snug layer of bubble wrap underneath. There was no return address. Raj tapped the outside of the package and deemed it safe. As he opened the wrapping, he read an artfully handwritten note.

"This man has caused enough pain. I think this might be the evidence that stops him. Please accept my prayers for your wife. One day I hope to offer my condolences in person. Sincerely, N."

Raj called Benito in such a hurry that his fingers fumbled through the process of speed-dialing his phone. He wasted no time in blurting out the news.

"I have something you'll like," he announced. "Natasha Semenova has sent me some forensic evidence. Come quickly, but not to my place."

Benito sped to an empty office building around the corner from Raj's PO Box. He accosted Raj as though questioning a suspect, so as not to arouse any suspicion of improper collaboration. Raj handed off the sealed plastic-wrapped package and Benito placed it into a small evidence bag, peeking at the contents as the exchange took place.

Benito and Raj discussed appropriate locations to get the evidence tested. Using a police lab in Washington was a dicey proposition. The killer might be on the lookout. But they knew a medical examiner, independent and out of state but approved by the city, one with a low profile and a stake in uncovering the truth.

"I wonder how the weather in Norfolk is this time of year," Raj mused as they drove away.

"What do you think the killer's figured out?" Raj asked. "Do you think he's even worried about being caught?"

"Don't worry man, we'll get him. This guy was on a mission of anger. And as my old partner Tommy used to say, 'Anger makes an eagle-eyed man blind'. Been the reason for us solving a lot of cases. The killer gets so focused on hate that they forget to cover their tracks."

"I hope so," said Raj. "Irina needs this. I need it."

"We'll get him." said Benito. "I owe you that much. You're the reason I could read well enough to pass the tests at the police academy. Don't ever underestimate how much that means to me, hermano."

"It's all good," Raj answered. And it was, for the moment.

Benito drove for a few hours until they arrived at the outskirts of town. He pulled up to a roadside café. The converted red barn featured a simple, yellowed signboard that announced, "DINER, open 24-7".

"It's 4:00. I need to recharge. You having anything?" asked Benito. "Man's gotta eat."

"I'm OK," Raj answered. "My stomach's all knotted up. But I'll have some tea."

They stopped at the counter. Benito ordered black coffee and a slice of apple pie. Raj ordered black tea with lemon.

"Apple pie and coffee. What a combination. Maybe it's all because of my mom's home-brewed café de olla, brewed with whole cinnamon sticks. The taste of the cinnamon in the pie, the strong coffee. Mmm, that's good!" he commented as he devoured a forkful of pie.

"Great memories," said Raj.

After their late afternoon snack, Raj and Benito headed into the dusk. Eventually Benito rolled his car into the wooded lake area where he had first spoken to the old medical examiner. A light turned on in the cabin, and a hand parted the curtains. As they approached the cabin, Raj saw the barrel of an antique shotgun pointed at the window.

"Put down the gun, doctor, we come in peace," he shouted from several yards away. The gun barrel moved away from the window and the old door hinges soon creaked open.

"Didn't your parents teach you not to sneak up on an old man?" McGonigle scolded them. "Could've given me a heart attack! Been a lot jumpier since you told me about Volk on the prowl. So, what can I do you for? Coffee, beer, information?"

"Pass on the first two," Benito replied with a wave. "But I have something for you that I think might help us with the murder investigation." He produced the package, still sealed, and handed it to the old man, whose hands started to shake as he regarded the evidence.

"Where did you get this?" McGonigle's eyes widened as he looked at his visitors. "Do you know how big this might be?"

"I do, and that's why I couldn't trust the DC forensics people with it," said Benito. "So, I thought of you. You said your license was still active?"

"Aye, it is," McGonigle commented. "But I've got no lab. Still, I'll see what I can do, and I've still got some friends who can do a lot with this. In the meantime, I'll take some, but you hold on to some of it as well. Chain of custody and all that."

"You may want to consider getting out of town, Doctor," Benito suggested.

"At my age, you can only run so long," McGonigle replied. "You know what karma is? Well, I believe in it, and if he gets me, maybe I will have deserved it. I should have stopped him."

McGonigle pressed Raj's hand between his two bony palms. "Thank you for giving me the chance to make amends," he said.

"No, thank you," said Raj.

The quiet afternoon was interrupted by a familiar sound. The incoming number was familiar.

"Bad news my friend," said Benito. "He just struck again".

"Oh my God," said Raj. "What makes you think that?"

"McGonigle's dead," said Benito. "They found him floating in his rowboat. Beaten to death. Damn, we warned him about this. I just, I guess I was hoping the killer wouldn't connect the dots so damn fast. Volk's a time bomb, and this proves it. Stay out of sight. You've been a big help, but we just spoke with McGonigle last week, and now he's dead. So you see why I'm saying, don't mess with this guy again. Please, I couldn't live with the guilt if he did something to you."

The news hit Raj like a blow to the head. He staggered sideways and caught himself on a wall. As he gathered his thoughts, he was flooded by a surge of guilt.

"It was me, wasn't it?" said Raj. "I shouldn't have messed with Volk. But I baited him. And now McGonigle's dead. Another innocent life sacrificed."

"It's true you shouldn't have gone rogue," said Benito. "But don't blame yourself for the actions of a guy like this. He kills because he likes it, because he thinks he is above the law. That's not on you. But from here on out, please, stay in your lane."

"I get it. I'm a family man, a lawyer, not a cop," said Raj. "And please follow your own advice. This guy sounds like he's only getting more dangerous."

"Trust me, I know," said Benito. "And to think he's one of my kind, a cop. It's hard to swallow. And it makes me extra concerned. He knows how we work and he keeps going. It won't be easy to stop him. But you have my word, we will."

As he said goodbye, Raj mulled the case. The killer may have known about the medical examiner's suspicions. If he knew this, what else would he be motivated to do? Volk may be feeling trapped, and a cornered predator is the most destructive force of nature.

Irina sat quietly at the table across from Benito and his boss, Sergeant Daniels.

"I brought the sarge with me today," said Benito. "I hope you don't mind, but he needs to hear your information."

"Would you like some coffee?" asked the Sergeant. His voice rumbled like distant thunder across cracked lips.

"No thanks," said Irina. "I might as well get to it. Raj told me he found some links in your case to a guy named Cherkasov. I know this man."

"Surely there are many Cherkasovs in your country," said Daniels. "How do you know this is him?"

"Andrei Cherkasov buys and sells whatever and whoever can make him money," said Irina. "I used to work for someone who worked for him. He was, how do you call it here, a pimp?"

"This can't be easy for you," said Benito. "Take your time."

Irina shook her head and waved away the tissues offered by the sergeant. Pity was not what she sought.

"We don't have time," she said. "The man who attacked me and killed me father. He spoke of making money from me. He saw my tattoo and knew what it meant. And now Cherkasov is connected to him. Don't you see? The killer . . . he's one of them."

She shifted her gaze between Benito and Daniels. It wasn't clear that they believed her.

"Let me show you something," she said. Irina carefully undid her blouse to reveal the tattoo under her armpit. "If you ask someone, they'll tell you this is how people like Cherkasov track their property. And that's what I was. What the killer thinks I still am."

"I can't imagine the horrors you've seen," said Benito, grimacing.

"I would not want you to," said Irina. "It takes so much time and energy to put those memories back in the closet. And they still don't always stay there."

"We'll follow up on this," said the sergeant.

"Don't just follow up. Catch him."

Irina picked up her purse and cleared an unruly strand of hair from her face before exiting the station. Did they take her information seriously, would it be shoved aside? Let them do with it what they saw fit. An honest voice must never be afraid to speak, or even to shout if necessary. Confronted with the enormity of fear's long shadow, Irina refused to be quiet.

Raj and Irina sat at the kitchen table. She leaned over and ladled a serving of borscht into his bowl.

"I don't like this," Lena complained.

"Vegetables are good for you," said Irina. "And besides, you have to eat them to get dessert, remember?"

Lena nodded and sighed.

"Mama takes good care of us all," said Raj. He gestured at the bowl. "Eat up."

The meal was interrupted by a knock at the door. Raj looked out and saw Benito standing on the porch.

"Come in," he said. "Why are you smiling?"

"Turns out McGonigle made preparations," Benito answered. "So whatever files Volk may have gotten are useless. And McGonigle passed the real info on to a pathologist at FBI labs."

"No chain of custody issues?" Raj asked. "Don't want to give this guy a sliver of an opening."

Benito shook his head.

"Dr. Lee says everything was done by the book. And it gets better."

"Spit it out, man" said Raj. "Don't leave me hanging here."

"We have Volk's DNA at the McGonigle crime scene, which probably hangs him for McGonigle's murder. And it has the genetic traits you told me to ask the pathologist about, so he looks like the guy who killed Alex. And it matches evidence from two early scenes, so if we can get a little more, he's facing multiple counts for the previous crimes," said Benito. "This is great news, no?"

"Yeah, I guess it is," said Raj. "I just wish nobody else had to die for our cause. I feel like maybe I goaded Volk into this."

"Don't," said Benito. "Don't go there. He chose to stay and help us, and we owe him many thanks. You gotta figure he knows what loose ends he might have left. It was a matter of time before he went after the doctor."

"I guess. I just wish I could say thanks to the old man face to face. He made the ultimate sacrifice."

"That he did. And we're going to make that mean as much as we can."

"Now that there's a single suspect, it should be easier."

"What do you think we should do next ?" asked Benito.

Raj clasped his hands together.

"I'm going to see if we can get a visual on Volk."

Benito's eyes opened wide. "You talking about surveillance? How? We need a warrant."

"Correction," said Raj. "You need a warrant. If you happen to get some anonymous information, who's to say where it came from?"

"You're going to give me a heart attack," said Benito. "And I'm too young and handsome to die."

Raj chuckled. "I agree with the 'young' part. But don't worry. I've got it planned out. He won't know what hit him. If I need backup, I'll call you."

Raj dialed Benito's phone. There was no answer so he left a message: "Project Eagle Eye is underway."

Raj entered the lobby of Volk's apartment building. Today he wasn't Raj Patel, Esq. Instead he assumed the mantle of Tariq Aziz, realtor. Irina was his co-agent, Larisa Korobkova. Raj was a pragmatic man. The ends didn't always justify the means, but given what he and Irina sought to accomplish, a small prevarication was easy to rationalize.

"I'd really like to see unit 318," said Raj. "I'm Tariq. I called ahead?"

The doorman furrowed his brow.

"Nobody told me anything about this," he said.

"Please, we came all the way from Fairfax County," said Irina.

"Well, I guess it can't hurt," said the doorman, who accompanied them to the unit and unlocked the door. "Just make sure to lock up when you leave, please. Never can be too careful these days."

As the door closed behind them, Raj made notes on the room's layout.

"We'll need to get the cameras in those vents," he said, pointing to air conditioning vents in the wall that bordered the neighboring unit. "Beyond that wall is where Volk lives. We have a saying here, 'A picture is worth a thousand words'. And these cameras can get us some nice pictures.

"I can get them in," said Irina. She smiled. "For once being small is a good thing."

When the cameras were installed, Raj watched from his computers at home and in the office. Days came and went, and there was no movement. The closet full of uniforms and blue shirts and pants hung undisturbed. Then Volk arrived. Raj noticed his eyes, his elongated frame, and the pale patch of skin on his forehead. He was just as Irina had described him. And he wasn't alone.

"Don't try anything," Raj heard him say to a petite brunette, one of two women accompanying him. As Raj looked closer he saw a tattoo under the woman's arm. Volk handcuffed her to the radiator and took the other woman, a statuesque bottle blonde, to his bedroom.

"Shit!" Raj whispered. "Time to call in the cavalry."

Chapter Twenty-Eight

Raj sat at Benito's desk, his legs crossed.

"You get my video," he asked.

"I did," said Benito. "Turns out Irina was right. I recognized those girls. They work for a Russian-owned agency. Thanks to your information, I traced it back to Cherkasov. And if they're with Volk, he's into this up to his neck. Too bad that tape isn't admissible in court."

"Yeah, but maybe if he brings the girls to his home, he's brought other stuff too," said Raj. "The weapons weren't found. Maybe that's for a reason."

"You think he'd be that stupid?" said Benito. "Wouldn't he have gotten rid of the slugs if he dug them out? Would he have used a service weapon?"

"Don't know," said Raj. "But I sure as hell would like to find out. He's a control freak, right? So maybe he can't risk having the evidence where it's out of sight. Let's hope so. What we need is a damn warrant for his apartment."

"Let me get this straight," said Benito. "You think a criminal mastermind is hiding evidence in his own place? And if it comes up empty, then haven't we shown our hand?"

"If he thinks he's in the clear, what better place to make sure he's in control of the evidence?" said Raj. "Not saying he does have it. But sometimes smart people make really stupid mistakes."

"Do we even have enough to get that warrant?" Benito asked. "I mean, I'd love to surprise that bastard and get him for all the murders, but all we have is DNA and some shards that may or may not come from his nightstick. For a regular case that would be plenty, but do you think it would be enough to arrest Volk?"

"As you know, the threshold for a warrant depends on the judge," said Raj. "Some of them would never want to be the one who served a warrant on a police officer. Too scared it will blow back on them. But some of these guys are climbers, looking for a bigger, brighter future. Those guys would just love to root out a dirty cop. Especially if they're thinking of higher office."

"Sounds like you have a guy in mind," Benito observed. "Do I know him?"

"If you read the papers, you do," said Raj. "Judge Marcus Wallace. He's ambitious, angling for the senate. Made his name taking on corruption. He's very pro-immigration and anti-trafficking. We've worked together in the past. Let me go with you and you'll get that warrant."

"Nameplate on the door says Hon. Marcus Wallace," Benito called out. "We must be in the right place."

Raj knocked on the door to the judge's chambers.

"Come in," said Judge Wallace. He was a scholarly looking man with a long, steep forehead, light brown skin and lively dark eyes. "Mr Patel. It's a pleasure to see you again. What can I do for you and your friend in blue?"

"We need a warrant, Your Honor," said Garcia.

"Eager young fella, gets right to the point, eh?" said Wallace. "I like that. Tell me about the case and what you have."

"What we have is an officer named Billy Volk. His DNA is at the scene of one of the early Russian murders, and also the murder scene of the former medical examiner," said Raj. "All told, if we're right, he could be responsible up to fourteen deaths. We also have a strong suspicion he's involved in sex trafficking: he's been receiving regular payments from a notorious Russian mega-criminal named Cherkasov. We're looking for a final nail."

"Ah, and you came to me because you know I'm not scared to piss off the police, is that right?" said Judge Wallace. He laughed. "It's OK. I don't mind that reputation. No great change ever comes without ruffling feathers, am I right?"

"I can't lie, Your Honor," said Raj. "Your reputation does precede you."

"McGonigle and the Russian murders? Connected?" Wallace asked. "Very interesting. Al McGonigle was a friend of mine. An honorable man. I'll give you a warrant for Volk's house and any vehicles or outbuildings. Safe deposit boxes or other off-site facilities aren't covered by this, OK?"

"Thank you, Your Honor," said Benito. He smiled and shook hands with the judge. "When we get Volk off the streets, DC will be better for it. We'll be strictly by the book. We want this guy as much as you do, maybe more considering what his actions do to the image of our shield."

"Well said," the judge agreed. "Good day."

The pounding at the door was sudden and loud, puncturing the quiet evening with the effect of a dart hitting a black balloon.

Billy Volk walked over to the window and peered out into the dimly lit air. He saw two police cruisers parked flanking the fire escape and an officer squinting up into the sky by the door. His stomach sank as he realized the game was drawing to an end.

"Police! Open up!"

He heard voices murmuring on the other side of the door.

"MPD," one of them said. "Don't make us bust in there. We have a warrant to search your place."

Volk opened the door. This was getting uncomfortable. He'd taken precautions but never anticipated a search of his residence. He wasn't prepared for this level of intrusion.

Volk watched as the team of officers perused his kitchen, the living room, and the closets. They turned over his linens, cut into his mattress, searched behind the vents. They wouldn't find anything there. The girls were safely stowed. Could it be that his colleagues would go away empty-handed?

A senior officer picked up the couch cushions. He shook and then unzipped them.

"Any of you happen to have a knife?" he called out. "I think I heard something."

A junior officer brought him a small utility knife.

"This seam, in the padding, cut through there," he instructed. "That seam between the halves of the filling shouldn't be there. Something's stuffed inside."

"There's something in here!" the junior officer shouted. With gloved hands he extracted eight bullets, all with faint but visible traces of blood remaining on them.

"What about the car?" the senior officer asked. "Anything there?"

A baby-faced Latino officer burst into the apartment. Having eschewed the elevator for the long stairwell he breathed heavily as he held an evidence bag aloft.

"Look what I found," he declared, staring Volk in the eye. In the bag were the nightstick and the old .40 caliber Glock that was his service weapon until the department upgraded to .45 calibers. He had them locked away in the car, in a self-made compartment next to the spare. He was such a careful driver that he assumed the weapons would never be found. And here they were, taunting him.

"There's more," said the baby-faced officer. "Look who we found in the storage shed."

A female officer ushered in two women. Their wrists bore the visible rope burns, and they recoiled at the sight of Volk.

Volk's legs quivered. He looked at the window, which was unguarded with everyone focused on sweeping for evidence. He glanced out at the street and tried to make plans. Logic told him that running was futile, but at the moment fear trumped logic.

The sunlight glinted off the ice crystals on the fire escape. It was narrow, rusty, and probably not fit to hold a large man's weight. The broken ladder ended in a jagged point just below the second floor window. Billy figured it for an eight-to-ten foot drop from there.

He could hear the door cracking as he slid the window open and stepped out into the frosty air. He dropped off the ladder and threw the two smaller officers that followed to the ground, kicking them with the heel of his shoe as he ran past. His legs could still cover ground in a hurry. He turned a corner, but the officers stayed close. Soon he began to regret the years of nicotine that had eroded his cardiovascular endurance, and he saw the others approaching.

A baton cracked into his ribcage, knocking him to the ground. He moaned and rolled over. Two officers loomed over him, with another three standing behind them.

"Cuff him Benito," said the senior officer to the baby-faced officer.

"Boris Volkov, Billy Volk, or whatever you call yourself, you are under arrest for the murders of Alex Petrov, Aloysius McGonigle . . ." said Benito.

Volk was stunned to hear the charges.

"On what grounds? What evidence could you possibly have?" he sputtered. But he'd seen it. And it was damning. He writhed against the cuffs. "You know I'll beat this in a heartbeat."

"You have the right to remain silent," said the senior officer. "I suggest you use it because you are a disgrace to the uniform and many of us would like to see you fry. Anything you say can and will be used against you in a court of law. You have the right to an attorney, and I suggest you get a good one, because you're facing fourteen murder counts and ten counts of human trafficking. See you in court."

The sun's last rays faded over the horizon as Raj and Irina heard a knock at the door. Raj looked through the peephole and saw his friend Benito. The officer wore a broad grin. Raj opened the door, sensing important news.

"We got him," Benito announced. "Of course, there's still the matter of a trial, but the evidence is pretty overwhelming."

Raj approached Benito, clapped him on the shoulder, and shook his hand.

"It better be," said Raj. "I know how things are. Juries don't like to convict cops."

"Yeah, and sometimes that's a bad thing," Benito agreed. "But I think we can overcome that. We all feel pretty damn good about this. This city owes you a debt of gratitude. You made us see what was right in front of us. It was there all the time, but nobody looked. Maybe they didn't want to. You made us do our jobs. Feds are even looking into arranging a deal with Cherkasov for his testimony against Volk. That's far from a done deal, though. Anyway, what I'm trying to say is that you led the way and because of that, the whole city will be safer."

"I'm glad we got him," said Raj. "But really, I couldn't have done it without you and Irina. To do anything that truly matters, we need more than ourselves. I've realized that now."

"You always were a deep one," said Benito. "But yeah, you're right. Anyway, I have mountains of paperwork to complete. I'll leave you and your family to dinner."

Benito departed in a hurry and Raj swung the door shut.

Irina hurried downstairs, her hair still wet from an evening shower.

"Is it really true? They caught him?"

"It's really true," said Raj. "Soon this whole ordeal can be over and done with."

"It will never be fully over for me," said Irina. "But having that man behind bars will be a good start. It will not bring back Papa, but maybe it means we have done something important. We have stopped a monster."

"Indeed we have," said Raj. But he would not feel safe until the monster was locked in a cage.

Chapter Twenty-Nine

Raj took a seat in the back row of the busy courtroom. He studied the defendant, whose right side was partially obscured by his corpulent, bespectacled counsel, Roy Lonergan. News shows had been buzzing in Washington and Baltimore. Dirty cops and government corruption were passé in the capitol, but the alliterative "MPD Menace Murders" captivated the region as few cases ever had.

Raj followed every detail of the trial. Unfinished business irked him, so obtaining closure became his primary focus. The media seemed to believe that Volk had a chance to escape conviction. Or perhaps they were just creating dramatic tension to boost ratings. Raj was concerned that the prosecution hadn't used its most powerful evidence yet. When were they going to swing the hammer?

He sat in the second row of the courtroom, a stone's throw from the defendant. The lead prosecutor, Jessica Goldstein, arose and sidled over toward the judge. She was young and tall, with broad, powerful shoulders, a crew cut, silver horn-rimmed glasses and a calm but somewhat diffident manner. She wore neon yellow suits that offended the eye, but were a privilege afforded to legal minds with elite talent like hers.

"The prosecution calls Natasha Volquez."

Raj hoped the jury would look past the lawyer's haberdashery to see the evidence Natasha could provide. If her experience was anything like Irina's, though, she might break on the stand. Could Goldstein protect her from the aggressive interrogation of Lonergan?

Raj turned his attention to the defense table. Volk was crouched over, leaning into the ear of his lawyer. Lonergan's size made it difficult for him to bend sideways, but he made an attempt and said something to Volk. Volk shook his head and shrugged.

A thin woman with glasses and sun-damaged skin walked through the courtroom doors. She hunched forward, her eyes averted toward the ground as she walked.

Volk stared at the woman for a few seconds. Then he raised his gaze toward the ceiling and slumped back in his chair. If the reaction was any indicator, this would be big.

"Please state your name for the record," said Judge Horace Barclay.

The judge had earned the moniker "Hang 'em Horace" for his Draconian sentences. Raj found that fact comforting.

"My name is Natasha Volquez," she said. "I used to reside here as Natasha Semenova, but I got married."

"Do you swear to tell the truth, the whole truth, and nothing but the truth?"

"I do, Your Honor," she said.

Goldstein sashayed towards the witness stand.

"Ms. Volquez, is it true you came all the way from Cuba for this trial?"

"I did," she said.

"Impressive," said Goldstein. "Please tell the court why you moved to Cuba in the first place?"

The defense attorney started to rise in objection, but Barclay motioned for him to remain seated.

"I witnessed the murder of my boyfriend at the time," she said.

"And when was this?"

"Ten years ago," she said. "I was a graduate student, and so was Slava."

"Do you remember the date?" Goldstein asked.

Natasha stared at Volk and then looked out at the audience.

"One does not forget a date like that," she said. "It was December twelfth. He had just told me he wanted for us to get married."

"Please take us through the events of that night," Goldstein said.

Raj clenched his fists. A growing lump in his throat restricted his breathing. Natasha's answers could go a long way towards Volk's conviction.

Her hands shook as she placed them on the stand. She grabbed the stand's wooden borders and her knuckles blanched.

"We were having a great time in the bar near Foggy Bottom," she said. "We ate, we drank a little. Not too much, Slava had an important experiment to do the next day. It was a beautiful night, cold but clear."

"And then what happened?" asked Goldstein.

"We were dancing on the sidewalk. He was a good dancer," she said. "It was kind of like a waltz, but I spun a few turns away from him, onto the sidewalk across the alley. And the suddenly the man came. He was very tall, wearing a dark blue uniform."

"Is that man in the courtroom tonight?" asked Goldstein.

She pointed a trembling finger towards Volk.

"That's him," she said. "He killed my lover, my fiancee. He beat him with his gun. He hit him with a stick, a big long stick that he kept by his waist. Slava had his hands up. He was a peaceful man. He was pleading, but that man wouldn't stop. Then Slava fell. His face hit the pavement, and when he tried to roll over to get up, the man shot him."

"Where were you when all this was going on?" asked Goldstein.

"There was a dumpster and a truck, a moving truck parked in the alley," she said. "I hid next to them but I could still see through the windows. I was scared. I wish I hadn't been. Maybe Slava would be alive. Maybe I'd be dead, but maybe that would have been better."

Her voice cracked and faltered with the last sentence.

"Would you like a recess, ma'am?" asked the judge.

She shook her head.

"I've waited years to let the facts be known," she said, clearing her throat and smoothing her skirt. "I need to let them know what he did. Let the truth be heard."

This lady was tougher than her frail build suggested. Raj knew she had to be, to emerge from that horrible night and become a productive researcher with a reinvented identity in a foreign country.

"The jury might wonder how you know it was him," said Goldstein. "After all, it was 10 years ago, correct?"

"I saw him there in the street light," she said. "Two meters tall, standing over Slava's body. Then he called him 'Russian pig' and he said, 'Your Russian whore is next'. I slid next to the truck, and then inside it, and waited for him to leave. I was terrified he would kill me too."

"Terrified enough to leave the country," said Goldstein.

"Objection," said Lonergan. "Counsel is testifying to the witness' state of mind."

"Withdrawn, your honor," said Goldstein. "What prompted you to leave the country, and to stay quiet all these years?"

"It was not easy," she replied. "I loved this city, my research, and Slava. But I saw the man's uniform. I knew he was police. In my country, you do not fight the police. Those who do, disappear. From what I saw, I was afraid our countries are no different from one another. I am so sorry I was not brave enough to come forward earlier."

Raj looked back at the courtroom door. The newspapers intimated that the prosecution had a surprise witness who would seal the case against Volk, whose was already guilty in the court of public opinion.

Volk crouched in his chair, his tall frame bending forward as though exposed to an invisible heat lamp. Raj almost felt sorry for him, but the pangs of sympathy were short-lived. Irina strode through the doors, her angular face framed elegantly by a snug yet demure black and white checkered dress. She held her head high and tossed her red hair back over her shoulders as she stared straight ahead toward the witness stand.

Raj glanced at Volk. He thought he detected a wince. He returned to watching Irina, concerned for her emotional welfare yet awed by her courage and resilience. She had no obligation to cooperate with a system that had ignored her. That she chose to stand up at this time spoke volumes on the size of her will, the purity of her principled heart.

"Do you swear to tell the truth, the whole truth, and nothing but the truth, so help you God?" intoned the judge.

"I do, your honor" Irina replied.

"Please be seated."

Goldstein approached, walking in a deliberate fashion with her hands interlocked in front of her. She stopped about four feet in front of Irina and smiled.

"It is very brave of you to be here today," she began. "Tell the court what you saw on the fateful night years ago, when your father died."

"He did not just die," Irina corrected the prosecutor. "He was killed. We were talking, having fun, laughing, not bothering anybody. My father never hurt anybody."

"What happened to interrupt the fun, Ma'am?"

"Suddenly, a very tall, thin man popped out of the shadows. He saw me, called me 'Russian Whore', hit me with a baton, and kicked me. My father, he was always protective. He tried to stop the man, but the man was too strong, too big, and he beat Papa. Then he looked at my father on the ground, and I'll never forget this, he just pointed the gun at Papa and shot him. Then, while I hid, too beaten and helpless even to scream, he dug out the bullets and left."

"Were there any specific features of the attacker that you recall?"

Irina scanned the crowd. She took a deep breath and fixed her gaze on Raj. Then she spotted Dr. Meyerstein in the rear right corner of the courtroom and sighed deeply.

"He was very tall, over two meters. He had two different color eyes, and a mark on his forehead like the white patch you see on horses sometimes. Just like him."

He long, thin index finger didn't waver as she pointed at Volk.

Volk's shoulders slumped perceptibly and he rubbed his forehead, as though he meant to expunge the damning blemish from his skin. A sense of relief mixed with apprehension ensued, as Raj realized that the ordeal was almost over, and a final resolution approached.

Raj perused the Sunday paper. This had become a comfortable weekend ritual for him to enjoy as the sun spilled through his front window. He sat in his wicker chair and read about the conflicts in the Middle East and Sub-Saharan Africa. Some of the innocent victims of these wars would one day show up at his office, and he would welcome them. They deserved at least that much.

Irina walked down the stairs barefoot and made her way to the chair. She pushed away the paper, sat down on his lap and smiled.

"You know that question you asked me?" she said.

"Uh, which one?" asked Raj. "I'm full of questions."

Her eyes glinted with mischievous excitement. "This one was about six years ago," she said.

He cocked his head to the side. "Do I know what you're talking about?"

Her smile grew wider. "You do."

She dropped to a knee in front of him.

"Raj Patel, will you marry me?" she asked. "I know we've done things backward, but now I'm ready."

Raj pushed the chair back and knelt in front of her. He pulled her to him and ran his hands up and down her back as he kissed her lips and neck.

"I do," he whispered. "For richer or for poorer."

"In sickness and in health," she said, her hands entwined in his.

"Till death do us part," he said. "As long as we both shall live."

Acknowledgements

Many thanks are due to those who have shaped and supported the creation of this book.

The critique group at Napa Valley Writers' Conference (Mary Karr, Warren Jones, Dwight Hilson, Emily Bogdonoff, Holly Myers, Roseanne Pereira, Peggy Prescott, Kathy Thomas, and Angela Hur) gave me belief in my identity as a writer, without which I may never have attempted to see the novel to its conclusion.

Thanks to Peter Ho Davies for his mentorship during the conference and his invaluable technical instruction that increased my consciousness of the art of storytelling.

A special thank you is due to my editor, Erin Young, who smoothed my literary rough edges, and did so with patience and good humor.

Most of all, thank you to Stevan Nikolic and Adelaide Books for choosing to publish and promote my book.

About the Author

Mukund Gnanadesikan is a 1992 graduate of Princeton University. His poems have been featured or are upcoming in the anthology Sheets: For Men Only, Adelaide Literary Magazine, The Ibis Head Review, Tuck Magazine, Junto Magazine, The Bangalore Review, Streelight Press, Poesis Literary Journal, Bloodroot Literary Magazine, Blood and Thunder: Musings on the Art of Medicine, Cathexis Northwest ,Dreams Walking, Meniscus Literary Magazine, Praxis, The Cape Rock, Crepe and Penn, and Paper Dragon.